LARGE PRINT

Killing
Time

LINDA

HOWARD

Killing

A NOVEL

Time

DOUBLEDAY LARGE PRINT
HOME LIBRARY EDITION
RANDOM HOUSE

Copyright © 2005 by Linda Howington

All rights reserved.
Published in the United States of America by Random House Large Print in association with Ballantine Books, New York.
Distributed by Random House, Inc., New York.

ISBN 0-7394-5618-0

This Large Print edition published in accord with the standards of the N.A.V.H.

Killing
Time

Prologue

Peke County Courthouse, Kentucky
January 1, 1985

THERE WAS A SMALL TURNOUT, ABOUT fifty people, to watch the time capsule being buried next to the flagpole in front of the county courthouse. The first day of the new year was cold and windy, and the leaden sky kept spitting tiny snowflakes down at them. A full half of the crowd was composed of people who, through office, ambition, or twisted arms, had to be there: the mayor and councilmen, the probate judge, four lawyers, the county commissioners, a few of the local businessmen, the sheriff, the chief of police, the high school principal, and the football coach.

Some women were also present: Mrs. Edie Proctor, the school superintendent, and the wives of the politicians and lawyers. A reporter from the local paper was there, taking both notes and photographs because the paper was a small one and couldn't afford to have a professional photographer on staff.

Kelvin Davis, the owner of the hardware store, stood with his fifteen-year-old son. They were there mainly because the courthouse was directly across the street from where he and his son lived over the hardware store, the New Year's bowl games hadn't started yet, and they had nothing else to do. The boy, Knox, tall and thin, hunched his shoulders against the wind and studied the faces of everyone present. He was oddly watchful and sometimes made the adults around him feel uncomfortable, but he didn't get into any trouble, helped Kelvin in the store after school, kept his grades up, and was generally well liked by his peers. All in all, Kelvin thought he was lucky in his son.

They'd moved to Pekesville from Lexington nine years before. Kelvin was a widower and meant to stay that way. He'd loved his wife, sure, but marriage was hard work and he didn't think he wanted to go through that again. He went out with different women now and then, though not so regularly any of them got ideas. He figured he'd get Knox through high school and college, then maybe he'd rethink his position on marriage, but for right now he'd concentrate on raising his son.

"Thirteen," Knox said suddenly, keeping his voice low. A frown drew his dark brows together.

"Thirteen what?"

"They put thirteen items in the capsule, but the paper said there would be twelve. I wonder what the other one was."

"You sure it was thirteen?"

"I counted."

Of course Knox had counted. Kelvin mentally sighed; he hadn't really doubted the number of items. Knox seemed to notice and double-check everything. If the newspaper said twelve items would be placed in the time capsule, then Knox would count to make certain the paper was right—or, in this case, wrong.

"I wonder what the thirteenth one was," Knox said again, still frowning as he stared at the time capsule. The mayor was placing the capsule—actually, it was a metal box, carefully wrapped in waterproof plastic—in the hole that had been dug the day before.

The mayor said a few words, the crowd around him laughed, and the football coach began shoveling dirt on the box. In just a minute the hole had been filled and the coach was stamping the dirt level with the surrounding ground. There was dirt left over, of course, but the coach didn't mound it up. The mayor and one of the city councilmen then took a small granite slab that had been engraved with the day's date and the date a century from then, when the time capsule was supposed to be opened, and dropped it with a thud on the fresh dirt. They had probably planned to place the granite slab just so, with the proper gravity for the reporter to record with his flash camera, but the weight of the slab evidently took them by surprise and they dropped it. The slab landed a little off to the side. The coach got down on his knees on the freezing ground and used both hands to shove the slab into its proper place.

The newspaper reporter took photographs to record the event for posterity.

Shivering, Knox shifted his weight restlessly back and forth. "I'm going to ask," he said suddenly, and left Kelvin's side to stalk the reporter through the tangle of people as they began dispersing.

Sighing, Kelvin followed. Sometimes he thought Knox was more bulldog than boy, because he found it impossible to just let something go.

"What do you mean?" Kelvin heard the reporter, Max Browning, say as he looked at Knox with a distracted frown.

"The time capsule," Knox explained. "The newspaper said there are twelve items but there were thirteen put in it. I counted. I wanted to know what the thirteenth thing was."

"There were just twelve. Just like the paper said."

"I counted," Knox repeated. He didn't get surly, but he stood his ground.

Max glanced at Kelvin. "Hey," he said in greeting, then shrugged at Knox. "Sorry, I can't help you. I didn't see anything different."

Knox's head turned and he locked his attention like a homing missile on the departing mayor's back. If Max couldn't help him, he'd go to the source.

Kelvin caught the back of Knox's jacket as the kid started in pursuit. "Don't go dogging the mayor," he said in a mild tone. "It isn't that important."

"I just want to know."

"So ask the coach when school starts back next Monday."

"That's six days!" Knox looked horrified at having to wait that long to find out something he could find out today.

"The time capsule isn't going anywhere." Kelvin checked his watch. "The ball game's about to start; let's go on in." Ohio State was playing Southern Cal, and Kelvin was really rooting for the Buckeyes because his youngest sister's husband had played for Southern Cal about ten years ago and Kelvin hated the son of a bitch, so he always rooted for whomever the Trojans were playing.

Knox looked around, scowling as he realized the mayor was already out of sight and the coach was driving away. Mrs. Proctor, the superintendent, was talking to a tall man Knox didn't recognize, and he didn't want to approach Mrs. Proctor anyway because she looked sour and fake, with too much makeup caked in her frown lines, and he thought she probably smelled as sour as she looked.

Disgruntled, he followed his dad back to the hardware store.

He never got to ask the football coach what else had been in the time capsule, because the next morning the coach, Howard Easley, was found hanging from a tree in his backyard. There was no note, but the cops figured suicide because the coach had gotten divorced the year before and had been trying without success to convince his ex-wife to give him another chance. He'd been hanging there long enough that he'd gone completely cold, and snow had collected on his head and shoulders.

The coach's suicide knocked all thoughts of the time capsule out of Knox's head. When he heard the detail about snow on the coach's head, he took off for the library to look up rigor mortis and how long it took a body to cool that much. There were a lot of variables, including if there'd been a wind that night that would have caused the body to cool faster, but if he figured right, the coach had been hanging there at least since midnight.

Fascinated, he kept digging, his interest caught by first one thing then another as he delved into investigative techniques. This was some cool shit, he thought. He liked it. Solving puzzles by taking tiny pieces of evidence—that was exactly what he enjoyed doing anyway. Forget taking over the hardware store: he wanted to be a cop.

1

June 27, 2005

"Hey, Knox, who dug that hole next to the flagpole?"

Knox looked up from the report he was writing. As chief county investigator, he had his own office, though it was small and crowded. Deputy Jason MacFarland was leaning in through the open door, the expression on his freckled face only mildly curious.

"What hole next to the flagpole?"

"I'm telling you, there's a hole next to the flagpole. I'd swear it wasn't there yesterday afternoon when my shift was over, but one's there now."

"Huh." Knox rubbed his jaw. He himself hadn't noticed, because he'd parked behind the courthouse when he came in this morning at four-thirty to wade through an ass-deep pile of paperwork. He'd been up all night, and he was so tired he might not have noticed even if he'd walked right by the supposed hole.

Having been sitting at his desk for three hours, he figured he needed to stretch his legs a bit. Grabbing his coffee cup, he refilled it as he passed by the coffeemaker, and he and Deputy MacFarland went out the side door, then walked around the side of the redbrick courthouse building to the front, their rubber-soled shoes quiet on the sidewalk. The new day was showing a cloudless blue sky, and the lush green grass was wet with dew. Colorful banks of spring flowers grew in carefully tended beds, but Knox would have been hard put to name any of them. He knew roses, and daffodils. Everything else was lumped under the general designation of "flowers."

The courthouse opened at eight, and the back parking lot was rapidly filling with em-ployees' cars. The sheriff's department had a separate wing on the right of the courthouse, and the county jail occupied the top two stories of the five-story building. The prisoners used to catcall down to the female employees and visi-tors to the courthouse, until the county installed slats over the windows that let in air and light but effectively blocked the prisoners' view of the parking lot below.

The flagpole was on the left front corner of

the courthouse square; park benches faced the street on both sides of the corner, and there were more of the neat flower beds. Today there wasn't any wind; the flags hung limply. And at the base of the flagpole was a nice-sized hole, about three feet wide and two deep.

Knox and the deputy stayed on the sidewalk; they could easily see from there. A granite slab had been flipped upside down and lay in the grass. The dirt was scattered more than seemed strictly necessary for digging a simple hole. "That was the time capsule," Knox said, and sighed. This was just the kind of shit high school kids would do, but it ate at his time just like any other crime.

"What time capsule?" MacFarland asked.

"There was a time capsule buried . . . hell, it was twenty years ago: 1985. I watched them bury it on New Year's Day."

"What was in it?"

"I don't remember, but nothing struck me at the time as being valuable. Things like a copy of the newspaper, a yearbook, some music and things." He did remember that the newspaper hadn't listed everything in the capsule, though, and in retrospect he was still pissed off about it.

"Bunch of kids, most likely," MacFarland said. "Thought stealing a time capsule would be funny."

"Yeah." Out of habit, Knox surveyed the surrounding ground. There were no footprints in the dew, which meant the vandals had struck hours ago. He stepped up on one of the park benches so he could get a better view, and said, "Huh."

"What is it?"

"Nothing. No footprints." The way the fresh dirt was scattered around, there should have been at least a partial footprint caught somewhere. But the dirt looked as if it had burst up out of the ground, rather than been dug up and tossed with a shovel. The flagpole was no more than ten feet distant from the park bench, so he had a very good view; there was no way he was overlooking any prints. There simply weren't any.

MacFarland climbed up on the bench beside him. "Don't that beat all," he said, after staring at the ground for at least thirty seconds. "How'd they manage that? I wonder."

"God only knows." He'd find out, though. Because the county jail was located at the courthouse, every corner of the building was equipped with a security camera, tucked up high under the eaves and painted to blend in with the building. Unless a person knew the cameras were there, he'd have a tough time spotting them.

He still had that report to finish, but the lack

of footprints around the hole fired his curiosity. Now he had to know just how the little bastards had managed to dig up the time capsule with a streetlight right there on the corner shining down on them, but with no one seeing them and without leaving any prints in the fresh dirt. Maybe First Avenue, the street right in front of the courthouse, didn't have all that much traffic on it during the wee hours, but there were always patrol cars coming and going. Someone should have seen something and reported it.

He looked across the street at the hardware store where he and his dad had lived; after he'd gone off to college, his dad had finally gotten serious about someone and remarried about ten years ago. Knox liked Lynnette just fine, and was glad Kelvin wasn't alone. Lynnette hadn't wanted to live above the store, though, so they'd bought a house out in the country. If Kelvin had still lived there, Knox thought, no kids would have managed to do anything without Kelvin noticing, because his bedroom had looked out over the square.

"Put some tape around the scene, keep people from tromping all over it," he instructed MacFarland.

MacFarland could have argued that there was nothing there but a hole, and that a missing time capsule didn't have any great value anyway—certainly not enough value to justify an investigation—but he merely nodded. Telling Knox when to back off was the sheriff's job, not his; besides, Knox was a source of great amusement to the deputies, who sometimes made bets on how far he would go to solve a puzzle.

He and MacFarland retraced their steps around the courthouse to the sheriff's department, where they parted company: MacFarland to carry out his instructions, and Knox to the jail, where the security cameras were manned.

"Manned" was a loose term, because more accurately they were "womanned," by a six-foot, fierce-eyed woman named Tarana Wilson, who kept fanatical watch over her domain. Her facial features were carved and strong, her skin burnished like dark bronze, and she had a brown-belt in martial arts. Knox strongly suspected she could kick his ass.

Because a smart man never approached a queen without bearing gifts, Knox snagged a cream-filled doughnut out of the break room and poured two fresh cups of coffee, one for himself and one in a disposable cup. Gifts in hand, he went up the stairs.

He had to stop and identify himself; then he was buzzed into the jailor's offices.

The actual cells were on the floors above, and access to those floors was rigidly controlled.

They hadn't had a breakout in at least fifteen years. Not that Peke County had any real hard cases in the county lockup; the hard cases were in state prisons.

The door to Tarana's office was open, and she was pacing in front of a bank of ten black-and-white monitors. She seldom just sat; she seemed to be constantly on the move, as if too much energy burned in her lean, long-muscled body for her to sit still.

"Hey, T.," Knox said as he strolled in, extending the cup of coffee.

She eyed the cup suspiciously, then looked back at the monitors. "What's that?"

"Coffee."

"What're you bringing me coffee for?"

"To stay on your good side. I'm afraid of you."

That brought her dark, narrow-eyed gaze swinging back to him. "Liar."

"Okay, so I really have the hots for you and this is my way of softening you up."

A faint smile curved her mouth. She took the cup of coffee and sipped it as she studied the monitors. "It might work, too, if me and my sisters hadn't sworn an oath to stay away from white boys."

He snorted, then extended the doughnut. "This is for you, too."

"Now I'm gettin' scared you really meant that about softening me up, but I got news for you: it takes more than any doughnut to do the job."

"It's cream-filled."

"Oh, well then, I might have to rethink my position." She grabbed the doughnut and took a big bite out of it, squishing white cream out both sides of the pastry. She licked the cream filling before it could splat to the floor, her attention never leaving the monitors.

"Now then, what can I do for you?"

"See the flagpole?" he asked, pointing at the appropriate monitor.

"Yeah, what about it?"

"There's a hole in front of it, where the time capsule used to be buried."

"Used to be?"

"Somebody dug it up last night."

"Son of a bitch. Somebody stole our time capsule? I didn't know we had one, but never mind that."

"I need to see the tape from last night."

"Coming right up. That's just trashy, stealing a town's time capsule."

In short order Knox was sitting in front of a spare monitor, rewinding the security tape and watching as everything went backward. He saw himself and MacFarland, then time spooled backward and dawn disappeared. Traffic had been light, as he expected. What he didn't expect, though, was to see no one approach the flagpole and spend a few minutes digging a hole. Not a single person approached. He was all the way back to sunset when he stopped the tape, frowning.

"You find the low-down rotten bastard?" Tarana drawled without looking at him, because she was still visually patrolling her monitors.

"Nope." Looking closely at the frozen image, he could plainly see that the granite marker was in place and the ground undisturbed at eight-thirty PM. The rich green grass was neatly trimmed around the marker.

"What do you mean, no?"

"I mean I didn't see anybody."

"Don't tell me somebody done dug up that time capsule a week ago, and you boys have just noticed."

"According to your tape, it was still there at sunset yesterday."

She wheeled, stared at the image. "If it was there yesterday, then whoever took it's on that tape."

"I didn't see anyone," he repeated patiently, and fast-forwarded through to dawn to show her. When he stopped the tape, they could see the hole at the base of the flagpole and the granite marker flipped off to the side. A ferocious frown pulled her brows together.

"Run it again," she snapped, coming to stand behind him.

He did, rewinding the tape yet again, and this time doing periodic stops of the tape to see when the vandalism first appeared. At 2:30 AM, the hole was there. When he stopped it again, at 1:53 AM, the site was undisturbed.

"Now run it in real time," she said, dragging a chair over. She gave her monitors a quick look, then settled her attention on the tape playing in front of her.

Knox punched **Play** and the time-counter began clicking forward a second at a time. Seven minutes later he said, "Shit, what was that?" A brief, white flash had glared on the screen. Then it was gone, and so was the time capsule.

He stopped the tape, hit **Rewind,** then almost immediately hit **Play** again. The tape had backed up three minutes. The same thing happened. The ground was undisturbed, then came that white flash, and when it faded, the capsule was gone.

"Somebody's messing with my camera," Tarana said in a voice of doom.

"I don't think so." Frowning, Knox rewound the tape over those same few crucial minutes. "Watch the timer."

Together they watched the seconds ticking away. At 2:00 AM, the white flash filled the screen. At 2:01 AM, the flash faded and the time capsule was gone.

"That's not possible," Tarana snapped, surging to her feet and kicking her chair. She turned and glared at all the monitors. "If somebody's messing with that camera, he can mess with all these, and that **ain't gonna happen.**"

Silently Knox watched the sequence again. He hadn't noticed the flash when he'd been fast-forwarding or rewinding. But it was definitely there, and the granite slab had been in place before the flash but was pushed aside afterward, and the dark hole gaped at the foot of the flagpole.

He rewound the tape all the way. The time display was exactly twenty-four hours before he'd come in here and Tarana had stopped the tape. He didn't know if anyone could tamper with the tape without messing up the time, or if it was even possible without someone coming into this office, in which case no way had a bunch of high school kids been responsible.

He scratched his jaw. He supposed he could sit with his watch in one hand and time the tape, but that would take twenty-four hours and be boring as hell besides. There was an easier way to get to the bottom of this.

Tarana was stalking back and forth behind him, breathing fire and muttering curses. Knox felt sorry for the next person who came through that door, because, deprived of a definite target, she might just take her ire out on anyone handy.

"I'm going over to the hardware store," he said, sliding his chair back and grabbing his coffee cup.

"Hardware store? What you going to the hardware store for? You can't just waltz in here and show me somebody's been messing with my cameras, then just waltz out again to go buy some nails. You sit back down!"

"Dad has security cameras, too," Knox said. "One of them is pointed toward the door."

"So?" she snapped, then realization dawned. "Oh, I gotcha. Glass door, big glass storefront, right across the street from the flagpole."

He winked at her as he went out the door.

The square was busy now as he crossed the street; people were coming to the courthouse, taking care of business like car tags, driver's licenses, boat registrations. Some of the stores were open, including the hardware store; the rest of them opened at nine. MacFarland had strung a nice crime-scene perimeter, blocking off a good twenty yards in either direction from the flagpole, thereby blocking the sidewalk and making people walk around.

The bell above the door dinged when Knox walked in, and Kelvin looked up as he was checking out a customer. "Be with you in a minute, son," he said.

"Take your time." Looking up, Knox located the security camera and turned to follow the alignment. Just as he'd thought, the flagpole was almost dead center opposite the front door. Whoever had done the vandalism might have somehow blocked the courthouse security camera, though he didn't see how, but this camera was inside the store and hadn't been tampered with.

The customer left and Knox went over to the checkout counter. "I need to see your security tape," he said to Kelvin. He nodded out the window. "Somebody dug up the time capsule last night and somehow blocked the courthouse camera. I figure your camera caught the action."

Kelvin looked up at the camera, following the path the same way Knox had. "Reckon so. I wondered what all that yellow tape was for. That's the time capsule we watched them bury, right?"

"The same one. Unless they dug it up and buried a fresh one that I don't know about."

"Nineteen eighty-five. Southern Cal won the Rose Bowl, and I had to listen to that asshole Aaron for a whole year."

Kelvin always referred to his brother-in-law Aaron as "asshole Aaron" because he liked the alliteration; he didn't, however, like his brother-in-law. Reaching beneath the counter, he ejected a tape and handed it over the counter to Knox. "There you go."

"I don't know when I'll get it back."

"Don't worry about it. I got extras."

Tape in hand, Knox went back to his office. He had a small TV/VCR combo and he turned it on, then slipped in the tape. With the remote in his hand, he rewound until he was close to the right time, then in fits and starts until 1:59 AM showed on the clock display. The detail wasn't as good and the glass distorted the view some, but he could make out the square granite marker right where it was supposed to be. He pressed **Play** and watched. There was always some variance in clocks, so he had no idea how long he'd actually have to watch.

At 2:03:17, there was a white flash. Knox sat up straight, staring at the screen. At 2:03:18, the flash faded. Now the pale square of the granite marker was lying off to the side, and the ground had been disturbed.

"Son of a bitch," he said softly. "What in hell is going on?"

2

A more careful examination of the scene revealed exactly nothing. The granite marker was polished on the side that bore the engraved dates, but a careful dusting picked up no fingerprints at all. There definitely weren't any footprints. The whole thing was weird.

By now, Knox wasn't the only one who was curious. Tarana was furious, still certain someone was messing with her security cameras even though Knox had tried to tell her his dad's store camera had shown the same brief flash, then nothing else. He figured when she calmed down some, he'd try again.

MacFarland was telling everyone how he'd noticed the hole when he drove by on his way in to work; others had noticed the hole, but hadn't thought anything about it. Now, if there'd been

a body lying there, that would have been different, but a hole in the ground hadn't seemed all
that suspicious.

Peke County was small, and not a hotbed of
crime. Pekesville had a comfortable population
of twenty-three thousand, just big enough to afford some conveniences that wouldn't be found
in a smaller town but not big enough to attract
gang activity or satanists, anything exotic like
that. The sheriff's department more normally
handled the garden variety of trouble: domestic
violence, theft, drunk driving, some drugs.
Lately meth labs had become real popular, and
since the labs were normally set up in remote locations, that meant most of them were in the
country rather than within Pekesville's city limits, which meant the deputies had fast become
experts in how to handle the literally explosive
situation.

But a hole in the ground? What were they
supposed to do with that?

When the sheriff, Calvin Cutler, moseyed
into his office and heard about the mystery, he
had to go look at the hole himself. Surrounded
by a group of deputies and two investigators, he
trooped down to the front of the courthouse.
"Don't that beat all," he said, staring at the scattered dirt within the area outlined by the crime-
scene tape. "Who in tarnation would want a
time capsule?"

Calvin Cutler didn't swear, which was so un-usual in a peace officer that his men sometimes referred to him, behind his back but with affec-tion, as "Andy." He stood six foot five, weighed close to three hundred pounds, and had hands that could swallow a basketball. He had started out as a deputy, worked his way up the force to chief deputy, and then when the sheriff retired, he'd run for the office and was currently in the middle of his fourth term. Sheriff Cutler knew the job from the ground up, and Knox couldn't think of a better man to work for.

"It's gotta be kids," he continued. "Nobody else would do such a fool thing."

"But how was it done?" Knox asked.

The sheriff turned and stared at the camera on the top corner of the courthouse. "Nothing but a flash on the film, huh?"

"And on the security camera in the hardware store."

Sheriff Cutler stuck his hands in his pockets and grinned at Knox. "Driving you crazy, I guess."

"It's got me curious."

"Guess this means you're going to spend de-partment money getting to the bottom of this mystery hole, if you'll excuse the pun."

Knox shrugged. On his list of priorities, this was way down at the bottom. There was no vic-tim, and nothing of any real value had been taken. This was vandalism, but the big question was, did anyone really care? And the bottom line was that the sheriff decided what he investigated, not him. "Only in my spare time, if you don't mind. It's puzzling, but not important."

"That's if you **have** any spare time," the sheriff said affably as they all headed back.

"Yeah," Knox agreed. Small county or not, the department stayed pretty busy because they were perpetually understaffed. Knox was the chief investigator, but since the department had only three investigators, total, he didn't figure that was any big thing. With just the three of them that meant eight-hour shifts were something they'd heard about but weren't quite sure they believed in; they were all pretty much on call twenty-four hours a day, seven days a week. Knox usually worked between seventy and eighty hours every week, but that was partly because the other two investigators had families and he tried to give them some home time. To his way of thinking that didn't mean he was a particularly good leader; it meant he was lonely, and he worked so he wouldn't have to go home except to sleep.

They'd wasted enough time pondering the theft of a time capsule, and he had a stack of paperwork on his desk that had to be plowed through, plus the cases in which he needed to do some actual investigating. After fortifying himself with another cup of coffee, he settled down to his job.

Knox liked working in law enforcement. Not only did he enjoy the camaraderie, but the job was a perfect fit for him. In what other field would he be paid for asking questions, poking around, solving puzzles? Okay, so maybe there were other jobs that would have let him do the same thing, but in law enforcement he got to carry a weapon. That trumped being, say, a reporter, every day of the week.

After about an hour of desk time, with maybe a quarter of his paperwork finished, he got to his feet and shrugged into a lightweight jacket. He wore a shoulder holster over a white polo shirt that was neatly tucked into a pair of jeans, and slightly battered athletic shoes. Considering the heat of the early summer day, he'd have gladly done without the jacket, except for the sheriff's dress code. Calvin didn't care if his investigators wore pajamas, so long as they also had on a jacket. Since the sheriff didn't also insist on a tie, Knox counted his blessings.

"Where you off to?" Helen, Sheriff Cutler's assistant, asked as she leaned in to toss another four inches of reports on his desk.

"Jesse Bingham's. Someone broke into his barn last night, slashed the tires on his tractor, killed a bunch of chickens."

"I've never met a man more deserving of

having his tires slashed, but I hate it about the chickens," Helen said, and strolled back to her office. Jesse Bingham was well-known for his nasty disposition, and he filed complaints just about every time anyone crossed him.

Knox hated it about the chickens, too. They were stupid birds, but surely they'd suffered enough, being owned by Jesse Bingham.

Leaving the parking lot, he took a left on Fourth Avenue, which led directly to the highway. When he stopped at the traffic light, his right-turn signal on, he saw a lone figure standing in the Brookhaven Cemetery just across the highway. He turned off his turn signal, and when the light changed, he drove straight across the intersection to the cemetery's entrance.

He parked under the spreading shade of a hundred-year-old oak, then got out and walked across the thick grass to the woman who was standing with her hand lightly resting on a white marble tombstone. Without looking, he knew what the inscription on the tombstone read: **Rebecca Lacey, Beloved Daughter of Edward and Ruth Lacey,** followed by the dates of her birth and death. If she had died three months later, the tombstone would have read: **Rebecca Davis, Beloved Wife of Knox Davis.** He put his arm around the woman, and without a word she tilted her head to lay it against his shoulder. They looked at the grave of the young woman they had both loved: her daughter, his fiancée.

"It's been seven years," she said softly. "Sometimes I go days without thinking about her, and then when I realize it, that's almost worse than the days when losing her feels as fresh as if it happened yesterday."

"I know," he said, because he did. The first time he'd realized that he hadn't thought about Rebecca at all the day before, the sense of having betrayed her had been almost more than he could bear. But time moved on, and the living either kept on living or they died, too; either way, life and events had a way of shifting around so the empty place was filled in. He could look at her grave now without feeling as if he'd been stabbed in the heart. He could remember her with distant affection, the sense of love having faded. He would probably always love the way they had been together, the promise of happiness, but she was seven years' gone and he was no longer **in** love with her.

He kissed the forehead of the woman who had almost been his mother-in-law. It was different for her; Rebecca would always be her child, and the quality of that love would never change. It was a love that wasn't dependent on hormones or chemistry to remain fresh, that didn't require close proximity. On the other hand, she too had days when the memories didn't surface, and maybe that was nature's way of keeping the pain from being unbearable.

Ruth Lacey was a slim, young-looking woman of fifty-three. There was very little gray in her hair and she kept it in a pixie cut that suited her delicate face. She'd been twenty when Rebecca was born, an age that now seemed to him to be ridiculously young. Ed, her husband, had been cheating on her practically from the day they were married, but she'd stayed with him, for reasons unknown to anyone but her. Maybe he'd soured her on marriage so much she didn't see any point in being free to try it with anyone else, so she'd stayed with him for purely practical reasons. Maybe she loved the son of a bitch. Knox knew there was no way of telling what went on in other people's private lives, or of understanding the bond that held certain people together.

She was a woman who seemed very open and giving, but who was actually very private. When Rebecca died, she had held her pain and grief inside—except with Knox. They had clung together then, and she'd let him see the depth of her loss. They'd helped each other through the dark days, and as the years passed, though they had less and less contact with each other, the bond and affection remained, as if they were soldiers who had fought side by side and never forgot that kinship.

There were always fresh flowers on Rebecca's grave. Knox had placed his share there, but over the last few years the effort had been mainly Ruth's. Last year, he didn't think he'd come to the cemetery at all. For three years before that, he'd come only on the anniversary of her death.

The funny thing was, the day after Rebecca's funeral, when he and Ruth had stood practically in the same spot where they were now, Ruth had told him how it would be. "For a while," she'd said, "you'll be here a lot; then gradually you'll be able to let go. You'll come on the anniversary, maybe, or her birthday. Maybe Christmas. Maybe you'll forget and not come at all. That's the way it's supposed to be. Don't feel guilty about it. You still have your life to live, and you can't do it if you try to hold on to something that'll never be."

He stooped and plucked a weed that had escaped the caretaker's eagle eye, remembering her funeral, and the grave covered with flowers. She had died in March, just before spring became full-blown. He'd spent the night at her house—despite being engaged, they hadn't moved in together—and when they got up that morning, she'd said, "I have a bitch of a headache. I'm going to take some aspirin." She'd headed toward the kitchen, and he'd jumped into the shower. When he had shaved and dressed, he went into the kitchen and found her on the floor, already dead. He'd called 911 then done CPR anyway, even knowing it was useless, but unable to **not** make the effort. By the time the medics arrived, he'd been exhausted and dripping with sweat but unwilling to stop because his heart was unwilling to accept what his brain already knew.

The autopsy revealed that a massive aneurysm in her brain had burst. Even if she'd already been standing in a hospital emergency department when it happened, there was no way anyone could have reacted fast enough to save her. So she was gone, at the age of twenty-six, two weeks before her bridal shower, nine weeks before their wedding.

That was when he'd started working so many hours, and seven years later he was still doing it. Maybe it was time he scaled back to, say, sixty hours or something like that. He hadn't dated much—you couldn't date when you were working all the time—so of course he hadn't become involved with anyone since Rebecca. He was thirty-five, and he sure as hell wasn't going to get any younger.

"What if we could turn back time?" Ruth asked softly, bringing his attention back to her. "What if, knowing what would happen, I could go back to the day before it happened and insist she go to the hospital?"

"I don't believe in 'what if,'" he said, though

he kept his tone gentle. "You deal with what is, and go on."

"You don't wish things were different?"

"A thousand times, and in a thousand ways. But they aren't different. This is reality, and sometimes reality sucks."

"This one certainly does," she said, stroking her hand over her daughter's tombstone.

"Do you still come here often?"

"Not the way I used to. I haven't been in a couple of months, and I wanted to bring fresh flowers. I haven't been bringing them the way I did at first, and it makes me mad that I don't remember all the time now."

"Like I said, you go on." He put his arm around her waist again and turned her, urging her away from the grave.

"I don't want to forget her."

"I remember more about when she was alive, than when she died."

"Do you remember her voice? Most of the time I can't; then all of a sudden it's as if I hear an echo of it and for a second I remember exactly; then it's gone again. Her face is always clear, but it's so hard to remember her voice." She stared hard at the trees, fighting tears and, for the moment, winning. "All of those years, all of those memories. Baby, toddler, little girl, teenager, woman. I can see her at every stage, like snapshots, and I wish I had paid more attention, tried to remember every little thing. But you never think about your child dying; you always think you'll go first."

"There's a school of thought that we come back to learn things, experience things that we haven't had in our previous lives." He didn't believe it himself, but he could see how the idea would bring some comfort.

"Then I must have had great lives before," she said. She gave a delicate snort. "And great husbands."

The comment caught Knox by surprise and he chuckled. Looking down at her, he saw her biting her lip to control a smile. "You're tough," he said. "You'll make it."

"So, what are you up to?" Ruth asked as they reached her car. She hadn't cried, and she might see that as a victory even though grief still lay like a veil over her fine-boned features. She asked the question to completely pull herself out of the past, not because she was really interested in the answer.

"I'm heading out to Jesse Bingham's. Somebody slashed the tires on his tractor and killed some of his chickens."

"Why on earth would anyone hurt those poor birds?" she asked, frowning. "That's terrible."

"Yeah, I'm getting a lot of concern about the chickens."

"But none about Jesse or his tractor tires, huh?" The frown eased from her forehead and she laughed as he hugged her.

He opened the car door for her and out of habit watched to make certain she buckled her seat belt. "Take care," he said as he closed the door, and she gave him a little wave as she started the car and drove off.

Knox returned to his own car, wishing he hadn't seen her. She made him feel guilty, as if he should still be mourning as deeply as she did. He couldn't. He didn't want to. He wanted to find someone else to love and laugh with, have sex with, someday get married and have kids with, though damn if he had much chance of that, considering the rut he'd dug for himself.

He pulled his mind back to the job and drove out to the Bingham farm to see what he could make of the vandalism. Sometimes people had a good idea of who had done it, or the neighbors had seen something, but in Jesse's case just about everyone who knew him disliked him, and he had no nearby neighbors. He was one of those people who blamed everything that happened to him on someone else; if he had trouble with the engine in his truck, he immediately thought someone had poured sugar in his gas tank. If he lost something, he thought it had been stolen and filed a report. But they couldn't just blow him off; they had to investigate every

time he filed a report, because all it took was for
him to be right one time and they'd catch hell if
they hadn't done their jobs.

Slashed tractor tires and dead chickens
weren't produced by Jesse's sense of persecution,
though. Either the tires were slashed or they
weren't, and the chickens were either dead or
running around pecking at bugs. At least there
was something concrete Knox could see.

The Bingham farm was set on a pretty piece
of property, with wooded hills and neat fields.
Jesse's one good quality was that he took care of
the place. The fences were always mended, the
grass cut, the house painted, the barn and sheds
in good repair. Jesse didn't have any help on the
place, either; he did it all himself even though
he was in his late sixties. He'd been married
once, but Mrs. Bingham had showed the good
sense to leave him flat more than thirty years before, and go live with her sister in Ohio. Word
was they'd never gotten a divorce, which to
Knox's way of thinking was a smart way to save
money. Jesse sure as hell wasn't going to find
anyone else to marry him, and Mrs. Bingham
was so put off marriage by her experience with
him that she wasn't interested in giving it another whirl.

Knox parked his car beside Jesse's truck and
got out. The house's door opened as he started
up the front steps. "Took your time getting

here," Jesse said sourly through the screen door. "I've got chores that I need to be doing, instead of sitting on my butt waiting for you to decide to show up."

"Good morning to you, too," Knox said drily. Seeing Jesse always surprised him. If there was ever a man whose appearance didn't match his personality, it was Jesse Bingham. He was short, a little pudgy, with a round cherubic face and bright blue eyes; when he opened his mouth, though, nothing pleasant came out. The effect was that of a rabid Santa Claus.

"Are you gonna do your job, or stand there making sarcastic remarks?" Jesse snapped.

Knox took a firm hold on his patience. "Why don't you show me the tractor and chickens?"

Jesse stomped his way toward the barn, and Knox followed. The tractor was parked in the shelter of a lean-to attached to the barn, and even from a distance Knox could see that the wheels were sitting flat on the ground. "There," Jesse said, pointing. "Little bastards got all six of them."

"You think it was kids?" Knox asked, wondering if a gang of kids had been extra busy last night.

"How the hell would I know? That's your job, finding out. For all I know, it was Matt Reston at the tractor place, so he could sell me some new tires."

"You said 'little bastards.' "

"Figure of speech. Don't you know what that is?"

"Sure," Knox said easily. "Like 'asshole.' Figure of speech."

Jesse gave him a suspicious look. In his experience, most people either took off in the face of his nastiness, or wanted to fight him. Knox Davis always kept his temper, but one way or another he made it plain he'd take only so much.

Knox carefully examined the ground; unfortunately, the prints in the dirt all seemed to be Jesse's, which he could tell because they were small for a man. "You walked around out here?"

"How else would I look at all six tires?"

"If there were any prints in the dirt, you ruined them."

"Like you could look at a footprint and tell who made it. I don't believe that crap. Millions of people wear the same size shoe."

Knox knew exactly where he'd like to plant a size eleven athletic shoe. He examined the tires, looked for fingerprints on the metal parts, but from what he could tell each tire had one slash in it: stab in a knife, pull downward. If the tractor had been touched at all except for that, he couldn't tell it. Maybe he could get a fingerprint that wasn't Jesse's off it, though—if Jesse hadn't wiped the tractor down this morning, and destroyed all the other evidence. Knox wouldn't put anything past him, though he guessed the old fart wouldn't slash his own tires, because that meant he had to spend the money to replace them. Unless—"You got insurance for things like this, Jesse?"

"Course I do. Only a damn fool doesn't have coverage these days, with people running around pretending to fall down on your property so they can sue you."

"What's your deductible?"

"What business is it of yours?"

"Just asking."

Jesse's face began to get red. "You think I did this? You think I'd slash my own tires?"

"If your insurance would buy new tires, and you have a low deductible, that would be a way to save money. You could get new tractor tires for, what, a hundred dollars?"

"I'll call the sheriff!" Jesse bellowed. "Get your ass off my land! I want someone else—"

"It's me or no one," Knox interrupted. "As for who cut your tires, I can't say. My job is to cover all the bases. You're a base." He walked around to the back of the barn, taking care to stay out of the soft dirt around the wall where Jesse kept the grass killed. There. The dirt was scuffed. He looked closer, and could make out what looked like one footprint on top of another one, as if someone had walked the same way, leaving as they had arrived. Bigger than Jesse's foot, too.

"What about my chickens? You think I killed my chickens, too? Just take a look at them!" Jesse had followed him, still bellowing, and practically jumping up and down he was so mad.

Knox held up a hand. "Don't mess up these prints, too. Just stay back, will you?"

"Changing your mind now, huh? Coming onto a man's property and accusing him of—"

"Jesse." Knox said it quietly, but the look in his eye when he turned his head to pin Jesse with his gaze said that he'd had enough.

Jesse stopped in mid-tirade, and contented himself with looking sullen.

"Show me the chickens."

"This way," he muttered, and led the way, back past the tractor, to a small chicken coop tucked up next to a trimmed hedge at the back of his house. "Look at that," he said, pointing. "Six of them."

Six hens lay scattered about the coop. There wasn't any blood, so Knox guessed someone had wrung their necks. The sheer meanness of some people never failed to surprise and disgust him.

"Did you hear anything last night?"

"Nothing, but I was tired and had trouble getting to sleep, so I may have been sleeping too hard. Weird night. All those lightning flashes kept me awake, but I never did hear no thunder. Finally stopped around midnight, and I went to sleep. I guess all this happened after that."

"Lightning flashes?" Knox asked, frowning. He didn't remember any lightning, and he'd been out and around.

"Kind of low to the ground, too. Like I said: weird. Not like normal lightning. Just these white flashes, like big flashbulbs going off."

White flashes, Knox thought. Wasn't that a coincidence. What in hell was going on around here?

3

"THE FLASHES MIGHT BE RELATED," KNOX said. "There was another vandalism last night where there was a white flash. Where were they, about?"

"Don't see how in hell any flashes could have something to do with killing my chickens," Jesse grumbled, but he turned and pointed toward the stretch of woods across the road. "Over there. My bedroom window faces that direction."

"You said they were low." Knox turned and surveyed the land: hilly and heavily wooded, like most of eastern Kentucky. "How low? Tree level, or higher than that?"

"Just above the treetops, I guess."

"Got any guess as to the distance?"

Jesse was a farmer, and farmers knew distances. He could probably pace off almost an exact acre. That it had been night would hamper him some, but he had the advantage of knowing every hill and curve of his land. He narrowed his eyes as he squinted at the hill, too interested to bitch. "About a hundred yards in, I'd say. Can't be much farther, or you crest the hill and go down the other side."

Made sense to Knox. "I'm going to take a look over there," he said. "Want to come along?"

"Let me put on my boots."

While Jesse fetched his boots, Knox opened the trunk of his car and took out his own pair of field boots, which reached almost to his knees. The heavy leather protected against snakebites. He was lucky in that he wasn't allergic to either poison oak or poison ivy, but so far as he knew no one was immune to snake venom. He sat down on the porch step to put on the boots.

Jesse came out wearing a pair of green Wellingtons, and together they tromped across the road and into the woods. Knox thought this had to set a world record for length of time for Jesse not griping about something; it had been—what—five whole minutes? He checked his watch so he could keep track of how long the peace lasted.

The temperature was cooler under the thick

umbrella of the trees. He wasn't much of a woodsman, but he recognized the red and white varieties of oak, the maple trees, the hemlock. Wild azaleas dotted the undergrowth with delicate color. The rich, earthy smell teased his nostrils, prompting him to take deep, appreciative breaths.

"Smells good, don't it?" Jesse observed, and for once his tone was quiet instead of strident. Knox made a mental note that the woods seemed to affect Jesse's personality; maybe they should build a pen out here and keep him locked in it.

The land began to rise, the slope becoming steep. They pushed through bushes, tugged their clothing free of briars that grabbed at them, climbed over some rocks and went around bigger ones. Jesse kept looking around, mentally measuring the distance, since the foliage was too thick for him to see his house. They were near the crest of the hill when he stopped. "Right about here, I guess."

Knox took his time, studying every detail around him. Just to the right, the foliage thinned out somewhat, but was still too dense to be called a clearing. The trees grew thick and tall here, with flowering dogwoods tucked up under the shelter of the bigger trees. As far as he could tell, none of the leaves looked singed or in any way disturbed, so whatever the flash was, either it hadn't been close enough to do any damage or there was no accompanying heat.

The ground, though . . . something had disturbed it, in a vague way. He couldn't find any prints, but clumps of decaying vegetation had been disturbed, with the darker, wetter side turned up. "Someone's been here," he said to Jesse, pointing to the forest floor.

"I see."

"Wiped out their prints, though. Wonder what they were doing up here." Knox did a full turn, looking for a break in the foliage that allowed a view of . . . something. "Nothing's visible from here. I guess some sort of flare could have been set off, but for what reason?" He sniffed the air again, but smelled only that same rich, loamy scent. No one had burned anything recently, or the smell of smoke would have lingered in the air.

"An animal could have done this," Jesse said, indicating the disturbed vegetation. "Two bucks mighta locked horns, or a fox could have caught a rabbit. Don't see no blood, though. And I don't see no point to this, other than wasting time."

Knox checked his watch: thirteen minutes, a new world record for Jesse Bingham. "You're right," he said, turning around and reversing his path downhill. "I was just curious about those flashes."

"I told you, it was heat lightning."

"Not if you didn't hear any thunder, it wasn't. This was right on top of you." Any type of lightning caused thunder. Moreover, the flash that had blinded the security cameras in town hadn't been produced by lightning.

"Then maybe there was thunder and I just don't remember it."

"That isn't what you said. You said you couldn't hear any thunder."

"I'm getting old. I don't hear so good anymore."

His patience shredded, Knox turned around and jabbed a finger into Jesse's chest. "Stop messing with me. Now."

Jesse glared at him, but before he could decide whether or not to risk pushing just a little further, the radio on Knox's belt crackled to life.

"Code 27," said the dispatcher's voice. **"Code 27; 2490 West Brockton; 10-76."**

Knox was already heading downhill at a run. **Code 27** meant "homicide/deceased person," and **10-76** meant an investigator was needed. He fished the radio off his belt and keyed it to give the dispatcher his 10-4 and ETA.

"Hey!" Jesse yelled behind him, but Knox didn't slow or in any way acknowledge him.

He was intimately familiar with all the roads in Peke County, even the back trails. West

Brockton began life in Pekesville as simply "Brockton," but once it crossed over the main highway it became West Brockton. The road was almost exclusively residential, upper-middle-class, though the farther you traveled from town the farther apart houses were. To the best of his recollection, 2490 was about a mile outside the city limits.

He got back to his car much faster than he'd gone up the hill. Grabbing the blue light from the seat, he slapped it on top of the car and turned it on, then jammed his foot down on the accelerator and left rubber as he rocketed onto the road.

He recognized the house as soon as he saw it, and not just because of the tangle of county cars and emergency vehicles parked on the far shoulder of the road. He knew the people who lived here—or at least he **had.** Right now he had no idea how many bodies he'd find inside.

No one had parked in the driveway or yard, at least not yet. He'd taught them well: let an investigator and Boyd Ray, their forensic guy, have a shot at finding some evidence before it was driven over, trampled, or otherwise obliterated—not that they had a big forensic department with all the newest equipment, but, hell, at least give Boyd a chance.

As Knox got out of his car one of the

deputies, Carly Holcomb, came toward him. The expression on her freckled face was as serious as he'd ever seen it.

"This is Taylor Allen's house," Knox said. Taylor was a lawyer, and Knox thought, judging from his dealings with him, a pretty decent one, as lawyers went. He was fiftyish, divorced a couple of years back, and had quickly acquired himself a twenty-nine-year-old trophy wife.

Carly nodded. "He's inside," she said, falling into step beside Knox as he strode toward the house. "When he didn't show up at his office, his secretary called but didn't get an answer. She tried his cell phone, and when she didn't get an answer on it, either, she called Mrs. Allen, who, incidentally, is in Louisville visiting friends. Mrs. Allen reported that she'd talked to Mr. Allen first thing this morning, and he hadn't mentioned anything to her about having to go anywhere before going to the office. The secretary was afraid maybe he'd had a heart attack, so she called the department and I was dispatched out here to check on him."

"You found him?" Knox asked sharply.

"Yes, sir. First thing, I checked the garage, and his car is still in there. I knocked on the door but no one answered." She pulled out her notepad and glanced at it. "This was at oh-nine-eighteen. The front door is locked. I tried both the back door and the sliding glass doors on the deck, but they also are locked."

"How did you get in?"

"I didn't, sir. No one has. I came back around front and tried looking through the windows. He's lying on his stomach in the middle of the living room floor."

"Possible heart attack?"

"No, sir. He has a spear in his back."

"A **spear**?" Knox echoed, startled and not at all certain he'd understood.

"Yes, sir. I estimate its length at roughly five feet."

They went up the steps together. The house was one of those newer houses built to make it look old, with a wide porch wrapping around two sides. The wood was painted white, and the shutters on either side of the tall windows were a neat dark blue. The porch itself was painted a medium gray, and looking down, Knox plainly saw one set of footprints on the planks. He pointed, and Carly said, "Mine."

There were no other prints. Not many people came to the front door, then. Taylor and his wife would normally have entered and left through the garage; because they were outside city limits, their mail was delivered by a rural carrier who put the mail in a box on the side of the road, instead of bringing it to the house.

Carly directed him to the bank of windows on the left. The curtains were partially drawn, so he stepped to the side and looked in. The porch provided shade, and the lights were on inside; he didn't have to press his face to the glass to see. A man lay prone on the living room carpet, his head turned toward them and—by God, it really was a spear in his back. A fucking **spear.**

Taylor Allen's eyes were open and fixed, and blood had run from his open mouth and pooled around his head. He lay in that particular boneless manner that was achieved only in death.

Knox had seen people killed by pistol, rifle, and shotgun; he'd seen people who had been run over by car, pickup truck, tractor, motorcycle, and big semis. He'd seen people who had been sliced and diced by a variety of sharp objects, from a pocket knife to a chain saw. This, however, was a first. "Not many people use spears nowadays," he said pensively.

Carly gave an abrupt cough, turning her back while she covered her mouth with her hand.

"You okay?" he asked, not really paying attention to her while he studied the scene in the living room. "If you have to puke, go out in the yard."

"Yes, sir," she said in a muffled voice. "I mean, I'm okay. Just had a tickle in my throat."

Absently he fished in his pocket, came up with a cough drop he'd been carrying around since winter and could never think to throw away when he was emptying his pockets, and held it out to her. She coughed some more as she took it from him, the sound stifled as she tried to control it.

Nothing looked disturbed inside, from what he could see. No lamps were overturned; the furniture all seemed to be in place. For all the world it looked as if Taylor Allen had been caught unawares by a spear-throwing intruder—who could still be inside, though that was unlikely. The locked doors didn't necessarily mean anything; most doors could be locked by turning a lock or depressing a button, then shutting the door as you left.

Boyd Ray came hustling up, carrying a tackle box of his gear. "Whatcha got?" he said as he puffed up the steps.

"A clean scene," Knox replied, stepping back. "No one's been inside."

Boyd's red, perspiring face lit up. "No shit. Well, hallelujah. Let's see what I can find." Not often did a forensics team find an untouched scene; usually it was already contaminated by the responding officers, or family members, or even well-meaning neighbors.

Giving Boyd time to collect his evidence wouldn't make Taylor Allen any less dead. Knox withdrew to the other side of the road and let Boyd work.

Collecting evidence was a painstaking process. Smooth surfaces were dusted for prints, photos were taken, tweezers were used to pluck tiny pieces of paper or cloth or other material out of the grass. Boyd made several circuits of the house, looking for footprints, tire prints in the driveway, anything he could photograph, lift, or otherwise preserve. The summer day grew hotter. Eastern Kentucky was usually cooler than the rest of the state, because of the mountainous terrain, but today the temperature had to be at least ninety.

Finally Boyd signaled he was finished with the outside, as he carried some of his gear to his van. Knox and one of his investigators, Roger Dee Franklin, tried to finesse all the door locks but were unable to get them open. The sliding glass doors had been secured with a safety bar. Finally, in frustration, Knox called for the heavy battering ram they used to knock down doors. He selected the back door for their entrance, as it was the farthest from the crime scene, and let the boys do their job. When the back door was reduced to separate pieces hanging lopsidedly on the hinges, he and Roger Dee, along with Boyd, stepped into the house.

The first thing Knox noticed was that the door had been locked with a sturdy dead bolt.

Ditto the front door. The dead bolt there was even bigger. The sliding doors were out because there was no way to fix the security bar in place from outside.

But the house was empty. An efficient search revealed that the only person inside, other than themselves, was the victim.

"How in hell?" Roger Dee muttered to himself. "All the doors are locked, and no one else is here. Don't tell me Mr. Allen speared himself."

"The garage," Knox said. "The garage door opener is probably missing from the car. Make sure Boyd dusts the car for prints." That was the only logical way for the killer to exit; he could then lower the garage door and the house was locked up tight. It was an excellent delaying tactic.

Roger Dee left, and returned to say, "No opener that I can see, but the car is one of the new ones with the garage door opener built in. He probably didn't have a separate remote."

"Bet he did. We'll find out from his wife. Most people don't go to the bother of programming the built-in openers when they've got the remote right there anyway. By the way, has Mrs. Allen been contacted?"

"A couple of friends are driving her home."

"She probably hasn't realized yet that she can't stay here. Make certain she's intercepted, and taken to a motel." Whenever someone was murdered, in the absence of glaring evidence to the contrary, Knox automatically suspected the spouse. He couldn't quite see the trophy wife doing the deed with a spear, but stranger things had happened. Until he checked out her alibi, she was a suspect.

He wandered through the house, seeing what he could see. A single coffee cup sat in the sink, along with a cereal bowl and a lone spoon. Breakfast for one, indicating that Taylor Allen had either been alone or merely eaten alone. Knox looked in the trash and saw the package for a microwave dinner, along with the black plastic container that still contained a few bites of what looked like broccoli. A wrapper from a candy bar lay on top of that.

Upstairs, only one side of the bed had been slept in. The bed was made up, after a fashion: the custom-made bedspread had been pulled up over the pillows, but the bed was nice and smooth on one side, and sort of lumpy where the sheet hadn't been straightened out on the other. Knox knew all about that sort of bed-making, because it was how he made his own bed. In the bathroom was one toothbrush, though the holder had a space for two. One basin still showed signs of dampness, while the other was bone dry.

All the signs said that Taylor Allen had been alone in the house. But someone had been here, probably someone he knew. He'd opened the door and let his killer in the house. Then, when he'd turned his back, the killer had . . . No, how could the killer have concealed a five-foot-long spear? Mr. Allen would have noticed. The only way a spear would have been unremarkable was if someone who collected spears had brought a fine specimen over to show Mr. Allen, who was for some reason interested.

Right offhand, Knox couldn't think of a single spear collector in Peke County.

4

KNOX SQUATTED OFF TO THE SIDE, NOT
touching anything, while Boyd carefully worked
his way inward toward the body, using a handheld vacuum to suction fibers and hairs from the
carpet. Next would come the body, and what
clues could be found on it. The wooden shaft
could have been homemade, though it looked so
smooth and uniform Knox thought it might
even be a broom handle. The metal head,
though, could be homemade only if their killer
had a metalworking shop in his house.

Roger Dee squatted beside him. "What're
you thinking?"

"I'm thinking about spears," Knox replied.
"And logistics."

"Such as?"

"I'm not an expert in spears, but it seems to

me a spear can be used two ways: you can stab with it, or you can throw it. Either way, it would be almost impossible for the angle of entry to be straight on. So you can stab up, or stab down. The M.E. will have to say for sure, but looks to me as if the spear is angled slightly downward."

"Stabbed downward. We can get a rough idea of the perp's height."

"Unless it was thrown. A thrown spear would have a slight arc to it, right?" Knox made an overhand throwing motion and imagined the trajectory of the spear. "A sidearm throw would arc out and then in, instead of up and then down. The spear would enter slightly right to left if the thrower was right-handed, and left to right if he was a lefty."

"Agreed." Roger Dee pulled at his lip, eyeing the prone body lying in the small pool of congealed and blackened blood. "He didn't bleed much, so he must have died almost instantly."

"Going by the location of the spear, I'd say it went through his heart." Had he dropped right there, or maybe turned around and faced his attacker, then collapsed? And had the spear been stabbed into him, or thrown?

Knox pondered the logistics of a spear, which, unlike a bullet, required a clear line of sight to be effective when thrown. Some prowess with spear-throwing was also required, either that or a lot of luck. "Logically, he was stabbed with it. Strange choice of weapon, but an ordinary method. But suppose the spear was thrown. Where would the killer have stood, so he had a clear line of sight?"

Roger Dee pointed into the foyer beyond the wide entrance into the living room.

"Had to be in there."

"Unless Mr. Allen turned, then went down, in which case the perp was standing in front of this window." Knox pointed to the side window. "Considering the size of the room, the length of the spear, he wouldn't have wanted to get much closer. We have two possibilities, and we need to give them equal attention."

"What if Mr. Allen only managed a half turn?"

"In my opinion," Boyd Ray said from his position beside the body, "if he'd made a half turn, he wouldn't be so perfectly prone. He'd have been sprawled more, because the fall would have been more awkward. As it is, it looks like he pitched facedown."

His men didn't work many murders, Knox thought, but there was nothing wrong with their thinking.

They did all the usual things, such as checking the answering machine, punching **Redial** on the telephone to see the last number Mr. Allen had called, and getting the number of the last call he'd received. In the first case, the last call he'd made had been to his office, and the last call he'd received was from a number in Louisville, probably the call Mrs. Allen had reported to his secretary.

"If I had a suspicious nature," Knox said, "I'd wonder if Mrs. Allen made that call this morning to make certain Mr. Allen was at home."

Roger Dee grunted. It was a truism that the spouse was usually the number one suspect, at least at first. The closer you were to someone, the more likely it became that you would either kill or be killed by that very person. "You're thinking she hired it done."

"Since I doubt U.K. offers spear-throwing as an elective, I'd say she didn't do the throwing herself." He'd heard it said that Mrs. Allen had had a double major at the state university: dating and primping. He'd never met her, so he had no personal reading on her. Interviews would bring to light whether she was disenchanted with her marriage and her husband, if she had any contacts with any knowledge of spears, if she was maybe slipping around and visiting other mattresses.

In the meantime, their biggest clue was the spear itself. Something as esoteric as spearmaking had to be noticed, and the spear had been made somewhere. The metal head would be analyzed, the type of wood studied, and eventually they would find out where it came from. Maybe it had been stolen from a collection somewhere. Maybe the killer had used a weapon from his own collection—stupid, but possible. Most killers weren't renowned for their brainpower, anyway. They all made mistakes. Even the smartest ones, the ones who made a game of it, eventually screwed up.

In this case, using such an unusual weapon was the first mistake, because it gave Knox something to go on.

The next night, a woman checked into a motel on the highway, just outside Pekesville. She was pretty, with dark hair and dark eyes, and a friendly expression that invited conversation. Pauline Scalia accepted that invitation and found out the new guest was from New York, would be in town at least a couple of days, and had an easy laugh. She paid with a credit card issued in the name Nikita T. Stover, and her driver's license matched her in both name and photo.

After getting the key, Nikita Stover pulled her car in front of unit 117, got out a small suitcase, and disappeared into her room. Half an hour later, the lights went out, signaling that Ms. Stover had retired for the night.

The next morning, Nikita dressed with controlled eagerness. Excitement kicked her heart rate up, and she could feel the pulse of her blood as it pumped through her body. She was here, she was really **here**! After all the years of studying, training, getting herself ready both mentally and physically, she was finally on the job. And what a job she'd been handed!

Not that the bosses had done her any favors; she was the third agent to be given this assignment. The first, Houseman, had been killed on the job. The second, McElroy, had failed miserably. Nikita was well aware of the danger she was facing, both personally and professionally, but she still felt the buzz of adrenaline burning through her system. She dearly loved a challenge, and she was as ready for the task as she would ever be.

She fumbled a bit as she tried to button her blouse, took a deep breath to calm the slight shaking of her fingers, then completed the task. She eyed herself in the mirror critically. Everything looked okay: white blouse, tailored black trousers, holster at her waist on her left side. She wore black pumps with two-inch heels, a plain wristwatch with a black leather band, and small gold hoops in her ears. She put on her lightweight black jacket and checked to make certain her weapon was covered. Frowning, she adjusted the fall of the garment just a bit to disguise the bulge. There; she was good to go.

She had a plan, and she was ready to im-

plement it. Where McElroy had failed, she
thought, was in trying to go it alone and not
using the local assets available to him. He had
gone the cowboy route, which was the safest
way in terms of protecting the secrecy of the
mission, but it had also been the route that held
the most personal danger and had also ham-
pered his investigation. Was safest necessarily
the best? By protecting one directive, he had
failed at the most important part of the mission.
She didn't intend to fail.

She found herself smiling at her own
thoughts. God, she loved the colorful idioms:
good to go, cowboy, go it alone. They were
all so culturally descriptive, while her own language was far more technical—and colorless.
She'd studied the dialect so intensely that she
now thought in those terms, which was good;
she was less likely to slip up and make a mistake. Accent had been less of a problem, because
she wasn't trying to pass herself off as a local.

Grabbing her camera and her small black
shoulder bag, she left the motel room and automatically checked to make certain the door
latched behind her. The heat of a Kentucky
summer swamped her, making her wish she
didn't have to wear a jacket, but a professional
appearance was important.

Her rented vehicle was parked directly in
front of her room. She hadn't precisely centered

it in the marked space, she saw, chagrined at her lack of skill. Training was valuable, but it couldn't take the place of actual experience. Driving on a training course wasn't the same as driving a strange vehicle in unfamiliar territory at night. At least she hadn't crashed into anything, or gotten lost. That would have been a humiliating way to begin her assignment.

A little remote device unlocked the vehicle, and she got behind the steering wheel. Always thorough, she took a moment to look over the controls and refamiliarize herself with the location of all the various knobs, levers, and buttons, then turned the key and grinned as the combustion engine roared to life. She took a moment to play with the radio; punching the **Select** buttons didn't produce much except static, but she'd learned the night before that the **Seek** button would find a station by running through the frequencies. She smiled at each music station she heard, but kept pushing the **Seek** button until the frequency search landed on what seemed to be a local talk show. She needed to know what was going on locally.

She had studied maps of the town and surrounding areas until she had every street memorized, but she kept a map handy as she carefully negotiated the traffic signals and stop signs. Locating the house she wanted wasn't difficult at all, and she was proud of herself. So far, so good.

The house was actually just outside the city limits, where the residences were farther apart and fields were beginning to appear. She parked in front and sat for a moment, studying the scene. Pretty. Nice tall trees and mature landscaping, lush green grass, and a house that looked affluent without being ostentatious. White, with dark blue shutters, and a nice deep porch that wrapped around the right side of the house. Four steps led up to the porch and directly to the front door.

Dark green bushes, covered with a multitude of pink flowers, hugged the foundation and hid the brickwork. Nikita wasn't much on horticulture, but she thought the bushes might be azaleas. Maybe. The bushes were neatly trimmed, the grass recently cut. Two giant oak trees— she did know oaks, at least—threw shade across the entire front yard and part of the house. Yellow crime-scene tape was strung between the two trees, blocking the driveway, and extended around the house in a garish perimeter.

Slinging her bag onto her shoulder, she got out of the car, camera in hand, and took several quick photographs to have something to back up her memory when she was writing reports, or working theories. Ducking under the yellow tape, she walked up the paved driveway, snapping photographs as she went. She didn't expect to see anything that would point the way to the killer, something that another experienced agent had missed, but she was fixing distances and measurements in her mind. Slowly she circled the house, noting every window and door, the state of the shrubbery under the windows, the distance to the ground from each window. Such knowledge might come in handy, might not. She already knew **how;** she just didn't know **who.** Or where the **who** was.

In back there was a small door in the foundation that gave access to the crawl space beneath the house. She studied the ground to make certain there weren't any footprints in front of the door, then crouched down in front of it; there was a handle, but she didn't want to touch it and disturb any of the local cops' evidence. Instead she worked her fingers into the seam until she could pull the thin slab of plywood outward, noting as she did so how the front corner dragged in the dirt. Taking a penlight from her shoulder bag, she directed the light on the ground directly inside the access door. It looked undisturbed, no scrape marks or hand imprints in the dirt.

The lack of marks reassured her that she was on the right track. Returning the penlight to her bag, she shoved the door back into place.

"What the hell are you doing in my crime scene?"

The deep voice, coming from directly behind

and above her, shot through her nervous system like a bolt. She jumped, but managed to stifle the shriek that rose in her throat. "Good thing I don't have a tricky heart," she said as she stood and turned to face the owner of the voice.

"Answer the question," he said, expression hard and blue eyes cold.

He was broad-shouldered and tall, a good six or seven inches taller than she, and she was five seven. He wore jeans, scuffed boots, and a blue jacket over a white polo shirt. His brown hair was a little on the shaggy side, not quite regulation. Maybe he just hadn't had time to get a haircut, but maybe he had a little bit of rebel in him.

At her hesitation he put his left hand on his hip, a deliberate move that opened his jacket and exposed the badge clipped to his belt, as well as the big weapon tucked into his shoulder harness. "If you're a reporter," he said, evidently having noticed her camera, "your ass is in big trouble."

Just as deliberately, Nikita opened her own jacket, showing him **her** weapon; then she lifted the flap of her shoulder bag and flashed her badge at him. "Nikita Stover, FBI," she said, and held out her hand to him.

His eyebrows lifted, and if anything, he looked even more displeased. "Last time I checked, murder wasn't a federal charge. What are you doing here?"

She shrugged and let her hand drop. Things would go better if he was friendly, since he was evidently in charge of the investigation; he'd called this "his" crime scene. This was the tricky part; she just hoped her documentation was good enough that he wouldn't investigate her. "Following a trail," she said, and sighed. "There has been a string of attacks targeting attorneys and judges, and we think it's the same person doing all of them. A federal judge was killed in Wichita last year, remember that? We're following up on every crime that could be remotely connected, looking for a break, because so far we aren't having much luck." She glanced at the house. "Mr. Allen was an attorney, so here I am. I'm not looking to take over your investigation; I was hoping **you** could help **me.**"

The set of those broad shoulders relaxed somewhat, but his eyes remained cold. "So why didn't you contact me?"

"You were my next stop. I just wanted to see the house first. I didn't intend to go inside, and I was careful not to mess up any evidence." Mentally she took a deep breath, then gave him a little smile and held out her hand. "Let's try this again. I'm Nikita Stover, FBI."

This time he took her hand. His palm was

slightly rough, and very warm. "Knox Davis, county chief investigator."

A sharp **crack** split the morning air, and splinters exploded from the wall almost directly behind her. The backyard provided no good shelter and they moved simultaneously, both of them sprinting for the far side of the house. He shoved her ahead of him, sending her stumbling. When she recovered her balance, she flattened herself against the wall, weapon in her hand, though she had no recollection of drawing it.

He too had his big automatic drawn, pointing upward as he took quick peeks around the corner. "Don't see a thing," he said, and grinned as he glanced at her. His blue eyes danced. "Welcome to Peke County."

"You think this is **funny**?" she barked.

"It's sure as hell interesting." His voice held a lazy drawl, as if he couldn't get too excited about something as mundane as being shot at. "Somebody evidently doesn't want you here, which makes me wonder how he knew you'd **be** here at this particular time." While he talked, he kept taking those quick peeks, and he pulled a radio from his belt. After keying it, he said, "Code 28, 10-00, 2490 West Brockton." He glanced at her. "The cavalry will be here in a minute."

"So I gathered."

"Who knew you'd be here?"

"No one. Not at this location, and not at this time." A chill went down her spine, because the ramifications of this were about as bad as she could imagine.

"Someone did. That bullet was aimed at you."

She couldn't argue with that. Considering the angle, either she'd been the target or the shooter had bad aim. Discounting the bad-aim angle, she was forced to confront an ugly conclusion: one of her own was trying to kill her.

5

INVESTIGATOR DAVIS REMAINED PLASTERED against the side of the house, looking for all the world as if he intended to stay right there until the cavalry, as he termed it, arrived. "Aren't we going after him?" Nikita asked in frustration, crowding her shoulder against him to nudge him along. She needed to know who had shot at her, and if this mission had perhaps been compromised from the beginning. Was this why McElroy had failed, and Houseman died?

"I must have forgot to put on my white hat today," he replied, not looking at her.

"So you don't have a hat," she said, driven almost to snapping because he was making inane remarks instead of **doing** something. "It isn't raining."

He glanced over at her, an incredulous,

slightly baffled expression flitting across his face. "I mean, I'm not wearing my hero hat today. You know, the good guy always wears the white hat? The cowboy?"

"Got it." **Uh-oh.** She should have made the connection, especially since she'd been thinking in cowboy idioms just a short while ago. She cringed inside at the unaccustomed mistake, and her cheeks began to grow hot. "Then you can stay here, and I'll go after him."

She started to move forward and his arm swept out, pinning her to the house. "No way. I didn't see any movement or smoke, so we can't pinpoint his location. There are a lot of places out there for a sniper to conceal himself, and a lot of open ground where you'd be a sitting duck. You stay."

"I'm a federal agent—" she began, fully prepared to pull rank on him. She used both hands to tug on the arm that pressed across her collarbones, too close to her throat for comfort. The effort was useless; she couldn't budge him, unless she was prepared to use a much more violent method.

"That's right, and I'm damned if I'll be stuck filling out a lot of paperwork explaining how you got your ass shot off. County paperwork's bad enough; with federal, I'd still be filling out forms a week from now. So you stay right where you are."

She pursed her lips while she pondered the situation, her dark eyes narrow as she stared at him. She needed to stay on his good side, but she also needed to find out who had shot at her, and obviously she couldn't do both at the same time.

On the other hand, he had delayed her long enough that whoever had shot at her was probably gone, and even if she dumped him on his ass and went after the shooter, she wasn't likely to find out anything. "Okay," she finally said. "You've probably waited too long to catch him, anyway."

"So put the blame on me when you write your report." He sounded completely unconcerned that she might do so, as if there was nothing she or the FBI could do to him on a professional level that caused him any worry.

She shrugged—as much as she could, anyway, considering she was pinned to the side of the house. "No, there's no point in whining and giving excuses. It'll still come down on me, regardless."

He gave her a quick searching look as he moved his arm from her chest, then resumed his vigil in the other direction. "Pull back to the porch. If the shooter can work his way around to change his angle, we're completely exposed here."

She looked around and saw that the angled

steps to the wide porch began just a few yards behind her. What he'd said made sense, so she moved swiftly in a low crouch to the steps, then up them and around to the front of the house. He was right behind her, watching their six while she guarded their front.

He said, "Anyone who's studied logistics will know that moving across that open ground was a death sentence."

He was trying to comfort her, and she was a little touched by his concern. "Yeah, well, TPTB aren't always well-versed in logistics."

There was a slight pause. " 'TPTB'?"

Now it was her turn to give him an uncertain look. She'd used a common acronym, one that had been around a long time. "The Powers That Be," she explained, a little warily. "Internet shorthand."

"Got it. I'm not much on the Internet thing; the guys who work juvenile cases have to stay up on the latest stuff, though."

Her life was so tied to computers she couldn't imagine not being totally conversant with them, but in a way she envied him the freedom to **not** be. Then it struck her that while she was on this assignment, she was essentially just as free as he was. She couldn't be monitored, and she had no way of contacting her superiors without physically returning to the base. At first that lack of a tether had bothered her, but a few minutes ago when someone had shot at her, her outlook had changed considerably.

Since she couldn't be monitored, the only way the shooter could have known where she was, was to have followed her. But why hadn't he taken a shot earlier, while she'd been alone? Or when she was walking to her car from the motel room? Why here, and why now?

The sound of sirens in the distance interrupted her chain of thought, but she knew she'd be returning to it, gnawing over the facts and possibilities until something made sense.

The cavalry arrived in the form of six county patrol cars sliding in on squealing wheels, followed by a large armored van built more like a tank than a van. The double doors of the van swung open and a squad of stalwart men, dressed in dark blue and armed to the teeth, swarmed out.

"A SWAT team?" she asked in astonishment. "You said cavalry, not the heavy armored division."

"They don't get a lot of action, so I guess they needed the practice," he said easily. "Besides, they love me."

She snorted, but didn't reply as they were abruptly surrounded by the deputies, all with weapons drawn and shouting a cacophony of orders at her. Belatedly she realized all of those weapons were pointed at her and she quickly said, "Federal agent," while she slowly raised her gun hand and with the other hand lifted the flap of her purse to flash her badge.

The weapons were immediately lowered, but no apologies were issued and she didn't expect any. If she'd been thinking, she'd have anticipated that reaction; the deputies had done exactly what they were supposed to do.

"This is Agent Stover," Davis said. "We were behind the house and someone fired a shot at her from the tree line across the back field."

"You sure the shot was aimed at her?" a deputy asked.

"Reasonably, considering the angle. If not, the guy was a lousy shot."

Davis walked off a few feet with the deputies, talking to them in a low tone. Nikita stood in place, effectively excluded and trying not to let it bother her. She was the outsider; these people worked side by side every day. But it was **her** life that was evidently most at risk and she not only wanted to be involved, she needed to be at least a half step ahead of them.

Until the area was secured, it would be foolhardy to leave the security of their position, so she was forced to remain on the porch. Walking a few feet away in search of her own pocket of privacy, she took a small cellular phone from her purse and punched in a series of numbers. The numbers were random and connected her to no one, because there was no way she could apprise her superiors of the situation. If what she suspected was true, one of them was possibly sabotaging the mission and she wouldn't contact them even if she could.

But for what reason would anyone sabotage her? It was to everyone's advantage if she solved this problem. That was what didn't make sense, but then a lot about this case hadn't made sense from the beginning.

A feeling of panic welled in her and she fought it down. So what if she was alone, cut off from any real help? Someone had made a tactical error in missing that shot and now she had the advantage in that she was forewarned.

She dug an electronic notebook out of her bag, propped it on the porch railing, and began making notes directly on the screen. Putting things in writing always helped her see the cohesive whole of any situation, and besides, she had to do something other than stand there looking useless.

Point one: She had picked her motel at random, so she had been followed from the time she arrived.

Point two: If that was so, why hadn't the killer shot her at the point of arrival, rather than waiting until today? Or broken into her motel room last night and killed her? She hadn't been on guard then, and now she was.

Point three: There weren't that many motels in Pekesville, so how hard would locating her have been? Maybe her exact arrival hadn't been known, and instead the killer had checked out the local motels, found her rental car, and followed her to a more isolated location.

"What kind of squiggles are those?" a familiar voice asked as Investigator Davis moved close to her side and squinted down at her notes. He reached down and took the EN from her and examined it, turning it from side to side.

"A sort of personal shorthand I developed to keep nosy men from reading over my shoulder," she said smoothly, though a smile twitched at her lips. She winked at him. "Seen any nosy men around?"

"Guilty as charged," he said, not sounding at all guilty. "This is a pretty cool gadget. Guess the feds have the budget to buy toys like this for their people."

"Guess so," she said.

He leaned his shoulder against a column. "Got any ideas about who would want you dead? Discounting the small possibility that you were in the wrong place at the wrong time and it was a random shot, someone firing without a clear line of sight. This isn't deer season, but people don't always obey the law, now do they?"

The area was definitely what she'd call rural,

even though it was just outside the city limits.
And things did occasionally happen for no reason; they just happened.

"I like the idea that this was an accident, but
I can't afford to believe it," she said ruefully.
"One other agent has been killed on this case;
we thought he'd gotten close to the killer, but
now I have to consider the possibility that his
mission was sabotaged."

"Meaning someone in your office is working
with the killer to eliminate judges and attorneys
who they think are working for the Dark Side."

"Plenty of those around," she said neutrally.
Dark side? That was so quaint she was charmed.
"What about the attorney who lived here? What
kind was he?"

"A pretty good guy, for a lawyer. He didn't do
many criminal cases, though he'd take some of
the small stuff. Mostly he handled property dis-
putes, divorces, wills, that type of thing. Not a
guy I'd say would attract anyone's attention."

"So there goes the 'dark side' theory."

"There's another angle. Mr. Allen's murder
may not be connected with your cases at all. But
whoever killed him could have been lurking
nearby, maybe watching the house for some reason, and when he saw you poking around, he
took a shot at you."

That theory had a bit more weight than
the "accidents happen" theory. Killers did tend

to hang around, for some reason, maybe because most of them weren't very intelligent. Except . . . "So why not shoot you? You're a bigger
target."

"There's that," he conceded. "But until we
prove one way or another what's going on, it'll
be safer for you to leave town and not tell anyone where you're going. I saw you talking on
your cell phone; did you report in?"

"No. I was checking a digital file."

"Won't there be a record of that?"

"If someone knows where to look, yes."

"Or they access your cell phone records.
Look, I know you're federal and have a lot
more resources than we do here, but if someone's out to kill you, then that means somehow
Mr. Allen's murder **is** connected to the Wichita
homicide, that someone in your office is involved, and the best thing for you to do is disappear. Those other possibilities are small, and
you can't afford to play the odds."

"I can't afford to walk away, either, not knowing who's behind this."

"Meaning you're going to stay here." He said
it as a fact, not a question.

"Unless you run me out of town, yes."

"All right. Then I'll see if I can find some way
to make you hard to find while you're here."

His easy acceptance of her decision took her
slightly off balance, and gave her a funny feeling

in the pit of her stomach. She narrowed her eyes at him. "Why are you being so accommodating? I know local law enforcement resents the FBI getting involved in their cases."

"Oh, it's just the way I am," he said, smiling. "I just love a good mystery."

6

THE SWAT TEAM AND DEPUTIES COMBED the tree line behind the Allen house and found where the shooter had likely stood, as evidenced by some scuffed-up leaves and a handy low branch on which to rest the rifle, but he himself was long gone. They had determined the angle by the simple means of sticking a pencil in the bullet hole in the house; since the bullet traveled in a straight line over a relatively short distance, the pencil would show the exact angle of impact and point toward where the shooter had been standing.

Nikita stood where the shooter had stood, Knox Davis beside her, and studied the geometry of where she and Knox had both been standing. From this angle, Knox had been on the left and she'd been on the right, facing him. The bullet had passed slightly behind her, imbedding itself in the wall. If Knox had been the target, the shot had missed by several feet; assuming the shooter had any degree of competency with a rifle, the person had definitely been aiming at her.

"Damn it," she said mildly.

His eyebrows lifted. "Damn it, what?"

"I wish you'd been the target."

"Gee, thanks."

"You know what I mean. If someone shot at you, that's fairly straightforward. You live around here. Maybe you got on someone's bad side. Maybe whoever murdered Mr. Allen wanted to take out the investigator, too."

Instead, she had lost her last hope that her mission hadn't been sabotaged. She was truly and completely alone, cut off from any help because she didn't know whom she could trust. She couldn't even return to headquarters, knowing what she knew and carrying a warning; she would likely be exterminated before she could pass on that crucial information.

"I've been thinking about the situation," he said, taking her arm and ushering her back toward the house. He used a light touch, so that she'd taken several steps before she realized what he was doing. She hadn't been quite ready to leave the site—in fact, she'd been hoping for a moment of relative privacy so she could scan the area for any telltale DNA left behind—but now she couldn't dig in her heels without raising his interest, which meant she wouldn't get that moment of privacy she needed.

He was good, she realized. That low-key approach took people off guard. She might not have been wise to him even now if she hadn't seen the steel in his eyes when he had first found her snooping around "his" crime scene, or been pinned to the wall by his arm to prevent her from taking action on her own. She needed him, but she had to be on her toes around him, too.

"Are you listening?" he asked with faint irritation.

"To what? You haven't said a word since the 'thinking about the situation' announcement."

"You looked like you were off in the ether somewhere," he explained.

He thought she looked sedated? She understood the gist of what he was saying, though, so she merely replied, "I was thinking."

"Can you think and listen at the same time?"

"Sure. Women are multitasking miracles of nature."

He chuckled as he steered her around a fallen log that she could easily have stepped over. She'd read that southern men were relatively protective, so she accepted the unnecessary aid.

"You can stay at my house," he said, and held

up a hand when she opened her mouth to immediately refuse. "Hear me out. I'll move into
Starling's bed-and-breakfast, tell people that the
house has to be rewired or something. None of
the neighbors will check, or even think twice at
seeing a light on there because I usually park in
the garage. I'm not there much, anyway, so it's
no big deal to me—"

"Except for the financial cost." How was she
supposed to deal with this? She couldn't repay
him, in fact didn't know if she'd be able to access any funds at all. The cash she had with her
might have to do.

He waved a negligent hand. "Don't worry
about that. You can pay me back later."

The offer, though outwardly kind, disturbed
her. Why would he offer her his home when
they'd just met, under less-than-perfect conditions? It wasn't as if they were friends. Moreover,
in her experience, those in law enforcement
were far more cynical and suspicious than the
average citizen.

The answer knotted her stomach. He **was**
suspicious—of her. He wanted her where he
could keep an eye on her while he checked her
out; he might even have already made a call to
start the process.

Casually, she pulled her arm out of his grasp
while she stepped around a tree; then she waited

for him and fell back into step. Her willingness to walk beside him would keep him from being suspicious of the little maneuver, but now her arm was free if she needed to take drastic action.

She thought furiously, trying to decide on the best approach to deal with him. He was crucial to her mission; her plan all along had been to approach the head of the local investigation, but the way he'd found her snooping around had started her off on the wrong foot and even getting shot at hadn't completely convinced him that she was one of the good guys.

"I don't know what to do," she finally confessed. "I'm . . . well, this is my first assignment, and the way things are going so far, I'll probably be working at a reception desk for the rest of my career if I mess up."

The expression in his eyes, instead of softening, cooled instead. "A rookie was given an assignment like this?"

"Legwork," she said, staring straight ahead. "No one thought I'd stumble into anything."

"Then why send you here? Even more, why try to kill you, because that sure let the cat out of the bag?"

Cat? Rapidly she considered the context of his statement and decided on the most likely meaning. "I don't know," she finally said. "I can't make sense of it. I've just been doing basic investigation, gathering rough data and sending it to Quantico for the brains to assemble." That, at least, was the truth—as far as it went.

"You saw something, questioned someone, and uncovered a crucial piece of the puzzle."

"I can't think what, and certainly nothing that the local investigators hadn't initially uncovered." She shook her head, then said, "Going back to the original subject, I'd feel very uncomfortable staying in your house—"

"Even if I'm not there?"

"Even if," she said firmly. "It's such an imposition—"

"Not to me. Like I said, I'm not there much. I work long hours, and the house is mainly just a place to crash for a few hours' sleep."

"You're not married?"

"No." An expression flitted across his face, so fast she couldn't read it. "The other investigators are, though, so I let them have as much time at home as I can."

That was nice of him, she thought. Overall, he seemed like a very nice guy. Suspicious, but nice.

They reached the house and she halted, looking around at the pretty home and the nicely landscaped lawn. The trees were in full leaf, and colorful flowers grew in neat beds. There were some places on earth where murder seemed to

fit in, as if it were some basic part of the surroundings, but not here.

"Has the bullet been recovered?" she asked,
indicating the hole in the house. "It'll be interesting to see if the ballistics match."

"Match what?" he asked.

She knit her brows, giving him a puzzled
glance. "With the one that killed Mr. Allen, of
course."

"Oh, yeah, that one."

Proof positive that he didn't trust her, Nikita
thought. She knew Taylor Allen hadn't been
shot, but that little fact had been held back
from the news item release. She'd given Knox
Davis an opening wide enough to drive
through, but he hadn't told her about the spear.

She was discouraged, the sun was high and
hot, and she wanted shade. Returning to the
front porch, she sat down in one of the white
wicker chairs. The green-and-white-striped cush-
ion cradled her, enveloping her in comfort. This
was a house kept with care and pride, she
thought as she took out her EN and began making more notes.

"I assume Mrs. Allen has been investigated,"
she said absently when her persistent shadow
propped himself against the railing in front of
her, his long legs crossed at the ankle.

"Ironclad alibi. She was with friends. I'm still

looking into the possibility that it was murder for hire."

"Big insurance policy?"

"Big enough."

"Boyfriend?"

"Not that I've been able to find."

She pursed her lips. "Girlfriend, maybe? His, not hers. Though hers would be a possibility, I guess."

"Again, nothing that I've found. They seemed to be happily married."

"Not so happily, if she had him killed."

"That's just a string I'm tugging on, one of many. You just tied a bunch of them in knots, though."

"Not deliberately." She tilted her head back and studied him, noting the calm intelligence in his lean face. Celtic heritage, she thought, remembering that this portion of the country had been heavily settled, pre-Revolution, by the Scots-Irish, and not diluted much in the two and a half centuries since. That lean, high-cheekboned, blade of a face was a look that could be seen in hundreds of carefully preserved old photographs.

"Where are you from?" he asked abruptly. "I can't place the accent."

And wouldn't it be amazing if he could, she thought with amusement. "Florida, originally, but I went to college in Washington State, and

I've worked in several different states." Again, that was the truth, and in this case the complete truth.

"That makes for quite a blend."

"It does," she agreed. "And you?" He was the one who had asked the first personal question, so she felt free to come back with her own.

"I've lived here since I was a kid. I was born in Lexington, but we moved here when my mother died."

"I'm sorry," she said with instant sympathy. "That's so hard on a child."

"Pretty tough. I was six."

"Did your father remarry?"

"Not until I was grown and gone."

"Where did you go?"

"To college, specifically, but the expression means I was old enough to leave home." His tone was neutral, but his gaze bored into her.

The colloquialisms were tripping her up, which was frustrating because the language was what she had studied most, enjoyed, and the area where she had felt most confident. Mc-Elroy had run into this, too, but his risk had been minimized because he hadn't had any contact with the local law enforcement, trying instead to be as unobtrusive as possible. Maybe his had been the better idea, but it was too late for her to worry about that now.

"Why don't you follow me back to the office?" he asked. "We can go over the file on the Allen case."

Instinct warred with dedication. She suspected he wanted her close at hand until he heard back about the inquiry into her status that he was certain to make, if he hadn't already done so, but at the same time she needed to see that file. She decided to take the risk, and trust that she'd be able to get herself out of any difficulty that might arise.

"Sure," she said. "Could we pick up something to eat on the way? I skipped breakfast this morning."

If she was FBI, Knox thought, he'd eat his badge.

The clothes were right: conservative, not too costly. She'd handled her weapon in the approved manner, and she was quick and bright. Most cops might not like dealing with the feds, but overall the ones Knox had met were smart people. Assholes, some of them, but bright assholes.

Maybe it was because she wasn't uptight enough. She had an open, friendly face and an easy smile, one that invited you to smile in return, and she was remarkably relaxed on procedure. No fed he'd ever known was very relaxed about anything.

Then there was the communication thing. A

few times he'd felt as if they were talking about different subjects completely, but then he'd noticed that where things went astray was when he used slang or idioms, and she would take him literally. Every section of the country had its own version of dialect, but "white hat" wasn't particular to the south. It was almost as if she weren't even American, but someone who had intensely studied standard English as a second language. This last possibility was what made his inner alarm jangle.

She could be from anywhere; there was no one ethnic look that he could say applied to her. She had glossy, dark brown hair that grew in a widow's peak from her forehead, big brown eyes, a wide, soft mouth, and even white teeth that definitely looked American. Braces, fluoride, nutrition, and regular visits to the dentist produced teeth like that. She wore very subtle makeup, and highlighted streaks fell on each side of the slightly off-center part in her hair.

She wasn't Middle Eastern, he thought, or Slavic. There was a warm tone to her skin and maybe she could be of Italian descent, or Spanish, but she was on the tall side for that heritage.

What it came down to was, he couldn't pin down anything about her, and that made him uneasy.

She sat across his desk from him, her chair pulled up close so she could use the desk for a table. He noticed that she seemed a bit hesitant when she first bit into her hamburger, as if she wasn't certain of the taste. Then she chewed more enthusiastically, but it wasn't until he picked up one of his fries and swirled it in the gob of ketchup that he'd squirted onto the spread-out hamburger wrapper that she did the same, copying his movements.

She's never eaten a burger and fries before. The thought sounded in his head with the certainty of a pronouncement. He tried to think of a place on earth, other than undeveloped nations, where McDonald's hadn't established an outpost or two. How could she not have eaten a hamburger, unless she'd been raised as a strict vegan and had only yesterday fallen off the turnip wagon, so to speak?

"Where did you say you're from?"

"Florida. Sarasota." She selected another fry and swabbed it in ketchup, then popped it into her mouth. Picking up her cup and guiding the straw to her mouth, she sucked up a big swallow of Coke—the sugared stuff, not the diet version drunk by almost every woman he knew. "Mmm, this is good," she purred.

While she ate, she was looking around his crowded little office as if it were a museum, and she was fascinated by the contents. He wondered what interested her the most: the piles of paperwork, the scarred and battered desk, his squeaky chair, or maybe the streaks on the window?

His phone rang and he picked it up. "Davis. Yeah." He tucked the receiver between his shoulder and jaw, pushing his chair backward so he could reach a file drawer and pull it open. He found a file and pulled it out. "Got it."

Agent Stover—or whoever she was—occupied herself while he was talking by getting up and wandering around the office. She couldn't wander far, a few steps in each direction, but she lightly touched objects with one fingertip, then moved on to another. He watched her bestow that gentle touch on his stained, ten-year-old Mr. Coffee, then move on to a clipboard of Wanted posters.

She was in good shape, he thought, but then she would be if she was a newly minted agent, fresh out of the academy. He eyed the shape of her ass, outlined by her pants, then felt like a jerk and looked away. A second later he decided to be a jerk and looked again; after all, it was a nice ass.

A voice squawked in his ear and he forced his attention back to the file he was reading, but he remained sharply aware of where she was and what she was doing. As small as his office was, that wasn't difficult.

She returned to his desk to retrieve her Coke. He watched her lips close around the plastic straw, an act that abruptly struck him as so rawly carnal he had to look away. Okay, so he was a horny jerk. Having a physical reaction to a woman he suspected of impersonating an FBI agent was unprofessional as hell, and he didn't like it.

Finally he finished his conversation and hung up the phone, then returned the file to the filing cabinet. Leaning back in his chair, he said easily, "Why don't you tell me where you're really from."

To his surprise, she gave him a crooked smile. "I knew you didn't believe me. I really am an FBI agent." Lifting the flap of her purse, she removed her shield and handed it over to him, then did the same with her ID card. "A genuine, authentic agent of the federal government. I suppose you've already put in a request for verification; am I supposed to stay here until you get it?"

"If you don't mind," he said, all politeness as he examined the shield and card. They **looked** real, but a good forger could do some amazing stuff. He had to be careful here; if she really was a federal agent, then he didn't want to make the mistake of disarming her and taking her into custody, which would cause all sorts of shit to come down on his head. On the other hand, he couldn't give her an automatic pass; he had to check her out, or he was a piss-poor cop. Finally he gave the shield and card back to her and she returned both items to their designated places.

"How about my driver's license," she offered. "Or a credit card. Want to see them, too?"

"If you don't mind," he repeated, and she actually laughed as she opened her purse and removed both cards from her wallet, handing them across the desk.

He studied the license with its holographic seal, closely examined it for signs of tampering, then compared the signature on the bottom with the signature on the back of the credit card. They matched, of course. He was beginning to feel foolish, while she was not only relaxed, she was amused as well.

"Good," he said as he returned the cards to her. "Now I don't feel as if I need to take your weapon away from you."

"**Try** to take my weapon," she corrected. "There's a point at which I stop being a good citizen and become a pissed-off agent."

"Then don't do anything that makes me nervous, and we'll get along fine."

She picked up another fry. "If I wanted to shoot you, I could have done it this morning when we were the only two people around, and my weapon was already unholstered."

"There's that," he conceded. "Have you had any other thoughts about how Taylor Allen's murder ties in with your other cases, and why someone in your office would obviously leak your whereabouts to a sniper who might or might not be the killer?"

"On the surface, I can't see any connection between Mr. Allen and the other cases. As for wanting me dead, that doesn't make any sense at all. Assuming I did find something that is threatening this someone in my office, I don't know what it is, and killing me would only result in someone with a lot more experience taking over. Killing me isn't cost-effective, as far as I can see."

"You've been pretty calm about the whole thing," he observed.

"What choice do I have? I suppose I could get hysterical and cry on your shoulder, but what would that accomplish, other than a stuffed-up nose?"

She hadn't been rattled when she was shot at, either, he remembered. He liked that kind of steadiness in anyone. There was a lot about her he liked, including that friendly smile. He just wished that damn verification would come in so he could feel better about liking her. Until then, he'd already let his guard down as far as he could without crossing over into total unprofessionalism.

The phone rang again and he answered it. He listened, said "Thanks," then hung up and smoothly pulled his weapon and leveled it at her. "Use two fingers and remove your weapon, then place it on the desk and step back," he said in a cool, level tone. "You're under arrest for impersonating a federal agent."

7

NIKITA'S HEART GAVE A QUICK THUMP AND
adrenaline burned through her veins. This was
it; she'd hoped events wouldn't bring her to this,
but she was a realist and she'd prepared. She
had to be more convincing than she'd ever
been before in her life, or her ass was burnt.
No, that wasn't it. A cooking term, though . . .
Burnt, cooked, baked—oh, yeah: her ass was
toast.

The ridiculous thought calmed her a little.
Without protest she opened her jacket and awk-
wardly used the first two fingers of her left hand
to pull the heavy weapon from the holster. She
laid it on his desk, barrel pointing to the side.
His big hand closed over the weapon and
moved it out of her reach.

"You have the right to remain silent," he

began as he lifted her to her feet and secured first her right wrist, then her left, in a set of handcuffs. The cold steel bit into her, so tight it felt as if her bones were squeezed together. She didn't bother listening as he recited the Miranda; she knew the drill by heart.

"Please empty my purse onto your desk," she said softly, looking up at him. He was still standing close, gripping her arm, so close she could feel his body heat. Cops were taught to use their own bodies to subdue and control, to grip, the agonizing holds that paralyzed a struggling suspect with his or her own pain. She didn't make even a tiny move of resistance, in fact leaned even closer to him, so close her hair brushed his shoulder. "Please."

His gaze was flat and remote, his face expressionless, all hint of affability gone. "Why?"

"There are some things in there I want to tell you about. Handcuff me to the chair or the desk if you're worried I'll try to bolt. I promise I won't, but you might feel nervous."

"Nervous?" he asked, briefly puzzled and his attention caught. "How's that?"

"Because I have training that you don't." Maybe this was working. She could see the flicker of interest in his eyes.

"If you were a real FBI agent, I might believe that."

"I **am** a real FBI agent, just not . . . now."

"Maybe you can convince a judge you're delusional, but I'm not buying it. They have no record of a Nikita T. Stover as an agent, former or otherwise."

"I didn't say 'former.' Please, just empty my purse on your desk. I'll tell you about everything that's in there."

For a moment she thought he'd refuse, but in the end his curiosity won out. He didn't take chances; he made her sit down, and he used a second set of cuffs to attach one of her ankles to the chair. Being cuffed was very uncomfortable, the way it pulled her shoulders back. Experienced prisoners didn't try to keep their shoulders balanced; they dropped one and let the cuffs ride more to the other side, which effectively relieved the pressure on both shoulder joints. She tried that, and almost sighed as the pain instantly faded.

Picking up her purse, he dumped the contents on his desk. After a moment he frowned at the array of gadgets. "What's all this?"

"First, look in my wallet. In the zippered compartment, there's a card. Take it out and look at it."

He unzipped the section she indicated and pulled out the card. It was thicker than most cards, about the same as three personal cards stacked together, and made of a lightweight, translucent compound that was virtually indestructible. It wouldn't burn, and she herself had tried to hack it to pieces just because they'd told her it couldn't be done. They'd been right.

On the left side a gold shield with an eagle on top had been laser-embossed, a shield that was similar but not identical to the one she'd showed him earlier. The shield read "Department of Justice" on the bottom and "Federal Bureau of Investigation" on the top. That hadn't changed, but the shape of the shield differed, being slightly more rounded, and the eagle looked more fierce. On the right side was a three-dimensional holographic photo of her, and below was her name and serial number.

"Cool," he said, holding up the card and tilting it so the hologram flickered. "What's it supposed to prove? That you know someone who can make 3-D pictures?"

"Try to destroy it," she said. "Go ahead, try anything you can think of. Cut it up. Melt it. Pour acid on it. See what happens."

"I don't have any acid with me today," he said, but he took a pair of scissors from his center desk drawer and tried to cut the card. Then he tried again, a look of concentration settling on his face. "This is thicker than a normal card," he said, bearing down with all the strength in his hands.

The rivet popped out of the scissors and the two pieces fell apart in his hand.

"Shit!" he said in surprise, and examined the card with more interest. "What's it made of?"

"If I told you, I'd have to kill you," she said, trying out the old joke. When he didn't laugh, she shrugged. "I don't know. It's called poly-di-something-something; I've never been able to pronounce it. The trade name is Ondite, for reasons I don't know. NASA developed it for spaceships about, oh, a hundred and twenty years ago. Sort of."

His gaze went flat again. "Stop fucking with me, lady. If this wild story is all the explanation you have, you're wasting my time."

"Because NASA didn't exist a hundred and twenty years ago? It didn't, counting from now. Try burning the card," she suggested, thinking he needed to be more intrigued before she tried explaining about NASA.

"I'll take your word for it," he said, and tossed the card onto his desk.

She was losing him. The key was getting his curiosity piqued enough that he would keep listening to her. He looked ready to haul her off to a cell, so she said quickly, "That silver case. Open it up."

"Why don't you just save your breath and—"

Abruptly her patience broke. She had to convince him, and she didn't have a lot of time to waste doing it. "Oh, for God's sake," she said in exasperation. "I'm from the future. The year 2207, to be exact. I'm federal agent Nikita Stover, sent back to catch a killer from my time who traveled back to this time to systematically kill—

"You don't believe a word I'm saying, do you?"

"You're kidding, right?" he asked rhetorically. He'd folded his arms across his chest and appeared to be waiting for her to wind down.

"The silver case is a DNA scanner. I was hoping I'd be able to get a reading in the forest behind Mr. Allen's house, but you stuck too close to me. Go ahead, open it. I assume you're bright enough to recognize technology that doesn't exist now."

Goading him probably wasn't smart, but she would do anything necessary to stay out of a jail cell. She would be useless there, and if her location became known, vulnerable to another attack.

"If it doesn't exist yet, then how can it be right here?" he asked, picking up the case and showing it to her, for all the world as if she hadn't noticed it before.

"I didn't say 'yet,' I said 'now.' There's a world of difference."

"Not that I can see. I'm holding it **now.**"

"Okay, so time travel messes with syntax," she snapped. "Do you want to get into an argument about past future tenses? The scanner exists temporarily in your now, but when I leave, it goes with me and it will then not yet exist."

Again she saw that flicker of curiosity in his expression when she mentioned past future tenses, which she'd hated studying in school. Time travel could tie language in a knot, making it possible for one person to both intend to do something, and at the same time to have already done it. But she didn't want to discuss language with him, she wanted him to look at the scanner.

"The lid is really a part of the scanner," she said, nodding toward the case. "It folds all the way back and connects to the bottom of the case. It won't work unless all the connections are made."

"There aren't any holes in the lid for connections," he pointed out, again showing the case to her.

Nikita rolled her eyes. "There will be. They stay closed until the initial contact, to keep out dust and debris. Just open the damn thing, will you?"

His lips quirked in amusement at her irritable tone. "You're getting a tad pushy, Ms. Stover. Remember who's wearing the cuffs and who isn't."

She narrowed her eyes. "Only because I let you cuff me, to show my goodwill."

"So you keep saying." He'd been fiddling

with the scanner the entire time, and now he opened it and slowly folded the lid all the way back, holding it up close to his face so he could watch for any hidden latches to spring open. Just as the two surfaces touched there was a quiet click as the two halves locked together. Immediately the self-test function began running, a series of different colored lights dancing over the scanner.

He tried to pull the pieces apart, but once the lid was secured, it stayed that way until the release button was pushed.

"Magnetized?" he asked, frowning.

"No. I told you how it worked. Press the triangular button at the very top to release the mechanism."

He studied the face of the scanner, pressed the specified button, and the lights went out as soon as the lid was released.

Silently he once more folded the lid back so it met with its matching half. Again came the quiet click and the lights flashing as the self-test ran again.

"Snazzy gadget," he finally said. "What's it supposed to do, other than look impressive?"

"I told you, it's a DNA scanner. It can recognize and process DNA. If you're in the data banks, the way I am, it'll give you my name, address, any prior arrests and convictions, where I work, where I live, my genetic heritage."

"How does it work?"

"It's sensitive enough to pick up DNA from skin cells that humans shed everywhere they go, and lead you to the sample. Since I'm sitting right in front of you, you won't have to go to that much trouble. To get a reading, just press it to my skin or clothing, and push the round green button."

"But you could already have programmed whatever information you wanted into this gizmo, couldn't you?" Smiling, he pressed it to his own hand and pushed the green button.

The lights danced, and information flashed on the three-by-two-inch screen. The scanners used one dimension instead of three, because that way the system was less complicated—and less expensive—for field work. It was the same video technology that was available to him, unchanged over two centuries. When something worked, like the wheel, it lasted, while other technologies fell by the wayside.

" 'Subject unknown,' " he read. " 'Genetic structure compatible with that of the northern European areas, specifically the ancient Celtic tribes, and to a lesser extent the Cherokee tribe of North America. Subject has blue eyes and brown hair. Require additional data for identification.' "

He stared at the little screen for a long moment, his expression unreadable. "How do I clear this?"

"Either scan something else, or close the lid. The information has been saved unless you push the delete button, which is the orange one next to the green."

He deleted his reading from the scanner, then silently put it against her cheek and pressed the green button.

"'Stover,'" he read. "'Nikita Tzuria. Age thirty, sixty-seven inches or 1.7179 meters in height, current weight unknown.'" He paused, eyed her up and down, and said, "I put you at around a hundred and thirty, maybe thirty-five, depending on how muscled you are."

Nikita couldn't help smiling, because the last time she'd had a physical she had weighed in at one thirty-three. That had been over a year ago, but her clothes still fit, so she imagined she weighed roughly the same now as then.

He continued reading. "'Subject has been employed by the United States Department of Justice, investigative branch, specifically the Federal Bureau of Investigation, for six years. Subject resides in Des Moines, Iowa. Genetic heritage, in order of influence: northern European, southern European, Chinese, Middle Eastern, Slavic, and the Aztec tribe of Central America.'" He glanced up at her. "That's quite a list."

"What can I say?" She hitched one shoulder; with her hands cuffed behind her that was all she could manage. "My ancestors got around."

"Middle Eastern." His gaze bored into her. "Where in the Middle East, specifically?"

"Israel. Tzuria, my middle name, is Hebrew. I don't know what it means."

"Your first name is Russian."

"Blame my mother. Her name is Nicolette, and she thought Nikita was a nice match. But I guess it sort of fits, since I have some Slavic heritage."

"How about the Chinese part?"

"That would be my . . . I forget how many greats. Six or seven, I think."

"Greats?"

"As in generations. My great-great-great-great-and-so-on-grandfather. That came about during the Chinese Revolution."

"I see."

Maybe he did, maybe he didn't. He was staring at her as if she had two heads. "And the Aztec?"

"I can't explain that one. Since it's the last one listed, the genetic influence is so small it's statistically unimportant."

He scratched his jaw. "I have to say this is all real interesting, but how is it supposed to convince me this wild tale you're telling is even remotely true?"

"I think you should do some more DNA scanning; scan your chair or your jacket; let it show you where the DNA samples are. Or take it outside and scan someone I haven't met, so there's no way I could have programmed anything about them into the scanner."

"It'll just tell me that the subject is unknown, like before. As for any particular genetic mix, how would I know for certain whether or not anything the scanner tells me is true? I don't know where everyone's ancestors came from."

"But they might. Pick the most unusual person you see. Go ahead. I'll wait right here."

Again his lips twitched with humor. "See that you do," he said, and he strolled out of the office with her scanner. At least he closed the door behind him, so no one could see that she was being held captive. While she waited she tried to ease the strain on her muscles by shifting back and forth, giving one group ease while another bore the pain for a while.

After about twenty minutes he returned, and placed the scanner on the desk. He sat down in his chair and studied her across the scarred surface. "I'll give you that you've somehow come up with a piece of technology I haven't seen before, but that's all. I do think the FBI—the **real** FBI—will be mighty interested in this little gadget. What else do you have?"

He wasn't convinced, but he was definitely

interested. Nikita was beginning to get a fix on his character. Anything that intrigued him had him caught; he could no more stop himself from trying to solve a puzzle than he could flap his arms and fly. Despite himself, he wanted to hear what else she had to say, wanted to see what her other equipment did.

She thought a minute, trying to think what would most impress him. She'd thought the DNA scanner would do the trick. Finally she said, "Do you see the little red tube?"

He fished around in the pile of her stuff and picked out a slim red tube, about three inches long and the diameter of a pen. "This?"

"Yes. That's Reskin. It instantly heals cuts and abrasions. Do you have a knife?"

His eyebrows lifted. "You want me to cut myself?"

"No, I'd never ask that kind of sacrifice of you," she said gravely. "I want you to cut **me.**"

He snorted at her dry tone, then paused and said, "You're serious."

"Yes, of course."

He grinned, shaking his head. "There are laws against a law enforcement officer using a knife on a prisoner, unless said prisoner is using violence against the officer or others. If I cut you even a fraction of an inch, you'd have me brought up on charges before the hour's out. Good try, though."

"Well, okay then, cut yourself. I don't care. Just cut **someone.**"

He was actually laughing now, as if he was enjoying the conversation. "I'm not going to cut you, myself, or anyone else. Dead end. Try another one."

"Coward," she muttered under her breath. "Give the knife to me and I'll cut myself. It shouldn't be difficult, even though I'm hand-cuffed. You can tell anyone who's interested that I somehow got a knife out of my pocket, and my fingerprints will be on it, so you'll be safe. Does that satisfy you?"

"I won't let you cut yourself," he said mildly. "Give it up."

"I can't believe you're being so stubborn. Has anything I've shown you so far **not** worked? You couldn't cut the ID card, the scanner worked. Why don't you try a little trust?"

"Because I'm not an idiot?" he offered.

"You're an idiot if you don't. A homogenized, close-minded idiot."

"Homogenized?"

He sounded as if he was enjoying himself; his eyes were sparkling, and his lips kept quirking before he'd catch himself and flatten them into a thin line.

"That's a delicate way of saying **inbred.** You have only two genetic sources? It's nothing short of a miracle you can function."

"I'm functional in all ways," he assured her, grinning.

She groaned and closed her eyes in exasperation. Now he was making sexual innuendos . . . she thought. The language differences were just enough that she wasn't certain. If he was, then she supposed men were men no matter what century they lived in.

"All right, all right," he said, suddenly capitulating. Nikita's eyes snapped open and she watched as he dug his hand in his jeans pocket and pulled out a knife that, when he flipped it open, showed a wicked four-inch blade. Deliberately he sliced the edge down the pad of his left thumb, and dark red blood immediately welled and began dripping down his hand.

"Open the Reskin," she instructed. "Brush it on the cut. Well, wipe off the blood first, then brush it on the cut."

"Now you tell me," he said, grabbing a paper napkin left over from their lunch and holding it to his bleeding thumb. "If you're bullshitting me, that's going to put me in a very bad mood," he warned.

She ignored him, watching as he held the thin tube of Reskin in his left hand and unscrewed the cap, pulling out a small brush that glistened with an opalescent liquid. "It doesn't take much; just a light coating will do."

"It had better." He pulled the napkin away

and quickly dabbed the Reskin on his cut. "Ouch!" he immediately yelped. "Shit! You didn't tell me this crap burns!"

Nikita laughed; she couldn't help it. "Look at your thumb."

He looked at his thumb and his expression changed in a way she couldn't describe: it wasn't shock, or disbelief, but a sort of numbness. Very slowly he recapped the Reskin and laid the little red tube back on his desk, then dabbed at the remaining liquid on his thumb.

He didn't say anything for so long she felt like screaming from the tension, but she held herself rigidly under control and waited for him to decide what he was going to do. He might reject what his own eyes had told him. People could sometimes be illogical, so she had to be prepared for that.

Finally he got up from behind his desk and walked around to squat beside her chair and unlock the set of cuffs that held her ankle to the chair. Then he cradled her hands in one of his as he unlocked the cuffs that bound her wrists.

Dropping both sets of cuffs on his desk, he resumed his seat and said, "Okay, start talking. Tell me everything."

"Everything? How long do you have?"

"Just start talking. I'll tell you when I've heard enough."

8

Now that he was really listening, she didn't know where to begin. She'd been rubbing her wrists, but she stopped and spread her hands. "What do you want to know? Give me a subject."

"You mentioned that you were tracking a killer. I'm not saying I buy into this time-traveler stuff, but I'm trying to catch a killer, too, so I'll listen."

She was silent a minute, trying to organize her thoughts. "We might need a chart for this."

He took a flip-top notebook and spun it across the desk toward her. "Draw one."

Draw one, he said. She smoothed her fingers across the lined page. If the man knew how seldom she had actually used a pen and paper, he'd probably laugh. She was familiar with them only because of her studies. Real paper was almost priceless, saved for archiving crucial information and teaching a very small selection of investigators about the past. There was so much mankind had learned and could do, but preserving digital information for longer than a generation or so had so far eluded them. Maybe she could take some paper back with her, she thought. The sale of it would go a long way toward establishing her financially.

"Pen?" she finally said, and he hooked one from inside his jacket, extending it to her.

First she drew a straight line crosswise on the paper, then small lines bisecting it. Starting with Monday, above each small line she put a letter for the day of the week: **M, T, W, T, F, S, S,** all the way across the paper.

Then she drew an arrow coming down between Monday and Tuesday. "Someone came through early Monday morning but we don't know who. Whoever it was knew enough to bypass the security at the Transit Laboratory, and to send himself. We know when he—"

"He?"

"For the sake of convenience, I'll say 'he' instead of 'he or she,' but it could just as easily be a woman. Anyway, because of the computer settings, we know when and where he transited. In the beginning, the weight of the transportee had to be known and the computer calibrated for that weight, but that was too dangerous, because what if he gained weight, even just a pound, in the other time? He wouldn't be able to get back. So that method was refined, and now the weight doesn't matter, just the links."

"Links?"

He was a master at one-word questions, she thought. "They're actual, physical links, worn around the ankles and the wrists, programmed to both send and retrieve."

"So where are yours?"

"Safely buried, where no one can find them. If I lose my links, I can't get back unless a SAR is sent with replacement links."

"When we say SAR we mean Search and Rescue," he observed.

"That's what it still means. They're a squad of specially trained commandos, because no one knows what conditions they will be going into. Usually just one SAR is sent, to diminish the chance of attracting attention."

He propped his chin in his hand and smiled at her. "If you're spinning a yarn, it's a damn good one. You have quite an imagination. Go on."

She gave him a long, level look. "If you thought this was pure fabrication, you wouldn't be wasting your time listening, and you know it. Not only that, if this were an interrogation we wouldn't be in your office, we'd be in an interrogation room and this would be taped. Maybe you don't want to believe me, but you can't explain any of my equipment, can you?"

"I'm listening. Don't ask for more than that."

She needed a lot more than that from him, but for the moment she let the subject drop and went back to the chart she was drawing. "A message was left on a computer at the Transit Lab, sort of a catch-me-if-you-can statement." She paused. "You need to understand that there are several groups who are against time travel, for whatever reason. Some see it as a moral issue—that you shouldn't tamper with what God hath wrought, that kind of thing. For others it's more practical, as in, don't change history because all hell might break loose."

"Theoretically, you can't change history."

"On a small basis, at least, that's wrong. Say someone in my time discovered records of a winning lottery number. He could come back in time and buy a ticket with that same number, and the winnings would be split between him and the other winner or winners. Only the amount of money each lottery player won would change, and there would perhaps be a minuscule economic ripple but nothing else."

"And the time traveler would then take his winnings back to his own time."

"Yes, but the currency would be of value only

to antiques collectors, so in effect he'd be taking back a specialized commodity rather than currency."

"How about changing history on a large basis?"

"Time travel is extremely regulated; not just anyone is allowed to do it, because of the possible danger. What would happen if, say, someone went back in time and assassinated Hitler before World War II started? What would the repercussions be? Without the war to invigorate economies that had been devastated by the Great Depression, what would life for the next century have been like?"

"You mean the United States wouldn't be a superpower."

"No one knows, and that's the danger of trying to change large-scale history. But if the United States hadn't been catapulted to superpower status, would the space race have begun? Would computers have been invented, without the driving need of space travel as impetus? Without the huge economy, would food programs to third world nations have been instituted, would medical advances have been made at the same pace? So you see the ramifications. The prevailing theory isn't that history **can't** be changed; it's that it **shouldn't** be changed because no one knows what would happen instead."

"So even bad things shouldn't be changed."

"Exactly. Everything, good and bad, has made up the path mankind has followed."

He sat back and surveyed her with narrowed eyes. "A lot of bad things have happened. You'd think the world would be a better place if some of them could be undone."

"You mean if people could live instead of die?" At his nod she said, "Can you guarantee that one of the people who died, if he'd lived, wouldn't have committed or caused an atrocity that was worse than what did happen?"

"No one can guarantee that."

"Exactly. So, not knowing, the Time Transit Council decided to leave well enough alone."

"And this renegade time traveler you're hunting didn't agree. Why leave a message, though? If you really want to accomplish something on the sly, you don't leave a message broadcasting it."

"There's no way he could transit without anyone knowing, though. The computers show every journey, when it originated and when it terminated. So I suppose he thought he might as well do a little taunting, maybe trigger an action that wasn't well thought out. Which is exactly what happened," she said bitterly.

"You weren't well thought out? Imagine that."

"The first agent sent through in pursuit was

killed," she said coldly, not liking his sarcasm. She drew another arrow that came in right on top of the first one. "The unauthorized traveler was waiting for him when he transitioned. His body was sent back to us."

"The **first** agent? How many have there been?"

"I'm the third one. Houseman was killed. McElroy was sent to arrive about half an hour later, but he couldn't make any progress and was recalled." She drew the third arrow showing the timing of McElroy's arrival, then her own arrival the next night.

"All this coming and going," he drawled, "you'd think someone would notice something unusual." As soon as the words were out of his mouth he froze, his gaze going blank as his thoughts turned inward. "Stay right here," he said, getting up and striding toward the door. "There's something I want you to see."

He was back in fewer than five minutes, holding a black rectangle. He turned on the small video screen sitting on top of a file cabinet, and slid the black rectangle into a black machine. **VCR,** whispered her memory. It was a primitive data-reader, which translated the data into video and audio.

A picture formed on the screen and he said, "Watch this," as he pressed the control that made the film speed forward. He stopped it with another control, then began feeding it forward frame by frame. She recognized the courthouse where she was currently being held, but there was no action, nothing going on. From the stark shadows and angles she knew the film had been made at night.

Then a bright white flash filled the screen.

She sat bolt upright, staring. The next frame was the same scene, except now there seemed to be a hole in the ground, when none had been there a moment before.

"You know anything about that flash?" he drawled.

"That's what happens when someone transits in or out," she said, stunned. "But—but the records don't show anyone coming in at this location. When was this?"

"Monday morning," he said, and tapped her chart showing when the killer had come through.

"He didn't transit here," she insisted. "The coordinates were several miles east of here. I've been there, I found the location. That's where he killed Houseman. He wasn't here."

"Then who was? Got any ideas on that?"

She shook her head. She'd seen the data; the only transits had been those made by the killer, Houseman, and McElroy—**unless someone else had come through since she'd transited.** That someone could easily have arranged to come through **before** the killer, before everyone else; it wasn't exactly a simple matter to set the time and space coordinates, but the computers could handle the task within a fraction of a second.

Someone else had come through. Who? Why? Was this someone also the person who had shot at her today? Again, **why**?

9

"I gather this isn't good news to you," he said, sharply watching her.

Nikita shook her head. "Someone came through whom I don't know about," she said, feeling a little numb. "Could be good news, could be bad news. I have no way of knowing if that was an authorized traveler or reinforcements for the killer." She pointed at the screen. "That hole in the ground . . . what was it?" She thought she knew, and wondered how she, how all of them, could have been so smart that they'd outsmarted themselves.

"Twenty years ago, the town buried a time capsule there," Knox said. "Monday morning, someone dug it up and stole it. You're saying one of your time travelers did it? First, why doesn't digging it up show on the film? Second—why in hell would anyone want a time capsule?"

"First, when someone comes through, it sort of—**freezes** time for a little while, as if everything has been shocked and can't move. That's one of the arguments the anti-time-transit groups use to prove that we shouldn't be doing it. The physicists haven't been able to explain it yet, but they have a theory that the traveler has to completely mesh with the new time on a molecular level before everything returns to normal."

"But while everything else is 'frozen,' is the time traveler? Shouldn't this last only a few seconds, instead of the time it would have taken someone to dig up the capsule?"

"Theoretically, the pause is very brief, a fraction of a second. It's so brief that I don't think anyone has ever thought about whether or not the traveler is also immobilized."

"You can't move a granite marker and dig up a capsule in a fraction of a second."

"No," she said hesitantly. "Unless there's technology that I don't know about, but the FBI makes a real effort to stay abreast of new technological developments."

"So that still doesn't explain how the time capsule went missing." He looked disappointed. "Unless the pause is much longer than anyone thought. I would say that's the only logical explanation, but the word **logic** doesn't really fit this conversation, does it? But how about the second part of my question: Why?"

"There was a paper buried in this particular time capsule that contained the theory and some of the process for successfully traversing time," she said. "If that paper isn't in the time capsule when it's opened in 2085, or if the time capsule itself is stolen, then the technology won't be developed."

"In **our** little time capsule?" he asked skeptically. "Who wrote something like that? I don't know of any quantum physics genius around here."

"No one knows who wrote the paper. Maybe it was known at one time, but the information didn't survive. A lot of digital information was lost or corrupted before people realized discs weren't a good way to archive anything."

"I was there," he said in an abstracted undertone.

"What? When?"

"When the capsule was buried. January first, 1985. The newspaper said twelve items were going into the capsule, but I counted thirteen. A research paper wasn't among the items mentioned. I never did find out what the thirteenth item was."

"Then it must have been that paper." She sighed and stared out the window at the gorgeous blue sky, with the occasional fat white cloud drifting by. "Have you ever seen a bunch of really smart people overlook the perfectly obvious?"

"Happens every day."

"Well, we did. In our defense, this is the first time we've had this kind of situation. When we were alerted that an unauthorized traveler had gone through all we thought about was sending agents to apprehend him. None of us thought of the obvious: go in ahead of him."

"Somebody did."

"I hope," she said with a wan smile. "That's the best-case scenario. The other possibility is that he isn't the only one. I was shot at, remember? So the bad buys could have the time capsule—or the good guys might. I simply don't know."

Knox checked his wristwatch, then yawned and rubbed his eyes. "There's a lot that isn't making sense, but enough of what you're telling me **is** that I'm going to cut you some slack for the time being. Those gizmos you have, and the card, have bought you some time. That doesn't mean I'm going to just let you go before I know for certain, one way or another, if you're crazy, pulling a con, or if you really did come through time. So I have to decide what I'm going to do with you."

"Instead of locking me in a cell, I suggest we

work together. We're both looking for the same killer."

"Uh, yeah—just how does the time capsule, the unauthorized time traveler, and all of that tie in with my homicide case?"

"Is it possible he wrote the research paper? All I've ever read on the subject indicated that the author was unknown, but archivists recover bits of old books, recordings, newspapers— things like that—every day. Some new information could have been discovered."

Knox shook his head. "Taylor sure as hell wasn't a physicist. He was a small-town lawyer, through and through. And what makes you so certain your time traveler killed him?"

"He was killed with a spear, wasn't he?"

"Well now," Knox said softly, leaning back in his chair and lacing his hands behind his head. "Just how did you know that? That little detail wasn't released to the press."

It was amazing, she thought, how eyes that blue could turn so cold. "McElroy was tracking the UT—unauthorized traveler—and found the body. He knew the UT had done it because of the spear, which you'll have an impossible time tracing because it was manufactured in China in the year 2023."

He flipped open a notebook and began making notes. "China stopped making nuclear bombs and reverted to spears?"

"I said it was manufactured there, not that it was used there. Do you think you should do that?" she asked, indicating his notebook. "Put this in writing?"

"If we're talking about one of my cases, I'm writing it down." His tone of voice said there was no room for discussion. "Why in hell would anyone start manufacturing spears? That's not exactly cutting-edge technology."

"For a while, spears were the terrorists' low-tech weapon of choice; they're cheap, is the main reason. When funds started running low, alternative means of murder were sought and spears were selected. There's something symbolic about a spear, especially when it's all of a sudden sticking through someone's neck. It's silent, which makes it a very effective weapon at night."

"So is there something especially symbolic about this particular spear, or was it just lying around and this guy saw it and thought, Hey, it'll be neat to kill someone with a spear?"

"This particular spear was in a museum, and it does have a special symbolism to certain people. That spear killed a heavily protected American general in 2025, so to them it represents human spirit over technology, or something like that."

"A victory for the Luddites."

"Exactly. To these groups that's exactly what

they're trying to do, save mankind from their own technology."

"I really hate people who try to save me from myself," he muttered.

Despite the worry gnawing at her, she had to grin. "Yeah. Good-doers."

He chuckled, and she said, "What?"

"Nothing. What's first on your agenda?"

She wanted to pursue the "nothing," because in her experience when someone said that, there was damn well something. But he was right, in that there was something more urgent that she needed to do, and she didn't know if he would go along with it. He might have uncuffed her, but at the moment he was still very much in charge unless she was willing to hurt a lot of people, him included, and matters hadn't progressed to that point.

"I need to go to my home time," she said. "I need to notify people that there's a mole, and if it wasn't one of us who went in early and stole the time capsule to protect it, then that's what we need to do, too, except we'll go in a day earlier."

"You're talking about zigzagging back and forth, until you're overlapping like fish scales."

"Yes, exactly," she said, pleased that he'd gotten the concept. "Like I said, this is new to us, but all we have to do is protect the time capsule and catch the killer. We know when he came over; one of us needs to transit in ahead of him. I can't believe we were so shortsighted."

"But if you come in ahead of him and catch him, he hasn't yet committed a murder and he's innocent of everything except unauthorized travel."

She gave him a helpless look. "We can't change life and death. We can't bring Taylor Allen back. But I can't think of anything else to do. I need to go back. When I make my report, it'll be out of my hands, but at least I'll have tried for the best outcome."

"Okay," he said mildly. "I'll go along with this—as long as I get to watch."

"You like watching, huh?" Damn it! Nikita had known she shouldn't say that, but it came out anyway. She had been doing so well, too, at keeping everything completely impersonal and focused on the matter at hand, because it wasn't fair to let this become anything more when she had no intention of staying in this time. But she liked his blue eyes and his lean features, and he had nice, strong hands, try as she might not to notice all that.

"I'm better at doing," he drawled, his eyelids drooping in a sleepy expression that made her heart pound.

Her stomach tightened, the sensation of physical response so strong she was disconcerted. She swallowed hard, then grimly got herself back under control. No, this could **not** happen. "I'm sorry," she apologized. "I shouldn't have said that, it was unprofessional."

"I don't mind unprofessional, every now and then."

"**I** do." Her cheeks burned with embarrassment. "It won't happen again."

"Guess you're right," he said with apparent regret. "If you really leave, it literally **can't** happen."

"Which is why I shouldn't have said anything out of line. I'm sorry."

"So you've already said." He waited a moment, then rose to his feet. "We don't have to wait until dark or anything like that, do we? For you to leave, or transit, or whatever."

"No." She was relieved by the change of subject. "I can go any time."

He grinned and shook his head at the double meaning. "All right, I'll drive you there, since your rental car is obviously known to whoever took a shot at you this morning. Wait here, and I'll get one of the deputies to pull my car into the secure area we use for special prisoners; that way no one can see you."

She might be crazy as hell, she might be pulling a con, she might be the actual murderer—Knox couldn't forget that she'd known about the spear—but whatever she was, she told a good tale. And just when he was ready to lock her up, he would think about those gadgets of hers and keep listening.

No matter what, he couldn't deny that her ID card, the DNA scanner, and that little tube of Reskin were things he'd never seen or heard of before. The cut on his thumb was completely healed over. That, more than anything, was what forced him to concede that there might, just **might,** be a kernel of truth in the yarns she told. The other stuff he might not have heard of, but something that healed a cut on con-tact—yeah, he and everyone else in the country would have heard about that. Wall Street and the company that had developed Reskin would have had commercials touting it running every fifteen minutes on every television station. The military would be buying the stuff by the shipload. So the fact that he hadn't heard about Reskin was a big point in her favor.

But he was a cop, and cops by nature had a hard time believing just about anything they were told until they had hard proof it was true.

He stopped a deputy and handed over his keys with a request to move his car into the se-cure prisoner loading area; then he knocked on Sheriff Cutler's door and stuck his head inside.

"What's up with our FBI agent?" Calvin asked, a mischievous glint in his eyes. "You've been in your office with her a long time."

"I have my doubts anything she told us was on the level," Knox said. "And she knew about the spear, which makes me twitchy. Either we have a leak, or she has prior information."

"Like from the killer? Well, now." Calvin leaned back in his chair. "Are you saying Ms. Stover is involved with the killer, or maybe is our spear-chucker herself?"

"I don't know. I don't think so, but she may know who it is, and that person may be who shot at her this morning. For whatever reason, she was definitely the target this morning. I'm going to do some digging. Whoever shot at her obviously knew her rental car and followed her this morning. There are some things I want to check out and I'm taking her with me."

The sheriff nodded. "Okay, but watch your back."

Knox felt uneasy about keeping things from the sheriff, but if he'd told the whole story, Calvin would have insisted on locking up Ms. Fake FBI Agent for impersonating a federal agent, at least. Knox held that option open, but first he wanted some answers that made sense. He couldn't accept that she had come from two hundred years in the future; that was too much to swallow. But something weird was going on, and he wanted to know what it was.

She was waiting patiently in his office, just as she had while he tried out the DNA scanner. He didn't know what to think of that; any guilty person would have taken advantage of the situation and tried to run, but she hadn't. Not that she would have succeeded, because he'd been ready for any move she might make, and it could be she was smart enough to realize that.

If she intended to run, her best chance would be when she was alone with him. He would see she got that chance.

"Come on," he said, and she got to her feet, stuffing things back into her purse. He still had possession of her weapon, and he meant to keep it. He'd have to be crazy to hand over a powerful weapon to her. She glanced at it, raised her eyebrows in a silent question, and he grinned as he shook his head. "No way."

She accepted the situation without argument. He stood back and let her precede him out the door. She angled herself to step past him, but he was still close enough that he could feel the heat of her body, smell the faint, sweet scent of a woman's skin. She didn't even glance at him, but he knew she was as aware of him on a physical basis as he was of her.

It had been a while since any woman had turned him on. Wanting sex wasn't the same as being turned on, and, yeah, he'd wanted sex. He was a normal, thirty-five-year-old man, and he hadn't died with Rebecca. But wanting a particular woman—no, that hadn't happened, until now, until Nikita Stover, with her big brown eyes and friendly smile. He had to be careful not to let the sexual attraction between them blind him to any guilt on her part.

His car was waiting for them, and she got into the front seat beside him, then leaned over so her head was almost in his lap and she wasn't visible through the windows. He glanced down at her; her head was almost touching his thigh. God, she had to know what that suggested. His hands tightened on the steering wheel as he imagined her head bobbing up and down in his lap. His johnson sprang to attention. **Shit.**

"Where are we going?" he asked, his voice level and cool. He'd keep this situation under control if it killed him.

"Take county road 73," she instructed. "And let me know when it's safe for me to sit up."

They were well away from the courthouse before he said, "Okay, you can sit up now." She did so immediately, tossing her hair out of her face. He breathed easier once she was safely buckled on her side of the car.

County road 73 led in the general direction of Jesse Bingham's place. There were no coincidences, he reminded himself. Whatever was going on with her was directly related to the flashes Jesse had seen three nights before. Jesse would probably say she'd killed his chickens, but somehow Knox couldn't see Nikita as a chicken murderer.

Nikita flipped open a mirrored compact, released the mirror by pressing on a tiny latch, and exposed a GPS unit. "Another two miles, approximately," she said.

Knox eyed the GPS with interest. The military GPS was far more accurate than the ones in cars and boats, and from what he'd seen, this was at least military grade. He wondered where she'd gotten it, if it had been stolen from a military base somewhere.

She carefully watched the GPS, and just before they reached the turn to Jesse's place, she suddenly said, "Here. Pull over here."

Obediently, he steered the car completely off the road, tucking it behind some bushes. She was already out of the car, walking swiftly toward a thick stretch of forest.

Knox followed her, watching her, watching the way she moved and the way her shiny dark hair swung with every stride. Then they were in the forest and the sounds of the occasional traffic faded, to be replaced by the sounds of nature: birds calling, insects rustling, leaves gently sighing in a light breeze. She stepped over fallen limbs, went around bushes, but didn't hesitate or veer from her chosen direction.

Then she stopped and pointed to the ground. "There."

He examined the earth. If she'd buried something there, she'd covered her tracks well. "Guess I should have brought a shovel."

"No need. I have this." She took another slender tube from her purse, this one black in color, and pressed the end of it. He'd thought it was a pen, or a laser pointer. He'd been half right. A thin beam of green light shot out of the tube and began to bore into the earth. She moved the light in gentle, ever increasing circles, digging as it went.

Then she turned it off, got down on her knees, laid the GPS unit to the side; he could see a series of concentric circles growing out of the center of its screen, expanding and disappearing, only to begin again. **Ground zero,** he thought. Nikita began scooping up loose dirt with her hands and tossing it aside.

Knox moved to stand in front of her so he could keep an eye on both her and anything she might uncover, but not so close that she could grab an ankle and topple him, or throw dirt in his eyes.

"That's strange," she muttered. "I didn't think I'd dug this deep before."

"Sure this is the right place?"

"I marked the coordinates on the GPS. I'm

certain." A moment later she made a soft sound of satisfaction and gripped the edge of a clear plastic bag, pulling it free from the dirt.

There was nothing in the bag.

Knox looked sharply at her. She remained on her knees, her face abruptly paper white as she stared at the empty bag.

"They're gone," she said in a tight, strained voice. "My links are gone. I can't get home. I'm stranded here."

10

NIKITA REMAINED ON HER KNEES IN THE dirt, barely able to speak. She felt numb with combined horror and shock. Who could have taken her links? Who could have known where they were? She had thought she was alone when she transited, but someone must have been nearby and watched her bury the links.

Logically, it couldn't be the person who had shot at her, because what better opportunity to kill her than when she was alone in this isolated spot?

Even more logically, if some unknown enemy had known she was coming through, why **hadn't** he been waiting here for her, to kill her the way he'd killed Houseman? Only one solution occurred to her that fit both parameters.

Still holding the waterproof bag by two fingers, she reached for the DNA scanner but couldn't manage to open it with just one hand. She held it up to Knox. "Would you open that for me, please?" she asked. Her voice still sounded strained, even to her, but it was level.

Silently, he took the scanner and flipped it open, then gave it back to her.

She aimed it at the bag and pressed the button. Any samples would have been contaminated by the soil, but the newest scanners were better at filtering out the contamination than the earlier models had been. With any luck, she'd get a reading.

The lights flickered, showing the locations of DNA on the bag. She pressed the scanner to one of the locations and the reading popped on the screen: **Stover, Nikita**—"Okay, the samples are clean enough to read," she murmured to herself as she cleared the entry. She glanced up at Knox. "The first reading was on me. Let's see what it says about these other samples."

The next sample was also hers. And the third. On the fourth, though, the screen flashed different information. She read it aloud: " 'Subject unknown. Genetic structure compatible with that of the northern European areas, specifically the ancient Celtic tribes'—Good God, Knox, it was you!"

"Ha ha," he replied. "I guess I don't have to tell you most people in this area will have a common genetic heritage. Don't tell me there's Cherokee in there, too?"

"No, you're clear. The rest of it is 'and to a lesser extent the southern Mediterranean area. Subject has green eyes and brown hair. Require additional data for information.'

"That description narrows things down to a few thousand people in the immediate area."

Nikita sat down in the dirt, staring at the little screen. How could this situation get any worse? But she'd been right in her supposition, cold comfort that it was. "You know what this means, don't you?"

"That you don't have any way to demonstrate to me that you can really travel back and forth in time?" he supplied with smooth irony.

"That this isn't anyone from my time," she explained patiently.

He hunkered down in front of her, blue eyes intent. "How do you figure that?"

"**Subject unknown.** If anyone from my time stole my links, the odds are he would be in the database."

"You have almost the entire world's population in this database?" he asked incredulously.

"Not everyone, not even close. But everyone in the FBI is in the database, as well as all Council members and all the personnel at the Transit Laboratory. Everyone ever convicted of a crime is entered. And since most people who belong to protest groups have committed at least misdemeanors such as disturbing the peace, they're in the database."

She rubbed her forehead, leaving smears of dirt across her skin. "No, the links were taken by someone from your time. I don't know if that's a relief, or not. An innocent civilian— well, maybe not so innocent, but a civilian—has those links and doesn't have a clue what can happen if he puts them on and accidentally activates them."

Glancing up, she caught an expression of patience and skepticism on his face, and she sighed. "You don't believe me. Not even the DNA scanner has convinced you, or the Reskin."

"Reskin comes close," he admitted, rising to a standing position and holding his hand down for her. "But get real; how can I swallow this, hook, line, and sinker?"

"I haven't asked you to swallow any hooks," she muttered resentfully, but she put her hand in his and let him pull her to her feet.

The light under the canopy of trees seemed suddenly brighter, and a low, almost inaudible buzzing filled the air. Frowning, Knox released her hand and pressed a finger to his ear. "What's that sound? Can you hear it?"

Nikita held up a hand to silence him, turning in a circle as she tried to locate the direction the buzzing was coming from. "Get down," she said urgently as she grabbed her laser pen. She dropped to the ground, flat on her stomach. "Get down!" she yelled at him, when he was slow to obey. She grabbed the boot nearest her and jerked it backward, toppling him; he would have landed on his face if he hadn't twisted, cat-like, to take the fall on his shoulder.

"Face down!" She put her left hand on the back of his head and ground his face into the dirt, half covering him with her body as she ducked her own head down and put her arm over her eyes.

She saw the white brilliance of the flash against her closed eyelids, even with her head tucked down, felt every cell in her body prickle as the energy washed over her. Static electricity danced over her skin, played in her hair. She felt what seemed like the briefest moment of immo-bility; then as the effect began to fade she forced herself to raise her head, which felt as if it weighed three times as much as normal. Every-thing seemed to be in slow motion, every move-ment took enormous effort. Beneath her, Knox was stirring, trying to rise, his head coming up.

Shimmering before them, solidifying, was the figure of a man.

As luck would have it, he had landed with his back to them. Nikita had a split second to recognize the weaponry in his hand. "FBI!" she rapped out. "Drop your weapon."

Slowly he raised both hands, then just as slowly turned his head to look over his shoulder at her. "Agent Stover," he said. "I'm Agent Luttrell."

"Maybe, maybe not. Drop your weapon, turn half a revolution to your left, and use your left hand to remove your ID card." She didn't recognize him, which by itself didn't mean anything, but after everything that had gone wrong with this mission, she wasn't about to take any chances.

Knox lifted slightly beneath her, his right arm moving, and she realized he had drawn his own weapon, but with her lying half on his right side, he couldn't maneuver properly. If he moved much at one time, or too fast, he would throw her off balance, and from the tight control he employed, she knew he'd realized that. He shifted again, and when he dragged his left arm out, she saw he'd switched his weapon to his off hand.

"Easy," the man said, slowly stooping to rest his weapon on the ground. He began turning, his balance shifting to his left foot. His powerful thigh muscles tensed . . . there was a second when she couldn't see his right arm . . . then he was a blur of movement as he whipped around, a thin line of green light shooting out from his right hand.

She fired an instant before he did. The laser

hit him at navel level and ripped upward, the stench of burning flesh filling the air. His shot burned into the ground inches from Knox's outstretched hand. The man dropped where he stood, his legs jerking spasmodically for a moment before they relaxed forever.

In the thick silence that fell, Nikita felt the quick lift and fall of Knox's breathing, felt her own heartbeat pounding, her pulse throbbing in her throat and wrists.

"Holy shit," Knox said, moving her aside and getting to his feet in one lithe action. He approached the dead man cautiously, holding his weapon two-handed and keeping it trained on the body, easing forward until he could kick the laser away from the man's outstretched hand.

"What other weapons is he likely to have?" he asked Nikita without looking at her.

"I don't know," she said dully. Nausea roiled in her stomach, hot and greasy. She felt herself break into a cold sweat. She'd never killed anyone before, never even discharged any of her weapons except in training or practice. She stared at the man stretched out on his back, his head turned slightly to the side and his eyes open as if he were staring at her.

He couldn't see her. She knew that, knew he was dead. He'd have killed her—and Knox—if she hadn't been faster, if she hadn't been forewarned. She knew that, too. But knowing and feeling were two different things, and she felt sick at what she'd had to do.

Knox went down on one knee beside the body and touched two fingers to his neck, feeling for a pulse. He then began swiftly and efficiently searching the man's pockets.

"You want to give me a hand?" he called to Nikita.

Which one? she wondered, shaken by the request.

"C'mon, don't just sit there—" He looked over his shoulder at her as he spoke, and he broke off. "You're as green as a frog," he observed. "Is this your first body?"

Slowly she shook her head. "It's the first one that's my fault, though."

"It was his fault, not yours. I won't say you'll get over it, but put it aside for now if you can. I need everything off him that can't be explained."

Shakily she stood. Approaching that body was one of the hardest things she'd ever done, but she made herself put one foot in front of the other until she could drop to her knees beside Knox. "How do you intend to explain the wound?" she asked. She was shaking in every muscle, a very fine tremor from head to foot.

"I'm not," he said. "We're leaving him here. Someone will eventually find him."

"This is against the law," she felt obliged to point out. She swallowed twice, hard, to keep from throwing up.

"Damn it, do you think I don't know that?" he snapped. "I'm risking a prison sentence, but you tell me what you think will happen if I call this in? How do we explain being up here in the woods and just stumbling over a body that, oh, yeah, happened to have become a body at exactly the same time we found it? Even without a pinpointed time of death, it's close enough that a lot of people will be suspicious, starting with the sheriff."

She fell silent, trying to think through all the possibilities. They couldn't call it in later, because the same question would still arise: what were they doing in the woods? "Maybe an anonymous call, later," she said.

"It's damn hard to make an anonymous call without all sorts of rerouting, or a secured phone. I don't have the last one and don't have a clue how to do the first one."

He was angry, and not without cause. She had put him in an untenable position, and though she couldn't have known someone would transit through almost on top of them, she was still the reason Luttrell was dead, and now they had to conceal their part in it. They were both law officers, and now they were breaking the very laws they had sworn to up-hold. At least this was her doing, while Knox must feel as if he'd been caught in a trap.

"I'm sorry," she said as evenly as possible. "The only way to make this right is to arrest me. I'm the one who killed him, not you. You shouldn't be in this position."

"No, damn it, I shouldn't be, but I am." His tone was savage, his blue gaze hard. "I can arrest you, yeah, but how did you kill him? Neither of our weapons has been discharged. Maybe you blurt out that you zapped him with a pen when he materialized in front of you, that he's a bad guy from the future, and all this other real believable stuff you've been telling me? You'll be in a psych ward before you know it. Or maybe you could demonstrate that little laser, which would bring up a lot of questions I sure as hell don't want to answer. What about you?—No, I didn't think so. This is my time and my county, so just do what I tell you. Now, what can't be explained and needs to come off?"

"His links," she said softly. Forcing herself to touch the dead man, she rolled back the cuffs of his sleeves and removed the thin metal bands clamped around his wrists, then pulled up his pants legs and did the same to the ones around his ankles.

"You have a set of links now," Knox pointed out.

She had already realized that and began inspecting them for damage. A laser hit could damage the connections and circuitry. She turned each link around and around, looking for scorch marks. She was beginning to feel optimistic until she picked up the one that had been on his left wrist. The outer edge at the hinge was darkened, which meant it had absorbed some of the laser's power. Time and light were interwoven like a braid, and they'd found that while bright white light didn't damage the links, other spectrums could, if strong enough. A laser was definitely strong enough.

"One of them is damaged." She tried to keep the disappointment out of her voice. She was an utter failure at it, but at least she tried.

"Three of them work, don't they? What could happen?"

"I'd fail to materialize in my own time. I'd still exist, I guess, but I'd just be a mitochondrial cloud somewhere."

"Bummer. Don't go that route, then." He was swiftly patting down the body; he found the shield card and slipped it into his front pocket, along with the laser, then picked up the other weapon and began examining it. "Was he really FBI? He has a card just like yours."

"Then he probably was," she said softly. "The cards are impossible to forge." Standing, she retrieved her DNA scanner and pressed it to the dead man's hand.

"Luttrell, Jon Carl," she read, skipping over the physical description. "Subject has been employed by the United States Department of Justice, investigative branch—yes, he really was FBI."

"Then it isn't safe for you to go back, even if all four of the links were in good working order. Someone in your office sent him gunning for you. How about the wristwatch?"

"Leave it. They still work and look basically the same."

"Obviously someone doesn't want you coming back," he pointed out. "Is the clothing made out of ordinary stuff, or is it some indestructible cloth?"

"It's synthetic. Unless it's given to a chemist to break down the molecular structure, no one will know the difference." She didn't need him to tell her she didn't dare go back now. She was all too sharply aware that she'd been virtually abandoned here.

"How did he just happen to materialize right on top of us? What are the odds against that happening?"

"It's fairly reasonable. Why would anyone expect me to be here? The physical coordinates would still be set in the computer, unless someone went through to a different location since I came through. Change the time by twenty-four hours and there shouldn't be any problem."

"Except we happened to be here."

"Because someone shot at me. Someone from your time. That's something they couldn't know, so therefore they wouldn't be expecting me to return so soon."

"My time? Here? I mean, now?" He sat back on his heels, staring at her with narrowed eyes as he mentally went over the evidence. "Yeah, I see what you mean. If it had been anyone from your time, the weapon of choice would have been laser, not rifle."

And she would be dead, she thought. Lasers were silent, the way a sunbeam was silent. Without the sound of the rifle shot, probably neither of them would have noticed the thin stream of light until it bored into her. They had been totally focused on jockeying for position with each other.

"Speaking of weapons, what about that one?" He pointed to the one Luttrell had dropped at Nikita's instruction.

"That's laser, too, for use at much greater distances than this one," she said, indicating the pen laser.

"A sniper laser."

"Yes." She went over to the weapon and picked it up, examined it. It was an XT37, the very latest model; only the crack antiterrorist teams had them. Someone in a position of power had to have authorized Luttrell's transition.

Luttrell himself could have been a good guy, told only that she'd gone rogue and had to be exterminated. If she'd had time to consider all the angles, she might have been able to wound him instead of killing him, though a laser wound was so disabling it was generally considered almost worse than death. The light beam could sever a hand as fast as a human could push the button and release it, faster, because the speed of light itself outdistanced even the control of a computer.

An amputation was considered a clean laser hit; contact anywhere on the torso was occasionally survivable, but the damage was horrible, calling for multiple organ replacements, and the energy surge often left the victims with neurological problems as well. A laser tag to the head was instantly fatal.

The XT37 was a substantial weapon, about three feet long, and weighed fifteen pounds. Disposing of it, or hiding it, wasn't going to be easy. On the other hand, they were the ones who now had control of it, which gave them an advantage.

"What else?" he asked, examining Luttrell's boots.

She returned to kneel beside him, placing the XT37 by her leg. "He might have a chip."

"A computer chip?"

She nodded. "As a precaution. For tracking him."

"Do you have one?"

"No." She had been asked to wear one, but she'd refused, and because the legal ramifications of a tracking chip were still being hashed out in court, for the time being agents still could opt out of wearing them. She had never liked the idea of her superiors being able to see every move she or any other agent made.

"If he had one, where would it be?"

"Usually it's attached to a piece of jewelry. Originally they were designed to be embedded in the skin, but everyone was ready to resign en masse, so that was changed." She shifted to slide her hand inside the dead man's collar, feeling for a chain. She located one and pulled it out; it was a St. Christopher's medal, but close examination revealed it was just that, a religious medal. No chip was attached.

"Try his belt buckle," she instructed as she lifted Luttrell's left hand and removed the ring he was wearing. It, too, looked clean.

Knox had unbuckled Luttrell's belt and was looking at the buckle, both front and back. "How big is this chip?"

"Tiny."

"Would it feel like a rough speck on the metal?"

She reached out to run her fingers over the buckle where he indicated, and her sensitive fingertips felt the minute rough spot, as if a speck of debris had been caught on the buckle during manufacturing. The light wasn't good there under the trees, though, and she wasn't able to see well enough to make certain that it was a chip.

"Do you have a magnifier?" she asked.

"Believe it or not, I do." He stretched out his right leg and wormed his hand into his jeans pocket, coming out with his knife. He opened one of the attachments and revealed a small, round magnifier.

Nikita took the knife and examined the speck. The magnifier wasn't a strong one, but it was good enough that she could make out the even edges of the "speck."

"That's it," she said, folding the attachment back into the knife and returning it to him.

"How do we disable it? Smash it?"

"No." She reached for the small laser, pulled the buckle end of the belt off to the side, and let it rest on the ground. Positioning the laser, she gave the button a quick hit and the buckle sizzled.

"That'll do it," Knox said wryly.

She felt more in control now. She wouldn't fall apart, at least not now. Maybe later, but for now she was thinking, and functioning. Together they finished searching Luttrell's body, and found some folded present-time currency sewn into the lining of his black jacket. He had come well-supplied, she thought, counting it. She handed the stash to Knox. They also found a credit card, which looked like any other credit card, and they left that. "It's forged," she told Knox.

"How do you know?"

"Do you think there are any authentic credit cards from this time left in **my** time? It's forged the same way mine is."

"Have you used it?"

"I had to, to rent a car and a motel room. We come prepared."

"So you're stealing."

"Essentially, yes. We knew what we'd be facing here, that we'd need some means of identification."

Knox rubbed his eyes, looking as if he didn't want to hear any more. "It isn't standard procedure," she assured him. "This was an emergency measure."

"What other laws are you breaking?"

"You know them all, now."

"God, I hope so." He looked around. "Let's get all this gathered, then wipe out our footprints and leave this scene as clean as possible."

She picked up the waterproof bag that had once contained her links, and slipped it into her purse. There was no point in covering the hole she'd dug; an empty hole told no tales. She retrieved the rest of her equipment, put it away, too, then looked around. She had everything.

Knox had everything they'd retrieved from Luttrell's body in his pockets, and he leaned over to get the XT37. "That's it. Now all we have to do is get to my car without being seen and recognized, and hope no one's seen the car and called in the tag number. And that the body isn't found for a couple of years."

Luck was with them. The highway had a fair amount of traffic on it, but at this time of day people hadn't yet gotten off work, and school was out for the summer. One pickup truck went by, and they heard it coming in time to crouch in the tall grass until it had passed.

Knox put the XT37 in the trunk, slammed it, and they both got into the car.

"Now what?" she asked, wondering if the day could get any worse.

He said, "I'm taking you home with me."

11

KNOX WAS SO ANGRY HE COULD BARELY contain himself, but none of what had happened was Nikita's fault, so it wouldn't have been fair for him to take it out on her. He was angry at finding himself in the position of having to lie to the people he worked with, who trusted him; to Sheriff Cutler, who was just about the best boss Knox could imagine. He was angry at having to break the law that so far he'd spent his adult life upholding, but he didn't see any way around it.

If he told the truth, not only would no one believe him and Nikita, but they would both likely be arrested for murder, not to mention that she would be charged with impersonating an FBI officer even though she really was a federal agent—just not right now.

He didn't want to believe what he'd seen. An old joke ran through his mind: A cheating husband, caught red-handed, says, "Honey, who you gonna believe, me or your lyin' eyes?" Almost more than anything, Knox wanted to believe his eyes were lying to him. Almost. Because he **had** seen it, and curiosity was eating him alive. Under his anger was a powerful need; he could barely contain his impatience to get Nikita home and pepper her with questions.

They were almost back to town when he glanced over at her. She'd been completely silent since getting into the car, either lost in her own thoughts or letting him stew—maybe a little bit of both. Killing that guy had shaken her, bad, but she'd held together and done what was necessary. If she hadn't been so shaken, he'd have already been asking the questions that burned on his tongue, but he thought she needed a little more recovery time.

She was in serious danger. That made twice, in just one day, that someone had tried to kill her. He agreed with her assessment that whoever had shot at her that morning was very likely someone from his time, meaning here and now—but who could have known she was coming, and where she would be? The most likely explanation was that it was a random attempt, some crazy with a rifle taking a shot at a stranger . . . which wasn't all that likely. Pekesville just didn't have that

many crazies and between the sheriff's department and the Pekesville police force, pretty well
all of them were known. About the only violence
that wasn't drug or alcohol related was domestic
violence, and those parameters didn't fit.

So the unknown traveler who had come
through time to kill Taylor Allen had, for some
reason, enlisted some local help. Great. Just
what he needed.

"Do you have anything you need to get from
your motel room?" he asked.

She jumped a little at the sound of his voice.
"What? Oh—sorry. My thoughts were wandering. What did you say?"

"Do you have any things at the motel?"

"A small suitcase. Are we going there to
get it?"

"No, I don't want you anywhere near there in
case whoever shot at you is hanging around waiting for another chance. I'll send one of the
deputies to get it. Does anything need packing?"

"I put everything in the suitcase this morning
before I left, and locked it."

"More future stuff, huh?"

"My clothing, some other things."

"What does your clothing look like? Does
everyone run around in silver metallic jump-
suits the way they do in the movies?"

She hesitated. "**Jump** suits? You have suits
that jump?"

He chuckled. "I think the term originally meant the one-piece suits parachutists wore to jump out of planes, but it basically means a one-piece outfit."

"I see. That makes sense. But, no, we don't."

"So what do you wear?" Despite his best intentions he was already doing it, he realized, throwing question after question at her.

"Normal clothing. When you think about it, there are only two basic types of clothing: skirted, and nonskirted. The skirt lengths go up and down, the pants may have wide legs or narrow legs, but that's all just variations on the basic themes."

"Zippers?"

Now she chuckled. "Zippers are still around, as are buttons. Think about it. How many hundreds of years have buttons existed in this time? Why would they completely disappear in just two hundred years? Zippers and buttons **work.** They're efficient."

"Are cars still the same?"

"No, internal combustion engines exist now only in a few museums and one or two antiques collections."

"No cars," he said, scandalized. He couldn't imagine a world without NASCAR. "Were they done away with because of global warming?"

"Um, no. Something better came along. But that wasn't until about a hundred years ago."

"Something better than cars?" He'd like to see that.

"I didn't say there were no cars; I said there were no internal combustion engines."

Okay, he'd pursue this at length later on; reluctantly he turned to a more immediately important subject. He glanced over at her. Some of the strain had faded from her face, so maybe what she needed was to be distracted. "How many changes of clothing do you have? Will you need to do some shopping?"

"I have what I wore here, what I have on now, and one other change of clothing. I do have currency for buying clothing, though; my mission allowed for that contingency."

"Is the money real?" he asked wryly. "Or is it forged like everything else?"

"No, it's real. By the late twenty-first century all developed nations had completely switched over to credit and debit cards, so the majority of currency was put in a secure underground vault."

"Why not just burn it?" In his mind's eye he saw billions of dollars of bills going up in smoke and felt his whole body tighten in rejection. That just wasn't right, but it was still a logical solution.

"For one thing, it has great historical value. For another, even in my time, there are still un-developed nations that don't have the computer capability for a totally digitalized economy. They use cash, barter, any means available."

Two hundred years, he thought, and some things still hadn't changed much. He was relieved to know cash hadn't been completely done away with, though. He was something of a dinosaur when it came to banking: he preferred to write checks. He did use his bank's ATM to withdraw cash when he needed it, but something retro in him was horrified at the idea of paying his bills by computer.

Nikita would probably get a big laugh out of that, but no matter how much she needed cheering up, he didn't think he'd tell her. He didn't want her thinking of him as just a few steps out of the cave.

Five minutes later he pulled into his driveway. His house was on the smallish side, a two-bedroom Craftsman style, with a front porch that went all the way across the front of the house and a small enclosed porch on the back. He parked in back, pulling around next to the door. Tall, mature hedges separated his backyard from those of his neighbors, while giant oak trees grew close enough together to cloak almost the entire yard and half the house in cool shade.

His house was over sixty years old but well maintained, and had been modernized several times over the years, so it was very livable. He'd bought it when he and Rebecca got engaged, thinking it would do for a starter house until the second baby came along and they would need more space. Rebecca had even picked out the kitchen appliances. But then she died, and there weren't any babies and he'd never needed more space. His life hadn't stopped when Rebecca died, but it had stagnated.

As he got out of the car he realized he was worried now not about any stagnation but whether there was any dirty underwear lying on the floor in the one bathroom. The time for a woman to see his dirty socks and shorts was after they'd made love, not before.

What felt like a small electrical shock ran up his spine and exploded in his brain. For the first time in seven years, he wanted a woman: not just sex, but the woman herself. He wanted Nikita in particular. He wanted to spend time with her, get to know her, find out what she liked and didn't like, if she was afraid of mice and spiders and snakes, if a little bug could make her squeal like a girl. He wanted to know if she slept on her stomach, back, or side, if she snored, if she liked showers or baths.

He wanted **her.**

It was a revelation. He'd forgotten how energizing that kick of chemistry was, like downing a pot of coffee, forgotten how it was to be so intensely focused on one person. The shape of her hand as she shut the car door, the way she absently pushed a strand of hair away from her eyes, the quick, questioning glance she threw at him—he noticed all of that, with a clarity that engraved those little things in his memory.

The big question was whether she'd be willing to indulge in what wasn't quite casual sex but was far from ever being a long-term relationship. Assuming she was interested, any affair was limited by the duration of her stay in this time. She might be here two weeks, or two days. They had no way of knowing what was going on in her time, whether anyone there would figure out someone on the team was playing dirty and send reinforcements or a SAR team.

She was waiting for him at the porch, a questioning look in her eyes, as if she was wondering why he was just standing there by the car instead of unlocking the door so they could go inside. Thinking about how long she'd be here made him look at her presence from another angle, and he asked, "How long do you have here before they'll come looking for you? There has to be a time limit, or they'd never know if someone was dead, injured, their links fried, or even in jail. There has to be a rescue procedure in place."

"We didn't know the exact parameters of

this case," she said, "so a really long time limit was set."

"How long is 'really long'?"

"A month."

That **was** long, longer than he'd expected. Most murder cases either were closed within a week or eventually became cold cases; either the leads were there or they weren't. Maybe something else was going on that he didn't know about. He didn't like that thought; what she'd sprung on him already would probably give him nightmares.

He opened the screen door, and they went up on the back porch; then he unlocked the door to the house and let them into the kitchen. Nikita stopped and looked around and Knox did, too, trying to see it through her eyes.

To the left was his tiny laundry cubicle, just large enough for a washer and dryer. The kitchen was an eat-in, with old cabinets that he'd stripped down to the original wood and stained. The tile on the floor looked like golden stone, and he'd splurged on the countertops, putting in solid surfacing because that was what Rebecca wanted. She had never cooked a meal here, never slept a night here. Whenever they'd spent the night together, he'd been at her place because it was just easier, he didn't have to cart around all the paraphernalia women needed to get ready for work in the mornings, all the hair and face stuff. A lot of what he'd done in the house had been for Rebecca, but in her absence the house had become completely his.

Nikita walked slowly to the big gas stove and ever so lightly trailed her fingertips over it, much as she had done with the things in his office. To her, he realized, everything in here, in his office, was a priceless antique. Some she had probably read about but never seen before.

"What does this do?" she asked, pointing at the electric can opener.

"It opens cans."

She actually leaned down and studied the way the can opener worked, pulling the little lever down and frowning in disappointment when nothing happened.

"Like this." He grabbed a can of chicken noodle soup from his pantry, showed her how the little magnet held the can in place, and let her press down on the lever. The can whirled around, and her face lit like a child's.

"There are so many details of everyday life we've lost," she murmured.

He leaned against the cabinet and crossed one ankle over the other. "How do **you** open cans?"

"We don't have cans."

"What does food come in, then?"

"Most food comes in clear containers that are edible themselves, and melt when heated. They're very nutritious."

He made a face at the idea of eating the packaging. "Yeah, but how do they taste?"

"Like whatever food they contain, of course."

"What if it's a food that isn't supposed to be heated, like ice cream?"

She looked amused. "There are other things, such as plastic cartons. Fresh produce is still fresh produce. I don't suppose the food itself is very different, just the containers and maybe preparation have changed." She took the can of chicken noodle soup and sniffed. "What do we do with this now?"

He pulled a small saucepan out of the cabinet and set it on one of the stove eyes, turned it on, and dumped the soup into it. "We eat it."

She played with the knobs, turning a burner on and off and watching the blue flame jump. Since she'd obviously never seen a gas stove before, he asked, "How do you heat your food?"

"Molecular agitation."

He laughed, thinking of his own molecules that were currently agitated. "Sounds like a microwave oven to me."

"A variation. So much of what we have was invented during this era," she said with an undertone of pure bliss, and abruptly he realized how much she was enjoying this part of her trip. Parts of it so far sucked, but this, the technology part, delighted her.

"Like what?"

"Oh, space travel, computers, lasers, things like that."

"Space travel" caught his attention, and he realized he could stand here talking to her until they collapsed from exhaustion. They had things to do—or he did, rather—but he didn't want to do any of them.

"That's really why I'm here," she said ruefully. "This time fascinates me, and I've studied it in great depth. I **begged** for this assignment."

"Be careful what you ask for," he said wryly.

She laughed, her brown eyes sparkling. "Exactly." Then she sobered as her thoughts turned to the people who had died, and all the complications that had arisen. Reading her mind, Knox touched her briefly on the arm in sympathy.

"Come on, I'll show you where you'll be sleeping." Which wasn't in his bed, unfortunately—at least not yet. He turned the heat down under the soup and led her through the house.

The house was small, with a living room–dining room combination, except he used the dining room for his home office and what few meals he had here he ate in the kitchen. The two bedrooms led off the short hall, one on the left and one on the right, with the bathroom between them. The front bedroom, the larger one, was his; the back bedroom was nothing extra, just a bedroom, with the requisite furniture. He showed her where the linen closet was, for fresh towels when she showered, then left her to take care of whatever needed taking care of while he went into the living room.

Instead of using his home phone, because he didn't want anyone to know where he was, he took out his radio and called in, passing along the request to have Nikita's suitcase picked up at the motel and taken to his office. He'd go in later tonight, when only dispatch was working, and retrieve it. He had to do something about her rental car, too.

An idea struck and he picked up his home phone and called his dad. Kelvin answered on the first ring. "Hardware store."

"Dad, is it all right if I stash a car in your barn for a while?"

"Sure. Whose car is it?"

"A rental. I don't want it seen."

"I can take a tarp home with me tonight if you want to cover it up, just to be on the safe side."

"That's a good idea. Thanks."

"When will you bring it?"

"After dark sometime. I'll call you."

"Okay. See you then."

That was another problem taken care of, Knox thought, if he could just get her car moved without being followed. He'd have to drive it, of course; no one else was going to get a shot at her if he could help it.

She came out of the bathroom, and he noticed how tired she looked. Today had been a hell of a day, for both of them, and it wasn't over yet.

"Let's have some soup," he said, taking her arm and turning her toward the kitchen. "Chicken noodle soup makes everything better."

"In that case," she said, "you should open another can."

12

NIKITA WASN'T HUNGRY BUT THE SOUP WAS comforting, and the air-conditioning in the house was set slightly too cool for her, so the hot liquid was doubly welcome. They sat at the scarred wooden kitchen table and silently spooned the rich broth and noodles—with a few tiny bits of chicken in the broth to justify the name—out of matching blue bowls. He had almost finished his when his radio crackled to life.

With a resigned expression he listened to the code, then picked up his bowl and spoon and took them to the sink, dumping the soup down the disposal, then turning on the water and flipping the switch. "I have to go," he said unnecessarily. "Stay inside and don't answer the phone, unless I'm the one calling." He scribbled his number on a pad of paper and pushed it toward her. "If that number isn't what shows up in the ID window on the phone, don't answer."

"All right," Nikita said. The technology was very similar to that in her own time.

He paused on his way out the door and looked back at her. "Will you still be here when I get back?"

"Of course," she said steadily, tamping down the spurt of resentment that he felt he had to ask that particular question. "I still have a mission to accomplish, and I need your help to do that."

He nodded and started out the door again, only to pause once more. "Shit," he said under his breath, striding back to her. Startled, she wondered if he intended to stuff her into the trunk of his car, or maybe handcuff her to a bed frame; she dropped her spoon and scraped her chair back, half rising, ready to fight.

Instead he bent down, propping his left hand on the table and cupping the back of her head in his right, and closed his mouth over hers.

Well, she thought in dim surprise. Then: **Oh.**

He was slow, very slow, and thorough—**very** thorough. His tongue curled into her mouth like an old friend, sure of his welcome. She put her hand over his on the table and he turned his palm up, capturing hers, lacing their fingers together.

A low, warm hum of pleasure, little more than a sigh, sounded in her throat. Of course she had noticed—several times—how attractive he was, but except for that one slip of the tongue she thought she'd been successful in keeping her thoughts to herself. Either his low-key persona had misled her about his self-confidence and boldness, or she had been as transparent as water in her appreciation.

She ended the kiss as leisurely as he had pro-longed it, only gradually pulling away. His eyes were heavy-lidded, intent; her own lids felt heavy.

"Do you think a kiss will keep me here?" she asked, her voice low.

He chuckled as he straightened. "No, but I damn sure wanted to know how you taste just in case you do split."

Split? He thought she would **split**? She didn't know if he was making a really lewd, disgusting reference, or if he thought she might not survive her assignment, and a laser attack did somewhat look as if the victim had been split open. Either way—

He burst out laughing. "If you could see your face . . ."

"Then my eyes would have to be on stems."

"**Split** means 'to leave,' " he explained, still laughing as he went out the door.

Nikita sat at the table, wondering how many

other times she had missed the meaning of slang expressions, and if he thought she was a complete idiot. Then she laughed softly to herself, because who cared? He knew why she wasn't familiar with all the slang he used. Some of it, yes, but not all. He had probably been laughing at her all day.

She didn't want any more soup, so she carried hers to the sink and copied what he had done: dump the food down the drain, turn on the water, then flip a switch that caused an awful grinding sound. When the quality of the sound changed, became a bit smoother, she turned off that switch and then the water.

He probably had one of those automated dish-cleaning machines that were common in this century, but she didn't want to push her luck. Until she saw him operate it, she would leave well enough alone. Instead, rummaging under the sink, she found a plastic bottle labeled "dishwashing detergent" and washed the dishes by hand, using a small, stiff-bristled brush that seemed to be there for just that purpose. Then she found a clean kitchen towel and spread it out on the countertop, putting the dishes upside down on it to dry.

Domestic duties taken care of, she decided to take advantage of his absence by thoroughly examining his home. If he had thought she would be too polite to pass up this opportunity to in-

spect an early-twenty-first-century house, then
his expectations were far divorced from reality.

She started with the little alcove in back,
where two white machines took up all the
space. She thought she knew what they were,
and by reading the various selections, she deduced she was correct. The machine that had
such selections as "Quick Wash" had to be the
"washing machine," which had been used for
wet cleaning. No one in her time ever used
water for cleaning clothing. The other machine,
then, was the drying machine. She opened both
and looked inside. The washing machine was
half full of socks and underwear, dry, so she assumed they needed washing and she quickly
closed that lid. The drying machine was full of
towels, and they were dry, so they had just as
obviously already been wet-washed.

She pulled one towel out and smelled it;
there was a delicious, faintly lemon scent to the
fabric. A tag caught her attention and she read
it, surprised to find that the towel was one hundred percent cotton. Cotton! Did he know what
a fortune these were worth? No, of course he
didn't. Only the very wealthy, the very very
wealthy, could afford clothes made from any
natural fiber. Cotton, silk, wool, linen—they
were more precious than diamonds. Almost all
clothing in her time was synthetic; certainly
everything she owned was.

The towel reminded her of the bathing apparatus in the motel. She had worked out how to use it, and though part of her was scandalized at the idea of using water to clean herself, she had greatly enjoyed the sensation of warm water cascading over her. Knox had the same arrangement in his bathroom, and after a day spent in these clothes, plus a lot of time out in the hot weather, she **needed** to bathe. Pity she didn't have her clean clothes to change into yet, but right now she'd be satisfied to wash off the old sweat and grime.

Putting thought into action, she hurried into the bathroom and locked the door, then stripped off her clothes. One of the advantages of the synthetic material was that if you were caught out in the rain, it dried very fast, within minutes. She quickly washed out her underwear and shirt, then hung them to dry before turning on the shower. She would have washed all her clothes, but doing the chore by hand seemed rather daunting. If Knox didn't bring her suitcase back with him, though, she would have to wash her clothes tonight before she went to bed.

After wrapping a towel around her head to keep her hair dry, she stepped under the warm water and sighed with bliss. Her time might be best in terms of convenience, but this time was definitely best in some things, a water bath being one of them. A plentiful supply of cotton towels was another. Oh, and paper! she thought, almost salivating at the idea of taking some paper back with her—assuming she didn't get killed, assuming SAR was sent with replacement links so she **could** go home, assuming a lot of other factors went in her favor.

The thought of home dimmed her delight in the shower. She couldn't let herself think that she might not be able to get home. She had family, friends, a job she loved. She was close to her parents and to her younger sister, Fair; her younger brother, Connor, had confounded everyone two years ago by giving up his wild bachelor days for married life, and he and his wife had promptly produced a fat, adorable baby boy whom she doted on. She couldn't imagine never getting to see Jemi's dimpled little face again, or listen to his infectious laugh. She **had** to go home, or she wouldn't be able to bear it.

Clean and smelling of an herbal-scented soap, she turned off the water and dried herself with the towel she'd wrapped around her head. On the vanity were a few items and she inspected them, recognizing a toothbrush and a tube of toothpaste—the tube said "toothpaste" on it, so there wasn't much chance of guessing wrong on that one—and a razor for shaving. Men still used razors in her time; it was another one of those objects that worked. In her time,

though, toothbrushes hadn't been used for
about a century; antiviral drugs had wiped out
tooth decay in the modernized world, and
mouthwashes broke down the sticky material
that got on teeth, dissolving it.

She found a bottle of moisturizer—un-
scented—and smoothed it over her skin, then
got dressed. Her underwear and shirt were dry,
and felt much better now that they'd been fresh-
ened. Comfortable and relaxed, she resumed
her exploration of the house.

In the main room, the living room, were a
couple of comfortable chairs and a large leather
couch, plus a much larger video screen than any
she'd seen before in this time. The one in the
motel room had been small compared to this
one. The floor was covered with a carpet that
didn't look as if it had seen much traffic. There
were a couple of lamps, some small tables, and
at the other end of the room was a desk with
one of the large, primitive computers and another small video screen. There were also books,
all of them paper copies, and her hand trembled
with excitement as she picked one up and
flipped through the pages.

Did these people realize how lucky they were,
that they had so very many books printed on
paper? One of the great tragedies of the late
twentieth and early twenty-first centuries was
that so much of their music, their books, their

culture, had been recorded on computer discs that hadn't stood up to time very well. Within two generations, the discs had deteriorated and most of the data was lost. Some of it could be re-created, of course; songs could be sung by other singers. But those original recordings were gone, never to be recovered. Manuscripts, research . . . so much of it lost. Paper seemed so very fragile, but there were fragments of paper hundreds of years old, proving that, with care, it was a viable medium for information.

She turned on his computer, and waited an interminable amount of time while it whirred and clicked before finally becoming operational. Absently she said, "Open communication program," then laughed at herself when nothing happened. Voice-recognition programs existed now, but they weren't the norm.

She sat down in front of the video screen and experimented with the manual operational system, fascinated with the little arrow that told you where you were on the screen. Computer knowledge had exploded in the late twentieth century, along with so many other sciences that had built her own world.

She was reluctant to do too much, though, because she was afraid she might inadvertently destroy the system. She clicked various icons until she found how to tell the computer to turn itself off.

Next she examined the bedrooms. His room was larger than the one he'd designated for her use, and the bed was larger. It was unmade, the pillows punched together in a lump, the sheet and blankets rumpled and thrown to the side. On the dresser was a photograph of a pretty young woman, and Nikita went closer to examine it. The woman's green eyes seemed to smile, and invite a smile in return. There were no other photographs. A telephone sat on a small table beside the bed, as well as a lamp, two books, a magazine, a glass with about an inch of water in the bottom, and one sock.

Something definitely hadn't changed in two centuries: men.

Having satisfied her curiosity, she returned to the living room and turned on the large video screen. Judging from what she had seen the night before in the motel, she could learn more about the mechanics of this culture by watching television than by ten years of intensive study in her own time.

She settled on the couch and was soon fast asleep.

The ringing of the telephone woke her. She scrambled to her feet and ran to the kitchen to grab the phone. First she checked the number in the lit ID screen, and it matched the number Knox had scribbled down. She pressed what seemed the most likely button and said, "Hello."

"So you're still there."

"I said I would be." She yawned, then peered at her wristwatch. It was analog instead of digital, and her mind was too clouded with sleep to make sense of all those hands. "I've been asleep; what time is it?"

"Just after six. I'll be through here in another fifteen, twenty minutes. Want me to bring something home for supper?"

She paused, then cautiously said, "Do you need to?"

"If you want to eat tonight, yeah. I don't have much in the way of groceries."

She wasn't particularly hungry, after having soup that afternoon, but she remembered how good lunch had tasted and said, "Could we have another hamburger?"

He chuckled. "You liked those, huh?"

"Yes. They're horribly bad for your health, I think, but I liked the taste."

"Everything that tastes good is bad for your health. It's a rule."

That hadn't changed, either. Every time something that tasted really good was developed, within a year there was a huge outcry about how unhealthy the product was. Not even vegetables and fruit escaped the notice of the alarmists.

"A hamburger," she said firmly. "And the french fries."

"That's the way to live. I'll be home in about forty minutes, depending on how long it takes me to get the burgers. Has anyone called?"

"No, it's been quiet."

"Good. I hope it stays that way."

While she waited for him to arrive, she splashed cool water in her face, and combed her hair. The nap had renewed her energy, and she felt as if she could function for another twelve hours if need be.

He estimated time very well, pulling into his driveway thirty-nine minutes later. She waited in the kitchen, aware of a warm sense of pleasure as she anticipated the opening of the door, seeing him for the first time since that surprising kiss.

He came in bearing her suitcase and white paper sacks from which wafted the most delicious aroma. His jacket was off, his weapon holstered in his shoulder harness. With his jeans and boots, he looked as if he belonged in an even earlier century, when horses were still the main mode of transportation. His jaw was dark with beard shadow, his hair hanging over his forehead, but he didn't look tired. Instead his blue eyes were sharp and alert, and he moved without any obvious fatigue dragging at him.

"What did you do besides take a nap?" he asked as he took two drinks out of one sack and slid one in front of her.

"Took a shower, and examined your house."

"Did you figure out how everything worked?"

"I think so. Nothing's broken, at any rate." She sat down in the chair she had occupied before, and he put a hamburger and a paper sleeve of fries in front of her. With controlled greed she began unwrapping the hamburger, but good manners dictated she wait until he was sitting down and ready to eat before she took her first bite.

They ate in silence, dipping the salty fries in ketchup. Reflecting on how many calories she had consumed that day, Nikita estimated she needed to run about ten miles just to break even.

"When it gets dark, we'll retrieve your rental car," he finally said.

"Is it safe for your father to have my car on his property?"

"No one will know it's there. No one will know where you are. I did some shopping for you today, bought you some clothes that will let you blend in better, something to cover your hair, sunglasses."

Those things would help. They were simple measures, but in their training agents learned that people often didn't pay close attention to the people around them, so she should be fairly safe. She was lucky in that no one really knew

her, other than Knox. This was still a small
town, however, and his neighbors would certainly notice a strange woman entering and
leaving his house.

She had come prepared for the eventuality
that she might have to change her appearance,
though. In her suitcase were some handy items
from her time.

"How would I look as a blue-eyed blond?"
she asked, grinning at him.

13

Half an hour later Nikita came out of the bathroom and did a slow turn in front of him. "What do you think?"

Knox had been watching news on the video screen, but he slowly got to his feet, staring at her. "Hubba hubba," he said, his deep voice going dark, his eyes getting that heavy-lidded look again. "I like. I like your dark hair better, but this is good. Real good. How'd you do it so fast?"

Distracted, she said, "It's a polymer product that coats the hair with a different color; it won't come off if your hair gets wet, but a simple shampoo will dissolve it. No bleaching and redying involved." She paused. **"Hubba hubba?"** She thought that meant something good, especially if she factored in the change in his voice tone. She could feel her cheeks getting hot as she reacted to the way he was looking at her.

"It means **yowzer.**"

She took a quick breath. That explanation hadn't helped any. "And that means—?"

"It means you look delicious."

That word she knew, but it meant something tasted wonderful. Obviously the slang in this time gave it a different meaning, unless . . . **oh.** Now her cheeks were really hot and she moved a step away from him, uncertain what to do. She wasn't a Naive Nancy, she had danced this dance before, but she'd been in her own time. Getting involved with him wouldn't be on the same level as stupidly getting involved with a **suspect,** which would be grounds for dismissal if not outright prosecution. In many ways Knox was like a fellow agent, but while the Bureau knew fraternization was going to happen, the official policy was still that it wasn't a good idea.

But how ethical was it to become sexually intimate with someone, knowing all the while one was here for only a short time? That was if everything worked right, SAR brought her some replacement links, she didn't get killed in the line of duty, and all the other possibilities. Her trainers in ethics classes had been realistic: sexual contact with people from other times was, given human nature, inevitable. Paradoxically, however, casual sex was perhaps more ethical than forming an emotional bond with someone from another time when you knew you would be transiting out.

She didn't think she'd had a casual thought about Knox Davis since first meeting him.

He closed the space between them, putting one hand on her waist; the heat of his hand burned through her clothing. "I've already thought of all the ramifications," he said, still in that slow, deep voice that affected her as potently as an aphrodisiac. "I know that, if everything works out, you'll be leaving. I know that I'm going to do everything I can to get you naked, but if you don't want to, all you have to do is say no."

In that instant, like hitting a solid wall, she realized that while she couldn't be casual about him, he could easily feel very casual about her. The trainers hadn't covered that possibility, instead focusing on any unfair actions by the agents.

Here she was, worried about behaving ethically—and he was worried about getting laid. **Men!**

There was a wonderful phrase that had stood the test of time; she took great pleasure in giving him a noncommital smile and saying, "I'll get back to you on that."

He tipped his head back and laughed, his

hand tightening on her waist. "You do that," he said in amusement. Then he kissed her again, and it was just as it had been earlier, slow and devastatingly intimate. This time, though, they were both standing; it was the most natural thing in the world to move close to him, to put her arms around his neck and rise on tiptoe so the fit was even better. She felt the shudder that rolled through him and suddenly the kiss wasn't slow, it was hungry and demanding, hot with insistence.

His scent and taste washed through her, awakening every female instinct and hormone she possessed. His penis was erect, pushing hard against her lower abdomen even before he slid his hand down to her bottom and lodged her even more solidly to him. How easy it would be to go to bed with him, she thought dimly, struggling to concentrate on anything except the pleasure igniting along her neural pathways. Whatever it was about that laid-back charm of his, it was lethal to her good intentions.

She fought for common sense and self-control, managing to put a breath of air between their lips, and murmured, "Shouldn't we be leaving?"

"Not just yet. It isn't good dark yet."

"Good dark, as opposed to bad dark?"

"As in, there's still enough light outside to

see." He pressed a quick kiss to the corner of her mouth, nipping lightly at her bottom lip.

Resolutely, she wedged her hands against his chest. She didn't have to push; just the position of her hands had him sighing with regret and easing back.

She took a few deep breaths, steadying herself, and dropped off of tiptoe. "I'm sorry; that was unprofessional of me."

"You keep saying that."

"It **is** unprofessional."

"Agreed. But you're sorry about it, and I'm not. Hell, after everything else we've done today, a little unprofessionalism feels like a breath of fresh air."

Meaning, at least now he wasn't being forced into breaking laws and betraying the focus of his life, so why not have a little sex? That thought gave her the strength she needed to put more distance between them; she wanted to have sex with him for a lot of reasons, but to be his consolation prize wasn't one of them.

"Just so you know my position," she said, "I obviously find you very attractive. But I won't be here long, so any relationship I have here is, by definition, casual. I've never had casual sex in my life, and see no reason to start now."

He whistled softly between his teeth. "That puts me in my place, doesn't it?"

Now she felt faintly guilty. "I don't mean to be insulting; it's just . . ."

"Hush." He touched one fingertip to her chin. "You don't have to apologize, or make excuses. If the time was right—no pun intended—I think we could have something solid between us."

The really sad thing was, she thought so, too. Her career kept her so busy she didn't have much time to devote to finding Mr. Right, or even Mr. Maybe. Now she had all but fallen into the lap of a definite Mr. Maybe who might even be Mr. Right, and she couldn't stay.

As fascinated as she was with this time, with all its energy and explosion of ideas and technology, she preferred her home time. Some travelers talked about picking an interesting time and staying, but she'd never understood how they could walk away from their families and friends, from everything they knew. Of course, she had to consider that perhaps they had no friends and their families were why they wanted to leave, which was even sadder.

Knox said, as though he were reading her mind, "But if you stayed . . ."

"I can't."

"Can't, or don't want to?"

"Never see my family again?" she asked softly. "Could you do that?"

"It's just my dad and stepmother, but . . . no.

I couldn't voluntarily walk away and never see them again." He reached out and fingered a lock of her newly blond hair. "Is there anyone other than family waiting for you?"

"A lover, you mean? No. I have friends, both male and female, but no one I'm interested in romantically." Since this seemed to be question-and-answer time, she lifted her brows in query and said, "Do you?"

"Not now."

Meaning there had been, but after seeing the photograph in his bedroom, she had expected that. "I was in your bedroom looking around." Snooping, yes, but she wasn't embarrassed. He had to have known she wanted to look at everything. "The woman in the photograph?"

She could almost feel him withdraw, his gaze turning inward, but into his memories rather than in anger. "Rebecca. She was my fiancée. She died seven years ago."

Sympathy had her touching his hand. "I'm so sorry. Yes, I know I say that a lot, but this is different. Has there been anyone since?"

"Just the occasional casual sex you're so set against, but no one close."

Seven years, she thought, and he was still emotionally faithful. This was a steadfast man. "You must have loved her very much. She would be honored."

His gaze refocused on her. "That's a quaint

expression, and a . . . sweet thought. Thank you. Yes, I did love her, and the grief was almost more than I could take. But it fades, after a while, and the cliché about life going on is true." He looked past her out the window. "On a different subject, by the time you change clothes, it'll be dark enough for us to leave."

And he had discussed his personal life as much as he intended, she thought as she got the shopping bags and took them into her bedroom. She didn't mind backing off a subject that was sensitive to him. Or perhaps, because he was a man, he thought they had already plumbed the depths and there was nothing else to talk about.

That thought made her smile, and she turned her attention to changing her appearance even more.

With only the light coming from the hallway to illuminate the room, she pulled the curtains closed over both windows, then turned on the lights in the room and closed the door. Opening the shopping bags, she pulled out a baseball cap, two pairs of jeans, two T-shirts, a pair of athletic shoes, and some socks. Just to be certain, she looked at the manufacturers' labels in her new clothing, and shivered with excitement. Prewashed, softened, bleached—yeah, yeah, yeah. As she'd suspected, they were **cotton.**

She'd never been able to afford even a single cotton shirt.

Hastily, she stripped down to her underwear. The two pairs of jeans were identical, so she grabbed the pair on top, tore off the tags, and pulled them on. The waistband was a little loose, but the length was good, and she loved the way the soft fabric felt on her legs. It felt substantial, without being restricting, and **comforting.**

That was a slogan the manufacturer could use, she thought in dizzy delight. **The comfort of cotton.**

She chose the pink T-shirt over the green one, and tucked the bottom into the waistband of her jeans. Surveying herself in the bedroom mirror, she squelched a squeal of joy. She looked . . . she looked so **twenty-first century**!

Even people who had met her that day would find it difficult to recognize her, with the different clothes and change of hair color. The color she'd chosen was a warm golden shade that went well with her skin tone. She also had colored contacts in her purse that would change her eye color to blue, but since they would be out after dark, she didn't think the contacts would be needed. For the daytime, the sunglasses Knox had bought would hide her eyes anyway.

She pulled the baseball cap onto her head

and stared at herself. Her own mother would know her, of course, and her sister, but her father and brother would probably pass by without another look.

After putting on her new socks and shoes, she returned to the living room and for the second time presented herself for his inspection. "Well?"

He nodded with satisfaction. "No one will know you. Take off the cap and pull your hair back in a ponytail."

Nikita obediently started gathering her hair back. It wasn't very long, not quite shoulder length, so her ponytail was short. He went into the kitchen and came back with a piece of plastic-wrapped wire that he gave her to wrap around her hair. She put on the cap again and pulled the little ponytail through the hole in back, feeling to make certain it was secure. "What's this wire thing?"

"It's the tie from a trash bag. I'm short on ponytail holders today, so we have to make do."

She ignored the dry tone and said, "I need another shirt, or a jacket, to hide my weapon." She paused, an awful suspicion blooming in her mind. She narrowed her eyes at him. "You **are** giving it back to me, aren't you?"

He shrugged, something really close to a smirk on his face. "Why do you want it? You have that little laser pen, and it can do as much or more damage as a nine millimeter."

"Yes, it can, and I'll use it if I have to. But if I can avoid attracting attention to it, don't you think that would be the intelligent thing to do?"

"Avoiding attention is the best thing to do, regardless. If you're seen carrying a weapon, you'll automatically be marked as law enforcement, which we want to avoid." He paused. "Your weapon is in the car. Carry it in your purse, not on your belt. On the other hand, it gets cool here in the mountains at night, so you do need something more than a T-shirt. I'll be right back."

He went into his bedroom and came out an instant later carrying a faded denim shirt. "Put this on."

The shirt was his, of course, and deliciously dwarfed her even though she was above average in height. She rolled up the cuffs to her elbows, and left the shirt hanging open and loose. "I'm ready, unless you can think of something else."

"Just one," he said, and kissed her again.

14

Knox glanced down at Nikita as she lay in the seat so no one could see her leaving his house. She would be seen eventually, of course, but he didn't want her appearance to be right on the heels of her **disappearance** as an FBI agent. He'd tell whoever asked that she hadn't found any connection between Taylor Allen's murder and the ones she was investigating, and left. She was a federal agent; local cops wouldn't expect her to do things the way they would. Put a day or two between one leaving and the other arriving, and people would be less likely to make a connection between the two.

Something about her bothered him, and not just the fact that she was from two hundred years in the future. She was either very calm about almost everything, or she was virtually emotionless. The only time that he'd seen a real reaction from her was when she'd killed the other agent from the future, Luttrell. For a minute he'd thought she was about to puke her guts up. Then she'd pulled it together, and functioned with almost robotic calmness.

Robotic.

His head suddenly tingled, as if his hair were standing on end. **No way.** What he was thinking was impossible. She felt like a real woman; she smelled like a real woman. Her skin was warm, she breathed—or she appeared to breathe, at least. He was abruptly tempted to stick his hand under her nose to see if he could feel the rush of warm air.

She had eaten two hamburgers, french fries, soup. Could robots eat? Why would anyone invent a robot that could eat, anyway? Wasn't that a waste of technology—not to mention food?

Depends on what the robot was used **for,** he thought. If, for some reason, a robot needed to infiltrate a group or army and had to appear human, then it would have to go through the motions of eating.

But she **kissed** like a woman, all soft lips and warm, moist mouth. No sooner had that thought brought some "What was I thinking?" relief than he remembered the movie **Blade Runner** and its replicants. The replicants had been human to all appearances, but they had been machines, programmed to "die" at a certain age. Could that technology exist in her time? Could it have progressed that far, that fast?

His common sense said, Why not? The space mission, after all, had gone from nothing to landing on the moon inside thirty years. The last fifty years of the twentieth century had seen such an explosion of technology that new change happened before the previous change had been completely absorbed. Another burst of creativity and inventiveness could have happened in her time, bringing God-only-knows-what.

In two hundred years, man had developed the means to travel through time. That had to be tougher than building a human-looking, human-functioning robot.

He tried to think of one reason why she couldn't be a robot. She had blushed; he remembered her cheeks turning pink. To blush, a person had to feel embarrassment. Could emotions be programmed? Or was it more a matter of programming to show certain physical reactions to certain events?

Other than when she'd killed Luttrell, she hadn't shown any strong emotion. She had been mildly exasperated, mildly amused, mildly annoyed. Considering how eventful the day had been, her evenness of temperament was either soothing or downright scary, and he didn't know which.

He couldn't believe he was actually wondering if he'd been trying to make love to a machine.

For Knox, wondering something immediately led to asking questions, because he couldn't stand not knowing. "What are you?"

"What?" she asked from the seat, twisting her head to stare up at him. Her brow was furrowed in puzzlement, but he got the impression she was abruptly wary. "Are we going to go through that again? I'm an FBI agent."

"That isn't what I meant. I mean, are you a human?"

To his surprise and stomach-clenching alarm, she didn't burst out laughing or act shocked, or do anything that would have reassured him. Instead she paused briefly, then in a measured tone said, "Why do you ask?"

"The way you act. No one can be that even-tempered. It's as if you have a baseline of behavior and never vary from it very much in either direction. You get annoyed, but not angry. You get amused, but you never really laugh. You get sort of turned-on, but not to the point of breathing heavy. Does your heart rate ever speed up, or are you some sort of robot?"

Again there was that telling pause, the even

voice. "Do you mean 'robot' figuratively or literally?"

"You tell me."

"I'm human," she replied, still in that controlled tone. "So that takes care of the literal question."

"And figuratively?"

"You tell me." Deftly she threw his words back at him.

A trap yawned at his feet, and he realized that if she was totally and completely human, he had just fucked up big-time by telling her that her sexual responses were robotic. Even the most calm-mannered woman in existence would get upset over being told that. Some women, when they got upset, let the whole world know. Others just got even. It was the getting-even type that he was afraid of.

When he remained silent, she sat up in the seat and stared straight ahead. "I'm sorry," she finally said. "I didn't realize I was acting inappropriately."

He had expected anger; what he sensed, instead, was fear. And that was the most alarming thing of all.

Nikita felt oddly frozen. She had done something wrong, obviously, but what? She tried to think what she should say, what she should do, what would be the normal reaction, but in light of what he'd just said, she obviously had no idea what "normal" was. When there was such a large gap in time, with a great deal of information either corrupted or lost outright, training could accomplish only so much. There were nuances she lacked, subtleties she didn't understand. In her job, such lapses could get her killed.

But what hurt was that he found her lacking. She had done something that repelled him, but she didn't know what. He had enjoyed kissing her; she wasn't mistaken about his physical response. So what had she done in the fifteen minutes since that had brought this on?

The frozen sensation ebbed, to be replaced by a burning sense of shame. She had always tried so hard to be as she should, to not let any difference be seen, to fit in; her legal standing at home was tenuous at best, so she had tried to never upset that delicate balance. Some of the others like her had been rebellious, but she had spent her entire life trying to please those in authority. The rebellious ones hadn't been destroyed, but they had been locked away, and the understanding had always been that when all the legal issues were decided, if opinion came down against them, they would be destroyed.

And if the bad ones were destroyed, how long would it be before public opinion demanded that all of them must be destroyed?

She wanted to ask what she'd done wrong, but she had spent her entire life blending in, not telling even her best friends about her situation; the inclination toward secrecy was so strong and reinforced over the years that she found it impossible to broach the subject with Knox. He already thought she might be a robot; it was best not to confirm any of his suspicions.

She sat rigidly and silently until they reached the courthouse. Knox once again pulled into the protected area where controversial prisoners were brought in, out of the public eye. "Let me have your car keys," he said, and she handed them over without a word.

"You won't have any problem driving this car, will you?" he asked, and she focused her attention on the controls.

"I don't think so," she said after looking them over for a moment. "Everything crucial seems to be in the standard position."

"Wait here five minutes. By then I'll already have left in your rental. Go back out the same entrance we came in, and turn left. Three blocks down there's a small grocery store on the right corner. I'll wait there for you."

Obviously he would be taking a different route, checking to see if anyone was following the rental car, though if the car was being watched, then whoever it was would see that a man was driving off in it, instead of a woman.

If so, then the supposition would be that he was taking the car to her. Either way, the car would be followed. He evidently thought five minutes would be enough time to evade any followers.

He got out of the car and she slid across the seat to take his place behind the wheel. The first thing she did was slide the seat forward, so she could reach the pedals.

"If by any chance I'm not there waiting, don't panic," he instructed. "Just stay put. I'll be there sooner or later. And one more thing: When we get to my dad's place, just stay in the car. It's dark, he won't be able to see you; he'll think you're one of the deputies."

Then he was gone, striding into the courthouse building. He would exit the building nearer the parking lot, walking boldly and openly, as if he had nothing to hide.

Nikita turned the car around, so she was sitting facing the exit, and watched the digital clock in the dash. The numbers seemed to change so slowly that she began silently counting off the seconds to herself, trying to exactly match her pace to that of the clock. What an odd thing time was, counted in the same sequence of numbers over and over again, never changing, and yet the quality of time was the subject of intense philosophical and scientific discussions and explorations. It wasn't just an artificial schedule people used to regulate their lives; it was a dimension unto itself, as real as the earth beneath them. But as complicated as time was, thinking about it was easier than thinking about herself.

At last the numbers showed that five minutes had elapsed. She buckled her seat belt, looked over the dials and controls one more time, then carefully put the gear in the "drive" position and pressed the pedal that fed gasoline to the engine. The car moved smoothly forward.

She didn't let herself hurry. She didn't see any other traffic, either motorized or pedestrian, in the parking lot. There were a surprising number of vehicles parked there, but then nights were always busy in the law enforcement fields.

She reached the parking lot entrance, and turned left. All the way to the store she checked her rearview mirrors for any cars that might be following her, but there was literally no one behind her for the entire three blocks.

As soon as she turned in to the convenience store parking lot, she saw Knox in her rental car. He gave one brief nod, then pulled back out into the street, and she sedately followed him.

Pekesville wasn't a large town, but it sprawled in the valleys between a jumble of mountains, seeking all the geographical cuts and crevices like water in a lake. It was a long, narrow town, with only two main roads and a warren of secondary streets running in all directions from and across them. That meant there was a traffic light at every corner, slowing their progress, so that it took them fifteen minutes to go about four miles. At last they were outside the city limits, though, and traffic thinned considerably. Streetlights faded behind them, and only their headlights illuminated the road.

Nikita fiercely concentrated on her driving, keeping a steady speed, not getting so close to Knox as to be unsafe, not letting him get so far ahead she might lose sight of him. That was how she had conducted her entire life: safely, staying within certain boundaries, finding expression in other things such as her work, where she not only was allowed to risk her life but in special circumstances was even expected to do so.

Not that she **wanted** to risk her life, she thought in muted agony. She simply wanted to be free to make mistakes, to maybe yell in public, to lose her temper without people wondering if some glitch had made her uncontrollable. She wanted to do silly things that had no reason other than she simply felt like doing them. She didn't want to live in fear of what might happen if she made someone uncomfortable.

Maybe being destroyed was better than the way she'd lived her entire life. Maybe the rebellious ones had the right idea, that it was better to live a short, real life than a long one in a prison of her own making.

By the time Knox turned off the highway onto a secondary road, she felt as if she could barely breathe, as if the air were too thick to pull into her lungs. She was drowning, had been drowning all her life, and only now had she realized it.

Are you a robot?

Why, yes, evidently I am. Thank you for pointing that out.

Knox's taillights loomed in her vision and she slammed on the brakes, shaking. He had let his speed drop, but she hadn't been paying attention, and she had almost collided with the back of the rental car. Damn him, why had he said that? And why did he have to be so observant and curious about everything?

He put on his brakes, slowing even more, then turned left onto a long driveway that curved up a small hill, where a one-story house sat among some tall shade trees. Several lights were on inside. Knox didn't stop at the house, but she heard him give one tap on his horn as they went past. Behind the house was a fence, and to one side was a barn. Knox drove directly into the barn. Nikita stopped and put the gear in "park," her headlights shining inside the barn.

An older man approached from her right—Knox's father, from the looks of him. They both shared that tall, broad-shouldered, slightly lanky build; even their heads were shaped the same. He turned on a light inside the barn, a single bulb that dangled from a rafter. Together he and Knox pulled a large tarp over the rental car so that even its tires were covered; then he turned out the light and they closed the double doors to the barn. Knox's father pulled a chain through the handles and secured the chain with a padlock.

Mr. Davis glanced at her, and though she knew he couldn't see her with the headlights shining at him the way they were, she felt his curiosity. Impulse seized her and she turned off the engine, then fumbled until she found the switch that turned off the headlights. Getting out of the car, careful not to stumble in the darkness, she walked up to the two men.

She didn't need to see his face to know Knox wasn't happy about his father meeting her, but sometime in the past half hour she'd stopped giving a damn about whether or not Knox was happy.

"Well, hello," Mr. Davis said. "I thought one of the deputies was driving Knox's car."

"You were supposed to stay in the car," Knox said, his tone cool.

"You told me to stay in the car," Nikita cor-

rected just as coolly. "You called me a robot because I wouldn't have sex with you, so why
would I do what you tell me?"

Knox made a choked sound, one echoed by
his father. She couldn't believe what had come
out of her mouth in front of his father, but she
just didn't care. Nothing and no one had ever
hurt her as much as Knox Davis had, and he
hadn't even been trying. It wasn't even his fault;
he couldn't have known that his choice of words
would slam her into a wall of reality and leave
her battered. She turned to Mr. Davis and held
out her hand. "Hello, I'm Nikita Stover."

His father took her hand. "Kelvin Davis.
Pleased to meet you." He sounded distracted, a
tone that instantly vanished when he turned to
his son. "Knox!"

"I didn't— I mean, I did ask you if you were
a robot," Knox said to her, "but it wasn't—"

"Why would you say something like that?"
his father demanded.

"It was a bunch of other things," he finished
raggedly.

"Oh, yes, I remember now. I don't get angry,
I don't laugh, and I don't get turned on. Two
out of three is really good, I suppose, but **guess
which one you're wrong about**!"

Mr. Davis shoved his hand through his
hair, uncomfortably shifting his weight from
one foot to the other. He obviously wished he

weren't in the middle of this. "Uh—are you two dating, or something?"

"No," Nikita said.

"Then how would he—?" The older man faltered to a halt.

Borne along on the flood tide of despairing rage, Nikita finished the sentence for him. "How would he know whether or not I get turned on?"

"Nikita, stop," Knox said.

"Don't tell me to stop!" She whirled to face him. "I've been **stopped** my whole life, afraid to do this, afraid to do that, afraid someone will think I'm too much trouble." To her horror, her voice clogged and tears welled in her eyes. "I don't cry," she said fiercely. "I'm afraid to even cry."

"I can see that." His voice was gentle now. "You don't need to cry. If you're mad at me, hit me. Come on, double up your fist and plant your best shot on my chin."

"Knox!" Mr. Davis protested.

"Don't patronize me," she said with muffled fury, her hands already curling into fists.

"If it'll make you feel better, go ahead and hit me."

It would, so she did. He didn't know what he was asking for. Nikita didn't telegraph her punch; she tightened the muscles in her arm and back the way she'd been taught and shot her arm straight out from her shoulder in a lightning fast, twisting motion. The punch landed solidly on Knox's left jaw and he staggered back, then abruptly fell on his ass.

"Holy shit," he said, holding his jaw.

15

"DAMN," SAID KELVIN DAVIS, STARING AT his son sitting on the ground. "You pack a punch, Miss Stover. Or should I say Ms.?"

She had read about the twentieth-century forms of address, preserved in business etiquette books that hadn't been digitalized, so she knew what he was talking about. "Call me Nikita." She sniffled and wiped her eyes with the heels of her palms, then said to Knox, "Are you going to get up, or just sit there all night?"

"Depends on whether or not you're planning on hitting me again," he replied. "If you are, I'll just stay down here, thank you."

"Don't be such a large baby," she snapped. "You've been pushing me around all day and I've been telling you and **telling** you—"

"That you've been letting me do it, yeah, I remember. And it's 'big baby,' not 'large baby.'" Warily he climbed to his feet, making certain he kept out of striking distance.

"**Big, large,** it all means the same." She was too upset to care if she'd made another language error. Events had unraveled; **she** had unraveled, to the point that it didn't make a difference to her now.

"You should probably come in and put some ice on your jaw," Kelvin said to Knox.

"Thanks, I will. I can just hear the guys tomorrow if I go to work with a big bruise on my face."

Kelvin turned politely to Nikita, extending his hand toward the house. "After you."

Nikita strode ahead of the two men, her thoughts and emotions still in turmoil. She could tell that on some level she didn't understand, both Knox and his father thought it was funny that she'd actually hit him. The violence hadn't relieved any of the pent-up emotion inside her; she wanted to hit him again, she wanted to cry, she wanted to scream her frustration to the skies.

The back porch light was on, and when they reached the house, she was able to tell it was a one-level redbrick home, far from new, with orderly bushes surrounding the foundation. The porch seemed to have been added on later, because it was made of wood and painted white. Kelvin opened a creaky screened door and ushered them onto the porch, then opened a wooden door that led, like in Knox's house, into the kitchen.

"Lynnette!" he called. "Company!"

"Is it Knox?" The voice preceded the woman who hurried in from another room. She stopped when she saw Nikita, immediately looking at her husband for an introduction or explanation, whichever seemed necessary.

"This is Nikita Stover, Knox's—uh—friend. Nikita, my wife, Lynnette."

"I'm pleased to meet you," both Nikita and Lynnette said at the same time. Lynnette was a comfortable fifty-something, attractively plump, with short red hair. She had a kind face, and an air of competence.

"Knox needs some ice for his jaw," said Kelvin.

"What happened?" Even as she asked, Lynnette was already going to the refrigeration unit, opening the side door and pulling out a package of something blue.

"Nikita knocked me on my ass," replied Knox.

Lynnette took a thin kitchen towel from a drawer and wrapped it around the blue pack, then gave it to Knox, who placed it against his left jaw. "On purpose?" she asked.

"Oh yeah." Knox pulled out a kitchen chair and sat down. "I asked her to hit me."

"You were probably expecting a girl-slap," Lynnette said shrewdly.

"Probably," he agreed.

"That wasn't what you got."

He chuckled. "I'll know better next time. She packs a Mike Tyson wallop."

He was laughing, Nikita thought. **Laughing.** Her insides were quivering and she thought she might be sick. Not because she'd hit him; he'd both asked for it and deserved it. In fact, she wanted to hit him again for laughing. Instead she stood frozen, staring out the kitchen window even though she couldn't see a thing outside.

"Sit down," Kelvin said to her, pulling out a chair and gently guiding her into it. "Would you like something to drink? Water? Milk? Maybe coffee?"

"Nothing, thank you," she said.

Knox swiveled in his chair and leaned toward her, blue gaze searching her face. She didn't know what he was looking for; some metal poking through her skin, maybe. He'd look in vain; metal hadn't been used in robot construction in over a hundred years.

"Let me see your hand."

He didn't give her time to comply, already reaching for her right hand and cradling it in his as he examined it. Her knuckles were red and already swelling, and there was a tiny split on one. "Ouch," he said. "Your hand is going to be worse than my jaw. Lynnette, do you have another ice pack?"

"No, but I can make do. I have some frozen peas." His stepmother again retrieved a bag from the refrigeration unit, and wrapped it in a towel. "Let's see," she said, taking Nikita's hand from his and carefully placing the cold pack over her knuckles, then tying the ends of the towel in a knot at her palm.

Nikita inhaled sharply at the biting cold, which seemed to intensify the throbbing in her hand. Stupid. She had been so stupid, injuring her hand when she knew she had to be in top shape for the investigation. She couldn't let herself forget why she was here, or that the mission was far more important than her feelings.

"What's this about?" Lynnette asked, sitting down. "I know I shouldn't ask, but I'm curious, and you **are** both sitting in my kitchen holding ice packs to various parts."

Kelvin snorted. "According to Nikita, she wouldn't sleep with Knox and he called her a robot."

"Slug him again," Lynnette promptly advised Nikita.

Nikita struggled against tears again. She had to stop being so emotional; she had to control herself until she was alone, at least. "I regret my inappropriate action," she said, her throat tight.

"If he called you a robot, the action wasn't inappropriate. I'd say it was downright restrained." Lynnette narrowed her gaze at Knox. "**Did** you?"

"In a way. Not exactly. There was another discussion going on at the time."

"And you aren't going to say what the other discussion was."

"No, I'm not." His tone was mild, but final. "And for the record, you don't know anything about Nikita. You haven't met her, never heard of her. She was supposed to stay in the car so you two wouldn't see her, but that didn't happen. She's incognito, because her life depends on it. If you see her in the street, I'll introduce you using a different name for her, but don't act as if you recognize her, okay?"

Both Kelvin and Lynnette nodded. It was obvious that questions were bubbling on Lynnette's tongue, but she held them back. Instead she brought out the age-old mother's question: "Have y'all had supper yet? Let me warm up something real quick for you."

"Thanks, but we've already eaten," said Knox, smiling with genuine affection at her. "And we need to be going."

"But you just got here."

"We're on a case together, and we still have a lot of legwork to do tonight."

"Depends on your definition of 'legwork,'" Kelvin muttered under his breath, earning an admonishing look from his wife and making Knox grin.

"The official kind," he told his father. He stood and put the ice pack on the table. "Thanks for the first aid."

"Take it with you," said Lynnette. "You have an automatic transmission; you can drive with your right hand and hold the ice pack with your left. Keep it on there for fifteen minutes, then off for fifteen, then on again. Keep doing that and you might not even have a bruise. And definitely take that pack of peas with you, because her hand will be in worse shape than your jaw."

Knox nodded and picked up the ice pack again. Going to Lynnette, he bent and kissed her on the cheek. "Thanks again. You're an acceptable stepmother."

She grinned and patted his arm. "I guess you're an acceptable stepson."

Nikita stood and added her thank-yous, then followed Knox out the door. Kelvin and Lynnette stood in the doorway and watched them walk to the car; when they reached it, Kelvin turned off the porch light and closed the door.

In the sudden dark privacy, Nikita felt even

more disconnected than before. She got in the passenger seat, while Knox slid behind the wheel. He tried to, anyway, banging his knees on the steering column and swearing under his breath as he moved the seat back enough to accommodate his long legs.

"That went well," he remarked. "Now they know about you, and they think I'm a jerk."

She wanted to say something along the lines of "The truth will come out" or "If the shoe fits," but clichés didn't appeal to her at the moment. She just sat silently as he started the car and reversed into the yard, making a three-point turn.

"Aren't you going to say anything?" he asked when they reached the road and he turned the car toward town.

She paused, gathering her thoughts. "When we get to your house, I'm going to sit down and draw up another time-line chart, list everything I know about Taylor Allen's murder—"

"That isn't what I meant."

"Oh, you want to talk about personal issues? All right. Don't kiss me again. How's that?"

He sighed. "Short, and to the point. I figured you'd feel that way. Look, I was just thinking about how calmly you take everything, and the technology that must exist in your time, and I thought it might be possible." A few seconds ticked by. "Is it?"

"Whoever killed Allen is a stranger to this time. He has to be living somewhere, eating somewhere. This is a small town; he shouldn't be difficult to find."

For a moment she didn't think he'd accept her change of subject, but then he said, "**If** he's staying here. He could be in the next county, or the next state."

"We won't know unless we look." Her tone didn't invite further conversation, and they sat in silence for the rest of the trip.

He had just unlocked the back door to his house when his radio squawked to life. He listened to the codes, his expression going cold. "There's been another murder," he said briefly, pushing the door open for her. "Same drill: keep the door locked, and don't answer the phone unless it's my cell number. Got it?"

"Yes, of course. This is probably connected, isn't it?"

"We don't have many murders in Pekesville," he said as he turned away. "What are the odds?"

16

THE OLD FORMER MAYOR, HARLAN FORBES, was in his eighties and deserved a more dignified death than being choked as he sat in his battered favorite easy chair watching the game-show channel on television. His bladder and bowels had released, and his kicking feet were probably what had knocked the lamp over. Choking was a violent death, with the victim struggling for long minutes before the brain finally died. It also took a tremendous amount of strength, or the knowledge to substitute technique for the needed strength.

The killer was perhaps strong, but he hadn't used his hands. There were no livid finger marks on the old man's neck, just a single ligature mark, meaning something had been looped over his head, twisted, and pulled. A belt, maybe. Could have been a rope, a long scarf, anything that was long enough and pliable.

It wasn't Knox's crime scene. The mayor lived within the city limits, so the scene was being worked by the city detectives. There was a great deal of cooperation between the two forces, though, effectively combining the experience, manpower, and budgets. They knew each other, formed specialized task forces together, and each helped the other as needed.

They didn't need Knox to work the scene, but the city detectives were always interested in hearing his observations; his reputation for being insatiably curious was well-known. He wasn't the only county investigator present; Roger Dee Franklin was also there, pretty much doing the same thing Knox was doing, which was watching.

The murder had occurred shortly after dark, by the next door neighbor's reckoning. She'd seen Harlan let his cat out as he did every day, late in the afternoon. It was the cat that had led her to check on Harlan, because the poor thing was standing at the door yowling to be let in, and he never ignored his cat. The racket had finally gotten on her nerves and she had called him. When he didn't answer the phone, she then called 911.

Roger Dee heard the cat story and drifted over to where Knox was standing. "Good thing the cat was outside," he murmured. If cats were trapped in a house alone with a dead person, they had been known to start snacking on the body. People forgot that cats were predators as well as pets. After seeing a few instances where someone old had died alone, with only a cat or cats for company, Knox swore to himself that if his lifestyle ever allowed him to have a pet, it would be a fish. He liked cats, but not enough to be their food.

Knox let his gaze drift back to the murder scene. There was nothing similar to the scene at the Allen house; the method was different, and on the surface the two victims had nothing in common, one being a fairly prosperous lawyer with a trophy wife, the other a retired, widowed old gentleman who owned a cat and had lived in the same house for fifty years. From what the neighbor said, Harlan Forbes didn't leave the house much, content to putter in his flower garden or sit on his front porch watching traffic pass by. His daughter or granddaughter usually brought his groceries once a week or so, or would pick him up to take him on an outing. He'd grown increasingly frail over the past year, and had begun talking about maybe selling his house and moving into an assisted-living apartment. The poor old guy didn't have to worry about that anymore.

With nothing to connect the two murders,

Knox was amazed at his own conviction that they were, somehow, related. He wasn't crazy enough to mention that to anyone, however. He'd be laughed out of the county. If he hadn't known Nikita, if he hadn't seen someone materialize right in front of him, if he didn't know a killer from the future was in the area, the idea would never have occurred to him, either.

The weird things that had been happening were all linked. The time capsule, the flashes out at Jesse Bingham's place, Nikita, the time traveling, Taylor Allen's murder—those were definitely linked, though Nikita didn't know exactly how Taylor Allen figured into it. She knew only that her UT had killed him, not why, and not who. So . . . how did Harlan Forbes's murder connect?

Harlan hadn't been robbed. There were no signs of forcible entry, but neither had his doors been locked. Most people around town didn't lock their doors if they were at home, until they went to bed. Both the method and the fact that nothing had been stolen said that the murder wasn't drug related, because an addict would have been looking to score some cash or something to sell.

"Poor old guy," said Roger Dee, echoing Knox's earlier thought. "Who'd want to kill someone like him? Retired, living off his pension—and God knows, being mayor of Pekesville never paid much. If he'd been robbed, at least there would be some sense to it, but to just come in and kill him—why? Reckon one of his relatives was in a hurry to inherit this old house and some beat-up furniture?"

"Could be." If Harlan had a hefty life insurance policy, maybe, or a nice nest egg in the bank. He hadn't lived as if he had money, but then a lot of old folks who'd gone through the Depression squirreled their money away and lived as if they could barely make it from month to month. Knox tried to think of all the possibilities, but the fact was he was still convinced this was somehow connected to Nikita's case. Well, it wasn't his scene to work; the city boys would check out the insurance/bank-account angle, and he'd help out here with interviewing the neighbors.

He and Roger Dee set out with their notebooks, knocking on doors and asking questions. This was an old, established neighborhood, and most of the residents were retired, which meant they were usually home at night watching television. None of them reported seeing anything or hearing anything unusual. They were all aghast at the violence done so close to home, and to someone they knew and liked, but not one of them was any help at all.

It was after two AM when he wearily drove home. The day had been a very, very long one, and when he pulled into his driveway and saw the lights still on inside the house, he knew it wasn't over yet.

Nikita sat at the kitchen table, a cup of coffee steaming close to her hand as she read one of Knox's books and waited for him. When she heard the car pull into the driveway, she got up and looked out the kitchen door to make certain it was him, then unlocked the door and opened it for him.

He looked tired when he came in, but why shouldn't he? It was late, he needed some sleep. Instead of going to bed, however, when he came in he sniffed the air and asked, "Is that coffee fresh?"

"I made it about an hour ago," she said as she returned to her seat at the table. She was proud that she'd figured out what the coffeemaker was, and how to work it. She had done the first because she'd seen a machine at Knox's office with the name "Mr. Coffee" printed on it, and though this one didn't have that name, it was essentially the same machine, the carafe differing slightly in shape. Without any instructions, she had puzzled out the procedure: the big empty space had measuring marks on it, so something went in there. The coffee? But if the coffee went there, then what was the box of paper coffee filters for? By experimenting, she discovered that the filter perfectly fit in the little basket, so that was where the coffee had to go. That meant the empty tank was for the water.

She found an unopened bag of coffee, read the instructions on how much coffee to use for each cup of water, and carefully measured both into the machine. Then it was a matter of pressing the **On** button, and after a moment the water began hissing and spewing into the carafe. Simple. And it tasted wonderful.

"Guess coffee's still around two hundred years from now," he said as he got a cup from the cabinet and poured some for himself.

"Definitely. It's the largest cash crop in South America."

"Even bigger than oil?"

"The oil market crashed when technology moved on." She remained in her position, book open, and kept her gaze on the book even though she was no longer seeing the words.

He pulled up a chair across from her and collapsed heavily into it. He rubbed his eyes, then folded both hands around the coffee cup. "The victim is a former mayor, Harlan Forbes. The MO is totally different, strangulation. Harlan was eighty-five, physically frail. There's nothing that ties his murder to Taylor Allen's, except my gut feeling."

"Could the mayor have written some sort of research paper that went in the time capsule?"

"No, he didn't even go to college. He was just one of those good old boys with the ability to glad-hand and schmooze, intelligent enough to be a good administrator, but not a go-getter."

Most of that, she mused, was in English, and she could understand the meaning of the idioms she didn't know by the way he used them. **Glad-hand.** She had to remember that.

"Perhaps it wasn't related to the other murder, then," she suggested.

He shook his head. "I've been thinking, and remembering who was at the ceremony twenty years ago when the capsule was buried. The football coach, Howard Easley, was found hanged the next morning. Coroner ruled it suicide, but now I wonder. The coach was close enough to see what exactly went in the capsule; in fact, he helped bury it. The mayor was right there. And now that I think back, Taylor Allen was there, too. He was just getting started in his law practice, and he was doing all sorts of civic things to build a network of contacts. He was part of the ceremony."

"But the coach died twenty years ago," she pointed out. "Why wait twenty years to kill the others?"

"I don't have an answer to that, but I think I'm beginning to see a pattern. I need to refresh my memory. First thing tomorrow we'll go to the library, look up the newspaper article, and see if it mentions who was there. There was a photograph, too, because I remember looking to see if my dad and I were in it, but the angle was wrong."

She nodded and looked back at the book.

After a minute he sighed. "Look—I'm sorry. I didn't ask if you were a robot because of the sex thing, I swear."

"There is no 'sex thing.' You've kissed me a few times, it was pleasant, and it won't happen again." She kept her expression as blank as possible, fighting down the urge to weep that swept over her again. She would **not** cry in front of him again.

She closed the book and got up. "I'm going to bed, if you don't mind."

"You won't be able to sleep, after drinking that coffee. We might as well sit here and talk."

"I didn't drink much, and I'm very tired. Good night." Taking the book with her, she went to the small bedroom he'd designated as hers and turned on the bedside lamp. She hadn't lied about being tired; she was so exhausted she could barely think.

He appeared in the doorway right behind her. "Do you have everything you need? Something to sleep in?"

"I'm fine, thank you."

"Are you sure? You can have one of my T-shirts to sleep in if you need it. The nights are warm, and the air conditioner in this house isn't the best. A T-shirt will be nice and cool."

"I have my sleep garments. I'm fine."

"Okay, then." He lingered in the doorway. "I'll see you in the morning."

"Are you asking for reassurance that you will, indeed, see me in the morning? I'm not leaving. I have a job to do."

"I know you're not leaving. You've had plenty of chances, if you wanted to go. It's just . . . damn. I hurt your feelings and I didn't mean to, but I don't know how to make it better."

"You've apologized. That's sufficient."

"No, it isn't. You're still hurt."

"Then I'll get over it," she said coolly. "I'm an adult. Would you close the door, please? I'd like to undress and go to bed."

He stood there for another minute looking extremely frustrated; then with a muffled curse he backed out and closed the door behind him. Nikita heaved a tired sigh of relief. She didn't want to deal with personal conflicts at all, but especially not when she was so tired.

Her clothing that she'd brought from her time wouldn't wrinkle, but she unpacked her suitcase and carefully hung the garments on some of the empty hangers in the closet, then did the same with the clothes Knox had bought for her. Those she was wearing, she removed and draped over the lone chair in the room.

When she was nude, she put on the single, seamless garment, a sanssaum, that she wore for sleeping. It was very comfortable, made of an opaque, fluid fabric that was gossamer in weight and adapted to body temperature. If you became too hot, the material wicked heat away from your skin. If you were too cold, it conserved heat. She couldn't imagine any of Knox's T-shirts were even half as comfortable as her sanssaum.

She turned back the covers on the bed and wearily climbed between the sheets, then stretched to turn off the lamp. In the sudden darkness she lay awake, far more aware of the strangeness of being here/now than she had been even when she first arrived. A scant thirty-six hours ago she had been full of plans and optimism. Now she was marooned in a time that wasn't hers, she had been betrayed by one of her own, and she didn't know if she would ever get back or if another assassin would be sent to kill her.

That must mean she would succeed, and they knew it.

Otherwise, why kill her? If she was destined to fail, they could just leave her here and no one would ever know. She hadn't been able to tell her family where she was going on her mission, because time missions were top secret, used only by the military and law enforcement. The technology was still too new—twenty years since the first one, and for the first ten years the transit had been fraught with danger, resulting in death often enough that every volunteer knew the odds of returning alive were, at best, fifty-fifty—the ramifications hadn't all been worked out concerning the effect of changing history, and the terrorist groups would love to have the technology.

If she didn't return, no one would ever know what happened to her.

So much had happened that she didn't understand. The time capsule was a surprise, but someone from her time had transited in and taken it. Who, and why? Knox knew the people in his town, and he said neither the lawyer nor the retired mayor could have had any sort of knowledge that could in any way be used to develop time-travel technology.

Who from this time was trying to kill her, and why? Who could have known about her?

A: The killer had been warned about her arrival—and probably about Houseman and McElroy, too.

B: The killer had recruited local aid. But why not just tell the sheriff that she wasn't a real FBI agent? Her credentials couldn't be verified in this time. She would be in jail, and out of the way.

Was it possible he hadn't wanted her in jail?

Just being out of the way wasn't enough. He wanted her dead.

She yawned, too tired to think straight. Turning on her side, she blinked her heavy eyes. Now that her vision had adjusted to the dark she could see the outline of the two windows, and she wished that she could open them. The room was a little stuffy, and some fresh air would be nice. But an open window was also a security breach; in her time, windows were never open. Training and custom kept her in the bed, wishing instead of doing.

The air here in these mountains was so fresh, and the rustling of the breeze in the huge old trees was an almost constant, soothing whisper in the background. The grass was green and fragrant, and flowers provided bursts of color and scent. Trees and grass and flowers still existed in her time; trees, in fact, had flourished now that they were no longer used to make paper. New varieties of flowers, in every color and scent, grew in great masses.

But it wasn't the same. This was . . . newer. And it wasn't home. It would never be home.

17

Knox got up at his usual time and heated two cups of the leftover coffee in the microwave. Reheated coffee never tasted quite right, but he couldn't see the point in letting coffee go to waste just because it had been cold for a few hours. Thank God Nikita drank her coffee black, so he didn't have to worry about how much of what to put in it. Right off the bat he couldn't find the single tray he knew he had, so he improvised and put the coffee cups on a baking sheet, then carried them both to her bedroom. As a peace offering, warmed-over coffee wasn't much, but it was the best he had.

He deliberately wasn't wearing a shirt, not to show off his manly physique, but because in his own experience the best way to get a woman to touch him was to take off his shirt.

Pheromones, he guessed. For whatever reason, it worked, and he needed her to touch him. Physical contact would help bridge the gap between them, pull her closer to him.

He knew he was invading her privacy in a big way, but that didn't stop him from knocking once, then twisting the doorknob and walking in.

Startled awake, Nikita sat up in bed. "What's wrong?" she asked urgently, pushing her tousled hair out of her face.

Knox's heart nearly stopped, and the baking sheet wobbled in his hand. The flesh-colored gown she was wearing was like some sort of fluid, pouring gently over her torso. It wasn't tight, and he couldn't see through it, but he almost didn't need to, so faithfully did it follow every curve, every outline.

He swallowed, and managed a halfway normal tone. "I brought you a cup of coffee. I figured you might need it to jump-start you this morning."

"Jump-start?" she asked, confusion wrinkling her brow.

He suppressed a grin. She probably wouldn't like it if she knew how much he enjoyed her verbal miscues caused by her too-literal application of the language. "**Jump-start** means use an external source of energy to get you started.

It's a car term." He took the tray over and set it down on the bedside table, then took a seat himself, settling beside her hip. He picked up both cups and extended one to her.

"Oh." She accepted the cup. "Thank you." She took a cautious sip of the steaming liquid, then made a face. "This doesn't taste like it did last night. What did you do to it?" She glanced at his chest, then looked away.

"Nuked it." He sipped his own coffee, glad for the hot liquid even if it wasn't the best in the world.

Appalled, she stared at her cup, and he had to laugh. "It's the same coffee from last night; I just reheated it in the microwave. It isn't really radioactive," he reassured her.

She took another sip, then said, "I would advise you to pour out the old coffee and make a fresh supply."

He chuckled. "It's hot, and it's caffeine. That's all I need. A fresh pot is brewing, but this tides me over until it's ready." He was chatting casually as he tried to keep his gaze from locking on her breasts, but, God, he was only human, and she had a fine looking pair: not too big, not too small, just round enough, and with soft-looking nipples. He wanted to pull off his clothes and climb into bed with her, but she hadn't given any indication that she would forgive him any time within the next decade, so he didn't push his luck. If she hit him again, she might break his jaw.

She was checking him out, too, with quick little glances at his chest and shoulders, but then she would devote her entire attention to the coffee. Maybe she wouldn't touch him, but she was thinking about it.

He fingered a loose fold of her gown, which happened to be on her stomach, where the fabric was a little bunched. "What kind of fabric is this? It looks like water."

She looked down at herself, frowning. "It looks wet?"

"No, I mean the way it sort of flows, as if it's liquid."

"That's the point. It's a synthetic fabric, of course, and the comfort of it is the whole idea. It keeps you warm if you're cold, and cool if you're too warm. All the really good sanssaums are made from it—"

" 'Sanssaums'?"

"What I'm wearing. That's what it's called. It means, literally, 'without seams.' The market name of the fabric is 'Elegon,' but who knows how it's made? Some chemists came up with it."

"I like how it feels." He rubbed the fold between two fingers, letting his knuckles rub against her stomach. He could feel the sudden breath she took.

Deciding that he'd pushed matters far enough, he got up. "I'm going to hit the shower," he said as he turned away. "I'll be finished in ten minutes; then it's all yours."

Leaving the room was almost more than he could do. She looked so damned sexy in that gown that showed every detail of her body without exposing her, her newly blond hair all mussed, her eyes heavy-lidded with sleep. She was getting to him, in a big way. Last night, when he'd seen the stricken look in her eyes, he could have kicked himself for even bringing up the possibility that she might not be human. His damn curiosity had made him open his big mouth and hurt her feelings. Robots couldn't have hurt feelings; **simulated** feelings, maybe, but not real ones.

So how did he know hers weren't simulated?

He shut that thought off as he stripped out of his jeans and got into the shower. She'd said she was human. He would take her at her word. She felt human, and that was good enough for him. If she was anything else, he didn't want to know.

He was going to have to work for her. He'd never **worked** for a woman before, not because he was such a hotshot lover, but because any attraction he'd felt had usually been mutual. The few times it hadn't, well, there were reasons why it just wasn't there, and he hadn't pursued the matter.

With Rebecca, the almost giddy sense of falling in love had been strong, immediate, and definitely mutual. It was as if they looked at each other and simply knew; the sex had been good because they were so in tune.

The way he felt about Nikita was unfolding differently, growing a little slower, but he was definitely feeling testosterone-driven urges that made him want to grab her up. He was a reasonable man, so he was taken by surprise at how **un**reasonable he felt about her. He couldn't just keep his distance the way she'd said; he **couldn't.**

Nikita sat in bed, sipping that awful coffee, and settled her jangling nerves. First he had startled her awake, though, oddly enough, she had seemed to instantly recognize him, because she hadn't reached for a weapon. Then her senses had been thrown into mild shock because he hadn't had on a shirt, and all that warm, bare skin made her want to cuddle close and feel the warmth wrap around her, to bury her face against him and inhale the scent of his skin.

Pheromones, she knew. It was basic biology: a woman's pheromones were airborne, capable of attracting men from a distance. A man's pheromones were mostly exchanged by touch. As close as he'd been, she had definitely felt the pull, urging her to reach out and stroke his chest.

Aesthetically speaking, it was a good chest, muscled and hairy—more muscled than she'd expected, given his relatively lean build. Either he worked to keep himself in shape, or he'd been blessed with excellent genes. Morning stubble had darkened his jaw—which was slightly darker on the left side, where she had hit him—and his hair needed brushing. She had wanted to pull him down on the bed with her, but her emotions still felt shredded. After a while she would get over her hurt, but right now all she could do was cling to her rather tenuous composure. When she was home—she had to believe she would somehow be able to go home—she would deal with the emotional issues he had exposed. In the meantime, she still had to work with him, regardless of how much she would prefer to just go away and hide.

The sound of the shower stopped. She waited five more minutes; then she heard the bathroom door open and Knox called, "It's all yours."

She didn't get out of bed until he'd gone into the kitchen. She gathered her clothing for the day and took it into the bathroom with her; it was still damp and steamy from his shower. The smell of him lingered in the air, mingled with that of soap and some minty odor.

The novelty of a wet bath charmed her once again, and soothed her nerves, though they were somewhat jangled again when she first looked in the mirror and saw her blond self; she'd forgotten about changing her hair color. Overall, though, when she was dressed in her new clothes, she felt almost ready to tackle whatever the day brought, and she followed the smell of cooking food into the kitchen.

He was standing in front of the stove, his back to her, and he still didn't have on a shirt. Helplessly her gaze traced the deep groove of his spine, followed the way the muscles in his back played whenever he reached for something. She felt as if she had been plunged into a heated pool. "I forgot my coffee cup," she said in a muffled tone, and fled to her bedroom.

The brief interruption to retrieve the cup gave her the time she needed to brace herself. He evidently didn't intend to put on a shirt until it was time for them to leave, so she would just have to ignore the provocation. When she went back into the kitchen, she asked, "What are you cooking? It smells wonderful."

"I didn't have much on hand; bacon, eggs, and toast is my limit, and I'm lucky I have that. I usually eat breakfast out." He glanced at her.

"You still eat meat and eggs in your time, don't you?"

"Some people do, and some people don't. Real animal protein can be very expensive. I usually eat a nutrition bar for breakfast."

He made a face, then pointed toward a section of cabinet. "Get a couple of plates down for me, please. If you don't mind."

She turned and opened the cabinet door, then took down two plates that were a sunny yellow color she wouldn't have expected in a bachelor's house. "These are pretty," she said.

"Lynnette gave them to me for Christmas last year. She said it was pitiful for a grown man to have nothing but paper plates in his house."

Nikita tilted her head and thought the matter over. "She was right," she finally said, passing the plates to him.

"Gee, thanks," he said wryly. He put the plates in the microwave and punched the one-minute button.

"What are you doing?"

"Warming the plates. I don't like for my food to get cold, and this keeps it warm longer."

The explanation made sense to her. She looked around. "Is there anything else I can do?"

"Set the table. The silverware is in that drawer there." He pointed with a spatula.

Place settings were another thing that hadn't changed much in two centuries: plates, napkins, and eating utensils. She looked around and didn't see any napkins, so she asked him where they were.

Again he pointed with the spatula. "Use the paper towels."

Marveling again at how plentiful and cheap paper was, she pulled two sections off the roll of towels, folded them, and put one each at the places they had used before. The microwave dinged as she was putting out the silverware, and Knox retrieved the plates, then began dishing up the food directly onto them.

He had an excellent sense of timing, because two slices of bread now popped up out of the toaster. He grabbed them, put one on each plate, quickly slathered butter on them, then handed the plates to her while he put two more slices of bread in the machine.

Nikita looked at the plates of food; they seemed identical to her, so she supposed it didn't matter which plate went where. "I've always wondered what cooked eggs looked like," she said as she put the plates on the table.

He looked around, his expression incredulous. "I know you said they were expensive, but . . . Surely you've eaten eggs before?"

She shook her head. "When I was young, my parents didn't have much money because"—**because they'd beggared themselves buying her**—"they had some unforeseen expenses.

Their financials are much better now, of course, now that all their children are grown and gone, to use your phrase."

"How many brothers and sisters do you have?"

"One of each, both younger." She never told anyone about the older one, the one who wasn't really a sibling. She had never known her, and tried not to think about her.

"Are you close?" He refilled their coffee cups with the fresh coffee, set them at their plates, then indicated her chair and waited until she had sat down before he did.

"Yes," she said, smiling. "My brother, Connor, has a baby boy whom we all adore. Fair, my sister, will be getting married next spring."

"So they're both younger, but they've both settled down. Why are you still unmarried?"

Because things like her didn't reproduce. "I'm married to my career," she replied as lightly as possible. "The training is unbelievably intense; then I did my specialized studies, too."

"Specialized in . . . what?"

"History. The last half of the twentieth century and the first half of the twenty-first, to be specific."

"Hard to think of **now** being history."

"It's probably even more difficult to think that in my time, you've been dead for about a hundred and fifty years."

"Ouch!" He gave her an appalled look. "Do you know exactly when I died?"

"No, of course not." Despite everything, she found herself smiling at his expression. "For one thing, I didn't know your name to search in the archives for it. For another, there are huge gaps in our records. For all the great gains your time made in technology, you were really dumb about archiving."

"Yeah, you've said so before. So my music CDs aren't going to last?"

"No, they'll be beyond use in about twenty years. I will say that, when the problem was noticed, it was swiftly rectified, but unless there was a hard copy of the music, book, newspaper—whatever—then there wasn't any way to regain those lost records. For instance, we know all of the music by the Beatles, but very little from about 1995 to 2020."

"What about books?"

"Printed material held up fairly well. Not all, of course. Some of it was printed on poor-quality paper that disintegrated. Others things held up well, though. Look how many of your banknotes still exist."

"Yeah, that's really good paper."

"Oh, it isn't paper; it's a special cloth."

He looked startled. "Are you sure?"

"Yes. It was analyzed."

"Well, how about that. Come to think of it, if you look close you can see the threads in the bills." He finally picked up his fork and began eating, and Nikita did the same—warily, at first, then with greater enthusiasm. She didn't care for the texture of the eggs, but liked the taste, especially when it was combined with that of the bacon. The bread was unremarkable, but edible.

"I wish I'd had your DNA scanner with me last night," he said after they'd finished eating, and she was observing how he placed the dishes in the dishwasher. "I don't know how I could have used it without attracting attention, but maybe I'd have had a chance."

"Could you use it today?"

"There were a lot of people in the house, scattering DNA everywhere. Would the scanner do any good now?"

She shrugged. "Possibly. It would be tedious work, trying to find a sample that's in our data banks, but if you had enough uninterrupted time, you might find something."

"The uninterrupted time would be the biggest problem. How about if we went back out to the Allen house, to where the shooter was standing yesterday? There was a heavy dew last night; would that destroy the evidence?"

"The conditions aren't optimal, and in any

case, we wouldn't be likely to find anything in our database because the shooter is almost certainly from this time."

"Yeah, I forgot. Shit." He sighed. "Okay, let's go to the library and look up those back newspaper copies. We'll find out what was supposed to be buried in the capsule, get some names, talk to some people. Someone is bound to remember something."

"Don't you have to go to your office to work?"

"I am working. And I'm never out of touch." He indicated the radio sitting on the table.

She watched as he put a small plastic pack in a slot in the dishwasher door, closed the slot, then closed the door. The settings would be easy enough to decipher, so she didn't bother scrutinizing that; all she needed was to learn the process. He slowly turned the dial until there was a click and a red light came on, and that was it. "Ah," she said. "I have it now."

"Have what?"

"How to operate the dishwasher. If you will show me how to operate the laundry machines, as well, I'll be able to take care of my own clothing."

"I'll do that when we get home tonight, unless you're running out of clothes and need to wash something now?"

She shook her head. "No, tonight will be fine."

"Do I need to wear the baseball cap today?" she asked when they were ready to leave. "If so, I'd really like to tie my hair back with something other than a trash-bag tie."

He gave a quick grin. "We'll stop somewhere and get something. I like the look, with the sunglasses and all, like a movie star trying to go incognito. You're kind of glamorous, you know."

"Glamorous?" she echoed, startled. That was certainly not a term she would ever have applied to herself. **Glamour** implied great beauty and style; she didn't possess the one, and couldn't afford the other.

"It's the way you walk, shoulders back, head high, like you're either in the military or have had ballet training."

"Neither. I would have liked to take ballet classes when I was young, but there wasn't enough money."

"I bet you'd have been cute as all get-out in a tutu," he said; then his eyelids got that heavy look as he studied her. "I'd sure as hell like to see you in one now."

Nikita froze, afraid he would try to kiss her again. She thought she had been doing a good job of acting normal, chatting, but that was all on the surface. Not only did she not want him to touch her again, she was afraid that if he did, she might start crying and not be able to stop. With one question he had torn the scab off a deep wound in her life, leaving her emotionally bloody and in pain.

He sighed at the stricken look on her face. "It's okay; I'm not about to grab you," he said gently. "I know I'm in the doghouse. Just—give me a chance, okay?"

She managed to nod her head, a very small nod but a definite one. He touched her arm, a brief, warm caress that was gone before she could pull away; then he tugged on the bill of her cap and turned to open the back door.

As early as it was, none of the stores he thought might have something for her ponytail were open, so they ended up driving to the Wal-Mart store. Nikita forced her thoughts away from her personal problems and looked around with delight. Knox led the way to what he called the "hair section," but she got sidetracked by the rack after rack of cotton clothing. By the time he noticed she was no longer following him and backtracked to find her, she had worked her way past the T-shirts and tops and was fingering some lightweight pants.

"Do you need more clothes?" he asked, which she was certain was a rhetorical question. She had four changes of clothes; she had intended to buy more clothing once she was here, anyway, unless by some great stroke of luck she had managed to catch the UT and return home within four days. Since the UT had obviously recruited local help, she didn't think that was going to happen.

"I do, yes, but I don't have to buy it right now."

He checked his watch. "You have a little time. The library doesn't open until nine."

In her time, the libraries were always open and accessible by computer; if you were away from home and needed some information, there were public computers everywhere. The closest thing in her time to a physical library was the Archives, but access to it was strictly controlled because of the fragile nature of the items.

She took him at his word, and while he went to get a cart, she began pulling hangers of clothing off the racks and looking at them. She knew there was a sizing system, but had no idea what size she herself was. All clothing in her time was custom-made by computer: you stood in a private room, your body was mapped, you chose the garments you wanted from a touch screen, and five minutes later the neatly wrapped items slid down a chute into the room. You had to use your Goods and Services card to open the door, the amount of the purchase was deducted from your card, and that was it.

When he returned with the cart, she was

holding a pair of cotton pants against her, trying to see if the size matched. "How did you know what size to buy for me?" she muttered.

"I did an intensive study of your ass," he replied. A woman standing behind him snorted with laughter, and beat a hasty retreat. Frowning, Nikita watched her go.

"I'm serious," she said.

"So am I."

"Very well, then: what size is my ass?"

"You're a very well-toned eight, edging slightly toward a ten. Slim, but not skinny. Basically, I lucked out—because there isn't a uniform size standard. You'll need to try things on. Or you can buy them now, try them on tonight, and we'll bring back what doesn't fit."

"You can do that?"

"Yeah, we can." He grinned at her astonishment.

"I'll do that, then. Size eight, you said." She returned to the racks, choosing four pairs of pants and four tops that she really liked. One even had sequins on it. From there she went to the underwear, where, to her dismay, the sizing was completely different.

"This makes no sense," she complained in frustration.

"Size five," he said, choosing a pair of minuscule black lace underwear and extending it to her.

She eyed the small garment, then shook her head. "I don't think so."

"How about these?" Returning the black underwear to the rack, he pulled out a pair of red ones that looked even smaller than the black ones.

"Definitely not." The back was nothing but a small strip, and she knew exactly where the strip would have to go.

Regretfully he returned his chosen item to the rack.

She decided on a six-pack of "natural cotton," tossed it into the cart, and moved on to the socks and shoes. Knox told her what size, she decided on a pair of sandals that looked forgiving about the shape of the foot, and finally they moved toward the front of the store and the hair section. Unfortunately, before they reached the hair section, they passed the makeup and lotion aisles, and Nikita found herself sidetracked again. She **had** to have a lipstick from this time.

She had just turned to Knox with a tube in her hand, saying, "What do you think about this color?" when a woman behind him said, "Knox?"

He looked around, and an expression she couldn't decipher changed his face. "Ruth," he said in that gentle tone he could do so well. He released the cart to hug the woman. "You're out early."

"I could say the same for you, except I know you're always out early—and late. When do you sleep?"

"Sometimes I don't." His arm still around her, he turned toward Nikita. "Ruth, this is Tina. Tina, Ruth Lacey. Ruth is Rebecca's mother."

Tina? Well, he couldn't very well introduce her using her real name, since she was supposed to have left town. She extended her hand. "I'm very pleased to meet you."

Ruth shook her hand, all the while sharply studying her. The older woman was pretty and neat, with a good figure and light makeup artfully applied. Because she was a woman, she also noticed what items were in the shopping cart. "Have you been dating long?" she asked.

"A while," Knox lied easily.

"I'm glad for you," she said in a soft tone. "It's been a long time." Still, there was a lost expression in her eyes. She hugged Knox, and said, "I really need to be going. Y'all have a nice day."

She swiftly left the aisle, and when she was out of earshot, Nikita looked at Knox and raised her eyebrows. **"Tina?"**

"I couldn't remember your middle name. I knew it started with a **T,** though."

"That's okay. **Tina** it is. My middle name would be too unusual here." She dropped her chosen lipstick into the cart on top of her clothing, and they moved on to the aisle with the hair products. She chose a small pack of multicolored bands for her hair, then was ready to check out.

"I felt sorry for her," she said.

Knox didn't have to ask whom she was talking about. "I know. I think it really hurt her, seeing me with you. When Rebecca died, Ruth told me to go on with my life, but I don't think she's managed to do that herself."

"No," said Nikita, her gaze turning inward. "Mothers never do."

18

At the library they went into a small, narrow room with three microfiche machines lined up side by side. The room was dim, but the microfiche files were outside in the library's main room, watched over by a bored young girl who made certain they signed their names on a list, along with which number microfiche they had. Evidently people had just been walking out with the microfiche sheets, though why anyone would unless they had one of the viewers, too, was a mystery.

Knox and Nikita hadn't had to hunt through file after file of microfiche film; Knox knew exactly which issue of the newspaper he wanted: January 1, 1985. They pulled chairs close together in front of one machine as he moved the slide around looking for the article he remembered. Nikita had to lean in to read the screen, putting her so close to him their shoulders bumped together. He put off enough body heat that she felt almost scorched, burning her even where they weren't touching. She could bear it only a moment before she had to move away.

He gave her a questioning glance, and she said, "The position was hurting my neck."

"You're lying," he said equably, turning back to the screen. "You want me but you're still mad at me, so you don't **want** to want me, and touching me is too much of a temptation. Do I have it about right?"

"Fairly close," she said, without expression.

"That's good to know," he said, and winked at her. "Now, slide back in here so you can read what I'm reading."

"There's no point. Just read off the list of items, and I'll write them down, as well as the people who were there that you can remember or recognize." She had his notebook, the one he made his investigative notes in, and he'd instructed her not to use her private shorthand.

"Coward."

" 'Discretion is the better part of valor.' "

"A coward said that."

"Would you find the damn article!" she exclaimed, then looked guiltily around to see if she had disturbed anyone. It was doubtful; there were only a handful of people in the library, and she and Knox were the only people in the microfiche room. Still, she felt herself go hot with embarrassment; she had spent a lifetime very determinedly not drawing attention to herself. She was distressed both because she had almost shouted in a public place and because he didn't seem to realize the depth of her distress. No, how could he? She would have to tell him about herself before he would understand, and that was something she had never done. From childhood she had been cautioned by her parents not to talk about her origins, or her legal status.

"Here we go," Knox said softly. "Max Browning wrote the article. He still works for the newspaper, too. We can ask him some questions. Let's see . . . the items slated to go into the time capsule include the 1984 yearbook from Pekesville High School, a cassette tape of the Top Ten in music along with a cassette player—smart thinking on someone's part—photographs and a written history of Peke County, a copy of the articles of incorporation—though why in hell they thought anyone would be interested in that in a hundred years, I don't know. There was also a copy of the local newspaper. That's it."

"That's seven," she said.

"That's all it lists. The article says, 'The mayor and others will place twelve items in the time capsule, including—' then it lists the things I just read. It doesn't itemize the other five. Shit," he swore softly in frustration.

"Who was there?"

"The mayor, of course, Harlan Forbes. Taylor Allen. The football coach, Howard Easley. Edie Proctor, the school superintendent. City councilmen Lester Bailey and Alfred 'Sonny' Akins. That's all it lists by name."

"Do you remember anyone else?"

"Max Browning, of course. The former sheriff, Randolph Sledge. He retired a year or so after this, and died about ten years ago. The probate judge was there. I can't remember his name . . . somebody Clement. He's dead, too. There were a bunch of businessmen, my dad included, the police chief, the county commissioners. I don't know their names, but all of that would be on record at the courthouse, and city hall will have the information about who was chief back then."

"Where do we go next?"

"I don't want you going to the courthouse, period. Cops are too good at recognizing people, especially if they're in the same place where they saw them before. Someone else may have been studying your ass."

"I was in your office, sitting on it."

"You were at the Taylor Allen site for a good two hours, plus they watched you walk into my office and they watched you walk out. Trust me."

"I refuse to believe that my buttocks are such an identifying feature," she snapped, disgruntled. It wasn't that she **wanted** to go to the courthouse; it was as if he thought her bottom was somehow so weirdly and differently shaped that people could recognize her by it.

"That's because you aren't a man. We men like to look at women's asses. In fact, we stare."

"Thank you for the explanation; I feel so much better."

He looked past her to make certain they were still alone. "C'mon. You can't tell me things have changed so much in two hundred years that men don't care about women's asses anymore. They still stare, don't they?"

She thought a moment, taking the question seriously. "Not on the job, they don't," she finally said. That was where she had spent most of the past eight years, she thought, either on the job, or in training, or studying. The agents with whom she trained and worked, male and female alike, had shared her circumstances, in that they were so busy in their chosen career they hadn't had much time for outside pursuits. Some agents, when they were off duty, had formed relationships with other agents, of course—and had promptly been separated. Not fired, but one or the other would be posted to another city.

They were then free to conduct their relationship as they saw fit, but they couldn't work
certain postings together. Research, teaching,
laboratory—yes. Field work—no.

Nikita hadn't had much off-duty time in the
past eight years. She had chosen to specialize,
and the study had required hours of extra work
tacked onto her regular duties. What free time
she'd had, she had spent with her family, except
for one relationship four or five years ago that
for a while she had thought would be the final
one, but it had faded away, too. No drama, no
fireworks, just a gradual shift of affection.

That was just like the rest of her life—no
drama, no fireworks. No heat, no passion, no
raised voices, nothing but a strict adherence
to the rules and the law.

"Hey," he said, putting his hand on her knee.
"Don't look so upset. If men don't look at
your ass at home, whenever you feel the need,
you just come here and we'll take care of the
problem. Scratch that—**I'll** take care of the
problem."

She removed his hand. "Thank you, but I
was thinking of something else. Now, what was
it you wanted scratched?"

He burst out laughing, and she sat back, chagrined that evidently she had once again run
afoul of some silly idiom.

"It means 'mark that out,'" he explained.

"Like this." He took the pad from her, wrote a word, then quickly marked through it several times. "See? This was scratched out."

"I understand," she said with dignity. "I should have known that one, because pens and paper were invented long before the late-twentieth-century gap in our records."

"Personally, I'm surprised you speak collo-quial English as well as you do. Say something in your normal accent."

"I'm not a monkey performing for your amusement," she said in her normal rapid speech, slurring the words together.

He blinked. "Wow. That was fast. You sounded like an auctioneer. Does everyone talk that fast?"

"No, of course not. Some speak faster, some speak slower. To me, the cadence of your speech sounds very slow and measured, almost formal."

"Well, you **are** in eastern Kentucky; that accounts for the slow part. I don't know about the 'formal.'"

Feeling as if their conversation had veered off course, as it so often did, Nikita tapped the pad with her fingernail. "I think we should concen-trate on our plan of action. You don't want me at the courthouse. I don't necessarily agree with your logic, but since you're a man, I'll take your word for it. Perhaps I could research the city councilmen's names, if you'll take me to city hall."

"You must have distracted me, because now that I'm thinking clearly, I remember where we are. We're in a library."

"Yes, I know," she said, bewildered. When had he forgotten where they were?

"All we have to do is look in the newspaper editions that came out the day after elections. Okay, let me think; elections are held in even-numbered years, and we didn't have any city elections last year so that means the last election was in 2002. Counting backwards, that means the city election we're looking for was held in 1982, and since the city and county elections are staggered, the county election was in 1984. Our city elections are held in June, so we need the June of 1982 newspapers, and November of 1984 for the county commissioners. Sorry I don't remember the exact dates."

"I don't think I'll be able to manage, with so little information to go on," she said drily, and he chuckled. Before he could reply, his radio beeped, and a voice called out a series of codes. He hooked the radio off his belt and called in, and that was when Nikita realized it was a combination radio and cell phone. She looked at it with more interest, wondering if he would let her examine it. This must be one of the first-generation dual-communicators.

"I have to go," he said, standing. He frowned as he looked down at her. "Will you be all right here by yourself?"

She rolled her eyes. "No, I'm just five years old instead of thirty; I don't know how I can possibly manage."

"You don't have to be sarcastic."

"Evidently I did."

"I just feel like you're in a foreign country, or something."

"I'm not, I'm in **my** country. I have money, I have your phone number, and I'm certain I can manage to make a call if necessary."

"All right, all right." He bent down and dropped a kiss on top of her head. "Is that cell phone of yours a real one, or is it just made to look like one of ours?"

She felt as if she should say something about the kiss, but at the same time it was so casual that mentioning it would almost be making too much over nothing. "I'm afraid it's fake. It looks like yours, but we no longer use the technology and none of the ones from now still exist."

"Okay, I'll get a real one for you. I want to be able to reach you at all times. Stay here until I get back."

"Are you serious? This is my idea of heaven, to be in a library. Just think of the research I can do!"

He paused on the verge of walking away, curiosity lighting his face. "I've wondered about something. To fill in the gaps where so much data was lost, why haven't your people just traveled back here and taken CDs and things like that back with you?"

"For one thing, your technology won't transit. We tried it. Books, somewhat, though they're damaged in the process. Your computers and discs—no. Anything organic transits best. We had to develop special fabric for our clothing, because natural fibers are so rare and expensive in my time."

His head tilted. "You mean someone wearing polyester wouldn't transit?"

"Oh, he would, but his clothing wouldn't."

A big grin split his face. "You mean he'd arrive stark naked."

"Exactly."

"Like the Terminator."

At her blank look, he explained, "That was a movie, where this assassin from the future arrived without any clothes."

"Then, yes, just like the Terminator. But you see why filling in those gaps is so difficult. I can research while I'm here, take photos—which most travelers have done, by the way—but there was just so **much** that was lost. And if this UT succeeds, then it'll be lost forever."

"He won't. We'll figure this out eventually. I'll be back as soon as I can," he said, and left.

Nikita moved to the chair he had exited. She wasn't exactly stranded—after all, her feet still worked—but without a vehicle of her own, she was limited in movement. But the library was a great place to be; not only could she research to her heart's content, she felt safe here. In fact, now that Knox's disturbing presence was no longer distracting her, her heart was racing with anticipation. A library! The research possibilities were endless. More excited than she could remember ever being before, she settled down to work.

"What's wrong?" Byron asked softly, lifting himself on his elbow beside her. His warm hand rested on her bare stomach, in a touch that was both possessive and comforting.

Ruth Lacey looked at the face of her lover. She still couldn't believe what she was doing, that after all these years she was actually being as unfaithful to her husband as he was to her. No, that wasn't true; one lover in thirty-something years didn't compare to dozens, perhaps even hundreds. She hadn't let Edward touch her in years, not since shortly after Rebecca's birth, because she was too afraid he'd give her a venereal disease. Later, there had been the risk of AIDS, which had completely destroyed the slight chance that she would ever resume sexual relations with him. She supposed he had somehow stayed disease free all these years, but she wasn't interested enough to ask.

She should have divorced him. She should have made a better life for herself and Rebecca. But she had kept putting it off, wanting to wait until she was certain Rebecca was settled; then her daughter had died, and so had any incentive Ruth might have had for moving on.

She sighed. There was no point in denying her melancholy. "I saw my daughter's fiancé this morning, with another woman."

Byron looked confused. "I thought you said your daughter has been gone for seven years."

"She has, but I still thought of Knox as **hers.** Logically, I know very few men would have waited this long before settling into another relationship, and, really, I love Knox and want him to be happy, but—but emotionally, I feel as if he's cheating on her."

"Ah. I see. How would Rebecca feel?"

That was what she loved most about Byron, the fact that he **listened** to her and didn't discount her feelings. Since Rebecca's death, she had lived in such an emotional desert that the attention he paid her was like water being poured on parched skin; she soaked it up, reveled in it, bloomed in his presence, and when she was away from him, he was all she could think about.

She made a wry face. "Rebecca would likely

fuss at him for waiting this long. They were good together; it was like they were two halves of a whole. They fit perfectly. She would want him to be happy. That makes me feel so selfish, but—"

"But?" he prompted, when she was silent for a moment.

"I feel as if I've lost him, too. He tried so hard to bring her back. The medics told me that when they got there, he was so exhausted from doing CPR that he just rolled over on his back; he couldn't even get up. And he was crying. Until now, it was as if we **shared** this—this emptiness where she had been. As if I didn't have to bear it alone."

He paused, then delicately asked, "Your husband doesn't—?"

She laughed, the sound bitter. "Oh, he cried, but when she was buried, that same night he went out looking to get laid. If he grieved, he showed it by doing what he's always done, chasing after every woman who'll look at him."

Byron's hand moved gently on her belly. "I would say I'm sorry, but if he were a perfect husband, then you wouldn't be here with me. I'm sorry I didn't meet you before he did, but would it be terrible if I admitted that I'm glad you've been unhappy with him?"

She gave him a tender smile. "No, it isn't terrible. It's honest. And flattering." Ruth snuggled close to him, turning so she could curl one arm over his shoulder and touch his hair. She loved touching him. Until Byron, she had gone so long without touching and being touched, without love or sex or any combination of the two, that she had felt like a virgin going into his arms. Everything had been new, and frightening; she had been so nervous that she hadn't been as ready as she might have been, and the first time had been a little painful, just as if she truly had been untouched.

To tell the truth, she had never felt like a very sexual woman; she had gone for security instead of love, and shut down those feelings. The choices she'd made had given her Rebecca, but when her daughter died, she had been left empty and bitter. All her days had passed in bleak sameness, without hope, until she'd met Byron. He had given her the affection for which she was starved, but even more, he'd given her a reason to live, to undo the pain and loss of the past.

There were a lot of things she liked about him. For one, he wasn't local. When they met, it wasn't in Pekesville, but in the next county to the west, so she didn't have to worry about running into someone she knew. To some people the next county might be considered local, but she'd lived in Pekesville her entire life and never traveled much at all, so local meant something different to her.

He wasn't a tall man, only a few inches taller than she, and Ruth found she liked that. They fit together very well, and Edward was a tall man, so she was glad that nothing about Byron reminded her of her husband—except that they both had penises, of course, but the way they used them was very different. Edward had always been sexually selfish; Byron was the opposite, kind and patient in bed, willing to give her satisfaction no matter how long it took, or how. He didn't seem to think his penis was the sole purveyor of pleasure; he loved her with his entire body.

He was younger than she, almost six years younger. She enjoyed that, too; it was a subtle stroke to her ego that she hadn't known she needed. Byron liked books, and movies, and taking quiet walks during which he held her hand almost the entire time. He would occasionally, and absently, lift her hand and kiss it, a spontaneous and unconscious giving of affection that almost made her burst into tears the first time he did it. He liked talking to her, and he was intelligent. He had theories and experiments that he explained to her, demonstrated to her, showing how much he appreciated her own intelligence. There were some details she didn't quite understand yet, but at this point she trusted him implicitly. If he told her something would work, she believed him.

"Who was the woman you saw with Davis?" he murmured against her temple. "Do you know her?"

"No, I'd never seen her before. She's some blond named Tina. He introduced us, but didn't mention her last name. They were in Wal-Mart, shopping—before eight this morning. I think they'd spent the night together."

"Because they were at Wal-Mart?" he asked, his brows wrinkling in confusion.

"No, because they were shopping **together** at Wal-Mart before eight, and she was buying clothes and underwear, makeup, ordinary stuff like that. You might run into the store that early to pick up one item that you're out of and need, but you don't go **shopping,** especially together. I think she spent the night with him, and didn't have what she needed this morning, so they went out to buy it."

"But why wouldn't she just go to her home?" He still had that confused look.

"I don't know." That solution did make more sense. "Maybe she doesn't live here. But in that case, why would she be with Knox? Why wouldn't she just drive her own car to the store? I mean, she would have to go home and get her car before going to work, or she'd be stranded. So there was no need to go shopping if he was taking her home anyway. That doesn't make sense."

Byron was really frowning now, the way he did when he was working out equations on his computer. "What did you say her name was?"

"Tina. Why?"

"And she's blond?"

"Do you know a blond named Tina?"

"No, nothing like that. I was wondering . . . that woman he was with yesterday . . . supposedly she left town."

"Yes. Jason MacFarland said that Knox told him she'd decided their cases weren't connected after all, so there was no reason to stay."

His brown eyes were kind as he stroked her hair. "But we know she wouldn't have said any such thing, don't we? She wouldn't leave, because Pekesville is where she needs to be. She and Knox spent a long time together yesterday. And it's very easy to change one's hair color, after all."

Ruth gasped in horror, sitting up in bed and twisting around to stare at him. "You think that Tina is— Are you certain?"

"No. I'll have to see her before I can tell. But

I think there's a good chance she's the same person, don't you?" He smiled. "If so, then knowing that's to our advantage. If you know where Knox lives, I can set up surveillance on the house. We'll know the truth very soon."

19

In less than an hour Nikita had gotten all the names of the city councilmen and county commissioners in 1985; because she had time on her hands and was nothing but thorough anyway, she also pulled up the article reporting the suicide of Howard Easley. The reporter, Max Browning, had nicely captured the shock and grief of the high school students and his fellow teachers, but especially that of the football team. Coach Easley had been a popular man. A sidebar listed the symptoms of depression, and warning signs of suicide. The obituary told where he'd been born and gone to college, how long he'd been coaching, where he went to church.

The list of pallbearers was interesting, in that some of the councilmen and commissioners mentioned in Nikita's list of names had carried Coach Easley to his final resting place. She made a copy of the obituary and article for Knox to read. She couldn't think how it would be relevant, but Knox had lived here most of his life and he might notice something amiss that went completely over her head.

Her official work finished, Nikita then spent a very happy couple of hours wandering the stacks. She slipped her miniature camera out of her bag and very discreetly filmed things she thought would be of interest in her time. The camera needed no additional light to take high-quality photographs, and the entire mechanism—indeed, everything she had brought with her—was specially made to mimic organic compounds in composition, so it would transit between times.

That human beings were carbon-based life-forms had greatly complicated matters for the scientists when they were working out the theories and practical applications of time travel. The matter of clothing was the easiest, because after all the fabric didn't have to **do** anything except hold together and provide reasonable covering. Adapting all their technology to time travel had been even more difficult than transiting the human body. In the original experiments, often the machinery casings would survive but the working parts of whatever equipment they'd used for the experiment would simply be fried—and that was the best-case scenario. Sometimes they were simply gone. Whether they materialized in another time and place was anyone's guess.

So her laser pen, the DNA scanner, her clothing, her camera, her EN—all of it was made to mimic organic material on the molecular level.

So how had the spear been brought through time?

The thought sent shock waves through her brain. Why hadn't this occurred to her before?

The spear in the museum had predated time travel, and the spear had been stolen. When McElroy had reported that he'd seen Taylor Allen murdered with a spear, and that he'd tracked the UT to the Allen house, what else were they to think other than that the spear was the same one, used because of its symbolic value to the ATT—anti-time-travel—groups.

So if it predated time travel and had been succesfully transited, what had it been made from? Not wood and steel; wood traveled well, but steel wasn't organic. At any rate, when China had been mass-producing the spears, they hadn't been using steel and wood. They had used ceramics and other materials, none of which had come from a living organism.

The only conclusion she could draw was

that the spear used to kill Allen hadn't come from the future, that in fact it was contemporary. And if it was contemporary, then it was traceable.

But why would the UT go to the trouble of finding a spear and using it to kill Taylor Allen if it didn't have symbolic value and he wasn't using it to make a statement? There were much easier ways for him to kill, such as by a laser, if he had access to laser weaponry, and if he had access to the Transit Laboratory, then it was at least feasible that he could get a laser weapon, as they were easier to attain than entry to the lab. Or, failing that, he could have acquired a weapon here; the gunpowder-propelled bullets were very efficient.

No, the spear had been used for a reason, but what? And a spear had been stolen from the museum. The coincidence was too large for her to ignore; it had to have some significance.

She sat down at a secluded table and took out her EN. Flipping it open, she began writing on the screen, muttering under her breath to herself as she did so.

"Did you find the names okay?"

She jumped, and the stylus flew from her hand to roll across the floor and under a stack of books.

Knox got on his hands and knees to retrieve it, his amusement plain on his face. "You were concentrating pretty hard on something," he commented, "to not hear me walking up."

"Sit down," she said urgently, indicating the chair beside her.

He lifted his eyebrows in question, but obediently sat. "What's up? Did you find something?"

"Not in the newspapers, if that's what you mean. I did get the names, but something else occurred to me." She bent her head close to his. "The spear. It **couldn't** have come from my time." She kept her voice low, almost whispering; the library was still sparsely populated, but as the morning had grown old, more and more people were coming in.

The eyebrows went up again. "How do you figure that?" Then his eyes narrowed, and she could practically see the thoughts churning in his head. "Organic. You said things have to be organic, or mimic an organic compound."

"That's right, and the spears that were in the museum were made before time travel, so the technology didn't exist to manufacture them out of materials that would transit even if someone had wanted to waste the money making them. If I remember correctly, the spears in the museum had fiberglass shafts, and the spearhead was ceramic."

"Looked like wood to me. The shaft did, that is. The head was buried in Taylor Allen's back."

"No, I've seen those spears. The shafts in no way resemble wood."

"Then our spear didn't come from your museum."

"A spear was stolen from the museum," she said slowly, running through the facts in her mind and trying to put them into a plausible scenario. "When McElroy reported that Allen was killed with a spear, it was a logical conclusion that the stolen spear had been used."

"Wouldn't everyone know it couldn't have been the stolen spear?"

"Only if they'd seen the collection. If a spear was reported stolen and then an agent says a spear was used to commit murder in the time that developed the beginning technology for time travel, in the place **where** it was developed, and if the stolen spear would have had a symbolic value to the ATT groups, then it would be eminently logical to assume the UT had stolen that spear and transited with it in order to kill the person who supposedly was the beginning of it all."

"Whoa," he said. "You're talking too fast, and I think that was all one sentence. Back up, and slow down."

Nikita took a deep breath, containing her impatience. More slowly, mimicking his cadence, she repeated the salient points.

"Okay, got it," he said. "So this other agent,

McElroy, wouldn't have known what the stolen spear looked like?"

"Not necessarily, no. I've spent a lot of time in museums because of the extra studies I undertook."

"I can see how the conclusion was drawn. Probably by your time everyone is so accustomed to the organic-only rule that it never occurred to anyone to check what the spear was made of."

She nodded. "It's also general knowledge, not security-coded."

"Then why use a spear that has no significance? There are easier ways to kill someone. Why not just shoot him?"

"Exactly my thoughts. The only thing that makes sense is if someone **wants** us to think it's one of the ATT groups. Someone went to the trouble to steal the spear in my time, and either locate or manufacture a spear in this time. But . . . **why**? If it's an ATT group, they don't have to use a spear, they can just do the murder and claim credit. It's as if the spear was used to deliberately convince us the murder was committed by an ATT group."

"Slow down," he cautioned. "I must be listening faster, though, because I caught the gist of that. It looks as if someone in your time is either trying to destroy the ATT groups by stirring up big-time action against them, or is diverting attention away from themselves."

"But who, and what would be the benefit?" She was silent a moment, then said, "The 'who' is obviously someone in the FBI, possibly even my own unit. We know that. But what would be the point, unless whoever it is holds a personal grudge against someone in an ATT, and in any event why kill innocent people because of it? Why send your own people in to be killed?"

"Because he has to," Knox said slowly, thinking hard. "Sending agents in is what he would normally do, so he can't deviate from that norm without attracting attention. But he somehow warns his accomplice, so the agents are either stymied or killed. My guess is McElroy must not be a top-notch investigator, because he never got close to this guy or he wouldn't have gotten out alive."

"It has to be one of my superiors." Nikita wondered if she looked as pale as she felt. "I would imagine the Transit Lab has been taken under FBI control for the duration of this mission, which would make it easier for this person to perhaps send information back, or even transit himself if direct communication was needed."

"Have you thought the killings may not have anything to do with the time-travel technology?

If the spear is a diversion, the reasoning behind it may be, too."

"Your time capsule was stolen," she pointed out. "By someone who traveled from my time to take it. But why take it if not for safe-keeping?"

"You're assuming a good guy has it."

"I'm still here," she said simply.

Again he thought hard as he stared at her. "If the contents of the capsule had been destroyed, and if something in there was crucial to the development of the technology, then time travel wouldn't exist and you wouldn't be here."

"Exactly. As long as I'm here, the paper or whatever still exists."

He looked horrified. "You mean I could be in the middle of kissing you and you'd, like . . . wink out?"

"Theoretically."

"Damn, don't do that! I'd have heart failure."

"**If** you were kissing me, which you won't be."

"Don't be so sure of that. But think: who, other than the ATT groups, want to prevent time travel from happening? What's the benefit? And why kill both Taylor Allen and Mayor Forbes, neither of whom would have known anything about time travel? Hell, from what I know about the old mayor, he wouldn't have admitted time travel existed even if someone vaporized on top of his ass. He didn't think the moon landing was real, either."

Nikita blinked in astonishment. "Are you serious?"

"As a heart attack," he said, raising his right hand in silent oath.

She was silent for a moment as she grappled with the magnitude of such denial in the face of a virtual avalanche of facts.

"Some people still think the earth is flat," he added.

"I've heard of them. They're in our history books. When our first colony on the moon was established, one of the Society's leaders was taken there. He was convinced, but his followers weren't. For a long time they still insisted it was a stage set, that he hadn't really been on the moon."

"How were they finally convinced?"

"The pope went."

He stared at her for a long moment, his face turning red. Abruptly he got up and walked at a fast clip toward the public bathrooms, his shoulders heaving. He managed to contain himself until he actually got inside the bathroom, and the closing door muffled his whoop of laughter.

Nikita tilted her head. What was so funny about the pope going to the moon?

When he returned, his eyes were wet and his lips kept turning up in a smile. "Sorry," he said in a strained tone. "It was just . . . I imagined him sitting in a rocket, wearing all his vestments . . ." His voice trailed off and he shook his head.

"Don't be silly," she said. "He wore a space suit just like everyone else."

Knox choked, and went back to the bathroom.

He was the most easily sidetracked person she'd ever seen, she thought. They could be having a serious discussion about the investigation and the next thing she knew she was explaining about how time travelers would arrive naked if they wore polyester.

While he was gone, she looked back at the notes she'd scribbled on her EN, and did some more thinking. **What was the benefit?** The why and the who were always tightly connected; find one, and you could find the other.

The killer—or killers, since there were certainly at least two, perhaps more—obviously hadn't found what he was searching for, and he was working his way down the list of people who'd had anything to do with that time capsule.

Knox finally returned, and Nikita forestalled any more possible outbursts of hilarity by tapping the list of names. "Someone on this list is the killer's next target. What can we do to keep them alive?"

That question wiped the last remnant of amusement from his expression. He stood looking down at the list, and he finally said, "Not a lot. There are too many of them. The sheriff's department and the city police combined don't have the manpower that would be needed. Several of them have already died"—he took his pen, leaned down, and drew lines through their names—"but that leaves twelve people. The best Sheriff Cutler could do would be to warn them. That's if any one of them would believe someone was out to kill him because of a time capsule that was buried twenty years ago."

"We have to interview them ourselves," she said.

"Nope. **I** have to interview them. **You** have to stay out of sight. Agent Stover left town, remember? You're Tina, my new live-in lover."

"I don't think so," she said coolly.

"I know so." He planted one hand on the table and the other on the back of her chair, leaning over her. "That's exactly what Ruth was thinking at Wal-Mart this morning, and exactly the way we'll act when we're out in public. It's the only way I can think of to keep you safe and keep you involved. The other option is for you to hide out somewhere."

She stood so fast he had to straighten or have

his head cracked. "Very well. But if you take advantage of the situation, the next time I have to hit you, I'll break your jaw. That's a promise."

"I never doubted you for a minute," he said, and grinned.

20

Knox had taken the time to acquire a new cell phone and charger for Nikita on his account, and paid extra for a battery that already had a full charge. Figuring he'd keep it when she left—after all, it wasn't organic, so it wouldn't make it back to her time—he splurged and got one that would take pictures, just because he liked gadgets. That meant he needed to upgrade his computer so he could download the pictures and print them, but what the hell, it needed upgrading anyway.

After he picked her up at the library, he took her to a drive-through hamburger joint, figuring that would be the most anonymous, and while they sat parked in the shade of a large oak, munching on greasy burgers and hot salty fries, he showed her all the features of the phone and how to use them. He was in the middle of an enthusiastic explanation about the digital-photo feature when he glanced up and saw the expression of profound patience on her face.

He stopped in mid-sentence. "I'm guessing you're either totally bored with all this, or you can operate gadgets like this with your eyes closed. Which is it?" he asked, beginning to smile.

"The latter," she said in a kind tone.

"Well, if you don't mind, let me finish telling you all about it, because some of this stuff is so cool I have to show someone."

What could she do but smile? "I'll listen."

When he was finished playing with her phone—setting the ring tones to a tune she liked, "Toréador," then setting it on **Vibrate** instead of **Ring,** which made the whole exercise useless; placing his cell number in her phone book, then putting her number in his—she had finished eating and his food had grown cold while he played.

While he was occupied with his food and his mouth was full, Nikita broached a subject she knew he wouldn't like. "I've been thinking; there's no need for me to be so dependent on you. It constrains both of us. You can rent a car for me, put it in your name, and who'll be the wiser? I'll repay you with my supply of cash."

Not to her surprise, he frowned, and swallowed a little too hastily. "I guess I like knowing where you are," he admitted. "After the screwup I made yesterday, I'm afraid you'll leave before I can make it right."

Nikita sighed and stared out through the windshield. She didn't want to talk about the devastating question he'd asked, because the reason it had been so devastating was none of his business. She glanced at him, saw the seriousness in his blue eyes, and felt her insides clench. Another reason that his comment had hurt was that she liked him too much. Given the time and opportunity, neither of which she had, she thought she would likely even grow to love him. He had that inner warmth she had always so admired in people, a bedrock sense of himself, and a relaxed sexuality that drew her like a beacon.

If she was successful at her mission, however, she would be leaving at the end of it, going to a place where he couldn't follow. If she wasn't successful, she would either be dead or "wink out," as he'd phrased it. She would be at home with her family and none of this would ever have happened, because there would be no time travel to bring her to this place and time.

She wished she were the type of person who could throw herself into an affair simply because she was attracted to a man, but she wasn't. She always had to be cautious. Until her legal status was decided, no one in his right mind would consider marrying her, and she refused to keep something like that secret from someone she loved. In a perverse little twist, if some man still wanted to marry her after she'd told him the truth, she knew she wouldn't be able to trust his judgment ever again, and did she want to legally ally herself to such a burden? Unfair, perhaps, but true.

"Say something." Setting his soft drink in the cup holder, he reached across the seat and lightly cupped her chin in his right hand. His fingers were cool and damp from holding the cup, but she could feel the heat just below the surface of his skin. His touch was light, a caress instead of actually holding her, but the sensation went all the way to her bones.

"You shouldn't touch me," she whispered. "It's a distraction we can't afford." She turned her head and looked at him, their gazes meeting there in the shady car, and her insides jolted again, this time stronger. The man looking back at her, blue eyes narrow and intent, wasn't relaxed. There were other words to describe him, such as low-key, but he wasn't relaxed. He was focused and determined—focused on her, and determined to get what he wanted. She remembered the hard-eyed stranger standing over her in Taylor Allen's backyard, and abruptly knew that was the real core of the man.

He could be patient, he could be understanding, but underneath all the little quirks and dents of his character was pure steel. He'd been holding back; he'd been courting her.

A primitive excitement whispered along her spine, bringing a particularly apt idiom to mind. "You're playing me." He was playing her like a fish on a hook, being given the freedom to run with the line patiently being fed off the reel, but slowly, so slowly, as the fish tired, it was being reeled in. So good was he at the technique that even though she suddenly realized what he was doing, she had no inclination to spit out the bait and run free. **Was he good enough to bring her in?** The challenge of it kept her here, because she wanted to know the answer.

She could rationalize that the job kept her here, and that was true. She needed his help. She was stranded, for the time being. But she didn't have to stay in his house, right at hand where he wanted her. There were other options available to her, now that she'd changed her appearance. Not many, but some, such as the bed-and-breakfast he'd mentioned.

One corner of his mouth quirked as he continued to touch her face, his fingers lightly rubbing along her jaw line. "I'm not playing, Nikita."

No, he wasn't. There were lighthearted, casual affairs, but the attraction that sparked between them was far too intense for that.

She understood the skin chemistry of it, the lure that made her hands almost ache with the need to touch him. She also understood that the circumstances were terrible, that she wasn't like other women and he had the right to know if she decided to accept him as a lover, that nothing they could forge together would be permanent even if they both wanted it to be. There were laws governing time travel, put in place for good and solid reasons. As much as she liked this time, she didn't want to stay here, and he wouldn't be allowed to go home with her. If by some miracle he wanted to return with her—a moot question at this point, since she couldn't get back herself—he would promptly be returned, and she would be incarcerated. Even worse, her illegal action would perhaps convince the lawmakers that even the most law-abiding of her kind were inherently unstable, and should be destroyed.

Trembling, she jerked her gaze away from his and stared blindly through the windshield again. "There are reasons why the answer must be no."

He let his hand fall. "Is one of those reasons that you aren't attracted to me?"

"No," she admitted in frustration, knowing that no matter what other reasons she gave, he would hear only this admission and act as if it gave him permission not only to continue his pursuit of her, but to actually intensify it.

"That's the most important one. Can you tell me any of the others?"

He already knew the circumstantial ones, she thought. He was well aware that she could "wink out" at any moment. So she moved on to others that hadn't been voiced, though the most important one of all she would keep to herself. "I'm not a man. I'm not comfortable with—" She gave a distracted wave, searching for a phrase more powerful than "casual sex," since she had already used that one and he'd sailed right over it without pause. Most of the slang phrases used in her time, he wouldn't understand, but one word had remained the same: "—drive-by fucking."

"Well, that puts me in my place, doesn't it?" he muttered. "Is that what it would be to you? Nothing more?"

"What else could it be, under the circumstances?"

"I'm not talking about the length of time we may have, but the emotion behind it. Yeah, I'm a man, but let's talk about emotion anyway. What's between us isn't casual, not on my part. But if you're just not that into me, then say so. Just don't lie about it, because that's throwing away something valuable."

Carefully Nikita considered what he'd said.

Most of it had been perfectly understandable, but one sentence had her stymied. She went over it in her mind, her lips moving a little as she repeated the words.

He burst out laughing. "I'm trying to be serious, and you throw me for a loop every time. I know what you're thinking. 'Just not that into me' means you like me okay, but you don't feel anything special toward me."

And he'd asked her not to lie, which of course didn't mean that she couldn't, but he was being honest with her, so he deserved the same consideration in return. "No," she finally said. "I can't say that."

"That's all I need to know." He gathered the remnants of their meal, stuffing papers and cups back into the paper sack, and got out of the car to take the sack to a bright red trash bin. Helplessly Nikita watched him, the easy way he moved tugging deep inside her. Like her, he was a cop, and there was always that authority about him that came from training, experience, and the fact that he was armed. The rest of it was just pure Knox, a man at home with his body, taking his time. If he made love the way he walked . . . oh, my God.

And because he was a cop, by the time he got back to the car, his mind was already back at work. "Do you have the DNA scanner with you?" he asked as he got back into the car.

Relieved that the subject matter had changed, she patted her purse. "Right here."

"I'm having a hard time applying your technology to our investigation, because it isn't in my norm and I keep forgetting about it," he admitted. "But the same night the time capsule was stolen, a citizen reported his tractor tires were slashed and his chickens killed. While I don't think that has anything to do with your UT, he also reported seeing very bright flashes in the woods across from his house. The location isn't the same as where you came through, but it's fairly close. Could you still pick up DNA samples after four days?"

"Has there been any rain?"

"No, not even a shower."

"Then it's possible." Excitement flowed through her. "In a secluded location, there wouldn't be a lot of confusing samples, and anyone who came through would be in the database. We'd know who we're looking for! I had no idea you knew the arrival location."

"Like I said, I'm having a hard time with the practical application of your scanner. I feel like an idiot for not thinking of this before."

She smiled at him. "Considering everything that's happened in the past twenty-four hours, I think it's understandable."

"Twenty-four hours? Is that all it is? Feels like weeks."

She knew what he meant. From the time they'd met the day before, they had been together almost all the time. A lot had happened, including the fact that he had stepped over an invisible line when he didn't report Luttrell's death. Her perception might be in error, but she felt as if she knew Knox better than she knew her fellow agents whom she'd worked and trained alongside of for years.

As he drove them out into the country, he explained about Jesse Bingham's cantankerous disposition. "Don't let him upset you; he's nasty to everyone. If he sees us across the road, he may get nosy about what we're doing, and come to see. In fact, I can guarantee it. So ignore anything he says."

She nodded her agreement, and squinted as the bright sunlight arrowed through the windshield. Taking out her sunglasses, she put them on, and almost sighed with relief. This mountainous state wasn't as hot as Florida, but it was hot enough; even her eyes wanted shade.

The terrain was really pretty, though. The mountains weren't towering beasts like the Rockies or the Himalayas; these were older, worn down by the billions of years of rain and erosion since the tectonic plates beneath them had crashed together and wrinkled the earth above. Everything about the Appalachians felt old, and slightly mysterious, as if all the years that had passed and all the people who had walked through these mountains had left some of their essence behind, to whisper in the wind and keep watch beneath the old trees.

She had never been to Kentucky before, but she promised herself that when she returned to her own time, she would make an effort to visit, to come back to this area and see how it had changed in two hundred years.

And perhaps to find Knox's grave?

She almost gasped at the pain that sliced through her. If she had been in her time, then Knox would be gone forever. She looked over at him, almost unable to bear the thought of him lying cold and unmoving, slowly decaying away to nothing.

This was why time travel was so fraught with danger, not just because of the physical risk or the temptation to change events that perhaps shouldn't be changed, but because they were human beings who couldn't leave their emotions behind when they transited. Humans formed pair bonds; it was a basic fact of life. Given enough contact between people from two different times, bonds would be formed. What would people do to preserve those bonds? No one from the past was allowed to be brought forward. Laws were in place that didn't allow a traveler to stay in the time he or she was visiting. If someone didn't return voluntarily, a SAR agent would be sent to retrieve him.

The laws had, in fact, potentially created a whole new criminal class. No one had broken the laws yet; some travelers had had to be rescued, because their links became damaged or lost or because of some other circumstance, but no one yet had voluntarily stayed behind. It was only a matter of time until someone **did** want to stay behind, or someone wanted to go forward. Because no one knew what chaos might result because of that, the Council had put in place strict rules and laws prohibiting cross-timers.

She couldn't stay, and Knox couldn't go.

She was jerked back to the present when Knox pulled over to the side of the road. She looked around, seeing a neat white house down a long driveway to the left, with equally neat outbuildings and a tractor sitting on flat tires. "That's Jesse's house," said Knox, then pointed toward the right. "We're going up there." He glanced at her feet. "I need to get you some boots. There are too many snakes around to go tromping through the woods in just sneakers."

He was wearing boots, as he had been the day before. She said, just in case he was thinking about telling her to stay behind, "I wasn't wearing boots yesterday when we walked into the woods. I'll take the risk."

He grumbled a bit under his breath, but he didn't argue. She was an adult and she was a cop, the same as he was. If necessary, he'd have walked barefoot through the woods, and they both knew it.

They got out of the car, and Knox locked it before they plunged across the ditch and into the woods. Bushes and thorns pulled at their jeans until they were beneath the canopy, where the undergrowth thinned considerably. The scent of rich earth and the perfume of hundreds of different plants filled her lungs. Birds flew among the tree branches, their liquid calls filtering down. An occasional rustle revealed the presence of a squirrel or perhaps a mouse burrowing for safety or an insect going about its business. The rustle might even be that of a snake slithering away, its daily hunt disturbed by the encroaching humans.

Knox had a good sense of direction, leading them on an upward slant without pausing to take his bearings. His head was constantly moving back and forth as he searched his surroundings in all directions. Nikita was a city girl, more at home on pavement than dirt, but she enjoyed the difference between this and her more usual surroundings. She herself had a good sense of direction, but since she had no idea where they were going, her internal compass was of no use. She simply followed him, though she mentally marked their path.

"Here," he said. He pointed at a patch of earth where the leaves looked as if they had been disturbed.

"Someone could have buried his links here," she said, trying not to sound as excited as she felt. All she needed was a full set of links, and she'd be able to go home. She had three of Luttrell's, but she needed a fourth.

Her personal concerns would come after the DNA scans, though, because she didn't want to disturb any samples. She took out the scanner and flipped it open, and took a reading. Numerous locations of DNA glowed faintly on the screen.

"Mine will probably be here," Knox said. "And Jesse's. If your analysis says the subject is a short, nasty-tempered little bastard, that's Jesse."

"The scanner doesn't indicate temperament," she said with a straight face.

"I know. That was a joke."

"I know," she returned, and gave him a sweet smile. "Gotcha."

He grinned, not at all perturbed that she'd turned the tables on him for once. She settled down to work, carefully locating the various samples and securing them for analysis. Some of the samples were duplicates, of course; humans scattered DNA like seed. She recognized Knox's description four times, and another unknown subject had twice that many samples; she assumed that was the "nasty-tempered little bastard." McElroy's DNA was present, which she would have expected, and a large amount of Houseman's. Houseman must have died here, she thought sadly. This was definitely the point of initial transition. She couldn't see any signs of blood, but laser weapons produced bloodless wounds. The disturbed patch of leaves might be where Houseman had fallen.

She knelt in the humus to scan another sample, and remained there on her knees, staring at the little screen.

Knox crouched beside her. "What is it?"

"Another agent. Hugh Byron. He's McElroy's best friend."

21

KNOX HUNKERED BESIDE HER, READ THE information off the screen. "Could he have come through since Luttrell did?"

"I don't think so. This was the faintest sample the scanner has been able to read, meaning it's probably the oldest."

He made a noise deep in his throat. "If it's the oldest, then he was the first one through. He's your UT."

She stared across the small clearing, not seeing anything except the scenario unfolding in her mind. "That's why McElroy didn't make any progress: he knew it was Hugh Byron, and he wasn't trying."

"Or they're in it together."

She nodded, depressed by the likelihood. "Or

they're in it together," she said in agreement. She shuddered in horror. This meant Hugh was the one who had killed Houseman, one of his fellow agents, and McElroy was likely a co-conspirator. The betrayal was staggering. If agents couldn't depend on each other, then the integrity of every mission was at stake, because if you didn't trust the agent who had your back, you couldn't do your job.

Identifying Hugh as the UT also explained why the security at the Transit Laboratory had been so easily breached, why McElroy, who was more than competent, hadn't been able to make any progress in the case. That must have been the plan, for him to return so he could keep an eye on things from that end. And heaven only knew what information and aid he had given Hugh when he was here.

Their only advantage, that Nikita could see, was that McElroy couldn't be in contact with Hugh unless he physically transited here himself. So if a superior had sent someone in to move the time capsule for safekeeping, McElroy had no way to let Hugh know it was no longer there. Hugh would still be searching for it, and for the person who had placed the critical item in the time capsule.

This also tilted her perception of other occurrences. "He couldn't have known, when he was here, that I'd be the next agent sent," she murmured. "McElroy, that is. Or what the co-ordinates would be. So he couldn't have warned Hugh, but Hugh would have known that an-other agent would be coming through and he must have been watching Taylor Allen's house. That's the most logical place I would go, that any agent would go, even though your people had already essentially sanitized it so thoroughly I likely wouldn't be able to get any information from the scene. I had to try, at least. He knows me," she added. "He would recognize anyone in the Transit Investigative Unit, because there aren't that many of us. But why use a rifle? Why not the laser?"

"What's the effective distance on the laser? Might have been too far."

"A laser is light," she said drily. "It goes until something stops it or the earth curves away from it, whichever comes first."

"Holy shit, you mean if you miss, it just keeps going and burns whatever gets in its path?"

"Okay, so I exaggerated, but in tests it's been proven effective at over a mile. That's earth-bound tests, because obviously you wouldn't want a handheld weapon that had no distance limitations. In space—"

"Wait, don't start telling me that stuff now. I have a bunch of questions I want to ask, and I don't want to get sidetracked. Let's go back to something you said. What do you mean, my people had 'sanitized' the scene?"

"I mean your forensics people had gone through it, chemicals had been used, plus so many other people had been there that—"

"It wasn't sanitized—it was contaminated."

"Let's say it was a combination of both." She frowned. "But McElroy could have gone in when he first discovered the body and used his DNA scanner to learn the identity of the UT. He must have made some excuse for why he didn't, maybe that he could already hear the sirens of the emergency vehicles."

"Tell me something else: why didn't you come in two or three days earlier, wait for the killer, and prevent him from killing Taylor Allen?"

"Because he had already killed Mr. Allen when we learned of it. Mr. Allen was dead. That's one of the laws: you don't interfere and bring people back to life. I explained that. You don't know what will happen. We've learned that the small things, the peripheral things, don't seem to be that important, but something like life and death can completely change history."

"Theoretically."

She gave him a long look. "Do **you** want to be the one to find out for certain?"

"No, thanks." He scratched his jaw. "I see

what you mean. Your Council erred on the side of caution."

"And even then the decision to begin time travel was so controversial there were riots in almost every developed country. A lot of people think no one should be doing this, that we're courting disaster."

"And you may well be."

"I know. That's why we're so careful. What we're doing now is the equivalent of dipping our toes in the water."

"In a big way. By my count, six of you have come through. You're bound to be making huge cosmic ripples, or something."

"Or something. Two are dead: Houseman and Luttrell." Luttrell's body wasn't very far away, either, she remembered with a shiver. "McElroy went back. I'm here, and Hugh Byron is here. I think we should probably expect McElroy to transit here again, if he can think of a reasonable excuse for doing so. But he doesn't know I've lost my links, so he must assume I haven't accomplished my mission or made any progress, or I would already have returned."

"He knows you have a DNA scanner with you, though, so shouldn't he allow for the possibility that you picked up something? Shouldn't he **expect** it?"

"For all he knows, I'm dead. That was the

plan. After all, that shot missed by very little. Until and if I go back, or he comes here, he doesn't know any differently. Hugh knows, but not McElroy. And I still think it was someone local who shot at me, because Hugh wouldn't be proficient with that type of weapon, even if he had been able to procure one. What laws do you have governing the sale of weapons?"

"Laws don't mean shit to someone willing to break them. You can always get a weapon on the street somewhere, or buy one from an individual, without going through an identity check. I can't think why Hugh wouldn't have used the laser, why he'd need to recruit someone local."

She shrugged. "Because he hasn't found the time capsule and he's busy looking for that? I don't know. When we find him, we'll ask. The thing is, **I** know what **he** looks like, too, so we aren't working blind."

He stood, looking around the little sun-dappled clearing. "We need to build a case board, so we're looking at all the pieces at the same time. This is so convoluted I'm afraid we'll overlook something crucial. A time line like you drew in my office would help, too."

"I can do that when we go back to your house. Can you send out a BOLO with Hugh's description, or would you have to make explanations that you don't want to make?"

"I have to justify actions I take or don't take. Sheriff Cutler runs a tight ship when it comes to spending the county's budget. So I could send out a BOLO, but there would be an accounting for it by this afternoon. The previous sheriff let things get a little out of hand with things being investigated for personal reasons."

No help there, then. He couldn't use the department's resources without explaining why, and there was no reasonable explanation he could give; unfortunately, the truth wasn't always reasonable.

Just to check, she briefly dug in the area where the leaves were disturbed, hoping Hugh had also buried his links, but she found nothing. They were taught that burial was the safest hiding place, but circumstance might dictate a more accessible location, so where an agent put the links was left to individual discretion. Hugh might prefer his links close at hand.

As they walked down the wooded hill to his car, Knox said thoughtfully, "I'm surprised Jesse didn't come nosing around to see what we were doing, but he might have been working in his garden and didn't see us. I wonder if he's noticed anything since Monday morning when I was here. Let's go ask."

They got into the car and Knox pulled straight across the highway into Jesse's driveway. A pickup truck was sitting in front of the house, and off to the right was the barn. Knox grunted when he saw the tractor sitting on its flat tires. "You'd think Jesse would've gotten those tires fixed before now." Abruptly his expression changed and he hit the brakes, stopping the car well short of the house.

"Get your weapon out of the glove box," he said quietly to Nikita.

Without asking questions, she did as he said, her instincts going on high alert to match his. Something didn't look right to him, and that was good enough for her.

Nothing was moving on the farm except the tree leaves, waving in a slight breeze.

"Jesse keeps chickens," he said. "The pen's out back, but usually you can see one or two around in the yard."

Nikita had never seen a live chicken before, but she knew what they looked like. Slowly, they each opened their car doors and half got out, heightened senses reaching out in all directions, but there was nothing out of the ordinary to see or hear.

"Jesse!" Knox called. "Jesse Bingham! Sheriff's department!"

Silence.

"What does he look like?" she asked.

"Like a short Santa Claus with an evil disposition." He paused. "You know Santa Claus, right?"

"Not personally."

"Har har. Very funny." He indicated she should go right, while he took the left.

She nodded and they split up, each holding their weapon in a two-fisted grip. Her head swiveled back and forth as she took in every-thing. A farm wasn't in her experience, but if she saw someone who didn't look like a short, evil Santa, she knew what to do.

Cautiously, she worked her way around the barn, checking both behind it and inside, but it was empty and silent. She had never been in a barn before; it had an interesting smell, seem-ingly composed of dust, straw, and machinery, with perhaps some more earthy scents mixed in. But overall it wasn't unpleasant, and at any other time she would have liked to explore.

She and Knox met in back of the house. A small chicken pen was nestled against the hedges, some white birds inside it pecking at the ground. The fencing was also used on top of the pen, keeping the birds from flying off, or so she assumed.

"Six of his chickens were killed Sunday night," Knox said. "He always opens the pen during the day so they can range around the yard, then closes them up at night so they're protected from owls and other predators."

It was well into the afternoon, and the chick-ens were still in their pen.

They went around to the front door. In passing, Knox laid his hand on the hood of the pickup truck. "Cold," he said.

Standing on the porch, Knox rapped hard on the door. "Jesse! Sheriff's department!" They listened, but there wasn't an answer.

"The tractor's sitting there with flat tires, and his truck is here, so he should be here. It isn't like Jesse not to get those flat tires fixed right away."

"Does he have any friends he might have visited?"

Knox snorted. "Jesse doesn't have friends, just adversaries." He put his hand on the doorknob, swearing under his breath when it turned easily. "And no way in hell would Jesse go off and leave his door unlocked."

They stepped inside, Knox first, then Nikita, covering each other. A window air-conditioning unit rattled away and the inside of the house was cool, which is what kept the smell from being worse. It was unmistakable, though, and Knox reached for his radio. He hesitated, meeting Nikita's gaze. She didn't need to be here, and first they needed to check the identity of whoever was making that smell, and ascertain how the person had died. The victim was almost certainly Jesse Bingham, but they needed to know for certain.

The farmhouse was two stories. Nikita took

the stairs, carefully touching nothing, and checked all the upstairs rooms. The house was amazingly neat, and there was no one upstairs, or any signs of violence.

The body was in the kitchen, sprawled just inside the kitchen door. Anyone trying to come in that way wouldn't have been able to open the door. There wasn't any blood, because the long furrow in Jesse's body had been cauterized by the intense heat of a laser.

"Shit," Knox said. "Shit!"

"How can you call it in?" Nikita asked quietly. "How can you justify being here?"

"I was here Monday morning when he reported the vandalism. It wouldn't be unusual for me to follow up on it, though I really should be working on Taylor Allen's case. Except I know who killed Taylor Allen; I just don't know where the son of a bitch is and I don't have the usual means of tracking him down, plus I can't prove he did it anyway. I just love this fucking case." His frustration rang in his tone, and he looked as if he wanted to punch something.

Before she thought, she reached out and touched his arm, offering what comfort she could. "I'd like to point out that this illustrates why I need a separate vehicle, but it's too late to do anything about that right now. Where should I go, that I won't be seen?"

"There isn't anyplace," he said savagely. "I have to take you back to my house; then I have to radio in that I'm coming out here; then I'll have to call it in once I'm back."

She couldn't come up with a reasonable alternative, other than not calling it in at all, but she knew that was further than Knox could go. Not calling in Luttrell's death had eaten at him. So instead of arguing, she merely said, "Wipe your prints off the doorknob, just in case someone else finds him before you can get back."

Swearing, he did so as they stepped out onto the porch. "This is a time bomb, just ready to explode on us. How many cars have driven past and seen my car parked on the side of the road? It's a quiet road, but it isn't deserted. How many have gone by since we've been here at the house?"

"I don't know," she said. "A few. Would your car be recognized?"

"It's a county car. Everyone knows what they look like."

They just had to hope no one would find out the exact time Jesse's death had been called in. If someone saw the county car sitting there, and then for some reason drove back by and noticed that the county car was gone, that would be a problem. The situation was getting so perilous for Knox that Nikita was tempted to tell him to call it in right then, that she would begin walking back to town. It was a long walk on a hot afternoon, but it wouldn't kill her.

In fact, walking back was exactly what she should do. "I'll walk—" she began.

Knox glared at her. "No, you, by God, won't walk. Someone's trying to kill you, remember, and it isn't Hugh, so you don't know who to be wary of. Let's just get you home as fast as possible, and pray for the best."

He didn't put his portable light on the roof or turn on his siren, but he drove as fast as he could without attracting even more attention, and got her back to his house in about fifteen minutes. He didn't get out, just pulled a key ring out of his pocket and gave it to her. "Here's the house key. It's the one with the big flat head. Usual drill: don't open the door, and don't answer the phone. If I call, I'll call your cell phone."

She nodded and slid out of the car. He was already rolling again before she got the car door closed, and she had to give an extra-hard shove to close it before he was out of reach.

Using his keys, she let herself in the back door and carefully locked it behind her. If the scenario went sour for Knox, if details came out that he couldn't explain, she would have to come forward. Secrecy was one thing, but this wasn't a matter of national security and she wouldn't let Knox take the blame for any of this.

Whether it would do any good, whether she would be believed, was the bigger question.

22

Nikita stood in the kitchen, looking around. This scenario was almost identical to the one the day before, but things had changed so much that she didn't feel as if she was even the same person. In truth, the only thing that had changed was herself, and her perception of herself.

Are you a robot? Sarcasm would have been bad enough, but the cautious seriousness in his tone had sliced through her.

She wanted to hate him, but that wasn't going to happen. She couldn't hate him. She hated the position she had been forced into, she hated the emotional cage she lived in, she hated the fear that made it necessary, but she would never hate Knox.

He was . . . special, and she didn't think he knew how special he was to a lot of people. When she'd been shot at and he'd called in reinforcements, and the entire damn SWAT team and half the sheriff's department had come running, he'd said jokingly that they loved him—and it was nothing less than the truth. They might phrase it differently; they might say he was a good guy, they liked him, and all the other ways people said they cared about another person; but the meaning was the same.

The affection in which he was held would cause people to give him the benefit of the doubt if any awkward questions were raised. So much of this situation depended on chance: who had happened to drive by and notice his car, if anyone had at all, if the time was noticed, if the incriminating detail was mentioned to the wrong person. Whether the troublesome details could be glossed over remained to be seen. If everything worked perfectly, they were okay. If not—she and her mission were exposed.

Idly, she wondered what would happen then. There were several possibilities, the first of which was that she wouldn't be believed, so she'd have to do some demonstrations, which might not convince people of anything. Knox had been intrigued, but he hadn't been convinced until Luttrell's appearance. Unfortu-

nately, any demonstration of the laser pen
would definitely convince the sheriff that she
was the one who'd killed Jesse Bingham.

But if she was believed, events would quickly
spiral out of control. Logically, the federal government would be contacted. The FBI, specifically. Her own agency, but an agency two
hundred years removed from her own reality,
would take her into custody. She would be in-
terrogated, examined, subjected to a barrage of
psychological testing, and held prisoner for her
own safety. She had a fake driver's license and a
fake credit card. She had a lot of cash with her.
Moreover, people in this time had social security numbers; she didn't. She had a serial number, engraved in her flesh. She was number
233704272177. The first four digits were her
order of creation: she was number 2,337. The
remaining digits were the date of her "birth,"
April 27, 2177.

The FBI would have a real party with that.

She could tell them so much, though. She
could talk to the scientists, tell them what she
knew about solid-state lasers, about antigravity
propulsion, space travel, warp drives—which
admittedly wasn't as much as a scientist from
her time could tell them, but she was an intelligent, widely read woman, and she had made excellent grades in the sciences she had studied in
college. She could make drawings of spaceships,

personal vehicles, but she didn't know if she could make them believe her.

Without links, without proof positive, she couldn't prove anything. Her laser pen and DNA scanner would be taken apart, and she imagined there would be a great deal of interest in them, but what would they **prove**? She couldn't point to a building and say, "These were manufactured here."

But all this worrying was wasted effort, because until she heard from Knox exactly what had transpired, she had no idea what would need doing. In the meantime, she was once again marooned, without any way to help him or even continue her own investigation. If she made it through the night without being arrested, come morning she would make certain the situation was remedied as soon as possible.

The afternoon was wearing down, and she was tired. The last two days had certainly been eventful: two days, two bodies. This was three bodies for Knox, because he'd been at the former mayor's house and she hadn't. He'd also been investigating Taylor Allen's murder. He had to feel overwhelmed by death and violence.

She could make an educated guess as to what had happened to poor old Jesse Bingham—or rather, why it had happened. He must have been nosing around where he'd seen those flashes, and for some reason Hugh Byron had returned there and Jesse had seen or heard something he shouldn't have. Perhaps Hugh's links **had** been buried there, and he had decided to put them somewhere else for safekeeping, and Jesse discovered him when he returned to retrieve them. Jesse had definitely been killed with a laser. The wound was distinctive.

A single burst of energy into a stationary target would produce a single bore, but the more usual method was to fire a single stream as you tracked onto the target. The tracking movement was what produced the long, deep, furrowed sear. What flesh the energy beam touched was vaporized, and surrounding tissue was cooked. Jesse had died immediately, but had he invited Hugh into his house or had Hugh intruded?

Hugh's willingness to kill told her that **she** had to be willing to kill **him,** or her chances of survival decreased dramatically. He was as well-trained as she, and had proven himself to be ruthless. He had an unknown ally. On the other hand, she had Knox as an ally, and her altered appearance would perhaps allow her to catch Hugh unawares. That is, she had Knox, provided he didn't get arrested, and provided she herself stayed out of jail.

The telephone rang.

Nikita jumped; she'd been lost in thought, and the sudden sound rasped along her nerves like a metal file.

It wasn't Knox; he'd said he would call on her cell phone. "Damn it!" Nikita swore, leaping for her purse and taking out the phone. Yes, it was on. She breathed a sigh of relief. Knox had turned it on to show her the features and play with it himself, and he hadn't turned it off before dropping it in her lap.

The call went to the answering machine after four rings. A woman's voice said, "This is Ruth Lacey. Please pick up." Nikita didn't, of course, and after a moment the call clicked off.

Ruth Lacey, Nikita thought. That was Knox's dead fiancée's mother. Why was she calling? And wasn't it a coincidence that she would call after seeing them shopping that morning?

Nikita immediately felt a little ashamed. For all she knew, Knox talked to her on a regular basis.

Just so she would know Mrs. Lacey's number, she picked up the cordless phone and looked at the little window, but it had already gone blank and she didn't know how to call up the number again.

A little on edge, she checked all the doors and windows to make certain they were secure, then decided she should once again take advantage of her privacy to shower and take care of her personal chores, such as laundry. The curtains were all pulled, she had both weapons at hand, and the cell phone was on. She wasn't likely to find a better time.

"She didn't answer," said Ruth Lacey, hanging up the receiver. Byron had rented a motel room in Pekesville so he could be close at hand, but they were at her house. Edward, of course, was out at some bar. He seldom came home before midnight, and if he did happen to come home while Byron was there, she simply didn't care. She and Byron were in the living room, both fully clothed, but even if Edward caught them naked in bed, she wouldn't care. He was nothing to her, literally nothing.

"She's there," Byron said. "I saw her go into the house."

"I don't want to leave a message that I can't explain," she said, worried. "That's the first thing the police do, is listen to any messages. No one, not even Knox, would think it unusual if I call to talk to him, but if I say, 'Tina, please pick up,' then that raises questions."

"I know. You were smart not to say any names. It's just that I couldn't see her face very well when she went inside; she was wearing a cap. I need to hear her voice, or get a better look at her face."

"I suppose I could go over there, knock on the door, but what if a neighbor saw me?" Ruth asked.

"Don't worry," he said, hugging her close and kissing her forehead. "If we don't find out today whether this Tina is actually Agent Stover, we'll have other opportunities tomorrow."

"I don't know how much longer I can wait." Tears welled in her eyes. "Yes, I do. As long as it takes. I'm sorry I'm not more help."

"You've been more help than you imagine." He framed her face with his hands, tenderness in his gaze. With his thumbs he gently wiped away the tears that overspilled her lashes, and kissed her soft mouth.

Ruth ducked her head against his shoulder. A week ago, she had been lost in despair, but since she and Byron had met in the cemetery, her entire life had turned around. He'd confessed that he'd seen her at Rebecca's grave on Monday morning, talking to Knox—though of course he hadn't known who Knox was—and with only a wisp of hope had gone back the next day hoping to see her again. She had indeed gone back the next day, because talking to Knox had sharpened the pain and she had felt the need to be as close to her dead child as possible. Byron had introduced himself, the next thing she knew they were having coffee, and within a few hours after that he was her lover.

The speed at which events had moved was bewildering, and exhilarating.

When Byron told her he was a policeman from the future who had been sent back to catch killers who were trying to prevent the invention of time travel, her heart had almost broken. Her affection-starved heart had opened to him without hesitation, and now she found he was a delusional schizophrenic. She had burst into tears, and he'd started laughing.

"I'll prove it to you," he said, smiling lazily at her, and he had. He'd taken her out into the country that night and demonstrated some of his weapons for her, as well as introducing her to his partner, a cool-eyed man named McElroy who had verified everything Byron said. McElroy had then completely convinced her by attaching what they called "links," four of them, one on each wrist and ankle, and . . . disappearing. Completely. Right before her eyes.

Byron had kissed her forehead then, too, and held her close. "I need help," he said. "If we can stop this killer, then I'll show you how to go back to the day before your daughter died."

"I don't want to relive it," she'd said, pain stark in her eyes.

"No, no. You'll go back with full knowledge of today, of everything that's happened. Time travel doesn't wipe out memories. If you can convince her to . . . I don't know, go to the doctor and have some tests run, maybe you can save her life."

"Maybe?" Ruth had been anguished. **Maybe?** She might have to live through Rebecca's death again? She couldn't bear it.

"There are some things that can't be changed," he'd explained gently. "Rebecca might not listen to you. Or there might not be time to have tests done. I'd actually suggest you go back to at least a month prior to her death."

"But won't I already be there?"

"No, of course not. If you travel a mile down this road, then turn around and come back to this very spot, you won't meet yourself. If you go back to before her death, you'll know everything that has happened in the years since she died, but physically there will be only one of you."

Temptation was a lovely monster, and hope was a tender bloom almost afraid to poke up its head. To see Rebecca again, to have her daughter alive and well—"What if she does listen to me? Will she come back to this time with me?"

"She could, but why would you want to? When you change something like that, reality . . . realigns itself. That's the only way I can explain it. You will have created an alternate reality, one in which your daughter lives, gets married, raises a family. And you'll be there with her."

And there it was, the thorn that tore at her heart. She felt it now. "But what about you?" she cried.

The smile he gave her was both tender and sad. "I won't be there."

So that was the choice he'd given her: she could go back in time and save Rebecca, but the price she'd pay was that she would lose Byron. He couldn't stay in this time, he couldn't wait for her. He had a job to do, and then he would be returning to his own time. If she **didn't** go back to save Rebecca, then she could go forward with him. He didn't ask her to, didn't flay her by asking her to choose between him and her daughter. But it was in his eyes, the knowledge that if he gave her what she most desired, he would never see her again.

For now, though, she would love him with every ounce of spirit in her. She would cherish every moment with him, commit every detail to memory: how he talked, how he moved, the scent of his skin, the way one dimple would peek out when he laughed. She would love him, and love him well, for the short time they had.

She would pay any price to have Rebecca back again.

Byron had brought a police scanner, and they had been listening to a flood tide of police chatter. Ruth didn't know the codes, but Byron did. He told her there had evidently been a death at someone's house, but she found the scanner difficult to understand and the constant noise got on her nerves, so she tried to tune it out.

"Do you have to listen to that?" she asked, trying not to sound irritable.

"Police activity gives me information," he said, though he turned down the volume some. "I can't just assume that Tina is the woman we're looking for. Stover may still be out there, and this at least gives me an idea of what's happening in the county."

"I know. I'm sorry. I'm just on edge." She rubbed her eyes and sighed. "Shall I call again? Sometimes sheer nuisance will make someone answer the phone."

He nodded, and Ruth dialed again. Again the phone rang four times, and again the answering machine picked up. She didn't leave a message this time, just quietly hung up.

"Still no answer."

"After it's dark," he said, "we'll go over there." He glanced out the window; the sun was setting, but there was at least another hour of daylight left.

In an hour, Ruth thought, surely she could annoy this Tina woman into answering the damn phone.

Ruth Lacey had mental problems, Nikita thought when the phone started ringing again for what was at least the fortieth time. She checked the Caller ID again; yes, it was the same number. Ruth hadn't left a message since the first call, but she didn't have to.

Nikita had taken her shower, then put her dirty clothing in the washing machine. Some of Knox's clothing had been in a hamper beside the washer, so she had put them in with hers. She was using his washer, his water, his detergent, so adding his clothes to the washer was the least she could do.

The phone had been ringing when she got into the shower, and it was ringing when she got out. It rang when the washing machine had finished its cycle and she transferred the laundry to the dryer. It rang while she looked in the kitchen for something to eat. She really, truly wanted to answer the phone and tell the woman she should find something else to do with her time, but Knox had said not to answer the phone, so she didn't.

"Damn it!" she finally shouted, and began examining the phone for a way to stop the infernal noise. There it was, a tiny switch labeled "Ringer Off." Using her fingernail, she moved the switch and the ringing stopped—on that phone, at least. The one in his bedroom continued to shrill.

She stomped into the bedroom and found the same wonderful little switch on that phone.

The silence that fell was wonderful. If the crazy woman wanted to leave a message, she still could, and Nikita would hear that, but at least she didn't have to listen to the ringing anymore.

Her cell phone, unfortunately, hadn't rung at all.

Calmer now, she searched Knox's refrigerator and found it woefully empty of food. He'd said that morning that he didn't have much food there, and he hadn't been lying. She looked in the cabinet where he had taken out the can of soup, though, and found more cans. At least she wouldn't starve, she thought, selecting one that read "Vegetable Beef," whatever that was. Vegetables given a beef flavor, maybe.

She looked out the kitchen window. It was twilight now; Knox had been gone for almost four hours. He might not be home for another four.

With nothing else to do, she settled on the couch in the living room and turned on the television.

Once she let herself relax, it didn't take long for her to drift to sleep.

She woke abruptly to the sharp knock on the front door. The curtains were pulled and Knox's door was solid, so she couldn't see who it was. The television was on, but she didn't adjust the volume because if she did, that was a dead giveaway that someone was home. Knox said he often left his lights on if he went out at night, so she wasn't worried about that, but televisions didn't adjust their own volume levels.

The knocking came again, more insistent.

"Tina," came Ruth Lacey's voice. "I know you're there. I want to talk to you."

23

Hmm, Nikita thought. To answer, or not to answer; what a question.

She'd have to be an idiot to open the door to a woman who was obviously having mental and emotional problems because the man her dead daughter had been engaged to seven years before was finally seeing someone else. Not that Knox was "seeing" her, but Ruth Lacey thought he was, and it had evidently pushed her into psychosis.

On the other hand, if the woman banged on the door as incessantly as she had rung the phone, Nikita might be forced into action to save her own sanity.

She eased off the couch, staying low so her shadow didn't fall on the curtains. At best, Mrs. Lacey was disturbed and, at worst, possibly violent. Add to that the fact that Nikita didn't know the identity of the person who had tried to kill her and she had to factor in the possibility, however remote, that Mrs. Lacey could be that person.

No, she was most definitely **not** opening that door.

Instead she got on her hands and knees, grabbed her cell phone off the coffee table in front of the couch, and crawled into her dark bedroom. If anyone shot through the window, she would be below the bullet's trajectory.

Her purse was on the bed. She hooked it by the strap and pulled it to her, taking her laser pen out of it and slipping the slender weapon into her pocket. Her automatic weapon, inside its holster, was lying on the bedside table—and right behind the table was a window that looked out on the front porch.

Cautiously, she eased up to the table and retrieved that weapon, too. She looked around; not much light was coming through the open bedroom door, since the only light in the house came from the lamp in the living room and the television, but if she moved the curtain aside, that was certainly enough light to betray her.

She closed her eyes so they could begin adjusting, feeling her way as she crawled back to the door and silently shut it, plunging the room into total darkness. When she opened her eyes, she still couldn't see anything, but after a moment she was able to make out the paler rectangles of the windows, and the sliver of streetlight coming through a tiny part in the curtains.

There were footsteps on the porch, and abruptly that sliver of light vanished.

Nikita froze in place. With the bedroom in complete darkness and the streetlight shining outside, she could make out the faint outline of someone standing on the porch in front of the window, with a darker blotch where a face was pressed to the glass as that someone tried to look inside.

She knew she wasn't visible, not with the bedroom darker than the porch. The human eye wasn't made to operate best when it was trying to see from lightness into darkness. So long as she didn't move, no one could see her. Even knowing that, though, her heartbeat was fast and heavy as adrenaline pumped through her. She was trained to act, but at the same time, the key was to choose the best course of action. **Don't just act,** one of her instructors had drilled into them, **act smart.**

In this case, the smart action was total avoidance. There could be no good outcome if she confronted Ruth Lacey.

The situation had abruptly gone from being nothing more than a nuisance to having the potential for violence. More accurately, she thought, the potential for violence had been there from the beginning and she was just now recognizing it.

The shadow moved away from the window, and she heard the footsteps retreating, then going down the front steps. There was a woman's voice, but it was too faint for her to understand the words. Who was she talking to?

Nikita crawled to the window, taking care not to bump into anything or let her knees thump on the floor. When she reached the window, she didn't touch the curtains, because any movement of the fabric could betray her presence. Instead she maneuvered so she could see through the same tiny crack where the edges of the fabric didn't quite meet, and slowly raised her head.

A car was parked at the curb, and Mrs. Lacey was talking to someone inside it. The tiny slice of vision Nikita had didn't allow her to see anything other than half of Mrs. Lacy's back and her right arm. The woman was gesturing back toward the house. Then, evidently having decided it was wasted effort to bang on Knox's door, she got into the car and it pulled slowly away from the curb.

Nikita shifted her position, trying to get a better look at whoever was with Mrs. Lacy, but her field of vision was too limited.

She remained where she was, crouched on the floor and watching the street in case Mrs. Lacey was wily enough to drive by again, perhaps hoping Nikita would turn on another light and thus verify someone was in the house. Nikita couldn't swear that the car hadn't parked just up the street and the occupants were not waiting to see if there was any sign of activity.

Nikita sank to the floor and opened the flip top of her cell phone; the little screen and the numbers immediately lit up, and automatically she shielded the glow with her hand as she punched in Knox's cell phone number.

"Yeah, Davis," he said after the second ring. He would have recognized her number, but the way he answered told her he wasn't alone and was probably still at the murder scene.

She kept her voice low, barely above a whisper. "This is just to let you know what has been happening; you don't need to do anything. Ruth Lacey started calling incessantly this afternoon. I didn't count the calls, but I estimate between forty and fifty times. Then she came here and began banging on your door, calling me by name—"Tina," that is—and saying she knew I was in here."

"That doesn't sound right," he said.

"I think she's having emotional problems. I didn't answer the phone or the door."

"Good. Don't."

"Any estimate on how much longer you'll be at the scene?"

"Probably another couple of hours."

"Any problems?"

"Not yet."

"I'll see you in a couple of hours, then."

She closed the phone and ended the call, then got up on her knees to once more peer out the window.

The car, headlights off, was parked at the curb again.

Nikita's heart gave a hard thump, and she forced herself to remain in place. She reminded herself that she could see them but they couldn't see her. All she had to do was remain quiet and still, and they'd never know she was watching them. They had turned around, so the driver's side was closest to the house. The shadows in the car were deep and she couldn't make out anything other than that two people were in the car, and she thought the driver was a man. Mr. Lacey, perhaps?

She wondered what they had hoped to accomplish. To tell her to get out of town and leave Knox alone, perhaps? Or maybe Mrs. Lacey was so far lost to reason that she would have simply attacked, in which case Nikita would have had to defend herself, and she had absolutely no doubt who would be the victor in any sort of physical confrontation with the other woman.

Jealous people did foolish things all the time; the two hundred years between her time and now hadn't changed that at all. But Mrs. Lacey wasn't jealous in the classic sense; rather, she must be desperate for everything to remain the same, for Knox to remain in love with her dead daughter, and in that way she could still cling to a little part of life as it had been before.

Nikita wondered what they would do if Knox drove up. She knew he wouldn't, not for a while yet, but **they** didn't know that. Had they thought what they would say, or were they simply operating without any plan?

Common sense had to prevail at some point, and they would go home. She hoped.

"There wasn't another car here," Byron said. "He came home this afternoon, let her out, and he left again. She unlocked the door and went inside the house."

"I don't think she's in there," Ruth said doubtfully. "I listened, and there wasn't any sound other than the television. No one was moving around. And only that one light is on; there should be a light on in the kitchen, too, if anyone is there."

"Why?" he asked, his tone betraying nothing but curiosity.

"Because people who watch television will go to the kitchen during commercials, to get something to drink or eat. So they leave a light on, usually the one over the sink, or maybe the stove light. Just a small one, enough that they can see. That's just what people do."

"But how could she have left? She doesn't have a car."

"I suppose she could have called someone to pick her up. You came to get me, and I tried getting her on the phone for at least two hours, maybe longer. There was plenty of time for her to do that. She might even have called a cab."

"I really need to get a better look at her," Byron said regretfully, drumming his fingers on the steering wheel as he stared at the house. He'd watched carefully, and there hadn't been so much as the twitch of a curtain. Even if this Tina was really Nikita Stover, she would have no reason to be suspicious of Ruth and surely human curiosity would have led her to at least look out. So perhaps Ruth was right, and no one was in the house.

He didn't like quarry slipping right through his fingers. He didn't like loose ends. And he especially didn't like having a highly trained agent like Nikita Stover out there somewhere, undetected. His skills were the equal of hers, but he was conducting two searches, while she was doing only one. He had to find that damn time capsule, or locate whoever had put the crucial information in the capsule. She, on the other hand, had only to locate him.

If McElroy had done his job correctly, she didn't have an inkling of the UT's identity, which was his, Byron's, biggest safeguard. Even if she saw him, she would likely think only that reinforcements had been sent. It would never occur to her to suspect a fellow agent.

On the other hand, perhaps bringing Ruth along had not been the smartest approach, but he hadn't known that at the time. Using her had seemed reasonable; she was a woman and, as such, less threatening to another woman. It was also possible that the multitude of phone calls had, instead of building up frustration, backfired by making Ruth seem a little less than sane.

But either no one was in Knox Davis's house, or the occupant was far more wary than he could have reasonably expected.

The next time, he would use stealth. People were far more careless when they didn't know they were being watched.

24

AFTER THE CAR LEFT AGAIN, NIKITA waited half an hour in the dark, watching for its return. She still couldn't be certain they hadn't parked up the street somewhere to watch the house, risking alarming the neighbors, but at least they were no longer parked in front of **this** house.

After half an hour, she moved quietly through the house, not turning on any additional lights as she did so. She had already checked all the windows to make certain they were locked, but now she checked to see that all the curtains were properly pulled, so no one could see in.

This entire evening had annoyed her almost to her limit. First the ringing telephone, over and over and over, and finally the sensation of being hunted, in the one place where she was supposed to be safe, had grated on her nerves. The evening had given her a whole new appreciation for harassment charges; federal agents didn't have to deal with those, but sometimes harassment was part of an escalating pattern that would end with federal statutes such as kidnapping being violated. After just one evening of it, Nikita was ready to do violence. She couldn't imagine people dealing with it on a continuing basis.

After an hour had passed without incident, she cautiously moved back to the living room, where the television droned on. Perhaps she was being **too** cautious, but she still kept low so she wouldn't throw any shadows on the curtains. She also kept her purse and weapons at hand, and slipped the tiny cell phone into her pocket. Then she stretched out on the couch and tried to watch television, tried to relax, but every time a car drove by, she tensed and lost track of what she was watching as she listened to make certain the car wasn't stopping.

Over an hour later a car did slow, and turn in to the driveway. She waited; logically, that should be Knox returning home, but she wasn't assuming anything. It wasn't until the car pulled around back that she made her way to the kitchen and peeked to make certain that it was Knox's car before she unlocked the door.

She held her finger up to her lips as he entered the dark kitchen. He wasn't a cop for nothing; he nodded, his entire demeanor changing from tired to wary. He shut and locked the door behind him, then whispered, "Why is the kitchen dark?"

"Because I didn't have a light on when she got here. If I'd turned on any additional lights, that would be a dead giveaway. But now that you're home, you can turn on as many lights as you want. Your keys are on the table, by the way."

He went to the sink and turned on the fluorescent light tucked up behind a wooden valance. The curtains over that window were drawn, too, but they covered just the lower half of the window.

"Tell me exactly what happened." He still kept his voice low as he went to the refrigerator and took out a soft drink.

"No, you first. Murder is more important than harassment."

They went into the living room and sat side by side on the couch, so they could more easily talk without being overheard.

"So far, so good," he said tiredly, sliding down on the seat so he could rest his head on the back of the couch. "The coroner is greatly interested in the wound, because he's never seen anything like it. The body has been sent for autopsy. The real test will come tomorrow when this gets out, because that's when people will start calling in that they saw a car at Jesse's place on such and such day, at such and such time. I think we're okay, though, because Jesse has been dead a couple of days, at least. He might even have been dead since Monday, which would probably make me the last person to see him alive. We'll be looking for reports of vehicles there earlier in the week."

She nodded. She should have thought of that earlier; they both should have. Even if Knox's car had been seen at Jesse's house earlier today, the time of death would render that meaningless.

"Tell me about Ruth," he said, rolling his head on the couch to look at her. His eyes looked tired, the lids heavy.

"You know about the calls, and her coming here. She knocked—banged—on the door for at least five minutes, saying she knew 'Tina' was in here. Then she tried to look in the windows. She left, and that was when I called you."

"Is that it?"

"No. Someone was with her—I think a man. I couldn't see well enough to get a description, but she was definitely talking to someone in the car with her, and from the bulk I'm fairly certain it was a man. They came back, parked at the curb and watched the house for a while, then left again." She checked the time. "That was about an hour and a half ago. It's been quiet since then."

"God," he said, closing his eyes. "I never figured Ruth would freak out if she thought I was getting serious about someone else. After Rebecca died, she even told me to go on with my life. I'll have a talk with her tomorrow, tell her one of the neighbors complained to me about the noise."

"Would your neighbors recognize Ruth?"

He thought about it. "No. Good catch. I must be more tired than I thought."

"Because you never make mistakes, right?" she asked lightly.

"Let's don't go there," he said with a slight smile. "I've made some real doozies, and they usually involved not keeping my mouth shut when I should have."

She blinked. "What, exactly, is a 'doozy'? I understand the general meaning from your usage, but—" She shrugged, lifting her brows to invite his answer.

"Hell, I don't know. In the context I just used it, it means some really bad mistakes. If someone had a really bad black eye—thank you for not punching me in the eye, by the way—I'd say he had a doozy of a shiner. If someone is a doozy of a cook, it means she's a really good cook. So it's a general superlative."

"I notice you said 'he' in reference to a black eye, and 'she' in reference to cooking."

"So sue me for gender profiling," he said comfortably, sinking even further into the couch.

He looked as if he would go to sleep where he was. "Have you had anything to eat?" she asked, before his eyes could completely close.

"Yeah, one of the deputies came to town and picked up a sack of burgers." His eyelids lifted. "Damn, I forgot about that. I don't have much food here. Did you find anything to eat?"

"Soup. I'm fine. But this entire situation isn't working. I need to be able to operate independently of you. And I can't stay here, with Ruth Lacey freaking out and watching the house because she can't bear the thought of you having another relationship."

"Where else can you stay?"

"You mentioned a 'bed-and-breakfast.' I assume that means one has a bed, and is fed breakfast."

"That's exactly what it means, but I don't like the idea." He yawned, and heaved himself to his feet. "I'm going to take a shower. We'll talk about this when my head is clear."

She watched him walk away, her gaze automatically dipping to his ass. **Yum,** as a character on television had said. It was a very descriptive word.

Somehow she wasn't angry with him anymore. Nothing in her personal situation had
changed, but during the day her hurt and anger
had slowly ebbed away. Truthfully, she hadn't
been angry so much as lashing out in pain, but
he couldn't have known how deeply his question would slice at her.

She stretched out again, cradling her head on
her hand. They were both tired; she'd probably
sleep soundly tonight, unless Ruth paid another
visit. She closed her eyes, and the next thing she
knew the room was dark and Knox was lifting
her in his arms.

"I'm awake," she said, reflexively clinging to
him lest he drop her. Her fingers dug into
warm, damp flesh and hard muscle.

"That's good. Making love's always better
when both people are awake."

Her heart pounded wildly in her chest, and her
thoughts scattered. "But—what—I didn't—"

"Hush," he said, and kissed her.

He smelled of soap and water, of man and
heat. His mouth was slow and persuasive, and
abruptly she thought, **Yes.** There were reasons
why she shouldn't become intimate with him,
and she didn't give a damn about them. She
wanted him, wanted that long, lean body
stretched on top of her, wanted him between
her legs and inside her body.

She pulled her mouth free, and he said, "No talking."

"I was going to say 'yes.'"

"Oh." He paused. "That's okay, then." And he laughed before once again taking her mouth with his as he finished the journey into his bedroom. She clung to him as he bent to place her on the bed, holding the kiss until he lost his balance and collapsed on top of her.

They both laughed like kids as they rolled on the bed in the dark, hands searching and learning. She stroked his muscled back, rubbed her face against his lightly haired chest, found the hard little peaks of his nipples and pinched them, then moved on to the serious stuff. She unfastened his jeans and found they were all he had on, sliding her hands under the loosened waistband to curve them over each ass cheek and squeeze. The hard-muscled globes were cool and smooth under her palms, warming quickly.

He was laughing again as he tried to wrestle her out of her garments. He was having a difficult time because she didn't want to release his ass. He managed to pull free and she took advantage, dipping her hands instead into the open front of his jeans. His penis thrust into her hands; it was amazingly hard, curving upward, and he grunted when she touched him. Hungrily she wrapped her hand around it, delighting in the thickness, the way it jerked as she slowly stroked up and down and with her other hand reached to cradle his testicles.

"Jesus. God. Get your clothes off," he groaned, falling back on the bed.

"You get them off," she countered, concentrating on what she was doing.

"I can't. You've got me by the balls. Literally." He groaned as she pumped him again. "Don't make me come, not yet."

"Don't worry about that," she whispered as she released him to hurriedly pull off her own clothes and toss them aside. He helped, their hands bumping together as they generally got in each other's way, but somehow they managed to get her clothes off and he kicked his jeans away, and they fell back naked onto the bed.

Quick as a cat she pounced, pushing him onto his back and straddling him. He made a deep sound of pleasure as she settled on the hard ridge of his penis, enveloping it with the damp heat between her legs. He lifted his hips, trying to angle himself for entry, but she shifted away. "Not so fast. I like feeling you this way." She settled again, sliding herself back and forth on him.

"It'll feel better from the inside," he said urgently, his fingers biting into her hips.

"We'll get there," she purred. "Don't you like

playing?" Teasing him was a lot of fun, she decided. It felt good to her, too, so good that she knew she could rub herself to orgasm this way.

He made a grunting sound again. "Fuck first, play later."

She began laughing and he lunged up, wrapping his arms around her and rolling again, but this time he ended up on top and the head of his penis edged into her.

All laughter stopped and he hung there above her in the darkness, waiting, waiting. Her breath caught in her lungs and heat swamped her, her entire body flushing as everything she was, everything in her, focused on the impending intrusion. Then it was there, slow and hot, pushing deep into her as her body pulsed in her eagerness to take him and hold him.

He pulled back, almost out, then eased forward again. Her back arched and she moaned, loving that sensation. "Yes. Like that."

He complied, and within a minute she was writhing, almost on the verge of climax, when he halted, panting.

"I can't," he said at her muttered protest. "I'm too close. You have to do it."

He pulled out and fell on his back, and eagerly Nikita slithered on top of him again. There was no teasing this time; she wanted him inside her again. She sank down on him as his hands closed on her breasts, and she fell into a duplicate of his rhythm, a slow up and down, enveloping, releasing, enveloping again.

Her climax swelled, almost within reach. She was dying for it, yet perversely she wanted this to last. Each stroke became maddeningly slow, the sensation so intense she almost couldn't bear it. Each time she sank down and he probed deep inside her, she shuddered in response, her rhythm fraying and becoming uneven.

"Faster," he groaned, grabbing her bottom as he bucked upward between her legs.

His action sent him deeper yet, into the realm of discomfort. She cried out and ground down on him as her climax broke over her in strong wave after wave, arching her back, tearing cry after cry from her throat.

He lifted her hips, pulled her back down on him, hard—once, twice, and he convulsed beneath her. Trembling, she collapsed on him while he was still holding her hips locked to him, groaning as he pulsed inside her.

Slowly he calmed, his strong body trembling just as she trembled. His chest heaved as he fought for breath, and she tried to move aside to give him more air, but he clamped his arms around her. "Stay," he said in a raw tone. "Like this."

Emotion unexpectedly swamped her, leaving

her near tears. She fought the urge to cry, instead burying her face against his neck and clinging to him. Bewildered, she wondered why she wanted to cry. This had been . . . wonderful. Their bodies were on the same sexual wavelength, without a single wrong move to mar the experience. She loved the feel of him, the smell of him, and maybe the very perfection of the experience was what had her weepy.

Their breathing slowed, became more normal. Drowsily, she nestled against him. She needed to get up, she thought; she needed to wash, and they were making an absolute mess of the bed. But she was so content right where she was, and they could always put on clean sheets . . .

"Hey, wake up," he murmured into her hair. He was stroking her back, her bottom, and she thought that if he wanted her to wake up, he really should stop those soothing touches. "Uh—this isn't a great time to ask, but are you on birth control?"

She smiled against his neck. "You mean you forgot about it?"

"Completely." His tone was rueful. "Are you?"

"Yes, I have about four months left on my yearly dosage."

She felt his interest sharpen. "A yearly dosage? You just have to take it once a year?"

"That's it."

"But doesn't taking it just once a year make it more likely you'll forget?"

"I receive an automatic notice. Everyone who signs up for the yearly control gets notified a month before the end of the dosage, then again two weeks later, then again the day before. It's up to you whether or not you follow up, and if someone decides to stop taking birth control, they're supposed to notify the system so it doesn't waste time with useless notifications."

"Is it just for women, or for men, too?"

"Women. The male system is different. The longest effective birth-control dosage perfected for men, so far, lasts about a month." And far fewer men than women signed up for birth control; but no matter how the social scientists argued, the fact still remained that men didn't get pregnant, so birth control was far more important to women. It didn't seem fair, but there it was.

She could practically feel the questions bubbling in him, but she placed her fingers over his mouth before he could start. "I'm so sleepy," she whispered. "We'll talk tomorrow. I just want to clean up and go to sleep."

"We can do that," he said, finally letting her ease to the side. "It's a waste of time, but so what; I have plenty of hot water."

25

KNOX WOKE HER TWICE MORE DURING THE night to make love. After the third time, as she began to surface from the sheer physical pleasure, her conscience awoke with a vengeance.

It wasn't fair of her to take advantage of his ignorance. There were certain things about her that he should know, that anyone who became close to her, whether in friendship or romance, should know. If he was then going to choose not to pursue any closer relationship, then it was better that she tell him now, at the beginning, when there wasn't as much emotional investment. She had learned the hard way not to wait.

After they had cleaned up yet again they returned to bed. He settled back on his pillow and pulled her close against his side, her head on his shoulder and his left arm around her. She listened to the strong, steady beat of his heart and sent up a silent prayer that this wouldn't be the last time she was close enough to him to hear his heartbeat.

"There's something I need to tell you," she said before she lost her resolve.

"That's never good," he commented after a moment's pause.

"What isn't?"

"Starting a conversation with those words. What follows is never anything I want to hear. Is this going to be any different?"

"Probably not," she whispered, dread making her throat tight.

"If you're married, Nikita, I swear to God—" he began with an undertone of fury.

"No, no! I didn't lie, I've never been married."

"Then what is it? You'll never convince me you're gay."

The old-fashioned term gave her a brief moment of amusement, but it was very brief. "Nor that. I'm a Copy," she said steadily, determined to get it said before he sidetracked her.

"A . . . what?"

"A Copy," she said. She had learned over the years how to keep her voice very neutral when she disclosed her origins. "I wasn't born, I was . . . grown. Like a vegetable."

"Shit. No kidding? All in a row, like carrots? What stuck up, your head or your feet?"

The image was so ridiculous she sat up in bed, abruptly angry. "I'm serious! This isn't a laughing matter."

"I'm not laughing," he pointed out, pulling her down to him again. "I asked a question."

"You can't—" She stopped, because he obviously **could** think that. His mind must have some real twists and turns in it, to come up with a carrot analogy.

"You said 'vegetable.' What was I supposed to imagine? Pea pods? Tomato bushes?"

"Would you just shut up? I'm not a damned pea pod! Or a tomato."

He pinched her bottom. "How about a peach? You're nice and juicy."

Exasperated beyond bearing, she snapped, "I was grown to provide replacement organs for my . . . sister. But she wasn't really my sister, because I'm her. I'm her copy. I'm identical to her, except I'm alive and she isn't."

There was a long, loaded silence, and she felt as if she were suffocating there in the darkness. She reached to turn on the bedside lamp so she could see his face, and also so she wouldn't feel as if the walls were closing in on her. He stopped her, his hand gentle on her arm.

"Leave the light off," he said gently. "Lie back down and tell me about it. In your time, people are cloned and the clones are killed for their internal organs? No offense, darlin', but that's damned barbaric."

"No, that isn't what happens." She could hear the upset in her voice, and tried to regain her neutral tone.

"Then what? How were you grown to provide organs? I don't think you're like a salamander, able to grow back parts."

"Would you please stop comparing me to vegetables and lizards? Please!"

"A peach is a fruit."

Goaded beyond control, she grasped a handful of hair on his chest and gave it a hard pull.

"Ouch!" he yelped. "Hey! Leave the body hair alone!"

"The next time, I go for your crotch," she warned. "Are you going to listen, or are you going to make smart remarks?"

"After a threat like that, I'll listen to anything."

To her surprise, she realized she was smiling, and she was glad he couldn't see her in the dark. Her feeling of dread had lifted a bit; maybe this wouldn't be so terrible, maybe he wouldn't be as horrified as people in her time were. When he pulled her down onto the bed and wrapped her in his arms again, she let him.

"Cloning is illegal," she said. "The results in cloning experiments never turned out quite right; the clones seemed to be genetically weakened. They became easily diseased, they died young for the most part, and if they did mature and propagate, their children were almost all born with severe birth defects. So cloning was outlawed, but billions upon billions were spent developing the technology to essentially grow replacement organs from a subject's own cells. The biggest problem was to grow the organs fast enough, because the donor might be in extremely poor health and not have the months needed for an organ to mature. So this huge experimental program was under way trying to speed-grow organs—"

"Hold on," he interrupted. "Any organ grown from someone sick would have the same genetic weakness that was attacking the person to begin with, wouldn't it?"

"If the problem was genetic, yes. But what if you were prone to heart disease, and when you were in your fifties you developed advanced cardiac impairment? A new heart could give you another fifty years, or longer, because you have to allow for new advances in medicine. Wouldn't you take the heart, knowing it was prone to developing the same disease in another half-century?"

"Hell, yeah. You can't beat those odds."

"The majority of people in the world feel the same way. The speed-grow program was at its peak about thirty-five years ago, when my parents had their first child, a little girl named Annora Tzuria. She was beautiful, healthy, but when she was two, she contracted a virus that so heavily damaged her heart and kidneys she needed transplants within a year to live. My parents immediately enrolled her in the speed-grow program, healthy cells were taken from her to grow the organs, and they waited."

"And instead, they got you," he interjected.

"Essentially, yes, but don't get ahead of me. There were different factions in the development program who competed for funding—"

"Some things never change."

"Definitely not that. The researchers in one faction believed they had perfected the cloning process and had eliminated the factor that made each copy in succession weaker than the one before. They were supposed to be growing organs. Instead, for about two years, they grew people. There were slightly more than four thousand of us when they were discovered and the program halted."

"It's hard to hide four thousand people."

"Four thousand **babies.** We grew normally; we didn't spring to earth fully formed. We were marked with serial numbers, which consisted of the number creation we were, added to our birthday, so my serial number is

233704272177. It's permanently etched in the skin behind my left ear. If the skin is tampered with, if I try to remove the number by surgical or any other means, a signal is transmitted to a security agency that oversees the copies and I'm to be immediately apprehended."

"But you're an FBI agent, not a criminal," he said, sounding angry on her behalf.

"I'm also a Copy. Copies' legal status is somewhat up in the air. Until it's decided, law prohibits discrimination against us. Federal agencies in particular have to be evenhanded in the application of their hiring policies, but I was accepted to the Academy on the basis of my grades. But that was later. Let me get back to the beginning."

"Okay, you were a fully formed, squalling baby."

"And it was discovered what they were doing. The experiment center was raided; all the experiments were taken into federal custody until it could be determined who was guilty of what and who were the original donors for these four thousand or so babies. Serial numbers were matched with records, and people were contacted."

His arms tightened around her. "That would be a hell of a shock. You think you're saving your life, or your child's life, and instead there's a whole new human being. What did they do? Your parents, specifically, but everyone else, too?"

"Some were too horrified to cope, and the babies were adopted out or remained in federal custody as wards of the nation. Some took their babies home with them. That's what my parents did. Whether or not my mother gave birth to me, I was genetically theirs, and identical to Annora when she was that young. But the fact that the Copies were complete humans meant that the people who were supposed to be saved, died, because by the time the experiment was discovered, there wasn't enough time to grow the replacement organs that were supposed to have been grown in the first place."

"God." That was all he said, but a wealth of understanding was in his tone, in that one word.

"They gave me the same middle name, Tzuria, in Annora's honor. She died three months after my parents brought me home. I don't remember her, and for a long time when I saw holograms of her, I thought they were of me."

"I can't imagine how your parents must have felt," he said thoughtfully. "They'd buried their child, and yet . . . there you were, that same child, only healthy."

"My mother said I saved her sanity, that she

could look at me and see this baby who needed her and depended on her. I looked like Annora, but at the same time, I was a different person. Annora spent most of her life in very ill health, while I was healthy and energetic. But Mother was always protective, and because the legal issues are still very much a hot button and because of the moral problems people have with the Copies . . . I've always been very careful in what I say and do. She told me from the time I was old enough to understand that I couldn't afford to get in any sort of trouble."

"That's quite a load to put on a little kid." He kissed her forehead. "No wonder you seem so—"

"Robotic?" she finished drily.

"I was going to say 'even-tempered.'" He chuckled. "I learned my lesson. The R-word will never pass these lips again."

"Robotic is exactly the way I am, and it went through me like a knife when you said that, because I realized how I had always held myself back. I never let myself get really angry, I never yelled, I never danced. I held everything in, because anything deemed too violent, or too enthusiastic, or too **anything,** could be used to have us legally declared a danger to ourselves and others."

"I can't tell you how sorry I am I said that."

He kissed her again, this time tilting her chin up so he could reach her lips. "When I saw how much I'd hurt you, I wanted to kick myself."

"And you were afraid you'd ruined your chances for sex," she added.

"That, too."

She yawned, suddenly exhausted. She still couldn't quite believe how matter-of-factly he had accepted her particular situation, when people in her time were aghast at the results of that experiment. "Some of the Copies haven't done well," she admitted. "Personality disorders seem to be more the norm than the exception. Violent crime rates are high among Copies, too. It's still being argued in the courts whether or not we should all be institutionalized for our own good."

"I don't guess it occurred to anyone that making a kid a ward of the nation, depriving it of a real family, always pointing fingers and looking for abnormalities, could cause personality disorders and a tendency toward violence, huh? Look at you. You were raised in a family with people who love you. The biggest problem is their childhood environment, not anything intrinsic in being a Copy."

"The prejudice against cloning is so ingrained, and with good reason, that most people react first with their emotions when they learn I'm a Copy. I've always told people I was becoming close to, so they could make the choice whether or not to remain my friend. Most chose not to."

"Their loss," he said briefly. "I'd hazard a guess and say that's the real reason why you aren't married, not just because of the pressures of your job."

"There's the birth control issue, too," she said, and despite her best efforts she could hear the echo of pain in her voice. She took a deep breath and regained control of herself. "Copies aren't allowed to have children. By law, I have to be on a birth control regimen. If I don't report in to have my birth control renewed, I will be captured and sterilized."

Held as closely to him as she was, she could feel the tension that invaded his muscles, feel the heat of anger wash over his skin. "Excuse the hell out of me for saying so, but sounds to me as if civilization has reversed instead of going forward. Never mind your technology, your society sucks."

"And yet, if you had lived in a time that saw the horrible birth defects caused by cloning, you would probably be more understanding."

"Probably not. I'm a Kentuckian; I'd more likely be in some underground militia, trying to overthrow the tyrants. To hill people, the Civil War was yesterday, and the Revolution the day before. The word 'taxes' still gets us riled."

"Then you wouldn't want to live in my time," she admitted.

"Probably not, but I sure would like to visit. What's it like?" He turned on his side to face her, and as she had with his anger, she could now feel the force of his curiosity. "What's the world's population? Is our form of government still the same? How many states are there? And what about cars?"

She laughed softly and looped one arm around his neck. "Stop worrying about the cars. They're called personal vehicles now, and they're powered by a variety of means: magnetic propulsion, hydrogen, electricity. There are free lanes and regulated lanes. If you choose the regulated lanes, the speed and traffic flow is controlled, so you never go very fast, but you don't get in traffic snarls, either. You program your route into the PV's computer, then sit and read or otherwise amuse yourself while the vehicle takes you to your destination."

"Have sex?" he suggested, laughing.

She had to laugh, too. "Yes, people being people, sometimes sex is had. If you see a PV with the privacy screens in place, you can be fairly certain what's going on inside. Occasionally a couple will be arrested for **not** having the privacy screen in place."

"What about those free lanes?"

"They're just as they sound: traffic isn't regulated. You have control of your vehicle. You choose the speed. There are horrific accidents on the free lanes, but every time someone brings up legislation to convert all traffic lanes to regulated, there's a huge outcry and that politician gets voted out of office in the next election."

"I imagine so. Is government still the same? Two-party, Democrats and Republicans?"

"There are three parties now, but no Democrats or Republicans. Those two parties died out in the early twenty-second century. No, 'died out' is the wrong terminology. Their identity changed, and they became something else. **Murphy?**"

"Murphy?" Knox echoed. "Who the hell is Murphy? Or do you mean **morphed**?"

"Yes, that's the word. They morphed into their present political identity."

"How about the rest of the world?"

"Some nations change, some don't. There are eight billion people on earth now. There would be more, but the great viruses of the late twenty-first century killed millions upon millions. The death toll from the viruses contributed to the changing political climate that did away with the Democrats and Republicans."

"And wars?"

"There are always wars."

"Yeah, figured. Human nature doesn't change much. Tell me about space travel. You have a colony on the moon?"

"And on Mars. The Martian colony was established underground, in the cave system; that was the only way to get enough protection. The moon colony is by far the most popular, because of earthrise. I think around four hundred thousand people live on Mars, but the moon has a population of over two million. There's a ban in place now to prevent any new settlers on the moon."

"I'd love to go to the moon and watch the earth rising," he murmured. "Have you been?"

"No, it's a hideously expensive vacation. Public servants don't make that kind of money."

"Something else that hasn't changed," he commented.

"I'm afraid not."

"No other colonies in outer space, though? No contact with other species? No faster-than-light travel?"

"No, no, and no. If we had the last one, we might manage the first one. But no one has ever made any form of contact with another intelligent species."

"I'm disappointed. In two hundred years, you expect to get a little farther out than your neighbor's house—metaphorically speaking, of course."

"Of course. But we did get the pope on the moon, so you have to give us credit for that."

"Now, that I'd have paid to see. The press coverage must have been wall-to-wall."

Wall-to-wall pertained to carpet, she was certain. She puzzled over the sentence, trying to work out the meaning from the context. Wall-to-wall, carpet . . . They were carpeted by the press reports? Yes, that made sense.

"The coverage was nonstop," she agreed, then gave an eye-watering, jaw-popping yawn that made him laugh.

"We don't have much time left to sleep, but we might squeeze in an hour," he said against her temple. "I'll hold the rest of my questions for later."

"Yes, that's a good idea." She yawned again. "Knox—thank you."

"For what?"

"For not being disgusted by what I am."

"You're a woman," he said quietly into the dark. "And I'm a man. We're together, and that's all that matters."

26

NIKITA LAY IN BED SLEEPILY LOOKING around while Knox took another shower before going to work. It was just after dawn, but the drawn curtains kept the room dim. She was slightly sore, utterly relaxed, and completely infatuated. On the physical front she had been overwhelmed by Knox's male pheromones during all of that bare skin contact, then emotionally ambushed by his easy acceptance of her circumstances. She suspected the combination had been too much for her defenses.

She couldn't make her feelings for him go away; it was too late for that. There was nothing she could do now except enjoy him for the length of time she had left, however much that was. She still had a mission to complete, a mission that was rife with complications. Even if she successfully apprehended Hugh Byron, her links were missing, stolen by someone who had no idea what they had, and the danger that person ran by having links and not knowing how to work them made her hair stand on end.

There was nothing like a little dose of reality to dim a postcoital glow, she thought. Duty gnawed at her. She would have liked nothing better than to snuggle down and sleep for several more hours, but she forced herself to throw back the covers and get out of bed. Yawning, she padded into the other bedroom and put on her sanssaum; she liked being naked **with** Knox, but that was entirely different from being naked in front of him while he was dressed and doing other things. She wasn't yet **that** comfortable with him.

He had put on a pot of coffee, and she followed the smell to the kitchen. As she went by, the door to the bathroom opened and a wave of warm, humid air rolled out. Knox stood there completely naked, rubbing his head with a towel. "Good morning," he said, his eyelids lowering as he swept his gaze down her. "Man, I love that gown thing you're wearing. It's sexier than a bikini."

Noting that he was definitely comfortable with being naked in front of her, she said, "Good morning," blew him a kiss, and continued toward the coffee.

She poured two cups, and carried both of them to the bathroom. Knox was standing in front of the sink, the towel knotted around his waist, while he squirted lather onto his palm. Nikita extended one of the cups. "Would you like a sip of coffee before you put that on your face?"

"God, yes." He set down the shaving cream can and reached for the cup, an expression of bliss crossing his face as he sipped the hot liquid. "Some people don't drink coffee," he commented. "I wonder about them."

She couldn't resist slipping her hand under the towel for a pat on that fine ass of his, which got her soundly kissed—as soundly as possible, anyway, since they both held cups of hot coffee and his other hand was full of lather. "Should I begin cooking breakfast?" she asked when her lips were free again. She pressed a kiss to his bare shoulder. "If you'll tell me what to do and how to do it, I'll manage."

He looked guilty. "I don't think we have anything here for breakfast."

"No food?"

"No food. We'll eat out. And I'll buy groceries today, I promise."

If he had time, she thought. He certainly hadn't had an extra minute for the past two days. Perhaps she could do it, after he rented another car for her. He had other cases he was working; he had to give them some attention. She was dependent on him to help her navigate the present, so until he was free, she might as well make herself useful.

While she waited for him to finish in the bathroom, she strolled into the living room and examined his stacks of books. A series of big, fairly thin books caught her interest; she pulled one out and, without looking at the front cover, flipped it open. It was full of photographs.

She looked back at the cover. It was white leather, and the words **Pekesville High School** were imprinted in the leather, along with the year 1986. It was a yearbook from Knox's high school. Smiling, she leafed through the pages until she found Knox, a gangly adolescent with a serious expression on his face. He must have been sixteen or so, with a hint of power already showing in his neck and shoulders, and a slight shadow on his jaw that said he was already shaving, and on a regular basis.

She put that yearbook back and took out another one. This one was from 1985, the year the time capsule was buried. She found Knox's class photograph again, noting the difference a year had made. He looked so young in this photograph, boyish, without the beard shadow he had the next year.

Out of curiosity, she went to the front of the yearbook and slowly began turning pages. The faculty pictures caught her attention and she looked for the football coach who had committed suicide, Howard Easley. He'd been a pleasant-looking man, she thought, his face not giving any hint of the sadness within that must have led him to his final action. Guessing someone's age from a photograph was tricky, but she thought he looked to be in his early forties, perhaps, with thick dark hair and striking pale eyes.

She read his list of credentials; he had several degrees, including a master's, and he'd taught both physical education and physics. He had attended the University of Kentucky, and the California Institute of Technology.

She was still staring at the page when Knox came into the room several minutes later, neatly shaved and partly dressed. At least he had on jeans. "What are you looking at?"

"Your yearbook from 1985." She looked up at him. "The coach, Howard Easley. He went to Cal Tech. I don't believe mediocre students receive master's degrees from there, do they? He taught physics as well as physical education. He's the only person so far who's anything close to being qualified to write whatever it is we're looking for."

He came to stand beside her, his head bent as he read the coach's credentials. "I didn't know him that well. I was just a sophomore when he killed himself, and I was into basketball instead of football, anyway. He didn't strike me as a genius, but what do kids know? I paid attention to girls and basketball, not some old guy in his forties. And, no, Cal Tech doesn't accept mediocre students."

"Does he still have family in the area whom we can talk to? Someone who would know if he was perhaps working on a hobby, or a pet theory?"

Knox put his left hand on the back of her neck, gently kneading. "I don't think he was from here, but I can find out. There are still people around here who knew him. I can find out what projects he was involved with when he was at Cal Tech, too." He glanced down at her. "You said 'Cal Tech' instead of 'California Institute of Technology,' which is what the yearbook says. I guess Cal Tech is still around, huh?"

"Cal Tech is the premier research facility for space travel. It has very close ties to NASA."

"Space travel is a long way from time travel."

"Not at all, actually. FTLT and time travel have a lot in common."

He narrowed his eyes, thinking over the acronym. "I get it. 'Faster-than-light travel.' Do we have that yet?"

"Not yet," she said regretfully. "But the team working on FTLT serendipitously developed time travel when prior research took them in an unexpected direction."

They looked at each other, their eyes lighting with excitement as the eureka moment sank in. Sometimes, even without all the pieces of the puzzle, you knew beyond a doubt what shape the puzzle would take when it was completed. This was one of those moments, and they knew Howard Easley was the key. The big problem was, he'd been dead over twenty years.

"There are still people around who knew Coach Easley," Knox said. "Max Browning, for one; he covered all the football games."

"Mr. Browning's name has been mentioned a lot," Nikita observed. Cops didn't believe in coincidence; should they be looking more closely at Mr. Browning?

"There were only two reporters for years, and they took their own photographs, too. Max may have files of photos that didn't make it into the papers, so he's at the top of my list of people to contact." He furrowed his brow. "I need to talk to Ruth and find out what the hell she was doing. There will be tips called in concerning Jesse's murder and I'll have to check those out—"

He wandered toward the bedroom still mumbling to himself, his mind racing as he tried to think of everything he needed to do that day. Smiling, Nikita followed him, but only to get some clean clothes from her bedroom and take her turn in the bathroom for a quick shower. She had to shampoo her hair, so there went her blondness, right down the drain. It was a simple matter to reapply a polymer color, though, and dry her hair.

When she came out of the bathroom, Knox glanced at her and choked on his coffee. Obligingly she went over and whacked him on the back. Through watery eyes, he stared at her red hair. "Wow," he finally wheezed. "I think I like this better than the blond. Just how many colors do you have?"

"Three. Blond, red, and black." She liked being able to change her hair color so easily, and she especially liked the red shade because it went so well with her warm complexion. "Your neighbors will think you're a real ladies' man."

"You mean they'll think I'm a hound dog." He sifted his fingers through the red strands, watching the light filter through.

"I hate to keep nagging about this, but I also need a vehicle. I can't sit here all day, and I can't sit in your office."

"Damn. Look, can you drive a stick?"

The look she gave him was completely blank.

"A manual transmission. A stick shift."

She arched her brows. "I can drive your stick shift, big boy."

He chuckled and gave her a quick kiss. "Damn straight you can; you put me in overdrive. But that isn't exactly what I was talking about. Some cars—mostly sports cars and trucks—have manual transmissions. You have to change the gears yourself."

"Then, no, I can't. I've never seen one."

"Then borrowing my dad's old truck won't work. Okay, I'll get a car for you; I'd been hoping not to use a rental company, but I don't see any way around it."

"What's wrong with using a rental company?"

"The cars are recognizable, for one. They all have that little company decal somewhere on it. Dad's old truck looks like a thousand others around here; no one would pay it the least bit of attention."

"Could you teach me how to drive a manual transmission?"

"I could give you the basics, but it's something that takes practice. Stalling out every time you accelerate would draw attention, and that's what I don't want."

"Not knowing who tried to kill me certainly is inconvenient," she remarked.

He growled, "Don't you dare be blasé about this."

Nikita put her hands on her hips and glared at him. "Have I been blasé? I've followed instructions to the letter. I didn't open the door even last night when I really, really wanted to throw that woman off the porch."

"And I appreciate your restraint. I guess I'm just saying, be careful. Got your cell phone?"

"Got my cell phone."

"Got your weapon?"

"Got my weapon."

"Got your laser?"

"Never go anywhere without my laser."

"You're set, then." He bent and kissed her, his mouth warm, the kiss slow. "Though I'd put you in body armor if I could. Let's go get some breakfast; then we'll hit the rental company and hope they have something available."

Nikita pulled her hair back and secured it, then put on her baseball cap and sunglasses. She was starving, so she was glad he'd listed breakfast first. She would have something other than eggs, though. She'd found that ova weren't to her taste.

Hugh Byron parked on the street several houses down. He risked having someone come out to complain about him being there, but several cars on the street were parked at the curb, so he hoped he was simply blending in. He had a pair of binoculars lying in the seat beside him, and he watched Knox Davis's house for any sign of life. The county's chief investigator should be leaving any minute now; Ruth said he had a habit of going to work early, and it was almost seven o'clock.

At last he saw movement at the back of the house, and he grabbed the binoculars. They were already focused, so all he had to do was train them on the two people coming out of the house.

He muttered a curse; Davis was between him and the woman. But he could see the woman's red hair even though she was wearing a baseball cap; sunglasses hid her eyes. She said something to Davis and smiled up at him, and his hand slid over her ass as he bent to kiss her. Then he opened the car door for her, closed it after her, and went around to the other side.

Ruth was right about one thing, Byron mused; Davis was definitely having sex. But they had seen a blond, and this woman had red hair. Either Davis had more than one woman keeping him happy, or the woman had changed her hair color.

Changing hair color was so easy it wasn't much different from changing clothes. Between the baseball cap and sunglasses, Byron hadn't been able to see enough of the woman's face to definitely identify her, but his instinct said this was Nikita Stover. She was about the right height and weight, and she was with Davis. Stover had last been seen leaving the courthouse with him; then later Davis had reported that she'd left town. Byron knew she wouldn't have done any such thing, so that meant Davis was lying.

Stover had made Davis her ally, maybe hooked him in with sex. How much she had told him was anyone's guess, but likely not very much; she was one of those by-the-book agents who either didn't have the imagination to improvise or was afraid to veer away from the rules. On the other hand, perhaps he'd underestimated her, because she had obviously improvised when it came to Davis. She was using him to provide shelter, and possibly using his resources to investigate.

For a brief moment he thought about taking both of them out, but cops tended to lose all sense of perspective when one of their own was murdered. The local ones were already antsy enough, with three murders inside a week in this little town that normally wouldn't see many more than that in a year. The citizenry would be on edge, too, and paying close attention to anything out of the ordinary.

No, this was better left to a more private time and place. It didn't matter. He knew where she was. She thought she was safe, but Davis was evidently called out on a lot of nights and Stover would be left at the house alone. He had her now.

27

KNOX DROVE SLOWLY DOWN THE TREE-lined street, his head swiveling. He already had his cell phone in his hand and he keyed it. "Get me the registration on this license plate." He recited the number, then said, "ASAP."

To Nikita he said, "Take a look at that car, the dark green one. Is that the one you saw last night?"

She gave it a quick look, but she didn't need to do that. "No, the one last night was a light color, either pale gray or white."

"That would be Ruth's car, then."

"What's wrong with the dark green car?"

"So far as I know, it doesn't belong to anyone on this street."

She wasn't surprised that he would recognize all his neighbors' cars. Cops simply **noticed** things. Without thinking about it, they registered clothing, body language, their surroundings. If she and Knox had been driving down a busy freeway, he could probably have described every vehicle he'd passed in the last five minutes, plus all the vehicles around him, and some of the ones on the other side of the freeway. Working the streets developed that kind of hyper-awareness. She had a form of it herself, not so much when it came to vehicles, but in analyzing evidence and reports. She knew what rang false, and what was important.

Law enforcement in her time relied too much on technology, she thought. Traffic was monitored by cameras almost everywhere, except for the long, empty stretches of highway out west; as a consequence, she didn't know a single cop in her time who really paid attention to traffic. They still noticed people, could expertly read body language, but part of their vigilance had been abandoned to the unblinking cameras.

Mankind had to learn the same lessons over and over; many battles in the decades-long war with terrorists in this century had been waged in cyberspace. Information and communication satellites had been targeted, not with missiles, but with spammers, jammers, and technoviruses. Secure defense sites had been hacked. When the computer networks went down, commerce had been first disrupted, then shut down. Having great technology was wonderful; completely relying on it was stupid.

Knox's cell phone beeped and a woman's voice said, "That license plate is registered to Enterprise."

"Okay, thanks."

Enterprise was the name of the rental agency where Nikita had gotten her car. "It's a rental?" she asked.

"Yeah, and I'm going to find out who rented it."

Nikita sighed. She didn't think she would be having breakfast soon, after all. On the other hand, something was disturbing Knox, and she had just been thinking how his instincts were probably much sharper than those of law enforcement officers in her time, so it followed that she should pay attention to those instincts. Probably one of his neighbors had guests or a family vehicle was in the shop, but it had to be investigated.

Not to her surprise, the rental office he went to was the same one where she had rented her car; it must be the only one in town, she thought. A town as small as Pekesville, without a commercial airport, wouldn't do a booming business in car rentals. The neat single-story building was of yellow brick, with a halfhearted stab at landscaping in the form of some sort of bush planted on each side of the door. The small parking area in front was shaded by large trees, while a fenced area in back held the vehicles available for rental. Unfortunately, from what she could see, the back lot was empty.

Knox pulled off his sunglasses as they went inside, and Nikita did the same, hooking one of the earpieces in the neck of her T-shirt.

"Hey, Dylan," he said to the diligent young man behind the chest-high counter. "Troy around?"

"He's in the back, Mr. Davis. Want me to get him?" Dylan gave a quick glance at Nikita, then another one. She smiled at him, and he flushed as he looked away.

"Yeah, I got a question I think he can help me with." Knox leaned on the counter, all lazy grace. "Won't take but a minute."

Dylan disappeared through a door. Nikita leaned against the counter beside Knox. "You know him, obviously."

"Yeah, I busted his ass for smoking pot back when he was twelve or thirteen. Scared the shit out of him. Never had any more trouble with him, either."

"Good job," she said, patting his ass in appreciation.

One eyebrow hiked up as he gave her one of those long, blue looks of his. "You keep doing that. You fixated on my ass, or something?"

"It's a fine ass," she murmured, because she

could hear Dylan returning. She propped both arms on the counter, the picture of decorum.

Dylan was followed by a stocky man who was wearing a short-sleeved white shirt and a tie, and drying his hands and arms with a towel. "I was cleaning up one of the cars," he explained, making Nikita wonder why the manager was evidently doing menial labor, but maybe he was the sort of person who preferred doing things outside rather than sitting at a desk. "Dylan said you have a question. Come on back to my office and I'll see if I can help you."

It couldn't be that easy, Nikita thought as she and Knox followed Troy back to his office. In her time, not one shred of information or evidence was given without the proper authorization. No matter how insignificant, no matter if a cop was talking to a member of his own family, everything had to be authorized.

"Tina, this is Troy Almond. We were in school together. Troy, Tina."

If Troy noticed that Knox had omitted her last name, he gave no indication, smiling and saying, "Nice to meet you, ma'am," and waiting until she extended her hand before he extended his to take it. In her time, no one shook hands anymore; that practice had died out during the great viral pandemics that had killed so many millions of people. She had read about the practice, though, and read that polite men didn't initiate a handshake with a woman; they waited until she initiated it, because she might not feel comfortable shaking hands. It was the pheromone-transference issue, she thought, that instinctively made some women wary about even casually touching men they didn't know.

Troy sat down behind his desk, and Knox and Nikita took the other two seats in the tiny space. He said to Knox, "What can I do you for, bud?"

Nikita blinked. She was certain the individual words were English, but once again she was left at sea. Knox, however, had no such problem.

"I've got the tag number of one of your cars; might have come from here, might be another location. I need to know who rented it."

"Knox, you know I can't give out that kind of information without a warrant," Troy protested.

Knox rubbed his jaw. "Well, I can go get a warrant; I just thought I'd save some time. It's a lead I got on these murders."

Troy gulped. "You think I rented one of my cars to a murderer? A murderer was in here?"

"I have to say it's possible. I just need a name—and the driver's license number. Right now I don't need to see the paperwork, though if this tip plays out, I'm sure a warrant will be coming through to cover your ass."

"Shit, I can't believe that," Troy said in disbelief. "Sorry, ma'am. A murderer!"

"I don't know that for sure; it's just a lead," Knox said patiently.

"Shit, Knox, I know you and how you are. Sorry, ma'am. If you're chasing something like this down, you're pretty fu—certain you have something. Sorry, ma'am. Okay, I'll see what the computer says."

Troy swiveled his chair around to peck at the keyboard and pull up a program on his computer. "What's the number?" he asked, and Knox recited the license plate number while Troy tapped it into the program. He hit the enter key, and waited. Another screen popped up, and he said, "I don't recognize the name. Dylan must have handled it."

"Who is it?"

"A Byron Hughes. California driver's license." He read off the driver's license number and Knox copied it down.

"Thanks, buddy, that's what I needed to know," Knox said, and clapped Troy on the shoulder. "Now, what do you have available? Tina needs some wheels."

"Nothing right now," Troy said regretfully. "One is scheduled to be turned in late this after-

noon, but that'll be the earliest I'll have anything."

"Can you give me a call when it comes in?"
he asked, scribbling a number on a blank pad of
paper.

"Sure thing. Uh—I won't say anything about
what you asked."

"Appreciate it."

"It's too big a coincidence," Nikita said as
they got back into Knox's car. "Hugh Byron,
Byron Hughes."

"Yeah," Knox said grimly. "And he was sitting right outside my house."

"He knows I'm there." Nikita stared through
the windshield. "Drop me off at the next corner.
If I'm with you, you're in danger." Her voice
was calm and flat. The chase was on, and she
could feel every particle in her beginning to
focus, concentrating on the task at hand. Hugh
might know where she was, but now she knew
where **he** was, or at least where he'd been. And
if he'd been watching Knox's house before, he
would do it again, waiting for a clean shot at
her. But she knew what his car looked like, and
he didn't know she knew. The advantage was
hers, and in fact, she had a better chance of taking him if she was on foot.

"I'm not dropping you anywhere." He shot a
furious look at her. "Don't even suggest it."

"I just did, so isn't it too late to tell me that?"

"Don't suggest it again, then. I have to get you somewhere safe—"

"Excuse me," she said gently. "Aren't you forgetting something?"

"What?"

"This is my job. Apprehending him is why I'm here."

He looked blank for a moment; then he said, "Fuck." He drove in silence for a couple of blocks before he added, "This sucks."

From the frustration in his tone, she deduced he had indeed forgotten why she was there and he'd simply been reacting with the protectiveness men were prone to exhibit. She reached over and patted his leg in sympathy. It was difficult when instinct warred with custom. That was why agents married to each other were never allowed to work in the same division.

Once he recovered from the shock of realizing he couldn't simply stash her somewhere and that, tactically, she would have greater insight into Hugh's probable actions than he would, he said, "Okay, we know what he's driving. I should have stopped when I saw the car; he might have been lying down in the seat to hide as we drove by. What's most likely to be his next move?"

"Be glad you didn't stop," Nikita said, her blood running cold at the thought of what could have happened. "You've seen what a laser can do. He wouldn't have been there unarmed."

"I'm surprised he was there himself. I'd have expected him to send his cohort, whoever that is." He narrowed his eyes. "That shot could have been intended to sidetrack you, and hamper your investigation, which is exactly what it's done. In the meantime, he's been free to search for the information."

She mentally examined the premise and nodded. If hampering her had been his intention, that one shot had certainly worked. She had been forced into hiding, unable to operate in her true role as an FBI agent, because she hadn't known whom she could trust, other than Knox. If the shot had actually killed her, so much the better, because then Hugh would have a clear field for at least a month before SAR was sent for her.

Abruptly the details jarred, as if something didn't fit. She rubbed her forehead, as if she could massage her thoughts into place. That didn't explain Luttrell. Why had Luttrell been sent here, evidently with instructions to kill her? McElroy couldn't know what was going on here, because Hugh had no way of communicating with him while they were in different times. Probably they had planned to kill whoever had been sent, but how had McElroy known the effort had failed?

Perhaps Luttrell had been part of the plot, whatever it was. At this point she didn't care why they were doing this; she only wanted to stop them. She'd find out the why of it later. Maybe Luttrell had been insurance, sent to aid Hugh, and it had been his bad luck to transition almost literally on top of her. That would explain his immediate reaction, which was to try to kill her.

This scenario made sense to her, and in a way it was comforting, because that meant she hadn't killed an innocent man. Luttrell's death had been weighing on her, even though she'd had no choice.

It made sense that Luttrell wouldn't transition at the same time Hugh had. If they waited, sent the third conspirator back later, then he could carry messages and report any worrisome developments. But if that were so, then they would have agreed on some means of establishing contact. Hugh must be worried that Luttrell hadn't yet appeared.

"What?" Knox demanded, as if he could hear her thinking.

"Luttrell must have been part of it," she said, and explained her reasoning.

Knox nodded, considering. "Makes sense. And since Luttrell didn't show, Hugh will be getting a bit anxious. He wants you out of the

picture. But won't he realize you'll have con-
fided in me?"

"No, he shouldn't. So far as I know, you're
the first person in the past who has ever been
told."

A pleased look spread over his face. "I'm the
first, huh? Cool."

"I wouldn't have told **you** if you hadn't been
about to arrest me," Nikita pointed out.

"About to, nothing; I did arrest you. I just let
you go without pressing charges."

He pulled into a drive-through restaurant.
"We'll pick up a couple of biscuits and cups of
coffee, and go talk to some people about
Howard Easley. We're looking for the same
thing that Hugh is looking for, but we're ahead
of him, so we have the advantage. We don't
want to blunder where he's concerned, since
he has a laser weapon, too, as you so kindly
pointed out. We need a plan."

28

"Course I remember when Coach Easley killed himself," Max Browning growled. Nikita thought that must be his normal method of speaking. He even looked like some peculiar breed of dog, with his bulldog jowls, bushy eyebrows, and humped shoulders. "I covered the story. January 1, 1985. Cold as a witch's titty. Sorry, ma'am."

"There wasn't any sort of suicide note, as I remember."

Max Browning leaned back in his chair. They were at his house, in a tiny, cluttered office that was closed off from the rest of the house by a pair of folding doors. His wife, white-haired and neat as a pin, had shown them in, then went off to put on a pot of coffee, just in case they weren't sufficiently wired for the day. Knox and Nikita sat side by side on a couch that sagged dangerously in the middle, throwing them together and threatening a complete collapse.

"No, no note of any kind. There was no sign of foul play, nothing indicating a struggle. I talked to him that night," Max said, and heaved a sigh. "Before he did it. Remember when the time capsule was buried?"

"Vividly," Knox said in a wry tone.

"You said you'd counted them putting in thirteen things, but the newspaper said only twelve things were supposed to go in. I went back and checked, and there were seven itemized out of the twelve."

"Yeah, I know; we checked, too."

"Well, I was standing fairly close; had to, so I could take pictures. But I was busy doing my job, so I didn't take note of each and every thing put in the box. You had me curious, so that night I called the coach and asked him if he remembered what all had been put in. He said no, he'd just been there to provide the muscle and he never listened to the mayor's speeches if he could help it, so he'd been thinking about some new plays he could put in the offense come spring training."

"Do you remember what time you called?"

"Sure. Right before the last bowl game came on at—what? Eight o'clock, maybe? It's been twenty years. But it was before the bowl game."

"He's thinking about new plays for spring training; then four hours later he hangs himself?" What had happened in those four hours, to cause that drastic a change?

"Some people are good at hiding their feelings, I guess. He was divorced, unhappy; it happens."

"I heard he and his ex-wife were trying to patch things up."

"Yeah, I heard that, too, but things must not have been working out. I remember she came to his funeral, cried her eyes out. Pissed me off. Sorry, ma'am. If she cared that much about him, looks like she could have given the poor bastard some hope—sorry, ma'am."

First Troy, now Max Browning. Why was everyone apologizing to her? Nikita wondered. She shifted restlessly, but a quick glance from Knox told her he'd explain later. She wondered when he'd started reading her mind—and when she'd started reading his.

"Anyway"—Max shook his head—"hell of a way to start out a new year."

"Did you ever ask anyone else what the other things were that were put into the time capsule?"

"Had more important stories to cover. Coach's suicide put it right out of my mind."

"Did Coach Easley have any kin around here that you remember?" Knox leaned back, his entire attitude saying that he wasn't in any hurry, had nothing urgent to do. Nikita had to lean back, too, or the sagging couch would have pitched her into his lap.

"Don't think so. They moved here from Cincinnati when he was hired."

"Were you good friends with him?"

"Good enough, I thought. If I needed a story, he'd always make time to sit down and talk to me. We weren't drinking buddies, if that's what you're asking."

"Did he have a drinking buddy? Did he have a drinking **problem**?"

"He'd have an occasional beer, as I remember. Not a heavy drinker at all."

"What about friends?"

"Well, let's see. He was closest to the principal . . . What was his name?"

"Dale Chantrell."

"That's right. Dale Chantrell. Haven't thought of him in a coon's age. He moved on to a school near Louisville. He and his wife, Arah Jean—if you ever saw her, you'd know why I remember her name and not his—were good friends with Howard and Lynn. Lynn was Howard's ex-wife."

Mrs. Browning entered the cramped little office then with a silver platter laden with an insulated carafe of coffee, three cups and saucers, a little pitcher of cream, and a choice of sweeteners—one of which was real sugar. She set the platter on a stack of papers on Max's desk. "Howard and Dale were good friends," she said serenely. "Lynn hated Arah Jean's guts."

"Thank you," Knox said, meaning the coffee. "Why did Mrs. Easley hate Mrs. Chantrell?"

"Like Max said, if you ever saw Arah Jean, you'd understand. She was one of those good-looking women who can't help but flaunt it. Everything she wore was just a shade too tight, or too short, or too low-cut. Too much lipstick, too much mascara. That kind of woman."

"Had plenty to flaunt, too," Max said, and his wife smacked him on the arm. "Well, she did!"

"I never said she didn't. I smacked you because, while I don't expect you to go blind whenever a good-looking woman shoves a set of 38D knockers under your nose, I **do** expect you to act like you have," Mrs. Browning said with considerable asperity.

Max grinned at his wife, clearly pleased she could still work up some jealousy on his account.

"Thirty-eight-D, huh?" asked Knox.

Because it seemed the thing to do, Nikita smacked his arm. Hard.

"That'll teach you," Max chortled, laughing at Knox's surprised expression. Mrs. Browning was smiling as she left.

"I'm just glad it was my arm and not my jaw," Knox said. "Do you think there was any-thing"—he rocked his right hand back and forth—"going on between Coach Easley and Arah Jean?"

"Naw, she was like that with everything in britches. Nothing personal. I doubt Arah Jean cheated; she was too smart for that. And Lynn wasn't the type of woman to put up with some-thing like that going on right under her nose; she'd have taken a horse whip to both of them. They were polite to each other because Howard and Dale were such good friends, but polite is all they were."

"Do you know where Lynn lives now?"

"Can't say as I do. Haven't seen or heard of her since the funeral. Now, if you could find Dale Chantrell, he might could tell you. Or maybe Edie Proctor."

"Edie Proctor," Knox said. "She was school superintendent back then."

"That's right. She's the one who hired Howard for the job. The board of education should still have his application somewhere, though if it's like all those other old paper records, they're boxed up in a basement somewhere. His application would probably list next of kin, but that would be Lynn, and you already know that." Max paused. "So. You gonna tell me why you're so interested in Howard Easley, after all these years?"

"It's part of our investigation into Taylor Allen's murder," Knox said smoothly. "I can't go into details; you know that. It's just a thread I'm pulling on."

"Uh-huh," said Max. "In other words, you're not saying. Okay, I understand. But when you figure out what's going on, I get the story. You better not call anyone else."

"It's a deal. By the way, do you know if Howard had any hobbies?"

"He was a football coach; he didn't have time for hobbies."

"Model airplanes," said Mrs. Browning as she breezed past the open door.

Knox turned to look at her. "Model airplanes?"

"That's right," Max answered, "I remember now. He built them in his garage. He built little motors for them, and radio-signal controls. Damndest thing you ever saw, back then. He'd get out in the field behind his house and fly those little airplanes. Crashed a few of them, too. What spare time he had, he was always fiddling with those things. He and some buddy he went to college with had this ongoing thing, to see what all they could come up with."

"What happened to his stuff when he died? Did Lynn get it?"

"Now, that I don't remember. The house stood empty for a while; then someone moved into it, lived there for a couple of years. It was empty off and on for about ten years; then finally it got in such bad shape no one would live there. It's about fallen in now, yard all grown up around it. You can barely tell there's a house there, the trees and bushes are so thick around it."

"Do you remember the address?"

"Not exactly. It was out on Beeson Road, past Turner Crossroads. About four miles down, on the left."

As they walked down the sidewalk toward the car, Nikita said, "Do we talk to Edie Proctor next?"

"I'm afraid so. She's here in town, so we might as well. Then we'll hunt up where Coach Easley lived. I know the general location; we'll just have to look for the place."

"You think something might still be there?"

"Probably not, but you never know. People

leave all sorts of crap behind in a house when they move."

"Whoever packed up his things should have cleaned out the house."

"We won't know until we look. There might be an attic space, or a partial basement."

And Knox wouldn't rest until he'd checked it out. Even when logic told him there wouldn't be anything left, he still had to see for himself.

Mrs. Edie Proctor was reluctant to open the door to them, even when Knox showed her his badge. She scowled at them through a latched screen door. "How do I know that badge is real?"

"You can call the sheriff's department and ask," he said without any hint of impatience.

"Humph," she said, staying where she was. From what Nikita could tell through the screen, Mrs. Proctor's mouth was drawn down in a permanent frown.

"What is it you want to ask?" she finally said. She didn't open the screen door, but she didn't close the wooden one, either. Cool air poured out of the house, evaporating the light film of sweat on their skin. The day promised to be another hot one.

"It's about Coach Howard Easley. He committed suicide twenty years ago—"

"I know how he died," she snapped. "What's that got to do with anything now?"

"You hired him, didn't you?"

"He was qualified."

"Yes, ma'am, he was. He had a masters degree in physics from Cal Tech. Any idea why he settled for coaching football at a little high school in eastern Kentucky?"

"I didn't ask."

That line of questioning was unproductive, Nikita thought. Knox must have thought so, too, because he smoothly changed course. "I'd like to see his application, if you know where it is after all these years."

"I didn't keep papers like that here at my house. I don't know why you're bothering me with all this. If you want to know something, go to the board of education. Likely all those old papers are still there in the basement."

Then she did shut the wooden door, leaving them standing on the sidewalk. Knox scratched his jaw. "That went well, don't you think?"

"Reasonably. We still have all our parts. Do we go to the board of education now?"

"Let me make a phone call first. It's summer; there may not be anyone there."

He had a phone book in his car and he quickly located the number. Thirty seconds later he ended the call. "Summer hours are eight to twelve, Monday through Thursday. No one's there at all today."

"You could call the present superintendent."

He tried that, and ended the call without speaking. "Another answering machine. Okay, that's a dead end for right now. Let's go see what we can find at Coach Easley's house."

29

COACH EASLEY'S OLD HOME WAS A DILAPI-
dated hull, badly overgrown with bushes and
saplings; one side of the house had collapsed,
and vines had overrun the wreckage, making it
impossible to tell anything about what the
rooms might have been or even where it was
safe to step.

There wasn't a yard anymore, just a more
level place for the weeds and bushes to grow.
The garage was to the rear of the house, and
what had been the driveway was choked with
waist-high weeds, honeysuckle vines, and ram-
bling blackberry bushes. "Chigger city," Knox
announced when they got out of the car to
see exactly what they were facing. "And this is
definitely snake territory; lots of hiding places
for them."

"I'm a city girl; I don't know what chiggers are."

"Tiny bastards that burrow into your skin and itch like a son of a bitch."

That sounded nasty. "The things I do in the line of duty," she muttered.

Knox removed his jacket and laid it on the seat, then opened the trunk and took out his boots. Today he had on athletic shoes, the same as she did. "Here," he said. "You put on the boots."

She stared at him in disbelief. "How would I walk in them? How would I even keep them on? You wear them; you'll have to be the point man, because you're big enough to fight this jungle." His chivalry touched her, because he was genuinely worried about her lack of protection and was willing to give up his boots to her.

To her relief he didn't argue, probably because he saw she was right about him having to be the point man. From a box in the trunk he took a green can and tossed it to her. "Spray that on every inch of bare skin. It's insect repellent. Spray your clothes, too."

Quickly she read the instructions, sprayed herself, then tossed the can back to him for him to do the same. While he was putting on his boots and getting other items out of the trunk, she clipped her holster to her waistband and slipped the pen laser into her pocket; she might need it, wading into that jungle. In a pinch she supposed she could use the laser to clear a tree out of the way, but then there would be the danger of setting everything on fire, plus the laser didn't have an inexhaustible power source. She didn't want to use it if she didn't have to. She wouldn't hesitate, however, to blast a snake.

When Knox closed the trunk, she saw that he carried a slim, round stick in one hand and a hatchet in the other. "Sawed-off broomstick," he said, seeing her looking at the stick. "Great for poking into places where you don't want to stick your hand."

Then he waded into the wild tangle of over-growth. He used the stick to poke the ground in front of him, and the hatchet to hack away at bushes so thick he couldn't push through them. Briars snagged at their clothing, bit through cloth; untangling themselves took time, but the only other option was to just jerk free, which left painful scratches. Within a minute they were both sweating in the humid heat and had covered about half the distance to the garage.

"Damn, what I wouldn't give for a rain shower to cool things off," he muttered. He paused to eye the sky, which seemed to have a yellowish tint to the blue. "Might get one this afternoon, from the looks of that sky."

"What makes you say so?" she asked. Nikita was always annoyed by people who would look at a perfectly sunny sky and announce that rain was on the way. Unless one lived in a desert region, rain was **always** on the way, sooner or later. She couldn't see anything unusual about the sky; it wasn't as clear as it had been, but there were no dark clouds, either.

"The feel of the air. It's too humid, which is thunderstorm-making. And the yellowish color is the leading edge of a front."

That she understood; his comment was based on science, rather than folklore. Not that folklore wasn't often right, but she was more comfortable with facts.

Their chances of finding something of value were small, but if anything remained from twenty years before, it would probably be in the garage. The house was far more likely to have been cleaned out before each occupancy, as whatever bits and pieces left behind would be swept up and put in the trash. A garage was different, the receptacle of things people no longer wanted but didn't want to get rid of, either. She supposed it was sheer stubbornness that made them try at all, that and that Knox evidently couldn't leave any stone unturned or any condemned property unexplored.

They disturbed swarms of gnats and mosquitoes, a field mouse ran across her shoe and nearly gave her a heart attack, and when they finally reached what remained of the garage, she

took one good look at it and shook her head.
"That's a death trap. I'm not going in there."

What remained of the rickety walls swayed at
the slightest touch. There were huge holes in
the Swiss-cheese roof; evidently an entire flock
of birds lived inside, because they noisily va-
cated when Knox experimentally shook the
frame.

"I don't want you in there," he said absently.
"It's dangerous enough with just one person
moving things around. But I think I'll cut some
saplings to brace the walls, just in case."

"If those walls are so rickety that a couple of
sticks will make a difference, then no one in his
right mind will go in. **Right mind** is the opera-
tive phrase, of course."

He gave her a quick grin. "You just have to
look at this as an adventure."

"**You** look at it as an adventure. **I'll** look at it
as dangerous and idiotic."

"Everyone has a role in life." As he spoke he
grabbed a sapling and bent over, hacking away
until he severed it close to the bottom. Another
few quick strokes trimmed away the limbs and
the willowy top. He was left with about seven
feet of fairly sturdy, green wood. He found
several more saplings that he judged strong
enough, and chopped them down, too.

Realizing she wasn't going to stop him with
an application of common sense, Nikita set her-

self to helping him. The saplings he'd cut were surprisingly heavy, which made her feel better because it meant they were stronger than she'd thought. She helped him drag them over to the garage, and stood ready to jam one against the wall if it showed signs of falling on him while he wedged the first one into place.

Finding a non-rotten place on the wall was the trick; even an iron railing wouldn't do any good if the end punched right through the wood. The outer framework was stable enough, and he put the first brace there.

While he was searching for a place to put the second brace, Nikita stepped back and studied the structure. It was big enough to house one vehicle, and there was no sign there had ever been doors that could be closed. It was essentially a large, three-sided shed, with some storage space added onto the right side. The storage space was an afterthought; even with the years of neglect, she could see that the wood on the right side was in better shape, as if it was newer.

She took the broomstick and worked her way around to the right, poking and prodding to dislodge any reptile bush-dwellers. From the front, it looked as if the overgrowth had completely swallowed that side of the building, hiding any openings that might exist. Once she moved to the side, though, she could plainly see

where a door had been. There wasn't one there
now, just the black hole of an entrance.

"There's a doorway over here," she called.
"Looks like a storage space."

Knox appeared beside her, wiping the sweat
from his dirty face. "Newer, too," he said, noticing the same thing she'd noticed. "This may be
where he worked on his model planes. Stay
here—"

"My ass," she replied equably. "I won't go in
that other side, but this part doesn't look as
suicidal."

"That's my girl." He grabbed her and gave
her a quick, warm kiss that wasn't enough for either of them. She fisted her hand in his T-shirt
and drew him back, holding him for a more
leisurely, deeper effort. He dropped the hatchet
and clamped both hands on her ass, lifting her
up and against the hard swell of his penis.

"God," he said, abruptly dropping her back
on her heels. "We can't do this now, and we especially can't do it here."

She blew out a shaky breath. "I agree. You
can't touch me again until tonight, not even for
just a kiss."

"I don't think you have to go that far."

"I do." She looked around; if the kiss had
gone on much longer, she might have been taking off her clothing right here, surrounded by

mice, briars, and assorted other unpleasantness. "Let's look around and get out of here. I don't like all of this out-of-control greenery. The forest is one thing; this is a bit spooky."

"Because Howard hung himself from that tree over there?"

"No, it's because people used to live here but now it's abandoned and rotting, and soon there won't be anything left to show they were here. Also, I think I'm bleeding in a dozen different places from these damn briars—" She stopped as she felt something crawling on her arm. She looked down, made a quick sound of disgust, and slapped a bug away. "I'm also not fond of bugs, and I hate mice."

"Got it. I'll hurry."

He bent and picked up the hatchet, then set to work clearing away the vines and bushes that almost obscured the opening. He poked his head inside. "There's a lot of stuff in here," he finally said.

"What kind of stuff?"

"Rotten cardboard boxes, for one thing. Some sort of clamp set up on a board; he must have used it to hold the models while he worked on them. A stack of **Playboy** magazines that I wouldn't touch for love nor money; looks like rats have been living in them for years."

She knew what the magazine was, because it

had existed for almost a hundred years before becoming defunct. Some carefully preserved issues
were occasionally sold at auction, where collectors bought them for ridiculously high prices.
They would cry to see these issues abandoned
and rotting. She thought it would be a mercy
not to tell Knox how much they would be
worth in her time.

"Wouldn't all of this have been thoroughly
searched at the time of his suicide?"

"I can't say. It should have been, but from
everything I've heard or read, there were no
signs of foul play; so I don't think there was ever
a criminal investigation. In a case of suicide,
you try to help the family as much as possible."

He stepped inside the storage area, and
Nikita carefully followed, watching where she
put her feet. The thick, musty smell of rot
filled her nostrils. Junk was piled helter-skelter
in the small space: folding metal lawn chairs,
discarded clothing, stacks of magazines and
newspapers, the cardboard boxes Knox had
mentioned. There were two of them, stacked,
taped across the top, which was useless now because their bottoms would probably fall out as
soon as they were moved.

"Why would anyone go to the trouble to box
something up and tape it, then just leave it behind?" she wondered aloud.

"I wonder why people do a lot of things," he said with a grunt as he booted a chair out of the way.

She didn't want to touch those nasty boxes, but she didn't see any way out of it. "Do you have a blanket or tarp in the trunk? Those things will disintegrate when we try to move them. If we can pull them onto a tarp, then we can drag them out of here."

He took his keys from his pocket. "There's a tarp. It's in the bottom of the box I keep in there."

She made her way back to the car and unlocked the trunk, then dug through a box of equipment and found the green tarp. She also plucked two pairs of plastic gloves from a package that was also in the box.

"Here," she said when she reached the garage again, handing him his keys, then a pair of gloves.

"Thanks." He snapped the gloves on like a surgeon, and took the tarp from her. She pulled on her own gloves, and working carefully, they spread the tarp out in front of the boxes. Knox used the hatchet to swipe down some monstrous spiderwebs that hung close to the boxes; then they each carefully moved into the cramped space, one on each side.

As gingerly as possible they shifted the top box, sliding it instead of jerking and lifting, while trying to support the bottom with their hands. It was useless; as soon as the weight of the contents weren't supported by the box underneath, the box tore apart and dumped the contents onto the tarp.

The same thing happened with the bottom box. As soon as they lifted it, the bottom tore out. By dropping and shoving, they managed to get half the box on the tarp. The spilled contents seemed to be mostly textbooks, stained and musty, but in fairly good shape. They began moving the textbooks to the tarp; they might have belonged to Howard Easley, in which case he might have written something in the margins, or left a paper stuck between the pages.

Knox made a soft sound, staring at a metal box that had been packed in with the textbooks.

"What is it?" Nikita asked as he picked it up.

He glanced up at her, his expression both surprised and gleeful. "I'm not certain, but I think it's the time capsule."

30

Nikita looked down at the box. Silly of her, but she'd been expecting something that was shaped like a cylinder, like a capsule of medication. The phrase "time capsule" brought to mind something sleek and capable of traveling through time, not a rather large metal box that was about eighteen by twelve inches, and perhaps five inches high. "Are you certain?"

"Not until we open it, no. The time capsule was wrapped in waterproof plastic before it was buried, too. But it was this shape; I think it was custom-made at a local metalworking plant."

The box was in surprisingly good condition, insulated as it had been all those years by the heavy textbooks. She squatted next to it, carefully looking it over but not touching it. "It's been here all these years; it wasn't buried beneath the flagpole at all."

"I watched them bury it. The coach must have come back that night and dug it up again. It was New Year's night, cold, snowing, the bowl games were on; I doubt there was any traffic at all in town, if he timed it right, waited until the third-shift deputies left on patrol." He squatted next to her. "There goes your theory that someone was sent in ahead of Hugh and got the box for safekeeping."

"Then the flash must have been Hugh transiting in; with a laser, he could have dug that hole in no time, found out the box wasn't there, and left before the security cameras caught up in time."

"Then he must have transitioned right back out, because there were no footprints, anything to show how he did it. I thought these links were like a two-lane highway, with no exit points other than the beginning and end. Wouldn't he have gone back to your time?"

"Theoretically, it depends on the link settings," she said slowly. "I heard that the Transit Laboratory was working to develop links that could be programmed in the field, but I haven't heard that they're certified for use yet. The regular links have two settings: one for the destination, and one for home. The traveler activates the setting needed. If Hugh is transiting short distances back and forth, then he must have stolen the prototypes."

"That's damn interesting," Knox drawled. "Explains how the killer got into Taylor Allen's house and out again without touching anything that we could tell. I thought he'd wiped his prints off the doorknobs and gone out through the automatic garage doors, but if Hugh is just popping in and out, he could show up any-where."

Nikita's hair lifted and she automatically looked around, then blew out a relieved breath. "He'd have to know exactly where we are and have the GPS coordinates before he could tran-sition to us. He wouldn't want to do that any-way unless he could be certain he was in a position where we couldn't see him. Remember what happened to Luttrell? The traveler is at a disadvantage until the transition is complete."

"If we go back to my house, he **has** the exact coordinates," Knox pointed out. "I don't know how he tracked you there—"

"I do," Nikita interrupted. "Mrs. Lacey."

Knox opened his mouth, probably to auto-matically disagree, then abruptly shut it. A look of cold anger edged into his eyes. **Cops didn't believe in coincidence.** First Mrs. Lacey had seen them together at Wal-Mart, and been visi-bly upset by Nikita's presence; that very night she had made a horrible nuisance of herself by calling repeatedly, something that Knox thought was very much out of character for her. Then she had done something even more out of character by going to Knox's house and beating on the door. There had been a man with her last night; then, this morning, a car rented by Hugh Byron was parked just a few doors down from Knox's house. No, that was stretching happenstance way too far.

"He didn't know for certain who you were," Knox said, thinking aloud. "Otherwise he would have tried to kill you last night when you were alone."

"He'd have had a better chance of succeeding once you got home and we were otherwise occupied," she said drily. "I wouldn't have noticed then if he'd transitioned right beside the bed."

"Good point," he said, and winked at her.

"Before that, I was very much on edge, and watchful. If I was just someone named Tina, then there was no point in killing me. I think all he was trying to do last night and this morning was get a look at me."

"Think your disguise held?"

She shook her head. "I wouldn't bet my life on it. Remember, he's from my time; he knows how easy it is to change hair color. And we've worked in the same division for a couple of years, so he knows me. The disguise was mainly to fool your guys, remember? To put out the

story that I'd left town. Hugh would know better, but he didn't know where to look for me
until that chance meeting with Mrs. Lacey;
then she must have told him about it and he put
two and two together."

"She can't have any idea what's really going on," Knox said. "She isn't . . ." His voice
trailed off and he stared into the distance for
a moment. "Shit," he finally said, very softly.
"There's only one thing that would pull her into
this. The son of a bitch has told her she can go
back and save Rebecca. She has no one else;
there was just Rebecca. She'd do anything to get
her back."

Nikita briefly closed her eyes as she instantly
switched from being extremely annoyed with
Mrs. Lacey to feeling such deep pity for her she
could scarcely bear it. She knew how her own
mother had suffered from the loss of a child,
even with a loving husband and three other
children to give her comfort. Mrs. Lacey was
alone. Damn Hugh Byron for being such a
cold-blooded son of a bitch, to use a mother's
grief and desperation.

"She must be the one who shot at me,"
Nikita said. "Do you know if she's proficient
with weapons?"

"I don't know. A lot of women know how to
shoot, especially if they grew up out in the

country." He looked down at the metal box, his expression grim. "I say we find out just what the hell is in here that this bastard has murdered three people for."

He picked up the box and carried it out of the rickety building. Nikita hesitated, then grabbed one end of the tarp and hauled it out with its load of books. Knox was already hunkered down in a sunny patch amid the weeds and briars, working at the lid of the box. It didn't have a padlock, but after years of not being opened, the custom fit of the lid had become even tighter. Finally he wedged the sharp edge of the hatchet under the edge of the lid and jerked upward; the lid flew open, exposing the contents.

Carefully he began taking out each item, handing them in turn to Nikita, who placed them on the tarp. They were:

A yearbook
A newspaper
A cassette tape
A cassette player
Pekeville's articles of incorporation
A written history of the county and town
Assorted photographs
A handwritten letter from the mayor,
    Harlan Forbes

The 1985 Peke County telephone book
A list of all the Peke County residents who
    had died in war
A carefully folded American flag that had
    flown at the Peke County Courthouse
A Sears catalog

Knox gaped at the catalog, then collapsed
on his butt in the weeds, holding his sides and
howling with laughter. "I don't believe it," he
gasped. "A Sears catalog! Who in hell put that in
a time capsule? Either they were drunk when
they thought that one up, or somebody had a
sense of humor."

Nikita had lifted the heavy catalog and was
gently leafing through the pages. "Oh, I don't
know. I think this would give a fairly good picture of what life was like in 1985. Look, it has
prices, descriptions, pictures. This could be very
valuable both as a collector's item and in the information it gives."

"Well, unless it gives the formula for time
travel, we struck out. I **know** thirteen things
were put in the box, so where's the thirteenth
item? Did Coach Easley take something **out**?"

"Then why not just take out that one item
and leave the box there?" Nikita asked reasonably. "There wasn't any need to take the whole
box if one thing was all he wanted."

"The man committed suicide a little later; he wasn't exactly in a logical frame of mind."

She lifted the heavy catalog and fanned the pages. To her utter surprise, because she hadn't really thought she'd find anything, a piece of white paper fluttered out onto the tarp.

Knox reached out and picked it up, read it.

"What does it say?"

"It's his suicide note, I guess. **'To hell with it. I'm tired of this fucking mess.'** Quote, un-quote. And why in hell he tucked it inside a Sears catalog, in a time capsule, then sealed the capsule in a box of books, I don't have a clue. I'd say he went nuts."

"Some sort of psychological breakdown. It happens; the brain chemicals alter, and we still don't know why."

"See if there's anything else stuck in there. We might luck out."

She shook the catalog again, but nothing fell out. Disappointed, she sat on the tarp and looked at everything he'd taken out of the box. Perhaps the newspaper— Carefully she examined it, because the pages already had a brittle feel to them, but nothing was inserted inside the folds of newsprint. The articles of incorporation were just that, without any extra sheets of paper added.

Knox went through the yearbook, without

results. They looked at the backs of all the photographs, but all that had been written on them were names, dates, and places. The mayor's letter was one page. The written history was just a written history. Frustrated but careful not to disturb the folds, Knox even searched the flag.

"Hell, all that's left to do is listen to the cassette, see if there's anything other than music on it," he said, picking up the tape and examining it. "Not that we can, because the batteries will be dead—assuming they even put in batteries, considering it would have been a waste of money." Dropping the tape, he picked up the small tape player and was about to turn it over when he stopped and said quietly, "There's a tape already in the player."

They drove to the nearest convenience store and bought some AA batteries, which Knox installed in the back of the cassette player. Sitting in the car, he punched **Play . . .** and the number one song of 1984, "Thriller," filled the air. Grimacing, he stopped the tape and took it out. "I always hated that song," he grumbled. "My favorite Michael Jackson song was 'Ben.' It was about a rat."

"That's scary," she remarked.

"You should see the video for 'Thriller'; now that's scary."

He popped the other cassette into place, and hit **Play.**

There was some static, then a very quiet voice began talking. "This is to David Li, Marjorie van Camp, and JoJo Netzer. You guys will know what to do." The voice then began to talk about gravity modification, and went into mathematical theories and formulas that made absolutely no sense to them, but was very probably what they had been looking for. The tape ended, "Sorry I won't be here to help. I'm checking out."

Knox rewound the tape, then took it out. "Well, that's the thirteenth item, and what Hugh is looking for. I don't think he belongs to any Luddite group, though; he's too willing to use the technology. He wants this tape, but not because he wants to stop time travel technology from being invented."

"No," Nikita agreed. "I thought—we were meant to think—that was the reason, but I agree that scenario doesn't fit Hugh. He isn't anti-time-travel; he was one of the most enthusiastic about it. I don't really care why he wants it. We have it, we need to keep it safe, and we have to apprehend Hugh. Everything else is secondary."

"You say he isn't likely to materialize in front of us. What's his most likely action, then?"

"He has a laser. All he needs is a clear shot."

"Then we're going to ground," Knox said. "I may get my ass fired, but I'm taking some time off work, starting right now. We have the advantage in that we know he's looking for you, so we pretty much know **where** he'll be looking. We just have to make sure we see him first."

"I have a gift for you," Hugh Byron said to Ruth as they lay together on a blanket next to a meandering stream. He was in a good mood; he knew where to find Stover, and within the next few hours he would eliminate that particular problem. She knew too much about everything. He couldn't take the chance that she would ever return to tell tales. McElroy was supposed to handle things on that end, but errors were occasionally made; witness Stover's presence here.

She smiled but didn't open her eyes. She was half dozing, tired after making love. "What?"

"Look," he said, and she opened her eyes. Her gaze fastened on the items he presented to her.

"What do I do?" she whispered, still not looking away from them.

"You put one on each wrist and ankle. When the time comes, I'll show you how to activate them. Promise me you won't try to use them without me; it can be very dangerous."

"I promise," she said, reaching out to touch

the links with trembling fingers. "They look so . . . ordinary. Are they yours? How will you get back if I have them?"

"They're not mine, they're Stover's. I found where she buried them." Someone had screwed up the timing of her transition; McElroy was supposed to make sure the next agent sent came through at a certain time and place, so Hugh could take care of that agent the same way he had Houseman, but when Hugh was en route, he saw the bright flash and knew he was too late. By the time he got there, Stover had already transitioned and disappeared.

The only satisfaction he'd been able to gain was in locating her links and taking them, making sure she couldn't return. Finding them hadn't been particularly difficult; the book said to bury them at the transition point so the agent would know exactly where they were, and Stover went by the book. All he'd had to do was locate the disturbed area of leaves and dirt, and dig them up.

"I can't wait to see her again," Ruth said. "I've been going over and over in my head what I'll say to her, to make her go to the doctor and have those tests run. She's so—she could be so stubborn sometimes. She was busy, with the wedding coming up and trying to get everything ready. She won't want to go. I'll have to make her listen."

"You'll think of something." He smiled a little. "You might have to demonstrate the links before she'll believe you."

"You'll show me how to do that?"

"Yes, but you have to be very careful and do exactly as I demonstrate."

"I will." She hesitated. "When will I go back?"

"When Stover's dead."

Pain flashed across Ruth's face. "I wish she didn't have to die."

"She has to for my mission to succeed. I don't want to kill her, I **have** to kill her. And if I don't succeed, if she manages to kill me, remember that she'll be hunting for those links and she's a highly skilled agent. She has to suspect I have them. She'll reconstruct my movements, discover where I've been, and then she'll come after you. If I don't kill her, Ruth, you'll have to. It's the only way you'll be able to save Rebecca."

31

"HE'LL BE WAITING WHEN WE GO HOME," Nikita said. "He'll prefer darkness, but if he has a clear shot at me, he'll take it, regardless of the time of day."

"Then I'll have to take someone home with me besides you."

She knew what he meant. He needed a woman, but someone who, when she got out of the car, was recognizably **not** Nikita. Hugh would be in his rental car; Knox would call Nikita's cell phone and give her the location of the car. In the meantime, she would be approaching on foot. While Hugh was watching Knox's house, she would be slipping up behind him. She and Knox would have him caught between them.

The plan wasn't without risk, to both of

them. There was no armor invented, in either this time or hers, that could withstand a laser weapon. But she had a laser, too, and come to that, a bullet could kill someone just as dead. They would have Hugh outnumbered. The odds were in their favor, but nothing was certain.

After their adventure at Howard Easley's old house, they were both sweaty and filthy. Knox called his father and asked if they could shower and wash their clothes at his house while he and Lynnette were at work. Kelvin, as usual, asked no questions.

Knox knew where the extra key was, so they drove straight out there. "You know how to work the laundry machine," Nikita said as they got out of the car. She pulled her T-shirt off over her head and tossed it to him. "You do that while I get in the shower."

Women in her time wore breast bands instead of bras, as they provided better support and were far more comfortable. They fastened by pressing the two overlapping ends of fabric together, so they were completely adjustable. Since her sojourn in the weeds and bushes, however, she felt as if tiny bugs were crawling all over her, and she was dreadfully afraid she had contracted a severe case of chiggers. The breast band came off, and she tossed that to Knox, too.

He fumbled for the key, not taking his gaze

from her as she bent to take off her shoes. "Are you going to completely undress out here?" he asked with considerable interest.

"If it takes you much longer to get that door open, then—yes." She threw her socks at him and unfastened her jeans, pushing them down her legs and stepping out of them. Grit scraped at her tender bare feet and made her toes curl. He'd finally found the key but was having a difficult time getting it to fit into the lock. She tossed her jeans over his shoulder and pushed her underpants down. "Hurry!"

"I can't," he said.

"You could if you'd look at what you're doing instead of at me!"

"I can't," he said again. "Jesus God!"

She tossed her underpants into his arms and shouldered him aside, unlocking the door herself. He dropped everything and reached for her just as the door opened. She burst through, skidded to a stop in the kitchen, and said, "Where's the bathroom?"

"Straight ahead, turn right, second door on the left."

The crawling sensation was so horrible she jumped into the shower before the running water had a chance to get hot. She yelped at the cold water, but even if it had been freezing cold, that was preferable to bugs.

She had already soaped down and rinsed off

when the shower curtain was jerked aside and a tall, naked man got into the tub with her.

"You're getting the floor wet," she said.

"I'll mop the water up later." He moved closer, crowding her, pressing her against the cold tile. His penis was so stiff it was curving upward, poking her in the belly.

She put her hands against his shoulders and pushed, moving him back. "I'm nice and clean, but you're all grimy and buggy. Just stand there and I'll take care of the problem."

His eyes were hot and narrow, but he did as she told him. His head was lowered and his gaze locked on her as she squirted a huge amount of liquid soap into her hands and started at his chest and shoulders, working up a great deal of lather. She washed his arms and back, his belly, then started at his feet and worked up. She darted a quick glance at him and saw that his jaw was locked and rigid, his throat working as he made himself stand there. She didn't look up after that, concentrating on what she was doing, smoothing her soapy hands over and between his buttocks. He made a choked sound, then was silent except for the harsh rush of his breathing.

She took a long time to wash his penis. By the time she finished his head was bowed and his entire body was quivering, one arm braced against the wall while his other hand was knotted in her wet hair. She simply leaned forward and took him in her mouth, holding him with her right hand and with her left gripping his ass and pulling him to her. A ragged sound tore out of his throat and his hips bucked; when she sensed he was on the verge of climax, she pulled away and stood.

Before she could wipe the water out of her face, he had her pinned against the wall, one thigh hooked around his waist, and he shoved himself into her so hard she couldn't stop the small scream that escaped. He didn't apologize, just pulled back and shoved again, and again. She had known that she was pushing him so far she likely wouldn't have time to climax but thought his response was well worth having to wait for her own pleasure; to her surprise, that hard, rolling rhythm pushed her into a fierce climax that left her weak and clinging to him for support. He lifted her completely off her feet and hammered into her, too far gone for even the pretense of consideration or sophistication, left with nothing but the blind, single-minded drive to orgasm.

Gradually she noticed that the water had gone cold. She fumbled for the control and turned off the shower. He remained collapsed against her, his chest heaving, his head resting heavily on her shoulder. If she hadn't been pinned against the wall, she couldn't have remained upright herself. She had wanted to play with him, tease him, but somewhere along the way they had both been sucked into a powerful whirlpool that had been too strong to deny or control.

"It's too soon to say I love you," he muttered against her shoulder. "We've known each other three days. So I'm not saying it."

"I'm not saying it, either," she whispered, as if by her silence she could deny the storm winds of emotion that were already swirling.

"I have an idea," Ruth said. Since Byron had given her the links, she had grown increasingly anxious. She could feel them burning into her skin, even though she wasn't wearing them. In her mind the links were snapped around her wrists and ankles; in her mind, she was seconds away from seeing Rebecca again, and snatching her from the cold hand of death. Why did she have to wait? What difference did it make to her if that Stover woman was still alive? She, Ruth, had the links. She had the means to reach her daughter. Byron made his lethal plans and was as patient as a spider, but it wasn't his daughter in a grave.

For days she had been drunk with passion and infatuation, but abruptly she was so impatient with him she wanted to grab him and shake him. How dare he give her the means to reach her daughter and then make her promise not to go until **he** decided it was time? She couldn't bear it.

He wanted to take this Stover woman when she was alone, something about not wanting to kill another cop. He meant Knox, of course, because Stover was a cop, too, but evidently she didn't count. Ruth had always loved Knox, but abruptly he didn't count, either. If it was he who was standing in the way of her seeing Rebecca again, then she didn't care if he got in the line of fire. Besides, when she went back to save Rebecca, he'd be alive then, too, wouldn't he? When she saved Rebecca, everything would change, and this would never happen, so it wasn't as if she were really risking Knox's life.

He was sleeping with that Stover woman. He had forsaken Rebecca.

But she knew Knox, knew his habits, knew how close he was to his father. A thought bloomed, and that was when she said, "I have an idea."

Byron turned to her, immediately attentive. Her impatience with him faded, because he always **listened** to her.

"I think I can find Knox," she said.

"How?"

"His father."

"How so? I refuse to kidnap his father in order to bait a trap. The more people are involved, the greater the chance for failure."

"No, no, of course I don't want you to kidnap him. All I have to do is call him and ask if he knows where Knox is. He might **not** know, but it's worth a shot, because they have such a close relationship."

He thought that over for a moment; she could also see him adding up the pros and cons. Finally he said, "Normally I would say it's too risky to connect your name to his, considering what our intentions are, but since you'll be leaving, I don't see that it matters."

It didn't matter anyway, she thought with another swift spurt of impatience. What mattered was getting to Rebecca.

She looked up the number of the hardware store and called it on her cell phone. Kelvin answered, his voice so much like Knox's that for a moment she was taken aback.

"Kelvin, this is Ruth Lacey. I've been trying to get in touch with Knox all day and I'm not having any luck. Do you know where he is?"

"Sure. He's at my house, taking a shower and doing laundry. I didn't ask any questions," he said, laughing. "I figure the less I know, the fewer gray hairs I'll have."

She laughed, too, then said, "Thanks. I'll get in touch with him there." She clicked off the call and with a triumphant expression turned to Byron. "He's at Kelvin's house, taking a shower and washing clothes, according to Kelvin. And if Knox is there, you can bet Stover is, too."

After Ruth hung up, Kelvin went back to stocking merchandise and waiting on his customers, but something kept nagging at him. When Knox had called to ask about using the house, he hadn't said not to tell anyone where he was, but maybe he figured he didn't need to say it, that Kelvin would automatically know what to keep quiet about and what didn't matter. Kelvin didn't automatically know, and that worried him.

Fifteen minutes later he gave in to his worries and called Knox's cell phone.

"Yeah, Dad, what's up?"

The wonders of Caller ID, Kelvin thought. "Are you all showered and laundered?"

"Showered, and the clothes are in the dryer. Is that why you called?"

"Reckon not. You didn't say, but was I supposed to keep quiet about where you are?"

"Meaning it's too late?"

"Yeah, afraid so. Ruth Lacey called, saying she'd been trying to get in touch with you all day. I didn't think anything about it, told her you were at my house. Has she called?"

"No, and she has my cell phone number anyway. She hasn't called it."

"Hmm. Guess this might be a heads-up, then. You should probably put your pants on."

"I'll be ready," Knox said. "Thanks for the warning."

Disconnecting the call, Knox turned to Nikita and said, "Ruth called Dad asking if he knew where I was. He told her. We'd better get dressed."

Their clothes weren't dry—except for Nikita's underwear, which seemed to dry within minutes—so they raided Kelvin's and Lynnette's closet. Knox was just a hair taller than his father, so Kelvin's jeans fit him fine. He grabbed the first shirt that came to hand and put it on, then pulled another one off a hanger and tossed it to Nikita. "Put this on, doesn't matter what it looks like. Just get dressed."

The first garment she'd pulled out was a pair of shorts, which thank goodness had an elastic waist, because Lynnette was about two sizes bigger. Nikita pulled them up her legs, her mind racing. "He won't just drive up. He'll stop and approach on foot, trying to take us by surprise. We can't assume his laser is like mine; he may have one like Luttrell's, with a much greater range. Get Luttrell's out of the trunk. I can show you how to use it; the aiming principle is the same except you don't have to allow for drop or wind. Just aim dead-on, and that's where the beam goes."

"You're his main target. You take that one, and give me your small laser."

"But he might **expect** me to have it. He doesn't know what equipment I brought, because I'm the one who chose it, not McElroy. You're more likely to take him by surprise than I am."

"Either way, we need to get the hell out of this house."

Nikita slid her bare feet into her sneakers, not stopping to tie them. Every second counted. Knox's sneakers were in the trunk of his car, and he didn't bother with his boots or take time to grab a pair of Kelvin's shoes. Instead he ran barefoot out the back door, grabbing his holster on the way out. Nikita jerked her purse from the kitchen table and was right behind him.

He'd just popped open the trunk when they heard the faint sound of a car on the road, moving slowly. Kelvin's driveway was so long that during the summer, when the trees and shrubbery were in full leaf, the road wasn't visible from the house. The sound stopped. Hugh had arrived.

There wasn't time for Nikita to show Knox how to use the XT37; he grabbed it out of the trunk and tossed it to her. "Over there," he said in a low, urgent voice, pointing to a thick line of shrubbery on the right. "Behind the shrubbery, on the ground. And for God's sake, don't get anywhere near the propane tank."

"The what?" she whispered.

"The big silver tank! It's gas." He pointed at the tank in question, closed the trunk, then took off running to the left. With any luck they'd catch Hugh in a cross fire. There wasn't any convenient shrubbery in this direction, which was why he'd sent Nikita the other way. He flattened himself behind an oak, hoping it was large enough to hide him, and drew his weapon.

The car started up again. He listened to the sound of the motor growing closer and closer; then it came into view as it crested the small, curving hill. Knox moved back just a fraction of an inch, trying not to make any sudden motions that would draw attention, but in that fraction of a second he'd recognized the car. It was Ruth Lacey.

She parked behind his car and got out. He glanced at her, slim and neat in oatmeal linen pants and a royal blue shirt, then turned his attention to where Hugh was probably working his way up the hill on foot. It broke his heart to see Ruth involved with the murdering bastard. She reminded him so much of Rebecca, the way she looked and moved, but in that instant he felt that soft spot in his heart crust over and harden. Because of her, Nikita's life was in danger. She had placed herself irrevocably on the other side.

She went up the front steps and rang the doorbell. If Kelvin hadn't warned them, if they hadn't already realized Ruth was helping Hugh, whoever had answered the door would have been a sitting duck. Knox studied where Hugh had most likely positioned himself, letting Ruth's location point the way to him. She would have been instructed to give him a clear shot.

Nikita wouldn't have been likely to answer the door, Knox thought; he himself would have done that. So had they planned to shoot him on sight, or try to draw both him and Nikita out of the house?

It didn't matter. Either way, Hugh planned on killing both of them, and Ruth knew it.

He saw a slight movement of the bushes. Could be a breeze, he thought, except it seemed to be right where he'd placed Hugh, and nowhere else.

Ruth rang the doorbell again, waited, then knocked vigorously. "Knox!" she called. "Knox Davis, you answer this door! Your car is parked right here, so don't think you can pretend you're not in there."

She waited and listened, growing increasingly more agitated from the sound of it. Knox risked another look at her. She was pacing back and forth on the porch, fiddling with a pair of

silver bracelets. Suddenly she burst into tears—
and did something incredibly stupid. Whirling
to face away from the house, she shrieked,
"They aren't here! There's no sound at all inside!"

Instantly Knox knew what Hugh would do,
knew the flash of rage that would overwhelm
everything else, and he stepped out from behind
the tree already firing. A laser burst bored into
the house just to Ruth's left, then swung wildly
to the side. Nikita launched herself from the
shrubbery, firing as she ran to keep Hugh from
targeting Knox. Both of them plunged through
the bushes at the same time, and almost stum-
bled over the man lying on his side.

Knox's lucky shot couldn't have been any
better aimed if he'd been standing not ten feet
away. The bullet had entered at an angle, the
entrance wound just under Hugh's left arm, and
the exit wound had taken out a chunk of his
spine. If he lived he'd be paralyzed, but Knox
knew immediately Hugh wasn't going to live.
The damage to his left lung, and probably part
of his heart, was too great.

Still, Knox kicked the weapon away from
Hugh's hand, just in case. Nikita went down on
one bare knee beside the dying man. "You won't
live," she said steadily. "It's over. Why did you
do it? What did you want?"

Hugh's eyes were glazing over, his internal

organs shutting down. He managed to blink, though, and a ghastly smile curled his lips. "Money," he gasped. "Patent . . . the . . . process. Always . . . money." His eyes didn't close, his lips didn't stop smiling, but in the next instant he was no longer there. Nothing was emptier than a dead man's eyes, Knox thought.

"Money," Nikita repeated numbly. "All of that . . . because they wanted to patent the process and get rich. Nothing about issues or standards, just . . . money."

A thin, unholy wail sounded behind them. They both spun, weapons raised, but Ruth wasn't armed. She stood there staring at Hugh's body and the anguish made her face almost inhuman. She was gasping for air as if her lungs weren't working, as if her heart wasn't pumping, as if her brain couldn't comprehend what her eyes were seeing.

"Noooo," she moaned, her voice like the rustle of dry cornstalks.

Nikita suddenly straightened, her body going rigid. "You're wearing links," she said.

Ruth held both hands up in front of her face, staring from one wrist to the other as if she didn't recognize the bracelets she wore. Then, slowly, she began to back away. "They're your links," she said rawly. "Byron found them. He gave them to me. If you were dead, he said, I could go back and save her. You're here to find out how time travel started, and make sure it doesn't happen."

"Is that what he told you?" Nikita asked, making a visible effort to keep her voice even and nonthreatening.

Ruth's head bobbled as she continued to back away from them. "I won't let you stop me. I'll save her this time, and she and Knox will get married and have beautiful babies, and I'll never tell her he was unfaithful. It's our secret," she said to Knox, though her eyes were angry.

"My links won't take you back," Nikita said. "They'll only take you to my time. If he told you they'd take you back, he lied. His could be reprogrammed, but mine can't."

"You're lying. He programmed them for me. I'll be there in plenty of time to make her have medical tests that will find the aneurysm. I'll save my baby, and she'll live a long time and be very happy."

"No, those won't work that way—"

"You're lying!" Ruth abruptly screamed at her. "You want them back, but I'll never give them to you, I'll never—" She began fumbling with the bracelets, and with a muffled sound of alarm Nikita started forward. Remembering the blinding flash of before, Knox grabbed her and whirled her against him, hiding her face as he ducked his own down to protect his eyes.

Instead of the silent flash there was a sharp

crack; then a fine red mist seemed to float up before settling to earth. Nikita made a raw sound, jerking backward and dragging him with her. They didn't make it quite far enough, and the fine mist turned their skin and clothes red.

In silence they stared at where Ruth had been.

"He killed her," Nikita said rawly. "He tampered with the links, and he deliberately killed her." She looked up at Knox and a tear trickled down her cheek, leaving a white trail. "I can't go home."

He didn't want her to go home, but he said, "They'll send a SAR team after you, when you don't show up within a month, right?"

Slowly she shook her head. "The links— they're literally a link. As long as they exist, the master board in my time can tell they're still there. It's the metal, a special metal. We can't communicate through time, but they can always tell if something happens. They . . . they know my links were just in a catastrophic incident."

What she was saying began to sink in. "They think you're dead."

Her lips trembled, and the sheen of tears blinded her. "Yes. They think I'm dead. No one will come for me. I'll never see my family again."

Gently he took her hand and began leading

her back to the house. They both needed another shower, and he needed to think what explanation he was going to make about what had
happened here today. Hugh Byron would have
no viable identification, and his prints wouldn't
be in the AFIS system. Ruth . . . no longer existed. He felt numb, and he knew that when the
numbness wore off he would be sick, but he'd
handle that when it happened.

Right now, he had to take care of Nikita,
who was in shock and hurting over suddenly
finding herself permanently stranded, with no
way home.

"Maybe you can make do with me," he said.

One night seven months later, they cut the
fence that surrounded a construction site in
Miami and sneaked across to where the footprint of a high-rise was being laid. The past
seven months had been eventful. In the end he
had decided to let all questions go unanswered,
and dumped Hugh's body close to Luttrell's.
They still hadn't been found.

So far as anyone outside the family knew,
Ruth Lacey had just disappeared. Knox was a
cop; he knew how to make a car disappear so no
one would ever find it. He spent two weeks in
his father's barn, dismantling it, destroying VIN
and serial numbers, and generally reducing the
car to scrap metal.

They had also reburied the capsule under the flagpole for it to be found at the right time. Knox had simply told everyone that he'd found it in Coach Easley's old garage.

They'd told the truth to Kelvin and Lynnette. They had needed to explain the damage done to the house by Hugh's laser, and Nikita's bag of gadgets had convinced them that neither Knox nor Nikita had lost his or her mind. It was a secret the four of them would take to the grave.

"You're sure this is the building that will be torn down two hundred years from now?" he hissed as they stepped around a wheelbarrow that had been tipped on its side. He was carrying a thick, heavy package.

"I'm sure," she hissed in return. "I don't recognize anything, but I know the name of the building. This is it."

He didn't argue, just placed the package inside one of the forms that were in place to mold the huge columns. Tomorrow morning, concrete would be poured inside those forms. "I hope this works."

"It has to," she said. Blindly she reached for his hand and clung to it, her grip so tight he could feel his fingers going numb.

"Maybe one day they'll come visit," he said.

"Maybe. When time travel becomes commercial, if it ever does. If they have the money."

"Well, you did your part in making it hap-

pen." He raised his hand, the one she was clinging to, and kissed her knuckles. "Have I told
you today that I love you?"

A smile broke over her face, replacing the
tears. "I believe you have," she said, and hand in
hand they slipped back through the fence, tugged
the wire back into place, and walked away.

Epilogue

Nicolette Stover took her grandson's plump little hand and steered him away from the potted geranium on the balcony, where a fat bee buzzed around the bright flower. Jemi was fascinated with both flower and bee, so it was best to remove him from temptation. He loudly protested and pulled away, toddling back toward the flower as fast as his fat little legs would take him. She scooped him up before he could reach it, swinging him high and blowing on his belly. Instantly his screech of protest changed to giggles.

She had to stay right with the little devil; their apartment was old, without the modern safeguards that would keep him safe. She and Aidan had once been comfortably established, but they had spent every credit they had for

Annora, then for Nikita. With two more children coming along, they had always hovered on
the edge of poverty, but she'd never begrudged a
penny spent on their babies. Things were much
better now, but they still hadn't been able to afford a newer apartment.

Since Agent McElroy had brought the news
of Nikita's death, Jemi was the only thing that
could lighten her heart. She had been through
this before, and survived because she'd had
Nikita. What would she do without her darling
girl, her miracle baby? How could she go on
without her? They didn't even have her physical
remains; according to Agent McElroy, there
weren't any. Time travel accidents didn't leave
even the smallest remnant.

She knew she wasn't the only one who was
suffering. Aidan often got up at night and wandered aimlessly through the apartment as if
looking for the daughter who would never return. Fair was distraught, lost without her older
sister. Even Connor seemed subdued. Only
Jemi was unaware of the sorrow that hovered
over his parents and grandparents, tackling each
day with the headlong fervor he'd inherited
from his father, because heaven knows, Connor
had never slowed down for a minute.

Jemi's very obliviousness was a balm to her, a
small, busy island of surcease. He played, he
jabbered, he shrieked and laughed and was for-

ever getting into places where he shouldn't be, and you didn't dare take your gaze from him for a single minute or he'd find something else to get into. She kept him as often as possible, not only to give Connor and Enya a chance to relax, but also because he was good for her and Aidan. He pulled them out of themselves and their sorrow, reminded them that life did go on and here it was right in front of them, in the form of an adorable toddler.

The security chimes rang, signaling someone wished admittance. Carrying Jemi, Nicolette went over to the video console and pressed a button. The image of a deliveryman dressed in brown appeared on the screen. She pressed the audio button. "Yes?"

"Nicolette and Aidan Stover?"

"This is Nicolette Stover."

"A package for you." He paused. "It was discovered by accident in the construction site over on Wilshire. It—uh—is very old."

"Who is it from?"

"It doesn't say. We scanned it to make certain it's safe." He paused, then reiterated, "It's **very** old."

Because he seemed to want her to ask, Nicolette said, "How old is it?" expecting it to be something she had ordered several years ago that was never delivered.

"Um—about two hundred years old. The delivery charge was prepaid, so we will fulfill our contracted duty. I do wonder if you could tell me, though, how a package this old could have your address on it?"

"I don't know." Since Agent McElroy had told them how Nikita had died, the issue of time travel had been very much on her mind. Obviously someone was playing some sort of joke, sending a package back in time to be delivered two hundred years later. If it was a joke, she absolved the person of maliciousness because the nature of Nikita's death wasn't generally known, but neither did she find it funny. "Do I have to sign for it?"

"No signature required."

She opened the old-fashioned delivery chute, and he placed the package in it, then gave the camera a two-fingered salute and rushed back to the street, continuing his daily mad rush to make all his assigned deliveries.

A soft bell signaled the arrival of the package. Still keeping a firm hold on Jemi, who was trying his best to wriggle free, she opened the delivery chute and took out the package. It was surprisingly heavy, and she dropped it; the thud made Jemi laugh.

It didn't sound as if the package contained anything breakable. "Aidan?" she called. "Would you either take Jemi for a few minutes so I can open this package, or you do the honors and I'll hold him?"

Aidan came out of his office. His thick hair was still dark, his eyes a warm brown that he had passed on to all of his children. After forty years of marriage, they still loved each other, and she hoped they would have at least forty or fifty more together.

"What is it?" he asked.

"I don't know. The deliveryman said it was found at the construction site on Wilshire, and that it was shipped to us two hundred years ago."

His face tightened. "That isn't funny."

"I know," she said, and sighed. "I don't understand it, either."

He picked up the package, weighing it in his hand. "Several pounds, at least," he muttered. The large, heavy-duty envelope was made of plastic, otherwise it would never have lasted so long. The delivery address had also been covered with a clear plastic film.

He tried to tear open the envelope, but it resisted his effort. He fetched the scissors to cut it open, dumping out several smaller clear packs and two single sheets that were each encased in more clear plastic.

He picked up the first sheet, read the first few words, and turned pale. He swayed, then abruptly sat down.

"Aidan!" Alarmed, Nicolette started to put Jemi down so she could check on her husband. The toddler, who had been struggling to get down, abruptly shrieked in protest at getting what he'd asked for, clinging to her like a monkey with both arms and legs.

"It's from Nikita," he whispered, and this time it was Nicolette whose legs wouldn't hold her.

"She sent it before she died." Without even knowing what was in it, this posthumous letter was like a knife through her heart. At the same time she reached eagerly for it. "What does it say?"

Even Aidan's lips were white. "It says, **Dear Mom and Dad, I'm not dead.**"

"Oh, dear God!" Nicolette burst into tears, in her frenzy holding Jemi close to her and rocking him back and forth. "Dear God," she said again. "Read it all!"

He moistened his lips and in a shaky voice began reading.

I suppose I am by the time you'll get this, but if you ever get the opportunity to come back to 2005 or later, I'll be around. I'm living in a little town in eastern Kentucky called Pekesville, with my husband, a wonderful man named Knox Davis.

My links were sabotaged and I wasn't able to get back. Agent McElroy is part of a conspiracy of murder, but whatever you do, DON'T try to confront him. If there is to be justice for what he's done, it will have to come from the hands of others. I hate that he can't be forced to account for what he's done, but the main thing you must remember is, he failed—and I didn't.

Because McElroy told everyone I'm dead—by the way, he truly thinks I am dead—no SAR was sent for me. I deeply regret not being able to come back and spare you the pain I know you must have been feeling, but in the end I couldn't have stayed. This time is more primitive, of course, but here I'm not treated with suspicion and horror. The man I love is here, and he doesn't care about my precarious legal status. Even more, here I don't have to worry that I'll be imprisoned for the rest of my life because of how I came to be.

And the most wonderful thing of all—Mom, Dad—I'm pregnant. I can have a family here. I'm free in a way I could never be in my own time. I miss both of you dreadfully, and Fair and Connor and Enya, and how I long to

see Jemi. **Kiss the little rascal for me
and tell him how much his aunt Nikita
loves him. I hope this letter eases your
minds, but it isn't safe for me to ever
return. Know that I'm happy and
healthy, and I'll hold you in my heart
and mind forever.**

> **Your loving daughter,
> Nikita**

PS: I hope the enclosed will be of use.

Nicolette was weeping so hard she could scarcely breathe, but she was laughing, too, squeezing Jemi and trying to hug Aidan all at the same time. Jemi set up a wail of protest, and she set him down, then went into Aidan's arms.

"She's alive," she wept. "She's there—two hundred years ago. I want her here, but just knowing—" She stopped, unable to say more.

"I know. I know." He was shaking violently. "She—we— Nic, we have another grandchild. Maybe more. We don't know how many we have!"

She gave a watery giggle. "And all of them except Jemi are older than us! We'll have to find our descendants. Nikita gave us the information we need. We know where to look. I don't know how much it will cost, but we'll manage—"

"Nic," Aidan said, his voice hoarse. He was strangely still, staring at the floor.

"I know, I'm rushing into things without planning, but we—"

"Nic," he said again, louder. "Look."

She looked. She felt the room whirl around, and she grabbed Aidan's arm for support.

"Oh, my God," she whispered. "That's—"

Paper. Packs and packs of it, vacuum-sealed and perfectly preserved. Nikita had sent them paper.